Also by Norman Mjadwesch

Richthofen's Reign

Broken Castle

Globall

Formula Won

FLEDGLINGS

First published 2015 by Tooth and Claw Productions

ISBN   978-0-9775956-4-8

Copyright © Norman Mjadwesch 2015

Visit www.toothandclawproductions.com to read more about and purchase our books and concepts.

For Sam, who understands fatigue better than most.

Acknowledgements

Though I have written a few other books, *Fledglings* is my first work of fiction and it was harder to do than I had initially anticipated. During my university years a typical essay was generally required to be two thousand words and I found them to be excruciating. If one of my lecturers had asked me to write sixty of them back to back on any topic I liked, I would most probably have declined, but that is exactly the level of commitment needed to write a novel. On any given day, the act of sitting at a keyboard is a very solitary experience, but in order to make it happen there are invariably other people around to get you over the line. I would like to express my thanks to those who have contributed towards the finished article:

To Samantha Wilson, who still hasn't gotten around to marrying me but pretty much does all of the graft every time I have a new book ready to go. Whether it's proof reading, preliminary editing, lay-out, design, preparing files for printing or refraining from excessive sarcasm as we stand around in the sun taking photos, poor Sam does the lot. And that's despite being snowed under with the ridiculous workload from her regular job.

To Col Cafferky, for volunteering his experience in editing. It cannot be emphasised enough how much a book is improved by objective input from those who know what they are doing. All authors think that their work doesn't need improving, right up until the point where they are proven wrong. Most writers will give credit to their editors and accept any errors as their own, and there is a good reason for that - if there are any mistakes in *Fledglings*, it's probably because I didn't implement all of Col's recommendations.

To Richard Halcomb, for taking the time to proof-read a book written by a complete stranger simply because they have an old friend in common (Hi, Matt!). Thanks for the feedback, man.

To Bob Bronkhorst, for once again going ballistic with the main photo on the cover design. All publications ultimately need to stand on their own if they are to be successful, but the cover makes people want to buy it in the first place. Bob also offered to edit this one, but I had to pass because he's ugly enough without having his eyes gouged out of his head.

To my parents, Norbert and Gerda, for so many things, not least of which has been the small matter of finance during desperate times.

To Andrew Ellaby, for assisting with the design of the smaller details on a model kit because I was too stingy to fork out ten bucks for decals. Plus the other stuff as well.

To everyone else who has believed in my ability to write. Thanks are due to all of you for your encouragement, but especially to my brother Ray, whose life revolves around fighting against the forces of evil but who still found the time to favourably compare an extract from one of my other on-going projects with that of the legendary fantasy author Hugh Cook. Those sorts of words can prop a man up for a very long time indeed.

Thanks, everyone.

List of characters

There are around a hundred different names mentioned in *Fledglings*. The principal cast of characters is listed below by the number of references made to them in the text:

Germany

Sebastian von Bülow – observer selected for *Jasta* service

Ernst Reinhold – long-time comrade to von Bülow

Max Beerenbrock – pilot initially under von Bülow

Lehmann – pilot initially under von Bülow

Falkenhoff – adjutant of the Fokker *Jasta*

Mellerhorst – adjutant of the Albatros *Jasta*

Karl von Bülow - Sebastian's cousin

Weber – replacement pilot

Kluth – Fokker DVII pilot

Rossler – pilot initially under von Bülow

Hockheimer – reconnaissance pilot

Bonninghauser – replacement pilot

Becker – original member of von Bülow's *Jasta*

Bartels – replacement pilot

British Empire

Adam Burrows – F.2B pilot

George Miller – commander of the Camel squadron

Percy Wiggan – F.2B pilot

Ross Burke – F.2B observer

Callaghan – patrol leader in the Camel squadron

Lewis-Hamilton – patrol leader in the F.2B squadron

Bowe – squadron scrounger

Limerick – armourer in the F.2B squadron

Barker – adjutant of the Camel squadron

Mary - nurse

Harding – adjutant of the F.2B squadron

Sloane – ground crewman in the F.2B squadron

Noone – replacement observer

Fenton – rigger in the Camel squadron

Drummond – F.2B observer

Ellington – Camel pilot

Elphinstone – Camel pilot

France

Yvonne Coiffard - prostitute

Dumont - pilot

Bonnet - pilot

Gaillard - farmer

Charlotte - brothel owner

Part I: Unleash the Jastas

Chapter 1

July 1916: The Calm before the Storm

The early morning air was cold and crisp, though nothing compared to the dead of winter. Normally, during these summer months, the warmth remained throughout the night. Songbirds had greeted the dawn with their various melodies, and now that they were done they were going about the rest of their daily business. In the distance, along the entire length of the Western Front, the rumble of the guns had never quite abated.

Puffs of foggy breath wafted from the mouth of the motionless figure standing quietly in the middle of the open field. Sebastian von Bülow had his hands shoved deep into his coat pockets, with his collar turned up to keep his neck warm. It was important to keep the neck warm. If it became chilled the muscles could seize in protest. A neck with limited movement was fatal for an airman; if a head couldn't behave as if on a swivel, a man's field of vision was impaired - and then: death. These days French aviators didn't have a very high regard for the well-being of the Germans whom they flew against.

Von Bülow reflected on the fact that flying was much like hunting on his family's estate. There was a slight difference: airmen's heads were not mounted and hung on a wall. But if a flier had a sore neck, he quickly became someone's trophy story.

3

He heard the soft tread of feet approaching. In a few months' time the footfalls would crunch a thin layer of frost with each step. *Will I ever see it snow again?* The war threw up those sorts of questions, and often answered in the negative. Von Bülow recognised the familiar figure instantly. If you live with a person for long enough, very soon you are able to pick out their mannerisms, every slightest movement, all of their habits. A man with his head covered cannot disguise himself from those around him when they know him as one of their own.

'Good morning, Basti.' It was a nickname von Bülow didn't like, but for the closest of friends you made allowances.

'And also to you.'

Hockheimer came to stand beside his companion and together they enjoyed the quiet part of a day that could yet bring anything. 'They are not back yet?'

'Not yet.' Losses had increased alarmingly of late. Their unit was comprised of various types of general purpose aircraft, and they were currently getting a taste of another phase in the see-saw war of aerial supremacy. Supporting the German army as it struggled with the latest Allied offensive on the Somme had been costly.

Germany had lost their recent advantage as more and more of the new diminutive Nieuport fighting scouts were encountered with greater frequency. It hadn't been long ago that heroes such as Max Immelmann had held the high cards. Now the Fokker *Eindecker* which they had flown had been surpassed, and Immelmann was dead.

Hockheimer scuffed his heel in the dirt, 'We should get something warm inside ourselves.'

'I'll wait here a little longer.'

'We're scheduled for midday.'

'Yes.'

Hockheimer shrugged. He wandered back to the warmth of their quarters, leaving the observer to resume a lonely vigil.

The sky remained empty. Eventually von Bülow went back indoors. Whether the missing machine was ever coming home would be decided sooner or later, and standing around waiting for it would have no bearing on the outcome at all. A hot meal would put some perspective on events.

Von Bülow shrugged out of his bulky greatcoat and washed his face and hands in a basin. He ordered breakfast, sat himself down at a table and tucked in a napkin. Presently his meal was brought to him, and he ate it undisturbed. Every movement of his fork was carefully orchestrated, every knife cut precise. To eat a meal was a civilised art-form; lesser men would use their utensils as a workman handles his tools. To chew carefully, to spill nothing, to avoid wolfing food or making farmyard noises – these were important to the young aristocrat.

His demeanour fitted his manners. Haughty and unruffled, von Bülow was equally at home surrounded by servants and he would have looked much the same. Only his hair was different. Curls had made way for a closely cropped scalp in deferment to military practicality. The fact that he was required to risk life and limb for Germany was little more than an opportunity to advance himself within his social circle. He already had the ribbon for an Iron Cross sewn into his button-hole and considered it as the first step in a steady progression should fortune smile upon him. He was still young enough to believe that it was his due.

Hockheimer found his friend settled down with a paper and a hot mug, 'Are you still intending to sit the pilot's course?'

'Yes.' Von Bülow glanced up from his article and raised an eyebrow, 'You know I was asked to?'

'It seems a pity, that's all.'

'Save your pity for Immelmann's mother.' He pondered the sentiment. 'Of course, it is only natural that others will be expected to fly in his stead. I should not want to miss such an opportunity simply because I have not learned every aspect of fighting from an aircraft. Learning to fly seems a very obvious step to take if I am to realise that ambition.'

'It is only that we fight well together in the air.'

The paper was put aside, neatly folded, 'So do the others, until they fail to return.'

The pilot gestured in exasperation, 'Ach, it happens. But you are good when it comes to shooting, I'll admit that much.'

Von Bülow frowned in bemusement at the remark, 'Anyone could tell you that for free.' Modesty was not his strongest suit. Nor did he require much of an invitation to tell of his skills, 'All of our comrades here have yet to bring down their first Frenchman.'

'None of the other observers have a pilot able to manoeuvre their flying machine expertly enough to make the shot possible.' The tone was half-mockery, but nevertheless dared the other to refute the statement. It was the same discussion that existed between authors and illustrators: the finished article relied on the contributions of both parties, yet one gets credit out of proportion to their efforts and neither will accept that this applies to themselves.

This time von Bülow conceded the point, 'It is as you say. Our achievement and continued survival must have drawn some notice. I see no other reason to have been asked to undertake pilot training. It seems backward, though, since we have shown our potential. Surely it would make more sense to utilise our proven skills rather than gambling on success in other directions?'

'That sounds most unlike you, Basti. I had an image of you as a man who could conquer every obstacle.'

'You know me well. But others who do not, how can they tell a man's character if they have not met him in person?'

'Character is always measured by an individual's actions.'

Von Bülow nodded at this, but he had had enough of the topic, 'I'll need to strip the gun again before we head out. One cannot be too careful when it comes to preparation, especially when a jam could result in a telegram to my parents.'

'As you wish. Finish reading your paper. I'll let the armourer know.'

'Thank you.'

Hockheimer departed, leaving his observer to complete the morning ritual.

*   *   *

Once again, another typical dank morning had enveloped London's East end. The sky outside was overcast, and Adam Burrows wouldn't have been at all surprised if it rained. Whether the weather could justifiably be called rain was a moot point; usually its unenthusiastic manifestation took the form of less impressive precipitation, and drizzle was a more apt description. As he pressed his nose close to the glass his breath fogged the window pane. The street below was empty.

Despite the grim aspect of the city, Adam was unable to contain his eagerness. He had celebrated his nineteenth birthday months ago, and now had the letter he had been waiting for in his hand. Finally.

Margery Burrows had been preparing morning tea. Now all thought of it lay forgotten. She knew what the news must be, from no further information than the look on the face of her only child. She had been dreading this day in levels directly proportionate to the awful excitement in her son. She looked across at her husband, and both understood what the other was thinking.

'Father, Mother – my papers have come through! I have been accepted for pilot training.'

The latest casualty lists were regularly reported in the *Times* and newspaper sales had increased because of it. No-one wished to miss out on news of friends and family, so poring over the endless columns had become a national pastime; week after week, month after month, hoping never to see a name, but devastated when it finally happened. It was a macabre lottery, one in which there were never any winners. Recently, there had been a marked increase in the number of losers.

Margery began to cry, and she realised that both her husband and her son had expected her to do so. *What else am I to do? Why are men so blind to death that they bask in its shadow, only to repent when it comes knocking on the door? Where does the curiosity come from to want to stare it in the face?*

'Father?' It came out as a quaver. Adam knew he had upset his mother, but didn't know what else he should have done with such an opportunity, especially given the expectations of the entire country. Some of his classmates had already gone to France. He looked towards his father, hoping that the old man could control the emotions of the foolish, weeping woman central to their lives.

Horace Burrows was not amused. He had played this out in his head many times, and all of them had ended like this. The boy would go to war, and Margery would spend her time reading every paper

8

with her heart in her mouth. The task caused parents to age, but many of them still outlived their headstrong sons.

'It isn't natural...'

Adam had heard it all before: flying machines were new; they really were not supposed to exist; ergo, they were evil. *Parents never understand anything.*

'They are new-fangled contraptions. Unsafe.'

The words were predictable. They had been uttered before, many times. Having Adam enter flight school had not been his father's idea. Though the Burrows family acknowledged that sooner or later Adam would be called up, the younger man had argued that if he volunteered for flying training, ultimately his introduction to the fighting on the Western Front would be slower than if he was called upon to undertake infantry training. No-one pretended that Adam was not basing his wishes on his personal agenda, but Horace and Margery had discussed it at length and Horace had agreed that Adam's reasoning had made sense at the time. The war could be over before he was ordered into uniform.

It had not worked out that way. Now the time was upon them, and Adam's turn had come around.

Learning to fly was a complicated and lengthy procedure, and it was inherently dangerous. Qualified instructors were few and far between, and because the art of flying was itself new, none of the teachers had a true grasp of their field. Horace was unsurprised to discover that trainees were regularly being killed in flying accidents without ever so much as seeing a Hun – that's what the Germans were being called these days - or even seeing France, for that matter.

Adam was confident in the same way that all young people are confident, 'Don't worry, I'll be all right. Arthur Reid has told us it's a marvellous thing to do. He's graduating from his course in a few weeks.' The endorsement of the school football team's captain was the only credential needed to persuade him that his peers knew what they were talking about. Their perspective had been obscured by a unified belief in their own immortality. Oddly, this view applied only to each person and they all privately acknowledged that some of their friends would die.

Normally a quietly spoken and thoughtful young man, Adam's obsession with going to war had changed him. Not even the death of friends had blunted his determination to follow in their footsteps. If anything, it added resolve to his mentality, driving him onward with ever greater purpose. He was repelled by the thought of being called a coward, and refused to be shamed by the sacrifices made by others while he sat back doing nothing.

The cavalry of the clouds. The phrase had been bandied about to boost morale and add allure to the war, following the ghastly losses over the last two years. Adam had been seduced by the idea that he could become a knight of the air, and nothing would dissuade him from the aspiration. Though he knew nothing of what he was about to embark upon, he nevertheless was no fool, and was nervous of the immediate future.

At an intellectual level, he knew he could die. There was an understanding that all of the caution he could practise would likely have little bearing on his future. Men were dying by the thousands every week and there was no way that all of them had been careless with their lives. He understood that.

Arthur had told them of a training accident that had killed some of the men on his course, though naturally Adam had omitted relaying the fact when talking to his parents. He suspected they knew of it anyway. As to aerial combat, well, the whole show seemed larger than life and altogether too exciting to miss out on. Some notion of the perils could be deduced without stretching the imagination, and there were the usual tales of derring-do to draw upon. But it was easy to read between the lines and understand that the best pilots were only achieving acclaim because so many others were falling to their guns. If nothing else, Burrows understood that if you could break a neck falling off a ladder, no less was to be expected from a thousand feet.

He understood it, but it still didn't feel real.

Many people profess to feeling the tug of fate, and it brought with it a sense of destiny. It was a sensation that God was protecting you, and that He would harm others to preserve you. It was an arrogant view, seldom with any earned foundation. This belief did not take long to dispel, but the cost was always a slap in the face - a very hard slap.

Adam Burrows had not yet received his slap, and felt that if others died so that he could rise, well then, that was the price of war...

Horace knew much of this himself, because he had also been young once upon a time, though his son may not have realised the fact. Youth has potential, but age has had time to acquire wisdom. Inevitably, his son would one day leave home and it was the role of a parent to prepare their children for exactly this eventuality. But sending a child to war was a far worse prospect to have to anticipate after investing in them a lifetime of love and protection.

Horace was reserved, unable to say aloud all of which he felt. He had no advice to offer, as young people never heeded it in any case. So instead, he shook the boy's hand. There was so much to convey in the grip, but none of it passed across, 'Be careful, my boy.'

'I'd best let Maud know. I'm going to ask her to marry me, if Mister Lanning will allow it.' After delivering news that would in other circumstances have been a bombshell, Adam excused himself from the company of his parents.

Horace hugged Margery. There was no other comfort that he could give. Unlike their children, most adults understand reality, 'Damn the Kaiser and all politicians.'

'And may God save the King.'

The pot of tea sat on the table between them, stone cold.

*   *   *

After two years of fighting, physical hardship had become the lot of every living thing. Humanity strove to kill their fellows in every way imaginable while domesticated beasts did as they had always done, providing the extra muscle. While most of the peacetime workforce was now employed by the army, others took up the baton in an endeavour to keep their respective economies from collapse. Non-combatants worked gruelling hours, producing or processing essentials such as food and clothing, or standing a twelve hour shift in a munitions factory.

Conditions in occupied France were terrible for the local population. Shortages in every resource, and particularly food, meant that times were testing. Typhoid and scarlet fever were rife, and for many the threat of starvation was never more than a stolen crust away. Civilian mortality had spiked.

Under martial law, strict rules applied to everyone. Forced labour was the order of the day, and in any other context it was forbidden to gather in large groups. Penalties were meted out according to the whim of the various regional authorities. Anything from beatings and deprivation to death could be expected for the smallest infractions. Women were encouraged to make themselves available to German soldiers, exchanging sex for protection and food. Those that accepted the mantle were branded as traitors by their countrymen. In truth, many of them had no alternative.

Hockheimer and von Bülow had driven into the nearest town. They intended to find a quiet corner and drink themselves into oblivion. There was not much else that they could do by way of entertainment.

'Drab.'

'Deserted.'

They passed a barber shop where the owner was preparing a customer for a shave. He waved to them as they drove by, a straight razor prominent in his hand. French civilians were not in the habit of acknowledging their conquerors, so Hockheimer assumed the razor was part of the message. Though the barber was taking his life in his hands with the affected greeting, the German officer pretended not to notice, 'It's a good thing the army organises our haircuts. I'm not sure the local civilians would be very trustworthy in the matter.'

'They'd be shot if they slit your throat.'

'Cold comfort if you're the customer.'

'If the French had that kind of determination, we wouldn't be driving on their roads.'

The streets were all but empty. Adults kept to themselves, not wanting to draw notice. Unless you had specific business to attend to, the best policy was to stay out of sight. Leaning against a run-down brick wall, two skinny boys watched the German car cruise past them. Von Bülow scowled, 'We should shoot them before they grow old enough to take up arms against us.'

'If they had known we were visiting they'd have probably packed their pockets with stones.' The looks directed at the Germans were carefully neutral. *When had children learned the need for circumspection?* As

13

the car drove past the youths, von Bülow saw a defiant gesture directed towards him. The driver stamped on the brake pedal, his reaction an automatic response that any adult would have had to a poorly behaved child. It was all the motivation the scamps needed to flee for their lives. Hockheimer was mournful, 'No point trying to find them. They'll have disappeared long since.'

'We'll shoot the next one.'

Two blocks later they spied another child. The girl's eyes were blank. 'Stop the car.'

Hockheimer leaned towards her, 'What is your name, little one?'

The empty look gave way to fear and a complete lack of trust, 'Would you like some food?'

Von Bülow nudged Hockheimer with an elbow, 'Don't waste it on the useless brat.'

The advice was ignored. After rummaging within his pocket, Hockheimer withdrew his fist and extended a crumbling chunk of pumpernickel in the universal gesture. Feral hands snatched the offering before the soldier could change his mind. The child darted away before other urchins detected an opportunity and stole the morsel for themselves.

Von Bülow wasn't afraid to voice his censure, 'Now you'll bring hordes of the little bastards down onto our heads.'

Hockheimer was unrepentant, 'Have a heart, Basti. They need to eat, the same as we do. What would you say if you saw a child starving at home?'

'Firstly, I would greet my family with, 'Hello, Papa, I have some home leave.' And then I would tell the little nuisance to go and pester someone else, with a boot in the backside to hurry it along.' He grew surly, 'If the French had fought harder their people wouldn't be in this predicament, and neither would we – looking after their soldiers' families while they shoot at us! What a joke, to expect us to be nannies to their brats.'

'If the French had fought any harder, you and I would be dead by now. Either that, or we'd be living in quarters a lot nearer to the Fatherland. Or behind barbed wire.'

Immersed in the moral implications of living near a garrison town, the two officers were not paying close attention to their surroundings. To their disgust, it began to drizzle in a fine spray that trickled down their collars and fouled the car's windscreen. 'Shit, where are the oilskins?'

Hockheimer recovered the wet-weather items, and they stopped the vehicle to put them on. Hurrying past to get out of the rain, a young woman in worn clothes paid them no heed. Hockheimer registered her existence and then refocused his attention once more to securing their personal comfort. Von Bülow's reaction was very different.

He had seen her before.

Memories came flooding back, unbidden and unwanted. The clean scent of her neck; that hair, soft and fine; the smoothness of pale, flawless skin; the delicate rounded crown of her head – it had been an intimate habit of his to tenderly cup it in the bowl of his hand; her beautiful voice and the words that were spoken by that perfect mouth.

He was stricken. *Please don't look at me.* He couldn't bear to see the accusation in those big, soulful eyes…

Her name formed on his lips, and he almost spoke it out loud. Only two things prevented the utterance. Firstly, von Bülow was dumbstruck in astonishment. More importantly, he knew it wasn't really her. The uncanny resemblance shook him to the core, but it was impossible that this was the same girl. His life unravelled until a

15

time before the war, and he tried to retreat from it, even as he was drawn like a fly to a spider's web.

The girl didn't see him looking at her. She simply went on her lonely way, oppressed by the harsh laws of a foreign power.

Hockheimer saw that von Bülow was acting oddly. He was no longer new to the business of living in the shadow of death, and the look on the other's face told a story of torment that was often associated with the things they had seen and done. Then Hockheimer noticed that his friend's attention was transfixed on the retreating form.

'The best cure of them all, eh? No better remedy for living with death than a roll in the hay with a willing maiden.' She diminished into the distance.

Von Bülow roused himself from his reverie. His next words were aimed at masking his initial reaction, 'You're probably right about the hay. Her bed probably has fleas in it.'

'No, that would be the Belgians.'

Von Bülow spat, 'Them, too. A pox on this war, and I hope that all Frenchmen die of envy, knowing that we have had our way with their womenfolk.'

'I've never seen a woman have that sort of effect on you. Did she have nice tits?'

The question was precisely the sort that von Bülow was normally happy to discuss at length. His terse answer had less enthusiasm than Hockheimer had expected, 'Yes. That would be it.'

Chapter 2

August 1916: Firefight

There had been relatively little action during the last week. Missions had been flown, but the French had been curiously absent. It didn't mean that they had vanished forever.

For now, von Bülow was happy to ride his luck. He doubted that the present situation would remain uneventful for very long, especially given today's objective. Three aircraft had been assigned the task of attacking the rail yards at Reims. Each of the Albatros CIIIs was loaded with four bombs, which amounted to over a quarter of a tonne of explosives. Von Bülow looked forward to seeing the results.

They stood in a small group, six men about to put their lives into one another's hands. Hockheimer was their natural leader. He had been in the army the longest and was one of the first men to join the aviation branch of the German armed forces. He had an easy manner that gave the others an affinity with him and those who knew him willingly followed his lead; it was because Hockheimer had asked von Bülow to become his observer that the newer man had a perception of elevated status within their unit - that, and the fact of his nobility.

The planned action was modest in scale, though this was nothing unusual. Small raids may have been little more than nuisance value, but they were hard to detect and even though the expected returns were meagre it was better than doing nothing at all. If all went well the French rail network would suffer a minor disruption and half a dozen fliers would make entries into their log books and then celebrate the fact that they had not been given a more perilous objective.

So they bent over the maps that they were studying and applied their intellect. Times, routes, known sites for concentrations of anti-aircraft defences – they perused it all. None of the planning was boring to them. How could it be when often it was the overlooked details that proved to be fatal? They plotted bearings and decided amongst themselves how best to execute the mission.

There was an edginess to their general demeanour that none of them tried to conceal. To say that they were frightened would be overstating the case; more accurately, they were tense because even on the simplest operations things sometimes go horribly wrong. They were tense, but that is not the same as scared.

To help deal with their mood, they smoked and drank in quantities that would have been considered excessive to the uninitiated. Coping with the stress of combat was easier if the brain was more alert but the nerves were deadened. Sometimes their mildly impaired state led to errors in judgement, but the men were far less likely to panic. The one offset the other by a wide margin.

Their aircraft were rather innocuous-looking. Most of the machines designed early in the war had a clumsy aspect, although the Albatros Works were less guilty of this than other design teams. The exhaust stack stood vertically, clearing the level of the upper wing. Consequently, it was something of an impediment to forward vision. The plywood skin of each machine was finished in multiple coats of varnish that gave them a honey-coloured appearance.

Every plane was loaded to the gills with bombs: four per plane, hanging vertically in the fuselage bay. All of them carried enough machine-gun ammunition to be a force to be reckoned with, enough to deter any Frenchman wandering about on his own in search of easy pickings. Keeping close formation usually gave them safety in numbers against marauding aircraft. It was the one advantage that a flexible mounting for a gun had over those that are fixed to fire forwards: though the Parabellum's ring mount didn't have the same stability as a shooting platform, this deficiency was compensated for by having a greater defensive arc of fire.

So much for protection against hostile airmen; that only addressed part of the problem.

Ground fire was just one of the hazards that could not be planned against as effectively. At some point the front lines needed to be crossed, and every soldier with a machine-gun or rifle was quite happy to shoot at anything with wings. Regardless of nationality, none of the infantry seemed to be remotely aware that the prominent markings on the surfaces of all aircraft identified friend from foe. Consequently, they took pot-shots at everything.

Sometimes the same affliction filtered across to dedicated anti-aircraft gunners, even though they were supposed to be able to distinguish between the various adversaries.

Unable to plan for every contingency, the men checked the time and counted the minutes before they were due to depart. There was no sense of urgency among them and none of them were as eager to go aloft as they had been when the opportunity had first arisen. Being repeatedly shot at had that effect upon the mind. All they were waiting for now was the return of the machine that had been sent out earlier to gather the latest intelligence.

From the ground, sound is usually the first sign that an aircraft is approaching. On occasion it can be spotted before it is heard, but for that to happen it needs to be at a sufficiently high altitude and someone needs to be looking for it to begin with. Today was not one of those days, and the assembled airmen heard the drone of the engine before they located the source. Sighting the home-bound machine as it came in, they immediately knew there would be trouble; rather than being an indistinct dot in the near distance, there was a dirty smudge.

The hedge-hopping two-seater couldn't possibly be trying to hide – it wore a pall of smoke like the Reaper's shroud. Trying to dodge the enemy was a pointless enterprise in the circumstances, as the stain in the air would be visible for miles. No doubt the crew's first priority was to get onto the ground as quickly as possible. In order to do so with any reasonable expectation of survival, they needed to come back to earth at an acceptable speed, and at an angle that would put the wheels onto the grass before any other part of the machine touched. Too fast or too steep were equally lethal. Landing gear in nineteen-sixteen was unforgiving. There was no suspension and the assembly would collapse if it was too badly abused.

To the experienced eyes of the handful of witnesses, disaster was imminent. The Albatros CI was clearly exceeding its landing speed. If the pilot tried to land, he and the observer would be pulled from the resulting matchwood and given a burial service – and if the men on the ground could see as much, then it must have also been painfully obvious to the fellows in the cockpit.

To attempt to go around again was hazardous. The machine was lucky to have made it home at all. To do another circuit of the airfield was perhaps putting too much faith in God, but they had made it this far...

The pilot tried to pull up. There was no other way.

When controls are not responding properly because wires are broken and flaps have been shot away – that is just about as bad as it can get. Oil and fuel leaks were not uncommon either, and fire was a huge hazard that could only be prayed against. Trying for an increase in altitude might have allowed extra time to set up a correct landing approach, but it came with the risk of stalling. When a machine is close down to the deck there can never be enough time to restart the engine once it cuts out.

The damaged aircraft's motor was labouring as it passed overhead and crossed the landing field's far perimeter. Something went wrong, either mechanically or from human error. The nose dipped precipitously and the pilot had no time to make a recovery. The reconnaissance plane and its shadow seemed bent on reuniting without regard for the consequences. Even from a distance von Bülow knew there would be no survivors. He looked at Hockheimer and they started running.

The manufacture of the earliest airframes was comprised almost entirely of flammable materials. The skeleton consisted mostly of wood, and the skin was usually fabric. Generally speaking, only the engine, control cables and tension wires were resistant to heat. Even then, the engine relied upon internal combustion for its power, and combustion has never been a concept that inspires thoughts of safety in the aviation fraternity. When fuel lines perish; when a seal fails; when any leakage of gasoline occurs at all – that is when life as an aviator is most fraught with danger.

The crash site was an inferno wreathed in a billowing black cloud of putrid smoke. The men inside were dead – there was no question of it. Those who had reached the scene first had been beaten back by the radiant heat of the flames. They watched helplessly as men they had known were barbequed.

The spectacle did not last long. With only a limited amount of fuel left on board, the volatile accelerants made for a quick ending.

Within the smouldering debris, the grisly forms of the crew were immediately visible. Their clothes had been mostly burned away. The bodies had been charred and crisped, fingers curled into claws as the skin shrivelled and tendons contracted. The black holes of their mouths were left agape in their last dying moments. Both men had certainly been killed on impact, but it didn't look like it. Fire had left them scoured of all semblance of a peaceful ending. They looked tortured.

Von Bülow noticed that the observer was wearing a pocket watch strapped onto the wrist, an innovation recently developed by airmen of all nationalities. It had quickly been discovered that delving into one's pockets whilst wearing leather gauntlets was not physically possible, so the simple solution had been to start wearing the timepiece in a way that could be easily accessed. He checked the burnt face of the item against his own and noticed that damage had stopped the recording of events when the man had died. It would make writing up the report a little simpler.

Hockheimer had served some time in the trenches and spoke what the others were thinking, 'God above, I've seen worse, but this is not something a man needs to have in his head before he fires the ignition switch.' He made no reference to whether or not the dead men had completed their mission or not – either way, whatever they had recently discovered about the rail yards was lost.

One thing was certain: the lone Albatros had met with opposition and that was all of the information that was really required. The airmen steeled themselves for combat. Each man had a different ritual, and none of them would ever be persuaded that their superstitions were foolish.

Hockheimer told Reinhold to break an arm and a leg. He nodded at von Bülow. Everyone climbed into their seats.

The gunfire over the front was desultory and barely worthy of notice. With novices, every bullet is thought to be potentially lethal. In time, only proven hazards were feared, for to tremble at every threat was the quickest path to insanity. To the six men sneaking through the sky, the small arms fire was dismissed as little more than an irritant - attempted pinpricks deserving only of disdain. Only when they had flown clear of the designated battlefield did they alter course with a dogleg towards Reims. If any word had been passed to a nearby airfield of the approaching raiders, they would have a difficult time determining the final objective.

They sighted the rail yards and made their attack. A dozen bombs tumbled to earth, destroying buildings and tearing up tracks. At least, that was how it appeared to the airmen from their elevated vantage. As the pilots steered an immediate course for home, the observers let fly with their guns, as much for the release of emotion as any intended effect.

To the human eye, there was enough damage to have made the trip worthwhile, as evidenced by the handful of new craters and the rising smoke that hung over the location. Though it seemed that nothing could have survived such a vicious assault, the truth was more prosaic: though they were badly frightened, none of the French railway men received worse than minor lacerations and befouled trousers.

Claude Dumont checked his watch. It was almost time to return home. The patrol had been uneventful. Though he had flown every day for the last two weeks, he had not fired his guns at a German in the entire time. It was most galling. This morning his squadron had sighted a solitary LVG, but it was at high altitude and he knew that they would never be able to make a successful interception. He had called off the chase almost as soon as it had begun.

The Nieuports accompanying him were ghostly in appearance, though in bright sunlight their silver doped finish could be dazzling to the eye. There were nine of them including the leader. In the distance, Dumont spied a pillar of smoke rising from the ground. *Someone has had a crack at Reims again. That will be for another patrol to attend to.* It was time for him to turn for home.

As the patrol made the necessary course alteration, Dumont saw three aircraft furtively picking their way along at treetop height as they attempted to dodge trouble. They were headed towards the German side of the lines, and Dumont's squadron was well placed to head them off.

He identified the planes as two-seaters, though his aircraft recognition skills were as bad as anyone else's. He thought that they may be C-types, but that was only a guess based on the fact that most of the enemy machines these days had that designation, irrespective of manufacturer. The 'C' configuration had the observer placed in the rear cockpit instead of in front of the pilot, armed with a machine-gun on a properly designed mounting. That was a relatively new development. Previous types simply flew with an *ad hoc* assortment of weapons, based on availability and personal preference

Dumont waggled his wings to draw the attention of the other pilots and pointed emphatically. The Frenchmen were not going straight home after all: they were first making a little detour. Setting a course to intercept, he started stalking the three troublemakers as they skimmed above the patchwork pattern of the fields below.

As the distance closed, he could tell that he had been spotted. It had to happen at some point. One did not simply expect the enemy to roll over for you when you came hard at him. Dumont had the lead, but discipline was still sometimes overruled by impetuousness and the other aircraft were almost jostling one another in their haste to have the first tilt at their quarry.

Tactics against single aircraft were different to those employed on larger formations. Dumont knew that he needed to get one of the machines to break away from the others before his men could work it over. He picked out the Albatros on the left and pressed home his attack. The other Nieuports broke over the trio like rough surf on a wading toddler.

One of the Germans drifted clear of the others, and four of Dumont's pilots gave it their immediate attention. The remainder stayed with the unbroken pair, intending to stay in a running battle with them as long as possible. It would end soon enough. Either the two-seaters would be destroyed, or the Nieuports would break off the engagement due to fuel shortage.

Dumont watched the other four pilots harrying their prey as they worked it like sheepdogs, coordinating each onslaught as they herded the Albatros further away from the protection of its friends. A frenzied pattern of gunfire was poured into the machine from every direction. Though his efforts were futile, the German observer had not given up. His options were limited and every time he tried to beat off an attack from one quarter he was immediately forced to respond to a new threat. To Dumont's eyes he was not being helped by the pilot, who had ceased taking evasive action. It was only a matter of time before the end came.

Von Bülow was in deep trouble and he knew it. His machine-gun was overheating but there was nothing he could do about it. Either he fired short bursts that would be completely ineffective against the blasted Frenchies, or he could try to pour more fire into them. If he let the barrel cool he had a better chance in the long run, but in the meantime he would be presenting himself as a sitting duck. Those were the choices: ruin the barrel or die. Maybe he would die anyway.

What in hell is Hockheimer doing? The pilot seemed to have frozen, and now was not the time to lose composure. He needed to snap out of his funk or they were both dead. The French quartet that had latched onto them was remorseless, and wouldn't easily give up when the fight was so one-sided.

More bullets hummed past von Bülow's head. The Nieuport that was shooting at him was following directly behind, screening itself from return fire by positioning itself in the blind spot beneath the tail assembly of the Albatros. *Zzziiip!* Von Bülow felt the disturbance in the air as another bullet passed by his ear. By the time it was gone it was too late to cringe. He flinched anyway.

In the air, the din of the engines killed any possibility of hearing anything other than the sound of each machine and the gunfire. The screams of the man sitting a few feet away were as audible as if he was on the dark side of the moon. Von Bülow was too busy fighting his own private war to see what Hockheimer was up to. Despite the fact that the two friends were unable to speak directly to one another, von Bülow was liberal with some abusive suggestions. He had no way of knowing that his friend had been struck in the initial attack, or that this was the principal reason that they had become separated from the others.

As quickly as it had begun, the attack ended. The pale hunters peeled away and left the stricken two-seater to its fate. The only reason that von Bülow could conjure was that they must have reached the limit of their endurance. No-one wanted to run out of fuel during flight.

He took stock, and his first thought was for Hockheimer. Relinquishing his grip on the smoking Parabellum, he twisted around until he could see the other man sitting there just a few feet away. Hockheimer was ashen, and seemed unfocused. Von Bülow reached across and grabbed the man by the shoulder. His friend half turned and looked back at him. Words were spoken, but they blew away. The pilot turned back towards the front.

Von Bülow thought that Hockheimer was injured, or that he was trying to address a problem with the oil pressure or other damage. *God knows there is enough of that – much of the aircraft has been shredded by gunfire.* Chips had been gouged out of the ply construction of the fuselage. The observer went back to wondering if Hockheimer had been hurt. If he had, there was no way for von Bülow to determine the severity of the injury, nor was he able to render assistance.

The only thing left to do was to resume his vigil at the gun and stay alert for hostiles. He would have to fight them off to the best of his ability, and rely on the fates to get them home in one piece. The rest was up to the pilot.

The memory of the Albatros CI spearing into the turf earlier that morning circled in his brain like a flock of carrion eaters.

They made it back but von Bülow was an empty shell. Hockheimer had been lifted out of the cockpit and into a waiting ambulance, then taken to an aid station. He died overnight. The main artery in his arm had been severed. Unable to manoeuvre the aircraft, he had tied his scarf above the injury in an attempt to staunch the bleeding, while the French had kept banging away at them. All the time, von Bülow had kept up a steady rhythm of fire to stave off defeat. Neither man had done anything wrong.

Hockheimer was dead and von Bülow had falsely believed that he had panicked. The thought was unworthy, but it could never be recanted. No-one ever needed to know what he had shouted at his friend, but the words had been said with God as his witness.

Reinhold and the others had gotten home in one piece. Someone laid a hand upon von Bülow's shoulder, but he was not comforted. A glass was put into his hand and filled. He drank from reflex.

Chapter 3

September 1916: *Jasta* Command

The men had been arriving singly and in twos as each made his way to the newly established airfield. The brainchild of the redoubtable Oswald Boelcke, new units known as *Jagdstaffeln* – literally, 'hunting units' – had been created with the specific task of seeking and destroying the enemy in the air. The personnel of these new and larger formations simply referred to them as *Jastas* and the most promising and aggressive airmen of the German Air Service had been selected to fly in them.

Each unit was comprised of a dozen pilots, and each man was allocated an aircraft to use as his own. There were several different examples of various designs in any one unit – standardisation of equipment was still many months away - but one thing had changed radically: gone was the concept of sending men into battle with inferior equipment. Where once men had been forced to fly anything at all that sprouted wings, now the outdated designs had been cast aside. The machines of the *Jastas* were built with a single purpose in mind and that was to destroy other flying machines. To this end, every plane was manufactured with a fixed forward firing armament - usually two machines guns, twice that of their enemies.

The most common machines parcelled out to the new units late in nineteen-sixteen were early examples of the Albatros D series, plus a smaller number of Fokker DIIIs and Halberstadt scouts. The 'D' designation referred to the double-wing configuration: though the earlier Fokker E was a monoplane, almost every fighter put into service after that time was a biplane.

Reliability issues and other problems ensured that the Fokkers and Halberstadts would gradually fall by the wayside. Only the Albatros was destined to remain and it would provide the backbone of the *Jastas* until well into nineteen-eighteen, and cause no end of headaches for the opposition.

Boelcke had ensured that the very best pilots were assigned to his own command, and his predictions regarding their individual potential were very accurate - some of the men who flew in *Jasta 2* would rise to fame very quickly. However, other units also required men to lead them. Pilots and observers who had shown an aptitude for aggressive flying were plucked from their units and reassigned.

In nineteen-fourteen, *Leutnant* Mellerhorst had seen some of the first shots fired in the war. Unfortunately, he was also one of the first casualties. Shrapnel had felled him near Liege as the German Second Army advanced into Belgium across the Meuse. Discharged after a two week hospitalisation, he had recuperated in the comfort of his family home and was feted locally as a war hero. Meanwhile his surviving comrades had sat in muddy holes throughout the winter. He rejoined them in the spring. A month later he had taken a bayonet between the ribs. This time when he was discharged he had gone home for good. Many of his friends thought he had died; there had been times in the intervening period when he wished that he had.

Bedridden and weak, he had started to read accounts of the early fliers. The novelty intrigued him so he made enquiries. Though his injuries precluded him from ever again taking up arms, he was offered an administrative posting to one of the newly formed *Jastas*.

He had been one of the first men to find his way to the new base of operations. Since his arrival two days previously, most of the other support staff had also set up shop. The new commander was due in later today. Mellerhorst looked at the clock on the wall in his office. Two hours. He wondered what the man would be like to work with.

There was one word that encapsulated the physical appearance of the new commander: compact. Mellerhorst mused to himself that it seemed to be a physique that suited most of the better pilots; being light enough not to strain an aircraft engine was critical to survival. Every kilogram of reduced weight in these flimsy inventions seemed to improve their performance. As such, life expectancy duly increased for those lacking in physical stature.

Mellerhorst measured the approaching pilot. He knew the bare details of the man from his file, and they were the blueprint for a typical army officer: early twenties, good family, career soldier. No doubt he had been brought up to believe that high status was his by birthright. He wasn't tall, but his bearing defied his height. There was a swagger that spoke of confidence and perhaps arrogance. Every movement was sure. *This is a man born to lead, a daring man - a man who holds his own destiny in the palm of his hands - and he believes it, too.*

Mellerhorst made all of these observations in the time it took the other to walk from the car to the doorway. He climbed to his feet and went to greet the new arrival. They saluted each other, then clasped hands, 'Franz Mellerhorst.'

'You are the adjutant, then?'

'Yes.'

The commander introduced himself, 'Sebastian von Bülow.'

'I will show you to your room.'

'Thank you.'

As they walked side by side, Mellerhorst found it difficult to keep pace. Von Bülow noticed immediately, 'You are injured?'

Mellerhorst gave a rueful smile, 'A required qualification for most young staff officers in these times.'

Von Bülow was sympathetic, 'Is it bad?'

'Bayonet. More than a year ago, now. It went straight through - carving meat still makes me nervous in the officer's mess.' He was not speaking in jest.

Von Bülow slowed his stride to allow the other man to maintain the lead. Mellerhorst was quietly appreciative of the other's consideration, 'Here.'

The young aristocrat looked at the empty space that was to be his quarters, 'Have my bags brought up and I'll meet you in my office in ten minutes.'

They exchanged nods. Mellerhorst departed.

Ten minutes later von Bülow was in his office. The adjutant closed the door behind himself, 'I met your cousin Karl at headquarters before I came here.'

'Oh, yes?' The commander's tone lacked interest and had suddenly become chilly.

'He recently received his flying certificate and was sorting out transfer orders. I was wondering if you wanted to get him assigned to this unit?'

'No.'

Mellerhorst checked himself. He didn't want to pry into matters that didn't concern him. All families had problems, and few of them appreciated outside interference. To cover his tracks, he dropped the topic and got straight to business, 'Things are still a shambles at this stage. The new *Jastas* have been formed, but everything is all theoretical at the moment. You don't simply create new formations out of thin air – we don't have anything approaching cohesion or adequate equipment.'

'What do we have?'

'Most of the ground staff is already here, but so far there are just nine pilots. It hardly matters, because we don't have enough machines for them, anyway.'

'What is the figure?'

'Five all told: two Albatros DIIs, a Fokker DIII, a Halberstadt and an *Eindecker*.'

Von Bülow raised his eyebrows, 'An *Eindecker*?'

Mellerhorst shrugged, 'It's better than nothing.'

'It's worse than nothing. No-one takes it up.'

'That leaves four, then.'

'One Albatros is to be reserved for me. Who are the best of the other pilots?'

The reply was prompt, as would be expected from a good adjutant, 'Reinhold, Bahlman and Rossler.'

'Reinhold I know. He gets the pick of the other machines. He'll probably want the second Albatros. Who are the other two?'

Mellerhorst dredged the details from the personnel files that he had committed to memory, 'Bahlman put in a claim for a Voisin a few months ago, but it was never confirmed. *Unteroffizier* Rossler - '

Von Bülow cut him off, 'Forget Rossler. No enlisted men fly until there is enough equipment for everyone.'

Mellerhorst looked at him askance, 'He comes highly recommended.'

Von Bülow interrupted again, 'If he was highly recommended, Boelcke would have snapped him up in *Jasta 2*. He's grounded until further notice.'

'That leaves Lehmann.'

'He can have the Halberstadt. What mark is it?'

'It's a DII.'

'Poor bastard. Maybe I should give it to Rosberg.'

Mellerhorst corrected him, 'Rossler.'

The interruption was barely noted, 'Well, I'm sure it's only temporary. Before we know it we'll have new machines straight from the factory, enough for everyone.'

'Will I write up the roster?'

'Who are the best of the spare pilots?'

Mellerhorst gave it one last try, 'Rossler.'

Von Bülow gave the adjutant a hard look, 'Not him.'

'*Leutnant* Becker, then.' Mellerhorst mentioned the man's rank to remove all possibility of doubt, 'May I enquire what it is that you don't like about enlisted men?'

Von Bülow's answer left no room for doubt, 'That you even need to ask tells me that I would be wasting my breath in trying to explain it to you.' There was no small degree of hostility in the response.

Mellerhorst was no longer so sure that he would have an easy relationship with the irascible man. Von Bülow did not let it rest there, 'I'd prefer us to agree on most things, Mellerhorst. And in front of the men we will.'

'Of course. In front of the men.'

Von Bülow gave the other officer a measured look, and allowed some leeway that ordinarily he would deny to new acquaintances; getting skewered with cold steel probably entitled a man to have an alternative view of the world.

34

Chapter 4

October 1916: The Ration Line

The civilians waited patiently as they queued for their ration hand-out. The armed guards looked uninterested, not expecting the slightest problem from the dispirited mass. Von Bülow was not involved in supervising the activity, but he watched also, as bored as the others but trying to alleviate his own state by studying that of others.

Then he saw a face in the crowd – it was the girl who had thrown him into disarray when he had first seen her just a few months ago. He again experienced a sensation akin to having ice water unceremoniously splashed into his face, but at least this time he had prior experience.

Unobtrusively, he edged closer to get a better view of her. Being a German amongst a group of French civilians naturally had an effect. Pedestrians made way as though he carried a plague in his blood. It was in fact a belief that many of them swore to be so.

The young officer was never going to shift these people from their opportunity to restock their supplies unless he resorted to force, but they edged away as far as they could without surrendering their position in the line to others. He made a detailed study of the woman. She was as he had remembered - very regal - if the attire could be discounted. In any case, given the limited availability of every resource, she could have worn those clothes to any opera theatre and still drawn attention. Von Bülow noticed differences this time. Her hair was a slightly darker shade than he had known; she was maybe an inch taller than he had at first thought; her eyes... there was no way to know about her eyes without giving himself away.

She was as close an approximation to perfection as he had ever seen. *Does she guard her virtue, or does another man hold her heart in the palm of his hand?* It was more than just idle curiosity.

Though his observations were made mostly through his periphery, any attempt at discretion was doomed to failure for no other reason than that he was dressed in field grey. Try as he might to be surreptitious, his notice drew the notice of others. Like any hunted animal, the girl felt his attention and looked straight at him, boldly, directly into his eyes, challenging his interest. And then, having conveyed her disdain, she looked away.

Now he had seen her eyes. They were not the same eyes as the ones he remembered. They were not innocent, nor lovely, but hardened to the world. He knew it with just one look. You could tell a lot about a person from their eyes; it identified them, and told of secrets even if they omitted the specifics. Seeing those eyes, he could now not do anything but ask. There was no alternative.

'Excuse me.'

She acted as if she didn't hear, or as if he must be speaking to another. The uneasy shift in her neighbours gave the lie away.

'Excuse me, Miss.' *There, that narrows the field.* He was not speaking to men or old women. She obviously wanted to flee, but was rooted in uncertainty. You did not openly defy one of the Kaiser's men.

'Come here.'

She looked for moral support from others in the line, but it seemed that they had all been struck deaf and blind. She pleaded her case, 'I shall lose my place in the line, sir.'

Von Bülow reassured her, 'No, I will move you to the front of the line after I have spoken to you.' The mood in the queue shifted once again. The promise of preferential treatment to a pretty girl was one they had seen many times. Where moments before she had been ignored without prejudice, now all regard for her well-being had frozen. With head bowed, the girl reluctantly stepped out of the long line and approached von Bülow.

'I do not wish to intrude.' Von Bülow generally reserved his bullying for subordinates, which although it included almost everyone that he met, was no way to treat a beautiful lady who reminded him of better days. She was still hesitant to engage him in conversation, and seemed intent on escape. He was determined to keep her right here in front of him, pinned to the pavement like an exotic butterfly on a board, 'You seem very familiar.'

She seemed startled, with perhaps a suggestion of embarrassment. The look evaporated, and she tried to fend him off, 'I do not think so, sir.'

Von Bülow was not so easy to dislodge, 'It would be difficult to forget your face. You are very beautiful.'

Somewhere from a well deep within, he beheld a change in her face, 'Yes, I may have seen you around.'

He was pleasantly surprised, but could not fathom how she could have ever paid him any heed? She must have seen thousands of German soldiers in the last few years. It was in fact what she had been hinting at, and now found the courage to voice it, 'You or someone like you. Your uniform stamps you as someone who is not local to the area.'

Ouch. There was nothing in the comment that could get her into trouble, but clearly she had teeth and was prepared to use them. The people in the line again shifted their allegiance. *They are so fickle.*

'I am not your enemy.'

'Our countries are at war, sir. What do you think it makes us?' Now she was treading on dangerous ground. She had an entirely captive audience. Von Bülow realised that his approach had been poorly executed and for one of the few times in his life he found himself embarrassed in front of witnesses. He walked a short distance away, and the girl was clearly expected to follow if she wished to be moved to the front of the line as he had promised.

He spoke more quietly, his best attempt at privacy in a public place, 'I apologise if I have given offence. It was not my intention. It is simply that you have a remarkable resemblance to someone I once knew.'

Her look became instantly frosty, 'So reacquaint with her again.' He looked awkward, almost as if he was physically trying not to squirm. In the space of a few words the tables had been turned. She rammed home the advantage, 'Or perhaps you will honour this woman by trying to bed another who reminds you of her?'

Von Bülow was stunned by the brazenness of the accusation, 'It is not what I meant…' The lie was written all over his face.

She rounded on him, 'What sort of woman do you think I am?'

'I am sorry if I have given offence.'

She stood there, splendid in her scorn, knowing full well that she had gone well beyond what a man could hope to get away with. The knowledge of the fact only increased her sense of injustice. Her next words were said without consideration of the possible consequences, 'Indeed? Sorry for being a pig? Or are you sorry for being a pig that escaped its pen and is now running loose, ravaging my country?'

There was an obvious answer to the insulting woman, and that lay in placing her under arrest. Von Bülow had inadvertently created a situation that he was not at all prepared for, but he could not bring himself to savage this girl who resonated so strongly with him. Instead of desisting after winning a major victory, she pressed him even further, 'Do you want to fuck me?'

The words were bold and shocking, and von Bülow knew that there was no right answer, even as there was only one true answer. Now he had become the butterfly, and the pin had gone straight through. She pressed him further, 'Just tell me, yes or no?'

That a woman even knew the word surprised the men who happened to be within earshot; that she had dared to say it aloud in a public place was scandalous; that she had said it to a German officer - unthinkable. The effect on the onlookers was mixed. Some stood spellbound; others were not at all interested in finding out how this scene would end. All Frenchmen knew that Joan of Arc was burned at the stake, and that Marie Antoinette had met the guillotine – women didn't get to say and do whatever they pleased and expect to get away with it, much as men don't. Those who were of a more timid disposition hurriedly scuttled away, all hope of provisioning abandoned for the day. For them, the loss of food was offset by the chance to live another day. They had no wish to be caught up in the inevitable backlash instigated by this outspoken female.

For von Bülow, it was as if the scene had been foretold. He knew this woman was wrong from the time she had looked him full in the face. She had nothing to lose, and was now backed into a corner. Her next words were spat out, 'Unless you force me, you can find your own whore, you Boche pig!'

Even the staunchest supporters were wavering now. Flinging insults at a German officer was a folly of the worst sort. A thrill of pride rippled through their ranks but it was mingled with a very large dose of impending danger.

Von Bülow could only be pushed so far. Unusually for him, on this occasion it was further than his peers would have found acceptable, 'I could have you killed or beaten for that remark.'

When the penalty is death, what else is there to lose? 'Yes? Is that how it ended with your other woman?'

The suggestion rocked him. Past events came flooding into von Bülow's mind in their entirety, swamping his senses. He could barely see, and shaded his eyes with his hands. He drew breath, exhaling slowly. He stared intently at her with pin-pricked pupils, ready to unleash a physical assault if there was one more word. On cue, she subsided.

Despite the woman's provocation, he was still under her spell. Irrationally, she would always be forgiven for having hips that were so clearly non-male, 'Good day to you.' He stalked off, experiencing firsthand the burning feeling of humiliation. He was sure it would pass, but the memory would simmer. No-one would have won a prize for surmising as much, either.

Now he knew what it must be like to be on the receiving end of a beating. The shock of open hostility was the last thing he had expected from the girl. It was not how civilised people conversed.

Well, that has cured me of her at least. Not at all like a dog with a bone, as I had feared. Further, von Bülow accepted that if slight physical differences were not enough to overpower his certain knowledge of bygone times, the deplorable manners of this exotic creature clinched it.

But by God, to behold her was to witness divinity given flesh. Such a pity that her vampire tongue drew blood so easily.

40

It was a lonely place, standing there on the cobblestones. The German officer had departed, though the remaining guards were looking at her as if she had performed an act of God. Regardless, she had lost her place in the food line. That was the tangible reward for her spite, and it left a bitter taste.

'Miss, I would be honoured if you would take my place in the line.' It was a young man, invalided out of the war if his shortened arm was any indication. She glanced at him, appreciative but suspicious. He seemed sincere. *What man doesn't know how to play that card?*

'Thank you, sir, but I could not ask it of you.' There was a protest from others in the line. They spoke quickly and to the uneducated ears of the Germans guards it must have seemed like a gabble. She heard references to the restoration of French honour, of courage and fighting spirit, of making a stand. It was precisely the kind of talk that got people arrested, and the reason that public gatherings were forbidden. It was all so much rhetoric.

The first man insisted, 'Please, just to be practical. There is no way of knowing if he will be back with company. Get your food and go home quickly.'

There was a general consensus in this regard. Unable to argue with the logic, she moved to stand with him, 'Thank you, sir.'

He seemed as pleased as a puppy. She studied those who were looking at her in admiration. Some of it was the usual speculative lechery; some of it had a different aspect – genuine respect. None of these individuals had stood by her when she was face to face with the despicable officer. On the one hand, it was understandable. To only fight battles that were winnable was a sound philosophy. And yet, some of these men and women had undoubtedly lost a large part of who they were. *Has this poor boy not made his sacrifice for France?* She elected not to prick him. There was no need to court more enemies than one already had.

'You had best hope he never sees you again.' *Typical. See a pretty girl and they all start blathering like asylum inmates. Have any of them ever considered that sometimes shutting up would work best?*

She smiled in a parody of confusion, 'What harm? He as good as admitted that all women look alike. He couldn't even distinguish me from one of his regulars.'

The ex-soldier tried for gallantry, 'He may be a bastard, but at least he has discerning taste.'

It never ends. How do they not see the insult?

One of the older women came to her rescue, 'Stop drooling over the poor child. Do you not see that she has had enough for one day?'

There were more loud protestations of denial.

She was having none of it, 'Pah!'

Fuel had been thrown onto the discussion, 'Quiet your tongue, woman! Where were you when you were actually needed?'

Where were you?

The old woman shut down. Gradually the line quieted and edged slowly forward. The amputee found his voice again, 'Miss, what you did was both brave and foolish. It is only your looks that saved you, I would think.'

'Do you not think it was those same looks that drew the pig's attention to begin with?'

He smiled, gently and slightly mocking, 'Your face is such a curse. What is your name?'

'I am sorry, sir. If I told you my name then they -' here she nodded meaningfully towards the soldiers, 'would be able to find it out from you.'

He nodded, disappointed but accepting the reason. Nevertheless, he knew a brush-off. The kicked puppy drew a shred of sympathy from her, 'If you knew me better, you would not sing so sweetly.'

Hope was again rekindled, 'If I knew you better?'

She regretted the comment immediately, and ignored further attempts at conversation. The silence was awkward, but welcome in its own way.

There was consternation at the head of the line, followed by mutterings of outrage. The gist of this filtered quickly to those nearer the rear. The food was gone. The supervising Germans bid them to disperse. The crowd disintegrated as everyone headed to their respective homes.

The girl walked away with nothing to show for her day other than a confrontation that would be better left forgotten. *Next time I will curb my tongue.*

Chapter 5

November 1916: Safari Hunter

Von Bülow sat at his table eating his breakfast. He saw one of the new faces approaching and sighed inwardly. *They will need to be taught not to interrupt me in the morning.* The man was making a beeline for him. As he passed a nearby table, Reinhold reached out and plucked the fellow's sleeve, then spoke quietly to him. A nervous glance was shot across the room.

Reinhold, he's dependable. Von Bülow crooked his finger at the veteran, who got up and strolled over, 'They'll learn, Seb.'

'Maybe. My father always said that youth was wasted on the young. I see now what he means; these fellows don't know a thing.'

'They're the same age as us, near enough.'

Von Bülow smiled, 'That was one of the other things he said, 'There's nothing like a good war to help boys become men'.'

Reinhold shrugged, 'That's one perspective. I'm inclined to think it prevents a lot more of them from becoming men at all – and that's from personal experience.' Briefly, they both thought of Hockheimer. The pain of the memory did not stab von Bülow as sharply or as deeply as it had done before.

Von Bülow waved a finger to indicate the others in the room. He didn't know any of them very well, 'He said that all young men make most of the same mistakes. I used to think that he was trying to goad me, but now I see the truth in it. It applies equally to men new to battle – they are unable to discern foolishness from experience, and they are at first unable to assess which response is more likely to be the correct one. If they choose poorly they are more likely to die, but given time they will sort out the truth of the matter.'

Reinhold made a pretence of peering into von Bülow's mug, 'Are you sure this is coffee?'

The comment elicited a quiet laugh, 'My apologies. It is a bit too much to discuss over a meal.' Von Bülow dabbed at his lips with his napkin, then rose from the table, 'Walk with me.'

He led Reinhold outside. As usual, the morning was cold. A thin dusting of snow lay underfoot. They barely registered the fact. Not far away the *Jasta's* aircraft were sitting side by side on the dead grass. There were now three additional Albatros scouts, but the Halberstadt had been written off in an accident a week ago. Someone was clambering all over the ageing Fokker DIII. Another figure was sitting in the cockpit. Von Bülow shaded his eyes, 'Can you make out who it is?'

'Becker, I think.'

They went to see what he was doing. A large dog was lounging underneath the aircraft with its shaggy head half propped up by the wheel it rested against. As they approached it got up and padded over to them, sniffing around their legs.

Von Bülow eyed it with distrust, 'If it pisses on my trousers I'll shoot the mutt.'

'You'd better get it right with your first shot, Seb. This one looks like he'd have your hand off.'

The distraction gave the man in the cockpit time to climb down and meet the other officers halfway. When he recognised von Bülow he lost some of his enthusiasm. 'I see you have met Typhus.'

Unaware that the commander had little interest in trivia, he supplied a morsel nonetheless, 'The German word is the same in English.'

'If that's your criterion, why didn't you name him Octopus?'

They were now close enough not to have to raise their voices. Reinhold knew what von Bülow would be thinking, and thought to get in first to soften the blow, 'Are you laying a claim on that battered thing now that you have wrecked the antique?' He wasn't talking about the dog.

Becker grinned sheepishly. He had still not lived down the incident with the Halberstadt, 'Sternberg has been trying to fix the problem with the rear cylinders. They're over-heating again.'

Reinhold nodded, 'They always do on this one.' It was a common failing of the type.

Von Bülow was not particularly interested. The sooner the Fokker was turned into scrap, the better – it was difficult to maintain proper formation in the air when one machine kept lagging behind the rest. Becker wasn't all he had been cracked up to be, either. The plane and the man were made for each other, if anybody cared for his opinion. He was prudent enough not to say it out loud.

Becker may have lacked some of the desired skills as a pilot, but it didn't make him an idiot. He knew what the commander thought of him after wrecking the Halberstadt, and he had a fair idea on how to divert von Bülow's attention if the man intended to discuss it further, 'I still can't accept what happened to Boelcke.' It was a low blow to bring up the name of a dead man simply to distract attention away from himself, even if no-one was hurt by the tactic.

Von Bülow nodded grimly, 'He was a lion among lambs – there will never be anyone to match him! Forty victories - imagine that? No-one else has even half as many, and only a handful have reached ten. I myself am still waiting on my fourth. But forty! That is a record that will stand forever.'

Becker agreed, 'Frankl and Richthofen – those are the two to watch out for now.'

'Give me a Prussian over a Jew any day of the week.' Von Bülow's attention was drawn to the men working on the Fokker, 'Excuse me while I have a word with Sternberg.'

As soon as he was out of earshot, Becker frowned, 'I'm sure that Sternberg is a Jew.'

Reinhold took Becker quietly to one side, 'I saw what you just did.'

There was only open-eyed innocence, 'Me?'

'What's in it for you, Becker? Why did you want to fly?'

The answer was cryptic, 'Last year.'

'What do you mean?'

'I joined the army to see what it was like to get firsthand experience of war.'

'Well, that would do it.'

Becker laughed, 'You don't understand. I wanted to write what the poets write, but I needed to understand it first.'

'You are a writer?'

'I worked for a newspaper.'

'So why didn't you become a war correspondent?'

Becker looked at Reinhold as if he was impaired, 'That's reserved for the senior journalists - the very senior ones. I was just the office boy.'

Reinhold back-tracked, 'So what happened last year?'

A far-away look came into Becker's eyes, 'The guns never stop. To learn how to distinguish between the various calibres of artillery shells isn't an experience I'd recommend. Within a few weeks I realised that I was going to die, so I decided to learn to fly before it happened. Humanity has been wondering about flight for hundreds of years – thousands. I took the opportunity.'

'That's it? You'd prefer to burn than to be blown to bits?'

'No. That's why you jump in the event of fire. There's fear, but no pain.' He was so matter-of-fact about it as he clapped his hands together, 'And the end is quick.' He grinned.

'Maybe one day they'll find a way to adapt parachutes for use in aircraft, rather than just for use in the kite balloons.'

'I think the static line would become fouled as you climb out. It'll never work.' They looked over at von Bülow, who was now standing pointing at something on the wing of his own machine. He appeared to be deep in conversation with Sternberg. Becker gestured towards them, 'He's got a death's head painted on the side of his Albatros. I'm guessing it means he came from one of the Hussar regiments?'

'Uhlan. That is to say, he was meant to have. He learned to fly instead. I'm sure the skull is in part to appease his father. They argued about it apparently. Seb said he'd just as soon plummet to his death in a plane as fall off a horse, and that the view would be better on the way down.'

'Fall from a horse? Can't he ride?'

'He can ride. He can do anything – if you don't believe me, ask him yourself.'

Reinhold's statement had been deadpan. Becker was unable to detect any irony, if any had been intended at all. 'If nothing else, I'd say he made the right decision, for no other reason than that machine guns are a better instrument of war than a lance.'

'There is that.'

Von Bülow had started making his way back to them. Becker nodded in his direction, 'You've known him a while. What does he want out of the war?'

'He wants to line his gun sight up on the man who killed Boelcke.'

'I thought he died in an accident, a collision with one of his own fellows?'

'Seb is quite unforgiving when these sorts of things involve men from within the ranks.'

Becker had his tongue placed firmly in his cheek when he mused, 'Why stop there?'

A gleam came to Reinhold's eye, 'Who said he stops there?'

Becker's curiosity was aroused, 'Who else?'

'Anthony Fokker for one. And before you ask, it's because he's Dutch.'

'What does he have against Dutchmen?'

Reinhold smiled, 'They aren't German.'

That got another laugh out of Becker, although why von Bülow would hate the man most responsible for advancing Germany's aircraft development was beyond him.

'Does he like anyone?'

'He likes Hermann.'

'Which one specifically?'

'One day you'll hear it from the man himself.'

'That's a bit unreasonable.'

Reinhold extended an inverted palm, 'Maybe you should take it up with him?'

Von Bülow was now within hearing, 'Take what up? Do you want to take the Fokker up?'

Becker's reply was bland, 'I was just curious as to your intentions once the war is over.'

'Well, we must have plans, eh? There's no use in thinking that this adventure will be the end of us all – that would just result in lying awake in bed all night. One needs to be well rested before you can expect to come home from the dawn patrol.'

Reinhold and Becker exchanged a glance. Von Bülow was oblivious, 'To answer your question, it is my intention to go on safari in South Africa. I have always wanted to shoot an elephant. To see how hard they fall.'

He tapped the toe of a boot with his victory stick. All pilots had such a stick; they were used to commemorate successes over the enemy and carved notches into the wood every time a kill was scored. Being the same size as a walking cane left ample room to keep a record of one's tally. 'That's why I call this fine staff The Tusk.' Von Bülow's men had in fact wondered about the name, having heard it mentioned on other occasions, but no-one had felt like subjecting themselves to one of the commander's lectures by asking. Until now. Not that they had asked.

Typhus was doing as dogs do, licking his scrotum without regard to that which may be said about the wholesomeness of the activity. Becker indicated the dog and joked, 'I wish I could do that.'

The expressed desire was crude but von Bülow only laughed, 'I'll pay you ten marks if you do, but if he bites you it will serve you right.' It had not been the precise meaning of Becker's comment, but the men had made the most of it.

Reinhold's attention went back to their discussion about firearms and he had some advice on the matter, 'You'll need a decent rifle.'

Von Bülow took a moment to get his bearings before he realised that Reinhold wasn't referring to Becker's pet, 'No, the art is in placing the shot. I'd like to think that my shooting skills will further improve the more combat I participate in. One day I'll use it to get a decent trophy – there must be some sort of record that needs breaking for using the smallest bore to down a decent sized bull. To place a shot precisely – that is a worthy goal. The heart, the brain, maybe the eye… so long as the weapon has sufficient penetrative capability, a hunter should always challenge his limits.'

'Well, no need to go to Africa. I hear Martinsyde send them over now and then.' Reinhold was of course referring to the British-built G.100, nicknamed the Elephant because of its excessive size and poor manoeuvrability.

Becker chuckled, 'I'm sure their mahouts are protesting about the nasty poachers that keep going after them.'

Von Bülow said, 'What's a mahout?'

Becker struggled to keep a straight face but managed it, 'I am sorry, gentlemen, but I should be getting back to the Fokker.'

Von Bülow watched Becker's retreating back, 'What's his story?'

'He fancies himself as a poet.'

The young *Jastaführer* ran a hand over the stubble on the top of his head, 'Poets don't survive wars, Ernst – though they write about people who do. People with martial spirit.'

'Who's to say that is even enough?'

'It's better than what he has. I give him a month. Will you take a bet on it?'

'Not if he has to fly that damned thing. No.'

Chapter 6

December 1916: Snowbound

Claude Dumont stirred the embers in the brazier as the snow continued to fall outside. Some units had decent quarters. His squadron did not. The only good thing about the tent that he lived in was that it was waterproof. It did not make up for the lack of heating. As night fell, so did the mercury in the thermometer. Winter was always at its fiercest in times of war.

Dumont sat on the corner of his cot, swathed in multiple layers of clothing. Beneath his uniform he wore two sets of woollen underwear. Over his uniform he had a sheepskin coat, plus gloves, scarf and a knitted cap. A blanket was pulled around his shoulders, another about his knees. None of it seemed to make any difference. In normal weather, Dumont was a neat little man with magnificent facial hair. His bristling moustache had enough character to write verse about – not at all like the anaemic examples that so many of the ridiculous English seemed to favour. Their tastes ran to excrement. Handlebar or pencil: how was there possibly any choice between the two?

For now, the miserable Frenchman hunched over his puny fire. The meagre heat did just enough to stop the snot from his runny nose from freezing in his moustache. He wiped it away with a sleeve, which now bore a wet silver streak reminiscent of a snail trail.

Upon the only other rickety bed in the tent, huddled under his own blankets, lay the squadron's latest replacement pilot. No-one knew what had happened to the last man to sleep in that space – that one had simply failed to return from leave. Whether he had deserted or fallen foul of misfortune remained a mystery. Dumont didn't spend too much time thinking about it. He looked at the motionless form. *Is he asleep?* In the veteran's opinion the new fellow should be giving thanks for the weather. It was keeping him away from the pointy end of the war.

'Wake up, Bonnet.'

He was answered with a muffled grumble, 'What is it?'

'Your foot is sticking out – leave it too long and you'll get frostbite.'

'I'm cold.'

You won't be making that complaint when you are shot down in flames. But he just said, 'Don't rub your feet too hard or the skin will come off. You don't want to get an infection.'

'How do you bear it?'

Dumont couldn't have been bothered answering. The pinch of the cold on his nose was making it run again. Absently, he wiped it once more. Inside his gloves, his fingers had become numb. He took the gloves off and placed them as close to the fire as he dared, the better to warm them. He then held his bare hands near to the flame, until the bite of returning sensation told him it was safe to put them back into the gloves. The process was a never-ending cycle.

The men eventually crawled beneath their blankets and tried to sleep. They pulled the covers up over their heads – the act prevented waking with eyelids frozen shut. Sleep was almost impossible in such conditions. Even exhaustion cannot keep out the cold, and each of them woke several times during the night wondering if it was killing them.

After another fitful night, they stayed in bed until they were driven outside by the desperate need to urinate. They could have performed the ablution in their chamber pot, but it only delayed the inevitable. Fumbling with buttons and fastenings was difficult enough, but shrinkage presented problems of its own. Each man's poor member was reluctant to emerge into the hostile sub-zero environment. The nature of the problem caused Dumont to piss on his fingers. *It isn't the first time and it won't be the last.* He curled his fingers and the urine, which had instantly frozen into a crust, crumbled away.

'Are you ready to go and get something to eat?' There was no point in bringing food back to their tent. The bitterness in the air would have defeated any attempt to transport a hot meal, so they shuffled to the kitchen together, hoping that the bread would be edible rather than frozen solid. If there was any butter it would be a lost cause - a solid brick impervious to knives. Coffee would at least be warm if it wasn't taken outside.

Together, the miserable pair carefully negotiated their way to the kitchen. The ground was frozen, and in places slippery underfoot. Wary of skating, they took great care not to fall; men had slipped and broken bones. There was no difference between earth and rock in these extreme conditions. *Amundsen and Peary voluntarily travelled to the Arctic? Idiots.* Dumont flapped his arms about to get his blood circulating better. He was careful not to do it with too much vigour; he didn't want to lose his balance.

How does anyone fly in this? Though it was true that combat was heavily restricted during the winter months, there were a few pilots who somehow found the inclination to get themselves airborne and do battle with each other. Dumont felt that it would have been more prudent to express one's aggression by playing dice indoors with mess mates and ignoring the war until the weather improved. *Napoleon was a bigger fool than the explorers. No-one in their right mind fights in winter.*

'Be careful of your footing, Bonnet. If you break your leg you won't see an ambulance for some time.' To have issued a coherent phrase had taken considerable effort. The cold had seeped deep into his mind, clouding all judgement and slowing his thoughts. If his lips had become too numb to properly enunciate his speech, he didn't notice.

Bonnet sat at the same table as Dumont, and the established pilot didn't have the heart to tell him to find someone else to befriend.

It didn't take very long until the new man started pestering him, 'What advice can you give to me?'

Though the intent of the question was undoubtedly related to battle tactics, he gave more immediately relevant information, 'Don't let your feet get wet. You'll get gangrene.'

Some of the other older men would have been amused by Dumont's predicament in other circumstances, but their discomfort had dulled their motivation.

'I mean about fighting the Boches.'

Dumont ignored him. He had a headache and needed to get drunk. If he felt ill, at least he should have a better reason than the bite of the raw air in his lungs. It hadn't been far from his tent to the kitchen, but that didn't mean the trip had been enjoyable.

Across the room Montagne was setting up his chess board, chapped fingers poking reluctantly out of a pair of ragged and fingerless gloves. Dumont doubted that anyone would want a game.

Once, chess had been used by some as a proxy for warfare. The thought made him disgruntled, mostly because the possibility no longer applied and he was risking his skin because of it. Dumont mused that maybe one day someone would invent low velocity bullets that didn't kill a man; then wars could be decided with pretend duels where no-one was harmed. Upon further reflection, he doubted that the world was made that way. Without the risk of bloodshed, there was no sense of honour. And without honour, there was no point.

'Get me a drink and I'll tell you a story.'

For his part, Bonnet was as weary as anyone else but he also recognised that once flying resumed, his life expectancy was poorer than that of any other man present. Determined to reduce the possibility of his early demise, he got up and did Dumont's bidding, 'Here.' He set the booze down with a thump. It was about the only thing that didn't freeze solid when you looked the other way.

Dumont drank straight from the bottle and passed it across the table. He weighed his words, 'The world and everything in it is for mankind to use as he sees fit. That's in the Bible. Everything: land, animals, slaves.' That was the sum total of his story. It made perfect sense to him, but he couldn't explain it any better. He could tell that Bonnet had not appreciated the imparted wisdom, and was expecting something more. *Too bad.*

'What does that have to do with flying?'

'Birds.' Dumont was sure he had already mentioned animals. Having reminded himself of birds, his thoughts meandered to flying against the Germans, each pilot twirling about the enemy in the dance of the dogfight, intent on not making a fatal error. 'Air fighting is a fair fight: one on one, except for the initial surprise attack which shows whether your opponent is a worthy foe – though if you kill him before he sees you, that answers the question. Also if you die.'

'How do I see him first?'

'You're new. You won't. Stay with your leader. Then you will learn.'

'What about shooting?'

'Forget that for now. Unless you are bullet proof, there is no way to make you believe that you cannot be shot. Very quickly you will understand how difficult it is to survive contact with the enemy. If you live, there will be little of use left for me to impart. The first few meetings with the Boches will be the most important ones. Forget about being a hero. You are not Pegoud or Guynemer, and neither are any of the rest of us.'

'Pegoud is dead, no?'

'You see? And you are not. So, you are not him. What is left to say?'

Bonnet seemed unconvinced, but he said nothing.

Though Dumont had claimed otherwise, air fighting was not chivalrous, though he would not say as much directly. Bonnet would work that out in his own time if he was lucky enough to live that long, provided that the winter didn't kill them all in the meantime. Dumont didn't derive any comfort from knowing that the Germans were also suffering from the cold – they deserved it.

Chapter 7

January 1917: The Crossing

Percy Wiggan craned his neck as he looked up at the immense ship looming ominously above him, whilst a myriad of men stamped a seemingly endless procession up the gangplanks. The ship was being loaded with the latest batch of reinforcements bound for France, and Wiggan could not but help to compare the activity to cattle bound for the knackers.

The hubbub of so many people all talking at once filled his head and could not be ignored. It lacked the intensity of a football stadium packed to the rafters, but it was the nearest approximation that he could imagine. The ship was adorned with an obscene number of banners and streamers, but these days the decoration was mostly to keep up appearances. Gone was the expectation that the war would be soon won, and though families still came to bid farewell to their boys, now it was a more solemn affair; many more of them expected their goodbyes to be final. There was no longer anything to cheer about. The losses had only ever gotten steadily worse and the aftermath of the Somme had left an expectation that there was still more to come. It was all too predictable these days. No-one pretended otherwise.

Volunteers were no longer enough to sustain the battalions. The Military Service Act was now in effect, and conscripted men made up the bulk of those who rubbed shoulders with Wiggan. Though there were still some who had volunteered – Wiggan was one such – the tone of the army was now that of an entity unwillingly doing the bidding of the state. Enthusiasm was at low ebb.

A generation had been shattered. There was the inevitable loss of life, but even those who managed to survive would never be the same again. The twentieth century had been ushered in with many wonderful expectations, yet all that had been delivered was loss of innocence. Those who had signed up for bloody adventures had gotten more than they had bargained for, and it would be fair to say that they now believed in being careful what they wished for.

Wiggan knew all of this, but there he stood with a satchel hanging by a strap from his shoulder, feeling part of something greater than himself. Not a stupid man, he could still not shake off the sense of being specially anointed. Part of his elation came from looking like he fitted in. Every button polished, belt and boots shining from careful ministration, he clearly took pride in being one of England's most recently minted officers. When he had seen his name printed in the *London Gazette* he had been very proud. He had cut out the small notice that bore his name and glued the clipping into a stamp book.

In his own mind, he had mapped out the probable path that he would walk. To begin with, he knew he would need to impress the veterans with whom he came into direct contact on a daily basis. The surest way to get their attention would be to claim his first victory quickly. It seemed that the best way to do so would be to force the other fellow to land. Shooting bullets into a German may be unavoidable over the long term, but it seemed too abrupt an initiation to begin proceedings. It would be far more sporting to wave a friendly cheerio to the vanquished and then be on his way.

Having thus shown his potential, the next order of business would have to be survival. Only then could he have a chance to further his successes. Wiggan was sure that further victories would come in time, though perhaps not enough to expect the most prestigious awards – no need to be too ambitious – but perhaps a Military Cross would be a good starting point.

Wiggan's instructors had left an indelible impression upon him due to the level of their expertise, and he felt that in time he would also like an opportunity to garner the same respect. What better compliment could be given a soldier than to be entrusted with training the next intake of recruits? After all, without capable reinforcements to replace those who had fallen, the war would very soon end in defeat.

After a stint as a flying instructor, he would probably return to active service as a patrol leader. Ultimately, he would like to acquire enough seniority to assume command of his own squadron. *In all honesty, that will take considerable time. Surely the war will be over before then?* Either way, he intended to be part of the victory celebrations – in Wiggan's view, live heroes were happier than dead ones. In the meantime, it was important to have plans.

Wiggan had an inkling that others may have had similar expectations, and that many of those dreamers had seriously misjudged their futures. Though some ambitions are modest, when everyone has the same goal even these can only be achieved by those who climb over the corpses of the ones who fail. *Moral fibre: that was the most important quality.*

He gazed once more at the troop ship. Most of those men were bound for life in the trenches. By all accounts that was a bad business. Wiggan did not consider that his job description was the more hazardous alternative. He patted the orders tucked into the pocket in his tunic. *The big adventure is about to begin.* He shrugged his carry bag more comfortably across his shoulder, then took bold steps onward.

Until this day, Wiggan had never been aboard a ship in his entire life. The sea surge was an eerie sensation, and because the novelty of it was enjoyable, he failed to understand how it could cause anyone to become ill. *Surely that should apply more to those of us who are on the water for the first time?* His mind wandered towards men who made their living on the sea, and speculated that part of the allure must be because it was so alien to normal occupations. And not only alien, but unforgiving. *In winter, if a ship sinks, do you freeze to death before you drown?*

The decks were filled to capacity, and knowing that he was just one of the writhing mass of khaki, Wiggan understood the value of submarine warfare. He tried to envisage the effect that a torpedo hit would have upon the vessel. It wasn't the most comforting thought. Both sides were trying to prevent supplies from reaching their respective enemies. From a certain perspective, Wiggan knew himself to be one such supply – a reinforcement.

Britain's surface fleet was more visible in their role of refusing admission to the continent, but Wiggan was more perturbed about German methods. Submarine warfare seemed more ruthless, and many neutral ships had been sent to a watery grave. Neither side was about to back down from their respective blockades.

U-boats had less inclination to delay merchant shipping for inspection than they used to when the war was new; now they skipped the formalities and simply sank their victims without warning. There were rules that applied to naval intervention, but Wiggan was unsure to what extent they were adhered to when countries were fighting one another in earnest. Piracy was internationally condemned, but when both sides considered the other

61

to be acting illegally, where did things really stand? He wondered how many articles of law were being broken, and if anybody cared, really?

The end justifies the means. By extension, it was no wonder that Germany did not hold back. Wiggan amended his thought, looking for a reason to show that his side was in the right. The Royal Navy blockaded ships without sinking them, at least that was what he thought to be the case. On the other hand, Germany was known to attack neutrals. Where did the line get drawn? Even if the torpedoed ships were indeed carrying war supplies, and Wiggan thought it likely, shooting civilians was unacceptable. It did not occur to him that the Allied governments were using non-combatants as a shield to ferry munitions to and from their shores. The *Lusitania* was but one example. Sinking an American passenger ship may have been in violation of international agreements, but there was a war to be won.

Still, the Germans were committing the greater sin. The perspective all depended on whose side you were on. *What would a true neutral say about it?* It would probably be something along the lines of, 'War is evil and you are all guilty.' Unfortunately, the world was not black and white. Like photography and cinema, everything was in shades of grey.

Wiggan had a brief notion that his vessel should be draped with a large flag denoting a hospital ship. The short trip across to France was making him nervous. If it meant improving his chances, he wasn't averse to a degree of subterfuge. And that was the heart of the whole issue. The trick was in successfully hiding unpalatable truths and convincing the voting public that they were on the side of justice. It wasn't even that difficult to pull off: everybody wanted to believe that they were on the right side of God, and quite often convenience provided enough reason to ignore damning evidence. Inconsistency has never been a crime in international law.

Wiggan guarded his thoughts. The complexity of just this one issue was tying him into knots. The whole mess was entirely more involved, and Wiggan was glad that he did not have to participate in constructing national policy. As a boy, he had once heard a saying that now made more sense: *In war, to reason is treason.* It was a pithy summation of the times.

He looked out over the expanse of water surrounding him, and had the first misgivings about boarding the ship headed to the meat grinder that was France. Somewhere out there, right now, a U-boat captain could be eyeing him through a periscope lens. There were many eyes watching the water, and the chance that he alone would spot something so small was infinitesimal. Nevertheless, Wiggan went back to staring at the slate sea.

Though he was preoccupied, he still noticed the activity around him. For the most part he was left alone, the enlisted men reluctant to converse with an officer. It suited him just fine. The ship was rolling gently, and now some of the soldiers were beginning to look unwell. Wiggan wondered what it would be like to feel their queasiness. He reached into his pocket to draw out a cigarette, briefly entertaining the thought that it would be interesting to suffer sea sickness firsthand - the better to round out his life experiences.

No sooner said than regretted. One of those nearby chose that moment to unload his breakfast. A small amount spattered Wiggan's boot. The offender realised his error and mumbled, 'Sorry, sir.'

Wiggan waved away the apology. There was no point getting upset over it, though he wasn't moved to offer belated tidings for the Christmas season. *There's no need to get too carried away with the full gamut of life experiences – secondhand vomit is unpleasant enough!*

A shower blew briefly across the crowded deck, turning to fine pellets of sleet. Wiggan squinted against the sting and bowed his head to keep it out of his eyes. The experience was uncomfortable, but no more than that. He had sympathy for those bound for life in the trenches, acknowledging that theirs would be the true hardship to endure. As a pilot, foul weather meant there would be opportunities to squirrel himself away in the comfort of his quarters with a cigar and a bottle of something strong.

The murmur of voices was constant. Wiggan idly allowed himself to imagine how much more raucous his fellow passengers would become if they saw the wake of a torpedo bearing down upon them. Feeling like a man apart, he didn't consider that such a circumstance would apply to him personally. He had unconsciously cast himself as an impartial observer in his mind's eye.

Wiggan leaned on the handrail, careful not to let go of it. He didn't intend to fall overboard; if he did, the ship would never be able to turn around in time to rescue him. He wondered again how cold the water was. Based on those times when he had washed his face in a cold basin, he expected it to be shocking. *If the ship went down, how long could a man last before he succumbed?*

Several yards away, Wiggan saw some Australians also leaning on the rail, oblivious to their surroundings. Their uniform was fancier than that of most others standing nearby. He could overhear snatches of their conversation. It appeared that they were returning to the front following a short hospitalisation. Wiggan wondered if they would speak to him if he went over to them. He intuited that having a King's commission would not be enough to engage the colonials as equals, at least not in their eyes, so he did nothing.

Their laughter drifted across to him. Wiggan only caught a snatch of what they were talking about, '...the Light Horse. So there I was, trading a white feather for an emu feather!'

Thank God I'm serving in an English squadron – no need to mingle with the men from the colonies and dominions. One of the Australians chose that moment to relieve himself over the side, amid great mirth from his fellows.

Chapter 8

February 1917: Pastimes

The German officers entered the empty hotel. Von Bülow approached the bar and sat himself down upon a stool. The publican made an announcement that seemed to give him some degree of satisfaction, 'The bar is closed.'

'Do you speak German?'

The sullen look could have meant either yes or no. Von Bülow was unperturbed, 'We shall converse in French, then.'

'The bar is closed.'

'What do you have for sale?' It was as if the owner hadn't spoken.

The Frenchman chose a more prudent course, 'There is some watered-down ale. That is all.'

'Horse's piss.'

'It is all I have.'

'Are you sure? I seem to recall that you said you were closed, and now you are willing to trade.' Von Bülow leaned conspiratorially towards Reinhold, *sotto voce*, 'The French, they sell their daughters too, I am told.' Reinhold did not re-join with commentary that could have implied rental instead of purchase.

The publican eyed them warily, 'I am sorry, but there is nothing else that I have left in stock.'

'Perhaps you would like to show me your cellar to prove the claim?'

The elderly man spread his hands in helpless innocence, 'Certainly. Please, I will show you the way.'

It was unlikely that the man was fabricating his tale; shortages were normal. Without bothering to answer, the uniformed men turned on their heels and left the premises.

Once outside, Reinhold mused, 'Of course, he could have been lying.'

'I'm not interested in chasing phantoms in a labyrinth. If he has a cask hidden away it would be too much bother looking for it. We have our bottle; it will suffice.'

'A word of warning: if he's holding out on us he'll be crowing to his friends about it.'

'The same way that he's crowing about living under German rule?'

Reinhold considered, 'I suppose we can tell some of the men to wreck the place next time they get leave. At least it will stop our own hands from getting dirty.'

'It's not too late to change your mind if you want to come with me.'

Von Bülow had never learned how to change to a new topic. Reinhold made an adjustment and shifted gears mentally, 'No, I've already told you that I have a girl.'

Subtlety was for others, 'She's no good to you at home.'

Here we go again. 'Maybe one day you will understand.'

Von Bülow felt that others could benefit from his wisdom, and he was not amenable to resistance. Consequently, his constant bulldozing only encouraged others to spurn his offers of help whenever possible. He could not understand the wilfulness of it all,

'What is there to understand? The frustrations of a Catholic priest as he listens to a whore's confession?'

Reinhold looked into the dreary sky, 'I will wait for you in the bar, Seb.'

He was given a hearty clap on the shoulder, 'In that case, I shall be back later.'

'Not too much later, I hope?'

A ghost of a smile played across von Bülow's face, 'Well, it has been a while. I shall apply economy of movement for maximum results. It's a bit like combat flying, if you think of it in a certain way.'

'Well, when you are out of ammunition, you know where to find me.' The two men laughed loudly at the wordplay.

Reinhold walked back into the empty barroom. The publican pretended to care, 'Where is your friend?'

'He is attending to a private matter.'

'Ah, I see…' A leer, 'Private, as in a bedroom?'

'Mind your own business.'

You tell me this – to mind my business - in my own country, under my own roof? I hope your bastard friend buys a dose of something very painful for his troubles.

But his face was expressionless, 'You wish for a drink?'

'I don't like horse's piss.' Reinhold reached into his coat and pulled out his own bottle, 'Get me a glass.'

The barman reached under the counter and recovered the one glass specifically reserved for such occasions. He had never told another living soul for fear of betrayal, but this glass has had the unwashed cock of a Frenchman rubbed around its rim. He casually placed the glass in front of the German.

Reinhold gestured with the bottle, 'Will you join me?'

The barman could not decide if he had been insulted by being offered a drink in his own bare establishment, or if the German was in fact a decent fellow. All else considered, he refused to believe the latter. He reached under the bar for a glass of his own.

Reinhold filled the first glass, ignoring the other. He took a swig from his bottle, 'Drink up, my friend.' His steely eyes seemed to bore into the Frenchman, daring him to decline.

Caught in his own snare, the barman made the most of a bad situation. *You sly Boche bastard.* At least it wasn't someone else's residue on his lips - a small consolation, but it was all there was. He drank down the contents in one go, not wanting to suffer the mental taste again, grimacing at more than the unaccustomed burn of concentrated alcohol.

Reinhold was sympathetic, 'It's been a while, I see. Hard liquor is very hard to consume when out of practice, no?' He poured the man another.

The publican eyed the glass. He would have to put his mouth on the same place as before for his own sake. What if the German noticed? Did he suspect anything was amiss? It was not as if he expected them to become familiar, surely?

'Drink up, my friend. We'll finish the bottle.' For his part, the visitor had only had a mouthful. The contaminated glass was obviously going to be filled a few more times before the ordeal was done. *Best to drink quickly and get it over with, otherwise the treacherous pig will never leave.*

Von Bülow walked briskly up to the plain wooden door and knocked. He immediately heard footsteps on the other side. The door was opened far enough for a head to peer through the crack, 'Hello?'

69

'Hello, madam. I have your address from a friend.'

'Of course, please enter.' He felt the older woman's eyes upon his person, surreptitiously measuring him.

Inside, the foyer of the brothel was tidy without being extravagant. 'How may I help you, sir?'

He was typically direct, 'How much?'

From long practise, the woman knew how much banter to lay on. She risked a saucy jibe, 'How long?'

Von Bülow gave a knowing grin, 'That is for your girl to find out. Ask her afterwards if you're still curious.'

The owner had taken careful note of the cut of his uniform. He was worth a bit. *These ones are always arrogant; they can't seem to help it.* She charged him double without batting an eye. If he was aware of the extortion, he didn't let it show.

He paid the money, 'Bring me some girls to look at.'

'Only to look at?' He stared back at her, an unblinking gaze suddenly as cold and empty as a fish's.

The madam disappeared, and returned with three candidates. Von Bülow's demeanour changed in an instant, docile to animated, as though he had been electrically charged. It was the girl: the one who he couldn't get out of his head. He failed to even register the other two. But this one… she made eye contact, recognising him immediately. She wilted before his eyes.

The madam was experienced in subtleties, and regretted not charging him even more. *Who is this officer?* His look had turned hard, 'What is your name?'

The girl was mortified. The silence extended between them.

He turned to the owner, 'Tell me this girl's name.'

The madam didn't even pause, 'Simonne.'

Von Bülow knew he was being lied to. No prostitute ever used her real name. He casually surveyed the room, pretending to notice things for the first time, 'You have beautiful furniture.' It was nothing of the kind, but it was all there was to be had. He walked over to the windowsill and picked up a vase, 'Expensive.' Again, an exaggeration. He gently set it back down, 'Tell me, how many items do you possess within this house that the German army would find useful?' The threat was very real. Anything could be stolen without recourse to compensation. The word most often invoked was 'requisition.' Nor would any penalty apply for wanton destruction of property.

The assembled women remained silent. They knew that this officer could break them with a word. *He looks so calm, but he can afford to.* He was relentless, 'How many rooms do you have?'

'Six, sir.'

'Six. Hmm.' Von Bülow leisurely considered the fact, savouring possibilities, 'Would you consider it to be an imposition should these…six…rooms…be used to billet some of my men?' There was no point in answering. The question was clearly rhetorical. No vacant rooms meant loss of income. It was a simple equation: a brothel with no rooms was doomed.

'Do you think I am threatening you?'

'No, sir.'

He raised his eyebrows, feigning surprise, 'No? Then kindly tell me what it is that I need to say to get the idea into your stupid brain.' Again, there was no right answer.

'Perhaps I can assist you?' Von Bülow drew his service pistol and pointed it at the madam's head. His eyes were strangely out of focus as he relived events that had happened elsewhere. It was probably the war, 'You will now tell me this girl's correct name, and she will produce her identity card to verify the fact. If you are lying to me I will shoot you.'

The madam was frightened by his bluntness, and judging by the reactions from the whores, she was not the only one, 'Yvonne.'

'This young lady will have a last name.'

'Coiffard. Yvonne Coiffard.'

He crooked a finger, 'Papers?'

Yvonne was furious, and stormed from the room. Von Bülow remained ominous, 'And you, madam? What is your name?'

The reply came out as a squeak, 'Charlotte Gerard.'

'I may call you Charlotte?' She gave him a shaky nod.

'If Miss Coiffard does not come back I will kill you. Do you believe me?'

Another trembling nod, 'Lucie, c-can you find...?'

Even as she faltered, the remaining whores fled the room. Von Bülow laughed out loud, 'I cannot believe they are both named Lucie? Perhaps for one it is a real name, and the other a pseudonym?'

Charlotte stood in abject terror. She could lose everything: her livelihood, her house, her life. Men like this one had turned the civilised world on its head. Before the threat to life and limb could be put to the test, Yvonne came striding back into the lounge, frightened but putting on a brave front. The pistol was tucked away with a flourish. She thrust the card into von Bülow's face with a defiant hiss, 'Here!'

He read the card and smiled, 'So quick to judge others, and yet I see you are married. Is he proud of you?'

Yvonne was crying frustrated tears of pain and rage, 'My husband is dead!'

Von Bülow's next words would have been no different had he been buying a sheep, 'I will have this one.'

Charlotte Gerard fought for some dignity. It was possibly all she had left in this life. Germany was in a position to wrench it all away. With the thought, she regained some measure of composure, 'She doesn't want to be with you.'

He idly toyed with his holster, 'I don't recall asking for her preference, or your opinion.' His tone was so mild, yet implacable.

The two women look imploringly at each other, neither able to help. Lucie and her colleague were nowhere to be seen. Von Bülow was losing his patience, such as he possessed, 'Come now, I'm sure she has been with Germans before. It's why you charge extra: we are very good for business. Perhaps you are aware that I am not obligated to pay for this service, but do so as a matter of personal honour?' *Did he even see the absurdity?*

He offered his arm to Yvonne, and she was compelled to accept it. Von Bülow smiled encouragingly at the small hand resting daintily on his forearm. As he led her away, he was moved to add, 'Maybe I'll return her without too much damage. Oh, and the business of threatening to shoot you? Of course I was only joking. You gave me little choice in the matter. We are not beasts.' His smile was a thin one.

Yvonne took the officer upstairs, the picture of abject misery. Each ascending footfall seemed one step closer to the gallows. She let him enter her room first, and he turned to her, 'Hello, my pretty one. It looks like I have found my own whore, after all.'

She refused to answer, or to meet his eye, but he didn't care, 'I tried to speak with you once before. That's not what I require from you now.' He was wasting no time with his clothing, and bid her to do the same. Not wanting her threadbare garments torn away by brutal hands, she complied. That mistake had been made before; new dresses were hard to come by and clothing that was once fit only for the rag basket had become one's Sunday best and needed to be cared for.

Even within the less respected professions some days are more degrading than others.

When he was finished he held her and even though he had already paid for her time, he told her that he was willing to continue paying extra if she agreed to be seen with him socially.

There was so little left to salvage, but the effort needed to be made, 'You cannot buy me!'

His callousness was never far away, 'I have already done so once. Tell me you refuse the offer and I'll just have you at no charge instead.' He studied her face, reading the flow of thoughts in her mind as tears streamed down her face in shame, 'If you think to avoid me by running away I will have your friends whipped.'

Yvonne's distress left him unmoved, 'Of course you won't. You asked me the first time we met what sort of woman I thought you were. There is no need to ponder the question any further, and I even know your price.'

He had been dressing quickly and looked down at her forlorn figure, 'I shall make the necessary arrangements with your employer.' He bowed, the perfect model of courtly behaviour. It was completely incongruous in the circumstances.

Charlotte was seated downstairs, waiting for the axe to fall. Von Bülow nodded curtly to her, 'Don't get up, I shall let myself out.'

She stared at him in a daze, unsure if he was being sarcastic or polite. He paused at the front door, 'You shall be hearing from me again.' *What can of worms has been opened now?*

Chapter 9

March 1917: A Sporting Chance

Sitting side by side on a rough-hewn plank resting on empty oil drums, the small group of men watched with detached interest the proceedings not far away. On the grassy expanse that doubled as their airfield, a friendly game of cricket was in progress. Sometimes these games were friendlier than others.

The sky was clear this morning. The fog had long since burnt off, 'Still a bit of a nip in the air.'

'You say the same thing every day, Burke.'

'Not used to this pissy climate. A sorry excuse for summer, if ever there was one!'

'It's spring.'

'Just as pissy.'

'I thought it was supposed to be the English who whinge all of the time?'

'The correct term is 'Pommy,' you stupid bastard. And your fucking habits are rubbing off on me.'

'Well, one can only hope that it is not reciprocated.'

'One can, can one?'

Ross Burke was an Australian flying with the RFC, and his distinguishing feature was a mangled ear which he told all and sundry had been shot off by a Turkish sniper two years previously. In truth, he had never been to the wild shores of the Ottomans.

Almost a decade older than most of the others in the squadron, in his early thirties, Burke was an old man by the unforgiving standards of frontline operational units. Though unusual, his age was by no means unique; there were other instances where men of his years still defied the deterioration that had begun to erode their faculties, especially their eyesight, and continued to serve faithfully in a combat capacity.

The men's attention went back to the game. It was the usual deal: the squadron's pilots versus their observers. The observers were batting, and had lost their first two wickets cheaply. Captain Lewis-Hamilton had brought himself on to bowl. Fielders crowded the new man at the crease. The bowler put one in short, the batsman ducked under it.

'Bit unnecessary, taking advantage of the uneven bounce like that. The poor chap hasn't even had time to get his eye in yet.'

Drummond sounded almost mournful, 'Why is Ryker even batting at four?'

'Because Dunhill decided he wanted to represent a different mob: bed and breakfast courtesy of Kaiser Bill.' Dunhill and his pilot had been shot down two days ago, but were seen to scramble safely from the wreckage of their RE8. They'd be sitting behind wire until the fighting ended. Others had been less fortunate.

Drummond didn't care about Dunhill. The man had the best chance to survive out of all of them, now that he was out of the war. Their attention went back to Ryker, 'He's useless.'

'You're bloody useless, but I let you sit next to me.'

'Listen to Mister Victor Trumper of Australia.'

'I should have opened the innings. It would have kept one end intact, at least.'

'On that surface? It's so poor it makes everyone who has a bowl look like Johnny Briggs.'

'What, they've got wonky eyes, have they?' It was an unflattering comment on the wily bowler's physical appearance, and entirely uncalled for.

'I saw Briggs play once, against Middlesex. Of course, at the time I was just a tyke. He took four wickets in a blink. Stirling effort, very deceptive.'

'Only a Pom would be proud of deception.'

'As a serving member in the armed forces of the British Empire, it is just one of many things to be proud of. Keeping company with boorish colonials such as yourself, however, is not one of them - strictly an impartial observation, of course.'

Burke scoffed, 'An observation? You must be an observer, then. Welcome to the fucking RFC.' He then affected his best King's English, 'That is what we call the Royal Flying Corps, if you are one of those not familiar with the airman's terminology.' He produced a pout that looked like he had eaten an un-ripened grapefruit: his interpretation of English snobbery.

The game pottered along. Nothing much happened in the way of runs being scored and Ryker looked like he had dropped anchor and was digging in. As usual, he was unexciting to behold. The fielders had fallen back to assume more defensive positions, except for Wiggan at short leg. The greatest rivalry was always between pilots and their own observers. Ryker saw an opportunity that he fancied and made solid contact. The ball cannoned into Wiggan. The close-in fielder fell to the ground clutching his ankle. The spectators roared with approval.

'Ha! Taken down by his own man; a modern rendition of David and Goliath!'

'I thought it was Goliath who had the club?'

'Ryker will live to rue it, mark my words. What happens if Wiggan is unfit to fly? Or worse, he thinks that he is fit and his ankle gives out at ten thousand with a Hun on his heels? Ryker will have to pay the butcher's bill with him.'

'I'm sure Wiggan won't feel his ankle much in those circumstances.'

'Probably trying to get himself grounded.'

'The C.O. wouldn't allow it. He's the best man in the squadron.'

'Bollocks. He's just lucky. Herman von Boring keeps wandering directly into his field of fire. Or at least he did until we were made to fly these damned things. I thought we'd have gone all right if we could only have hung onto the FEs a little longer. But RE8s? The only things worse are BE2s.'

'The only thing worse is having to sit here listening to you bitch and carry on the way you always do.'

In the meantime, Wiggan gave his smarting leg a vigorous rub before climbing gingerly to his feet. He resumed his position with no small degree of stoicism.

Drummond leaned forward for a closer look, oblivious to the fact that over such a distance the minimal body movement made no difference to his eyesight, 'He looks unperturbed, but I'll wager a pound that he'll flinch if Ryker has another crack at him.'

'I'll take that bet.'

Drummond instantly back-peddled, 'Ah, I was only speaking hypothetically.'

The others seated on the plank piled scorn upon him, 'Cheap, that's what you are. All talk.'

'It's just that I don't have the money on me.'

'Because you're cheap.'

Lewis-Hamilton came back on again for another spell of bowling. Ryker played and missed, and then again. The next ball climbed into the area of his ribcage, caught some bat handle and lobbed straight to Wiggan, who plucked it out of the air more easily than an apple from the tree of Eden. Ryker cursed in disgust, tucked the bat under his arm and made his way back to the makeshift bench.

Burke was nudged in the ribs, 'You're in.' The Australian clambered to his feet and prepared to face the Old Enemy.

As he sauntered in to the take his guard, he was greeted at the wicket by the familiar commentary, 'Here he comes, the flag-bearer of the Players.' The taunt implied that the pilots represented the better-bred Gentlemen, the much-lauded amateurs of the sport. No doubt many of them aspired to such an ambition, although it also meant that the observers were relegated to representing the game's working class. The fact that one of them was an Australian added spite to the label.

Burke was happy to engage in some gamesmanship. He looked at the bowler, the same man who brought him home safely every time they flew into combat, 'And who are you then, a hyphenated version of Sid Barnes?'

Lewis-Hamilton gave him a cheery wave and doffed an imaginary cap, 'Dear boy, no doubt you wish to emulate your precious Trumper again?'

Burke pointed at the aircraft parked at the perimeter of the airfield and declared, 'I'll clear that bloody contraption in this over to prove it.'

The bowler drew himself up, indignant in spite of himself, 'How on Earth do you propose to do that, you braggart?'

Burke knew that he had gotten under the man's skin, 'Easily. Everyone knows how Trumper batted.'

Lewis-Hamilton saw an opening, and exploited it without regard to propriety, 'Exactly my point. Past tense. The poor man is dead, is he not?'

It was as plain as the nose on his face that the civilised world was involved in a war that was well on its way to killing millions, but the insensitivity of the remark incensed Burke. In a world that was increasingly sordid, there were elements that should have remained sacrosanct. Trumper had died relatively young after an extended illness only two years previously, and it was something that many of his countrymen had been deeply affected by. This was despite the fact that at the time of Trumper's passing, Australian troops were embroiled in the star-crossed Dardanelles campaign at a God-forsaken place called Gallipoli, where thousands of their fellows had died more horribly than the sporting champion, 'You'll pay for that insult, you low bastard!'

Lewis-Hamilton made a show of strutting back to the start of his run-up. He turned on his mark, paused for half a heartbeat, then came striding back like a roaring locomotive. Lacking an umpire to penalise him for the act, he deliberately over-stepped the crease by half a yard in order to extract an extra advantage, and let fly with a thunderbolt.

Burke charged at him and gave a mighty heave of the bat. His lusty swing failed to connect with the ball. There was the dead sound of leather on wood that all players of the game know. The pegs sat askew and both bails tumbled through the air, fetching up with soft thuds in the grass a few feet away.

Lewis-Hamilton gave Burke a send-off, 'And that's how Barnes disposes of the redoubtable Trumper.'

Burke pointed a forefinger, enraged, 'A no-ball!'

'Sorry, old cock, you must be mistaken. I'm afraid the umpire didn't pick it up.'

Some of the players closer to the action looked sheepish, but they were disinclined to interfere with a superior officer, especially when he was virtually going toe to toe with his own observer.

Burke fired another shot in a confrontation that had escalated well beyond niggling, 'You must be a friend of Grace's. What's his full name? Oh, yes, Doctor DisGrace. That fat bastard has pride of place in your smug hoity-toity black heart, and was notorious for his cheating ways. He taught you well!'

Lewis-Hamilton reddened at the aspersion cast upon the great man of English cricket. Knowing that he had contributed to the current situation, he simply responded with a lift of his nose and an exaggerated accent, 'There's the pavilion, you uppity Orstralian lout. Be a good sport and make way for the next man in. Even a *player* as esteemed as your Victor made his fair share of ducks without quibbling about it.'

The disparaging class reference to the dead Australian Test opener was not lost on Burke. Instead of braining the bowler with the bat, as he so richly deserved, Burke stormed off, smashing at clods of turf at his defeat by dark forces.

The victorious bowler made light of the incident, 'Dear me, these southern folk are such sore losers. Who's the next man in?'

'Looks like Humphrey Drummond, skipper.'

'Well, let's make him welcome.'

The abusive chatter was more restrained this time, in part to rein in the effects of the previous incident. In reality, it had more to do with Drummond not being an Australian national.

Burke resumed his place on the bench, disgruntled that he had let his own pilot get the best of him. The same ruthless streak had gotten them through many scrapes together, but a line had to be drawn somewhere. Lewis-Hamilton was a man who simply could not bear to lose. He was very compatible with the Australian in that regard, but it usually led to confrontation when they faced one another at twenty two yards. It was as well that they weren't carrying pistols.

Drummond was making a decent fist of his time at the wicket. His usual playing style saw him work the ball around for singles, with the odd two thrown in for good measure. He was known for a stubborn willingness to stand behind a straight bat, forcing the opposition to prise him out. Out of nowhere, he struck the ball cleanly over the infield. There was a call from short leg that alerted the field, 'Cat shit!'

Burke exchanged a look with Ryker, 'That's something you don't see every day.' He was referring to the shot itself, not having accurately heard the comedy call made by Wiggan. It was part of Wiggan's subtlety, and the man had no intention of ever letting on. It was enough that he amused himself.

'Here, look! Barry's under it.'

The men on the bench took a sudden interest. Barry was completely unaware of the event, tethered to a stake and content to nibble grass. They all wanted to see how the goat would react if it was hit. The ball missed. The goat looked on with mild interest as the ball bounced along the grass, before resuming breakfast.

Everyone was still looking in the general direction of the dumb animal, when movement in the background caught their eye, 'Someone coming for a visit.' It was an aircraft on a direct bearing for their position. It sharpened their focus.

'Blimey, I think it's a Hun!'

There was no time for preparation as every man looked after himself, abandoning the familiar routines that had preoccupied them during the ritual of an organised sport. The cricket game disintegrated as the various RFC members ran pell-mell for the nearest available cover. Burke and Ryker upended their plank and lay it on its side. They cowered behind the makeshift barricade knowing that bullets would tear straight through it, but at least aware that they were shielded from the notice of those eagle eyes peering down at their exposed position. Machine gun fire rattled in their ears over the sound of the rapidly approaching aero engine. Ryker poked his head up for a look, 'Looks like a Roland to me.'

'Get your head down, you stupid bastard!' Ignoring his own advice, Burke also peered over the top of the plank to get a better idea of the state of things. So far as he could tell, the cricketers had abandoned the airfield. Every one of them had fled to safety wherever they could find it. The only living thing in sight was Barry, desperately straining at the rope and bleating in terror, but barely audible over the roar of the engine and the staccato sound of the machine gun.

Burke looked up. A small object could be seen leaving the German machine, flung from the confines of the open cockpit. It landed near the parked aircraft and exploded. Another bomb followed. This one landed next to one of the parked RE8s.

Clearly satisfied with the effect, the impertinent pilot circled overhead once, then headed back the way he had come - in and out, as elusive and mischievous as a will-o-the-wisp.

In no time men emerged from their hiding places to assess the effect of the surprise attack. One of the planes was burning like a bonfire, its skeleton exposed as the skin was eaten by flames. The initial shock of unexpected action was quickly wearing off, and it was expressed in unusual high-spiritedness. These were men who had seen a whole lot worse in recent times. A piddling strafing run ruining their game was almost beneath their notice.

Lewis-Hamilton came to stand beside his observer, but addressed Drummond, 'Do you still think that all Huns are called Herman von Boring?' Though he had not heard the comment from that morning's play, there were many other occasions in which he had. Englishmen were nothing if not creatures of habit.

Burke answered in Drummond's stead, 'Cobber, I'd say that was the work of Fritz Trumpermann, a distant cousin to a slighted man of considerable repute.' It would take more than a few paltry bombs for the Australian to forget the most recent under-handed tactics of his captain.

Lewis-Hamilton wondered if he had permanently soured things with the gunner. Perhaps offering an olive branch was the best balm? 'The business of shooting men in the back seems to have made us less disposed towards fair play in matters not associated with life and death.' It was barely adequate as an apology, but the admission was as close as the commander of 'B' Flight was able to bring himself to express.

It merely reaffirmed Burke's view of the world. The war was forcing too many men with different backgrounds deep into one another's lives. Many of them found it to be very difficult to accept that others were equal in at least one area: the job of survival. Concepts of brotherhood were all very well, but the average Englishman still found it irksome to have to rely on men from the colonies and dominions - men whom they held in low regard because of their origins. Burke was sure that he was not the only one who hoped they choked on their ingrained sense of superiority.

'Will someone shut up the bloody goat, or I'll put a bullet in the flaming thing.'

'Here, steady on, old boy. Barry's had a dreadful fright. We shan't get any milk from her today, I should think.'

'Who calls a nanny Barry? Didn't anyone think to lift its tail before naming the stupid thing?'

'Show some respect, Burke. Barry's the squadron mascot, and a source of milk and cheese to boot.'

'Piss off, Drummond. It's as useless as you are. That's why you tried to kill it with a cricket ball just now.'

'Oh, ho! It took the Kaiser himself to get me off the wicket – how poorly does that reflect on you, with your own feeble performance?' No matter which cricket team one played for, squadron allegiances were more commonly rooted in one's place of birth. Further, if a man happened to be born in the same country as another, it filtered across to postcodes. Human beings are wired for rivalry. No wonder there was a war on.

In the distance, a faint voice was reciting a familiar refrain. The words were far from original:

'There once was a man from Leeds,
Who swallowed a packet of seeds.
Great tufts of grass,
Sprouted out of his arse,
And his balls were covered in weeds.'

Chapter 10

April 1917: Bloody April

The early part of nineteen-seventeen was a golden time for the German pilots of the *Luftstreitkräfte,* at least so far as combat losses were measured. Throughout the entire war, a typical *Jasta* averaged just a dozen men killed, and as many wounded. The scale of these losses was progressively more severe as the Allied air forces increased their own resources. When the first *Jastas* were formed, they were comprised of a largely hand-picked cadre of highly motivated pilots who were the cream of the flying units. Fighting in concentrated formations, these men re-wrote what was possible, and Allied losses jumped alarmingly. The events of the previous year paled in comparison. Casualties in the *Jastas* were negligible.

For the Germans, new fighting aircraft had reached the front in significant numbers. The most sought-after machine was the Albatros DII. It was one of the first of a new generation to be powerful enough to be able to carry two machine guns as standard armament. The increase in firepower would prove to be decisive and spurred the Allies into developing their own response.

During the preceding winter, the DII had been further upgraded, resulting in the remarkable DIII. The 160 hp Daimler engine fitted to the earlier type had been replaced with a Mercedes power unit resulting in an increase in performance to 180 hp. This greatly improved both acceleration and rate of climb. Its fuselage was of semi-monocoque construction whereby the plywood skin was wrapped around the airframe. This method of manufacture gave it the same strength afforded to any animal with an exoskeleton. If the Albatros had a weakness, it was that the wings would sometimes fail if the machine was handled too aggressively in battle. Combat pilots, being what they were, often found this out the hard way.

By April nineteen-seventeen the Albatros DIII was the most numerous German fighter in action, and though only a few *Jastas* were operational at this time, their effect upon British and French forces led to this time being referred to as 'Bloody April.' Though more than three hundred Allied machines were destroyed during the month, this was just a taste of things to come, especially when placed into the context of the final year of the war. However, it was by far the most destructive period in the air fighting to date, and was very instrumental in the rise to fame of Manfred von Richthofen, whom the English knew as the Red Baron. His unit was *Jasta 11*, and his men ran amok: Richthofen and Kurt Wolff claimed over twenty victories apiece that month. Germany's premier pilot became the first man in the world to celebrate fifty aerial victories.

Ultimately the DIII would be replaced in service by the DV, and though the latter type was another improvement, by the time it was in widespread service it was too badly outnumbered in the air to have the same dominance over the enemy as the first models had enjoyed.

Another mission, another kill. Von Bülow was satisfied as he took stock. His men had fought well again today. This morning's success brought the commander's overall score to five. Reinhold was the next best with two; four other men had one victory each. Against this was just two men killed in action, though one of those had been today.

All in all, though, in accountancy terms von Bülow's men were well and truly in the black.

Prior to April, only the commander and Reinhold had troubled their victory sticks with carved notches. Now the other men were learning at an accelerated rate, and von Bülow was leading the way. He had expected nothing else. Almost half of the pilots in the *Jasta* had registered their first victories. The remainder were champing at the bit, not wanting to be left behind in what had become a feeding frenzy along the entire length of the sector.

Oskar Lehmann was one of those striving without success, and feeling very aggrieved that none of his comrades had supported a claim for a machine he had destroyed. Three witnesses agreed that they had seen thick smoke emanating from its engine, but it was not enough. It didn't help matters that no wreckage had been found in the location that he had indicated.

He reached out a hand, 'Can I try it?'

'You don't smoke.'

'Last year I didn't fly, either.'

Reinhold passed the cigarette, 'They calm the nerves.'

Von Bülow smiled, 'That's not all they do. Try grabbing a cat and hold an ember to its arse – you'll get some entertainment for sure.'

Lehmann looked appalled, 'You've done that?'

'Life is cruel, but that doesn't mean it can't be funny.'

Reinhold laughed at the picture in his mind, 'Didn't it scratch you?'

The commander smiled, 'He was running too fast to be thinking about drawing blood.'

Lehmann sought some clarification, 'Was it a pet?'

'Undoubtedly, but I never found out whose.'

Across the room a heated discussion was underway following the most recent briefing, and tempers had started to fray. The German system of confirming victories was black and white, and pitted men against one another in a competitive manner. Each aircraft that was proven to be destroyed needed to be credited to someone. Unfortunately, there were many cases where two or more pilots felt that others were trying to grab recognition for work that wasn't rightfully theirs. If any disputes couldn't be resolved within the *Jasta*, the case would be put before an arbitration commission that had been established for exactly this purpose.

This morning, Rossler was furious, 'Two! Just because it hasn't been done until now doesn't mean it can't.'

Beerenbrock may have been new to the *Jasta*, but he was having none of it, 'Garbage; I was onto him as soon as he killed Becker.'

'And then I shot him down. How could you see what I was doing? You were fixated on the bastard and didn't notice that I was in your blind spot.'

Mellerhorst was almost at the point of restraining them, but his choice of words showed the direction in which he was leaning, 'Rossler, you'll never convince anyone that you got two, especially in view of the fact that this is your first combat claim. It's the first for *Leutnant* Beerenbrock as well, so share the joy.'

'No. That Nieuport is mine. I have witnesses.'

'They all say that both of you were shooting at it together.'

'And that I got the other one first.'

'That is an unrelated issue.'

'The first one proves that I can shoot straight. What does Beerenbrock have to support his claim?'

Beerenbrock rejoined the fray, 'I was on him first, and he went down. I'm not saying you weren't part of it, but I was there first!'

'Doing what? Following him home, for all anyone can tell.'

Von Bülow had been listening to the argument, and now he had heard enough. He weighed in, 'My recommendation on this dispute will influence the final adjudication if you can't agree, and that could takes months. One or both of you could be dead before a decision is reached.'

Rossler glared at the commander. He knew exactly what was coming. To say he was disappointed would be inaccurate, because he expected to be denied by his class-conscious superior and the unfairness of it all was anticipated and probably even inevitable.

Von Bülow saw the look and derived a spiteful satisfaction in denying the insubordinate tyro, 'Rossler, the word of an *unteroffizier* will have far less credibility than that of an officer, and especially so when you have no support from anyone else. That you even think to question the honour and ability of your betters is something I find personally offensive. You want two? Not even I have ever shot down two!'

He dared the enlisted man to speak against the biased decision. Rossler was furious, but knew he was up against impossible odds. Von Bülow nodded in grim satisfaction that a point had been proved, 'You will accept my decision as the correct one, or you will find it very difficult to get confirmation for anything in the future.'

Mellerhorst cast his eyes down upon hearing the threat. It was unnecessary and not conducive to maintaining the morale of the men. If the non-commissioned ranks felt that they were being treated poorly by their officers, things would quickly turn sour. The adjutant was under no illusions concerning von Bülow's prejudices, but speaking them aloud was another matter entirely.

Rossler held his tongue. Beerenbrock knew he had inadvertently contributed to the scene, and looked as though he had eaten an apple and found half a worm in its core.

Von Bülow tapped his boot with The Tusk, 'So. Congratulations to both of you for your first victories. I shall have you written up for your Iron Crosses.' He smiled in a way that belittled their achievement while indicating his own tunic, 'Not the one worn on the breast; just the button-hole ribbon for now.' The two men would have had to have been both deaf and stupid not to hear the condescension. In any case, they were fully aware that there was an order of progression in the state's military awards system; von Bülow was only pointing out the difference in the varying classes for his own aggrandisement. It was his way of rewarding himself for leading his men on the scoreboard. To him, no other kind of leadership mattered.

Once dismissed, Rossler lured Mellerhorst away from the others, 'His family owns an estate, is that correct?'

Mellerhorst was unsure where this was going, 'And?'

'They'll fall upon hard times once he starts managing affairs. The seeds he sows will only ever grow weeds.'

Mellerhorst was no fan of von Bülow, but the officer corps was still required to appear united, 'Either way, the hired labour isn't placed to offer criticism.'

Rossler knew when he had run up against the establishment and accepted the rebuke in silence.

For von Bülow's part, it was nothing to put the morning's unpleasantness behind him. He was in any case otherwise preoccupied. *Damn Richthofen – he has all the luck when it comes to running across the hapless Englishmen. The man seems to bag one every other day, and we get hardly anything on this part of the front.*

*　　*　　*

Von Bülow and Yvonne made a picturesque pair walking arm in arm, both dressed to kill in their own way. Behind closed curtains, disapproving eyes bored holes into them as they strolled past. Yvonne felt the scrutiny as though it were cigar burns. Von Bülow for his part was oblivious.

Outwardly, they were a young couple trying to get along in a world being torn down around their ears. Only a very select group of individuals knew differently, curious to see what this unholy alliance would bring.

They talked of inconsequential matters, mostly. Every so often, one would probe for weaknesses in the other. They were not hard to find. Although von Bülow saw himself as master of both their destinies, Yvonne bowed to no man, notwithstanding the necessity of what was essentially an exchange of currency. Nor was she blind to his motives, 'I see what it is that you are doing when we walk these streets. The looks I get from passersby must give you a great deal of satisfaction.'

'On the contrary, I only refrain from shooting them like dogs because it would upset you if I did so. They are your own countrymen – you love that they hate you for your collaboration.' And once again, no opportunity to inflict a wound had been passed up.

'Listen to yourself: a preening peacock who loves the sound of his own voice and believes that he has some secret knowledge because of his name. In truth, you spend more time looking in the mirror than reading poetry.'

Von Bülow paused in mid-stride, 'It seems that I am unable to follow the train of your thought. I can tell by your tone that you are denigrating me, though for the life of me I am unable to find fault with your observation.'

Is this his attempt at wit?

'Yvonne, why is it that you resist me? My intentions are well motivated.'

'Is that what you call it: The Intentions? I had heard that men give peculiar names to their parts.'

'Why must you use love as a weapon?'

She was incredulous, 'Love? What misguided belief is this? I think you are mistaking your pizzle for a sacred concept.'

He sneered at her, 'Very clever choice of words. You think everything I do is out of malice. Need I remind you that the first time we met I was interested in getting to know you, and you abused me for it?'

'No, my comments were directed towards your boorishness and your limp-handed Kaiser.'

Insulting Wilhelm's disfigurement didn't bother von Bülow at all. He was a firm believer in physical perfection and though he wouldn't say so for fear of it reaching the wrong ears, the thought of a malformed monarch offended his sensibilities, 'If you wish me out of your life you need only say the words.'

'The words.'

He did a double take, not sure what he had lost in the translation. She glowered at him, 'Would that it was so easy.'

He was now bordering on exasperation, 'What do you want of me, Yvonne? I can give you more than just tins of coffee and biscuits.'

'You say these things, but it doesn't disguise the fact that you only buy my time with blackmail.'

'No, I have a far better price than that.' His smugness was impossible to ignore.

They argued in undertones so as not to be overheard. Von Bülow wanted to maintain an appearance of harmoniousness. Yvonne for her part simply didn't want to push her luck to the extent that she had on their first encounter. She doubted that there would be as lenient a let-off were it to happen again.

He took her hand. She endured the touch, though it would never wash off – she had given up trying. Von Bülow had turned gentle again, 'I look into your eyes, and they tell of your wounds. One day I would like to feel as though I am drowning in their depths.'

Yvonne would never be swayed by false sentiment, 'When I look into yours, there is no risk of drowning; your soul is far too shallow.'

His attempt at conciliation had been slapped down again, 'I am tiring of your waspish tongue. I'll walk you home.'

'And when we get there, of course I'll let you fuck me. It's all part of the arrangement, no?' To minimise her regard for his manliness was a poor strategy, but it was better than nothing.

'You should be thankful that I don't beat you instead.'

'Yes, I'm sure that I am eternally grateful for your consideration in the matter.'

He became enraged, 'You say anything that you can think of: you throw crockery, you never hold back! Me? I show restraint. I could bash you for your insolent tongue, and am entitled to do so. But I refrain! At least one of us has feelings.'

'The only feelings you value are those felt between the sheets.'

'Can we please not argue, for once? We sound like an old married couple.'

Yvonne graced him with her most withering look, 'No, we don't. Firstly, I was happily married until your army marched into my life and ended my reason for being. I happen to know what married life is really like. Secondly, you have no basic understanding of the concept, and that is demonstrated by your addiction to visiting brothels.'

'Do not forget it is where I found you.'

'No woman has ever met a decent man in such a place.'

He was getting the wild look again, and Yvonne wondered if he would strike her. He had never done it, but if it was to happen, she wanted it done in public. Witnesses would despise her for putting herself into the position in the first place, but at least they would see her fighting. She drew a modicum of comfort from the respect she had once garnered from others during her first meeting with this vile man, not so many months ago.

He must be deranged. How else to explain the sudden mood swings? He doesn't even seem to notice them. Are all soldiers like this? Was Jean-Pierre? Is it best that my love is dead, that I never saw him diminished in this manner?

Von Bülow's dangerous mood passed, though the rest of their time together went depressingly according to script.

Chapter 11

May 1917: Incomprehensible Allies

There was a restrained sense of relief within the squadron now that their RE8s had been exchanged for Bristol Fighters. The F2.B, colloquially known as the Brisfit, came with quite a reputation - one which had not yet been caught out. 'Yet' – that was the operative word.

Adam Burrows was the newest member of the squadron and had never flown the recently replaced 'Harry Tate' operationally. He took the stroke of fortune as a good omen, though omens had an uncommon knack of only sometimes foretelling the true course of events.

Burrows got on well with his observer and had already seen limited action. His first close look at the German Albatros scouts had been alarming, and though he had been on the receiving end of their gunfire he had survived the ordeal. Despite this baptism of fire, the veterans didn't act any differently towards him. Those that had survived the last month said that a novice's life expectancy was measured in mere weeks, and that perception had not yet had time to dissipate. He was still within the timeframe.

Things had quieted since April, but none were sure if the lull was temporary. Just to be on the safe side, replacement crews were still being treated as though they carried leprosy. Burrows couldn't say that he blamed the experienced crews for their reluctance to welcome the new men, since forming bonds with strangers was easier if the latter could first prove that they had the ability to survive. It wasn't an unreasonable expectation, though it set the newcomers apart when what they really needed was good advice.

One Bristol had been lost during Burrows' first battle with the Germans, and he had seen the effect that the death of the crew had left on those who returned home. Places had been set at the table for the missing men, and the survivors had gotten royally drunk to honour them. If losses had been so much worse before his arrival at the squadron, Burrows doubted that anyone could have been sober for two days straight. What with a perpetual hangover and the effects of the ever-present residue of the castor oil used to lubricate their machines, it was no wonder that everyone had a poor complexion and most complained of diarrhoea. The ones who didn't complain - those were the stoic ones.

Burrows' attention moved to the pair of French aviators who had found their way onto the British base. The visitors were attempting to communicate with some of the squadron's senior airmen. Whether the Englishmen were happy to converse with the Frenchmen because they would never know their allies well enough to mourn them, or because they recognised survivors of similar backgrounds, was unclear. Through a mixture of gestures, broken dialect and animal noises, men without a common language were relating their experiences to one another.

Burrows was not included in the conversation, but simply watching and listening allowed him to be able to ascertain that the Frenchmen had recently been involved in an incident involving the shooting up of a transport column drawn by horses. Apparently, the horses had fared rather badly.

Burrows liked horses and didn't approve of shooting them. Certainly there was a need to disrupt enemy supplies, but deliberately machine-gunning innocent beasts seemed excessively cruel, even allowing for the fact that some cruelty was inevitable. And whilst it was no more cruel than shooting people, at least the people had a sense of why. Burrows gave no thought at all to the endless procession of cattle, sheep and pigs that went to market, or the reason for their existence as domestic animals. At the end of the day, all living things were bred to die. War was just an extreme example of the fact.

Who had the horses belonged to? Burrows didn't speak any language other than that which the King approved of, and he was unable to decide whether the excitable pilots were bragging of their own deeds, or were indignant about something that they had witnessed the Germans doing. Eventually he reasoned that the horses must have been German, for no reason other than that he doubted that the French would have been fond enough of the species to carry on to such length about their destruction at the hands of the brutal Hun.

There was more discussion between the Englishmen and their French visitors. A misunderstanding had occurred in the nature of the strafing attack. The horses had not been pulling ammunition, as the English had first believed. In fact, they had been carting hay to the front. Without either article being available in sufficient quantities, the war would have quickly stalled.

From the time that the first shots were fired in nineteen-fourteen until the cessation of hostilities, artillery fire accounted for seventy percent of all casualties during the course of the war. Machine guns were deadly, gas attacks were terrifying because of their very nature and bayonet charges harked back to the old days. But it was the big guns that were part and parcel of the everyday experience of life in the trenches.

Yet for all of the destructive impact of the thousands of artillery pieces available to the various warring nations, it was horses that every army relied upon. Without equine muscle, very little could be packed up and moved to and from the rail yards. And horses ate hay. As inoffensive and innocuous as hay may have been, it was the lifeblood of the army. Men without food could still fire their weapons, but if too many horses grew weak from hunger or died of other causes, the war would be lost.

Idly, Burrows wondered if snipers went out of their way to shoot horses. As much as he was repelled by the thought, it seemed logical to do so. So far as he could tell from such limited exposure, the war had little to do with logic. Logistics, yes – logic, no. Not wanting to give anyone ideas, he kept his peace about marksmen deliberately targeting dumb animals.

What have I got myself into? Burrows did not fit in with this altered reality. He had thought it was terrible enough that some of his classmates had died during training without even leaving England's shores, but it was no preparation for the reality of actual warfare. Ties of comradeship bound his fellows to one another, but he had never questioned why it was so. Ultimately, it hinged on mortality: in a nutshell, no man wanted to die alone. Civilians lived in families and communities, and they understood the need for togetherness. They laughed, traded, married, raised children, grew old, and accepted that this was the correct order of things. However, nothing really equated to relying on people who could - and in all probability, would – die within the next few weeks or months.

Do populations band together thus during pestilence or famine? Even having such a thought come to the fore made him think that his life was forever diminished, no matter what the future held. *When everything is going well, why do we dwell on catastrophic possibilities? What is wrong with the minds of men that we dare fate to answer our questions?*

Burrows concluded that Maud was the sensible one after all. He decided that when next they were reunited they would debate these sorts of things. Furthermore, he vowed that he would not be so sure of himself in those discussions. When one's core beliefs were so clearly built on the unfounded opinions of youthful innocence, harsh experience was bound to impart some unwanted lessons. *Next time that she speaks, I will listen.* Adam Burrows had no recollection of any similar conversations with either of his parents.

Returning to the present, he heard one of the men asking whether anyone thought that the Frenchmen would be appreciative of some English flavour, by way of a recitation. The one that he had in mind had purportedly been invented by an armourer in their squadron, and without fanfare, they belted out a noisy rendition with gusto:

> A doughty one was Albert Ball,
> He was given a VC and all,
> His preferred means of attack –
> Shoot the Hun in the back!
> Now he's missing from the daily roll-call.

The performance came complete with hand gestures intended to emulate the course of Ball's battles with the enemy, but despite every best effort, all that the Frenchmen heard was nonsense. They failed even to comprehend the name of the great pilot, because his name was not pronounced in a way that registered to their ears.

For his own part, Burrows' sensibilities were offended. Albert Ball was dead, and not even long dead, and his receipt of Britain's highest award for valour had not been announced until after he had gone missing. The young Londoner was unable to understand how it was that within days of learning the details of such a tragedy, there were callous souls capable of composing ditties to mock the same losses that others found traumatic. He was unable to fathom whether it was a coping mechanism, or simply a way to proclaim one's immunity to the considerable suffering that surrounded combatants embroiled on the continent. Nor could he understand why others let such insults pass without comment. *Are they still all boys at heart, lacking the fortitude to do the right thing without adult guidance if the price is risking isolation from their circle of friends? How can such a thing be harder to do than volunteering to fight a war?*

He had no answers to any of the questions. Despite his indignation, Burrows bottled his disapproval inside himself, saving the words for those who may one day appreciate them. Whether anyone ever would – that would depend on who read his diary, and Burrows certainly intended to be selective about such an audience.

The veterans interacted as though he was invisible and most of the time he may as well have been. 'I doubt that the poor Frogs understood a word of it. I mightn't be able to speak their lingo, but they're looking at us as if we have escaped from a loony bin.'

'Well, you do sound barmy at the best of times. How much worse must it be for a foreigner?'

'Strictly speaking, we're the foreigners.'

'Not really. Going back a few generations now, I have reason to suppose that some of my forbears had their way with the local lasses in the aftermath of Agincourt. Or maybe it was Crécy... either way, it practically makes these garlicky fellows family.'

'Best not to say it to their faces, would be my advice.'

101

'Why not? They don't understand the King's English.' Mention of the medieval battles with the French may have got a rise out of the visitors, but the English pronunciation of French locations almost approached the level of butchery sustained on the Somme, and they were oblivious.

'If you can't communicate with the men, how on earth do you talk to their women?'

There was a knowing smile, 'Sign language.' And the fellow illustrated the point by pursing his lips in a parody of seduction. The patchy stubble of a man not yet old enough to shave on a regular basis detracted from his attempt to pass muster as a female - French or otherwise. Burrows' sensibilities were offended all over again.

After much shaking of hands and back slapping, the two Frenchmen went on their merry way. Another generation may have considered the fraternisation as good public relations, but at the end of the day the men shared common experiences that rendered their language barriers almost insignificant. It was a small matter that they knew nothing at all of each other. Burrows felt that the French may have benefited from their ignorance.

'What sort of people eat snails, frogs and mushrooms?' In Burrows' opinion, that was the first sensible question that anyone had asked.

'Bloody Frogs, getting us involved in their stupid war. If they had a proper monarchy none of this would have happened.'

'Don't agree with you, there, chappy. The whole trouble started because the Arch Duke was assassinated.'

'Bollocks. Royalty gets bumped off all of the time and it doesn't always start a war. Whoever uses that for a reason has blinkers on their eyes or a white cane to get around.'

'Any country that doesn't have a king is in a parlous state - Australia, for instance. Scrabbling in the dirt for survival – what hope have they ever got of learning cleanliness, let alone decorum?'

'The damned French are lucky we're in it on their side this time around.'

'They just need to toughen up and kill the Hun bastards more efficiently. The Frenchies are all too soft. It probably comes from their having to say *'merci'* all of the time.'

'I must profess that I don't understand much of their mindset. For instance, they take vulgarity to new levels by lionising their fliers the way they do. Where is the concept of working together?'

'Our chaps get the same treatment in the press, else how did Ball become popular?'

'An isolated incident. The Frogs keep scorecards, as though the whole thing is a sport to them.'

'Yes, that does go beyond the pale.'

Burrows quietly removed himself from the company of men who were clearly not deep thinkers.

'Have I any further need to prove to you that the English are crazy?' Dumont's observation on the sanity of the English was due in no small part to their execrable singing. The limerick was not a form of verse that was to be found in French culture. To them the entire concept was an incomprehensible curiosity.

Claude Dumont had warmed to Bonnet in the last few months mainly because Bonnet had proven to be reliable in combat, though he had not yet killed any of the invaders - not worthy ones, at any rate. Horses and their teamsters didn't count.

'Could it be that they were mocking your sister?' Bonnet's deference to the senior man was somewhat more familiar than it had been when he had first arrived at the front during the winter. Rather than a neophyte's awe at the incomprehensible, his affection was now tempered with respect born of appreciation of the other man's skills, for though Bonnet had not shot down any Fokker or Albatros scouts himself, he had witnessed Dumont adding to his personal tally of victories and understood the difficulties involved in the deed. To emphasise the significance of these achievements, the older man had also now been elevated to the command of their *escadrille*. It followed the usual method: the previous incumbent had been killed.

A gleam came to Dumont's eye, 'To do so would only prove my point. In my family, it is only my mother who was born ugly.' The words were said in jest, though they masked an underlying uncertainty. Claude Dumont had not seen his sister in a long time, and feared for her safety. The war was many things, but happy was not one of them.

'Lieutenant Dumont, I will have to say that the King, Kaiser and Czar could sort this entire mess out if only they would sit down to a family dinner together. Then we could all go home.'

'Perhaps the cousins could, though that would require the sort of sense only the French possess. In any case, I won't rest until you have shot down your first Albatros.'

Bonnet smiled, 'I don't think the world is holding its breath.' He didn't specify which part of the conversation he meant, but it hardly mattered.

'Speaking of holding your breath, did I ever tell you about the time I was in a cemetery when an artillery barrage came down on my head? Of course, I didn't know it was a cemetery, as there were no markers to identify the place, but the number of bodies that were unearthed told their own story.'

Bonnet had heard the tale many times, but Dumont never seemed to remember who he had told it to. There was still the same old ending to hear, 'The worst part was that they were Germans - '

'…which enhanced the stench.' Bonnet finished the sentence, and Dumont looked momentarily startled until he realised why the other man must have known the story.

Dumont gave an equivocal shrug, 'You can understand that I haven't forgotten the incident.' Incident. At any other time in a person's life, being strewn with body parts would not be dismissed so lightly, but frequent proximity to danger lent a certain perspective.

Bonnet pointed with his chin in the direction of the aircraft lined up on the grassy expanse of the airfield, 'Is that goat a nanny, do you think?'

Dumont shoved his corpses back into the mental box that they had leapt out of, and looked at the tethered animal, 'Are you thinking what I'm thinking?'

Bonnet grinned, 'That depends on whether you think we should steal it. Milk, butter, cheese.'

'Do you want to risk getting shot for it?'

'I already risk the same for pay that can't buy very much of anything useful. Not because of the inadequacy of the pay, but because useful things are in short supply. But a goat…'

'What about a dress?'

'I don't wear dresses, contrary to that which you may believe.'

'I meant as a gift for your girl.'

'For all I know she's already getting a supply of anything she wishes from one of the others boys in the neighbourhood. You understand? Anything?'

Dumont laughed evilly, 'There is so little left of you to be corrupted.'

'That's why we should steal the goat.'

'Maybe we should offer to buy it?'

'When the English refuse to sell, who then will get the blame if it goes missing?'

'Where is your faith in humanity, Marcel?'

Chapter 12

June 1917: Heraldic Beasts

Ross Burke was counting the days. In little more than a week, he was due for a posting to England. His first six months in France were just about done. Only two things stood in the way of that occasion. The first was if he got himself killed; the second was if leave was suspended because of an unexpected increase in the intensity of the fighting. Like the first possibility, the second could also be fatal.

'Excuse me, Ross, do you mind if I have a word?'

Burke didn't know what Burrows wanted, but he could hardly tell the boy to go away, 'Yes?'

'I have a letter from home.'

The Australian could tell from Burrows' face that nobody had died, nor had the boy been notified of a new love interest on the part of his girl. But what other news would require the counsel of another? Burke was sure he was about to find out.

'My fiancé has written me, and it appears that her sister has done something incredibly foolish.'

Burke didn't have anything against Burrows, but there was a distance between them that went beyond generational. The kid was too inexperienced in life as a whole, and he still seemed to have a large target painted on his back whenever he flew against the

Germans, 'What business is it of mine that I should care?' The question was more abrupt than he had intended.

Burrows looked at the ground, 'None of the others have done much more than their schooling; the same for me.'

How do you deny that? 'I'm surprised you noticed, but give it time.' The conversation was awkward. Just because he was past his twenties didn't mean that Burke had become a know-all old codger, though he would have been the first to admit that he had a decent head start on the other men he flew with.

Burrows was struggling with his need to confide in someone, 'I think that up to a certain age a person lacks sufficient experience to properly understand the world, so they make up theories to fill the gap, but the theories don't have a proper foundation.'

Strewth, a fucking philosopher! 'Give it up, Burrows. The only thinking you need to do for now relates to getting yourself back on the ground after each jolly jaunt to Hunland. After that: reload, refuel, get drunk. The rest is decoration.'

'You're older. You've got more perspective than the others here. They don't have opinions worth listening to, but you might.'

Might I? Burke sighed inwardly. Better to just get it over and done with, 'What do you want to know?'

'Maud is really quite upset. Her sister has disgraced the entire family.'

'Pregnant, I suppose?'

Burrows' expression was solemn, 'Worse! She went and got married to a total stranger. They hardly even know one another, and the cad didn't even ask her father for permission.'

Burke was unable to keep the amusement off his face, 'Unlike you, no doubt.' *Please Sir, I wish to bed your daughter.*

The earnestness of the younger man prevented him from detecting Burke's tone, 'Exactly. It's a terrible scandal.'

'Well, be thankful the lecherous cove isn't a sailor.'

'But he is!'

Burke laughed out loud. Burrows was shocked, 'It isn't funny!'

'It's only your puritanical upbringing that blinds you to the fact, but I'll tell you something for free: if it wasn't funny I wouldn't be fucking laughing.'

'I thought I could rely on you for advice.'

'Maybe you should revise your theory in that regard?'

Burrows' thunderous expression told that his disclosed confidence had been utterly betrayed.

Burke couldn't have cared less for the other man's distraught look. The fellow was completely over-reacting, 'You want me to write a letter to the scoundrel and tell him to return the wanton wench to a state of chastity? I'm thinking it's a little too late for that - notwithstanding that I am a complete stranger to the pair.'

Burrows was torn between running away and trying to salvage something from the shambles, 'Maud will never forgive her for the deed.'

Burke planted himself down, 'I'll tell you a story.' Burrows had a look on his face that said he was about to be taken for a ride and didn't appreciate the fact. It irritated Burke that people had less faith in him than they ought, 'When I was a lad my mates and I, we shared possession of a foldable blade which we had found, and which would have gotten us a fair hiding if our fathers had found out.'

'Fair enough, too.'

Burke didn't require the input of a Lost Boy and he talked right over him, 'One afternoon I was walking home and a swaggy waylaid me. I thought the smelly old blighter was going to murder me, and my hand went straight to my pocket. He didn't even see me do it.'

Burrows had no idea what a swaggy was, but he understood the gist, 'Did you cut him?'

'No. As soon as he got close enough to breathe his fumes into my face the bugger asked if I had some coin to spare. The next day I gave the knife to the kid whose turn it was next, and never handled it again.'

'See, your old man was right.'

Burke gave up. If this kid wanted to get killed in the war, then that was his business. You did what you had to do, but there were consequences if you made an error.

For his part, Burrows had heard the tale, but it was someone else's lesson. His woes were closer to home, and not in the least related to the violent mentality of those who hailed from a far-flung former convict settlement.

Burke saw that none of what he had imparted had made the slightest effect, 'What's her name, the sister?'

'In truth, Ross, I am ashamed to speak it out loud.'

'Then how about you learn to kill some Huns? The lass probably got carried away with things because of the war, and who better to blame than the ones who started it.'

'There's a grain of truth in that.'

'Just a grain? I'm flattered.'

'Maud always said that of the entire family, her sister was the sensible one.'

'Well, from all the carry-on, I'd say your girl's probably onto something. So given that she's worth your eternal devotion, what the hell are you doing in France?'

'Excuse me, but there is such a thing as honour.'

'That may be, but if you are here and she is not, what chance do you have of getting on-her?' Burke got the nuance just right, and Burrows flushed in indignation as tears welled in his eyes.

*   *   *

Smoke curled from the end of Oskar Lehmann's cigarette as he perused the newspaper he was reading. He had poured schnapps into his coffee to cool the beverage to an acceptable drinking temperature. The other pilots considered his concoction to be an abomination. Their opinion did not alter its flavour. He took another sip, unperturbed.

Reinhold grimaced at him, and was answered with more than a sardonic smirk, 'You fuss worse than my mother, Ernst.'

'Probably she'd disapprove of your excess when everyone else is doing without.'

Lehmann sounded bored, 'Probably.'

It was likely that the combination of liquids was specifically designed to incite ridicule. Even so, Reinhold was unable to resist the bait, 'Why don't you put your cigarette out in it if it's execrable flavour you desire?'

'You are already complaining about shortages but you'd approve of three ingredients? You don't consider that to be excessive?' Reinhold saw no profit in explaining exactly what constituted an ingredient.

They were joined by Beerenbrock, who scraped his chair out from beneath the table. Leaving drag marks upon the floor did not bother him, especially since yesterday when a bullet had nearly taken his arm off. He was still undecided whether the resulting holes in his sleeve

111

were a mark of distinction, or damage that would result in some personal discomfort now that it was ventilated and could let in the rain and cold. He brushed his cuff unconsciously.

Reinhold aimed a query at him, 'What is your view on Lehmann's tastes?'

Beerenbrock deliberately misunderstood the question, 'He likes boys? So much the better - there's less competition for the girls. I'm all for it.'

Lehmann snorted scornful amusement, 'The day you talk to a girl I'll eat a cigarette, lit end first.' Beerenbrock reddened at the remark and retreated from the conversation. Reinhold and Lehmann exchanged knowing grins. The day Beerenbrock first bedded a girl they'd put him in for a medal.

The grins vanished as von Bülow made his entrance. He seemed ebullient, 'Have I missed the party?'

Lehmann was happy to poke fun at his fellows, but the commander was definitely off limits. That one had no sense of humour if you applied the dictionary definition of the term. 'No, *Herr Leutnant.*' They had the same rank, but von Bülow was not one to let that stop the other officers from deferring to him.

'What are we talking about today?'

Von Bülow had not played any part in the conversation but no-one was about to point out the fact. The junior pilots looked in unison at Reinhold. The commander did not hold the veteran in thrall to the same extent, 'The usual. Drink. Women.'

The unsurprising answer fell on deaf ears. Von Bülow hadn't actually asked the question out of curiosity; it was his custom to interrupt a conversation and then steer it in whichever direction he was inclined to take. They all knew the routine by now. 'Who designed the damned Albatros, anyway?'

Everyone knew the answer, 'Robert Thelen.'

'And Schubert.'

Von Bülow waved his hand irritably in the air, 'Yes, yes, but which of those imbeciles is responsible for the placement of the radiator?' It was a fair question. The cooling system was situated on the top wing immediately above the pilot. In the event that it became punctured by machine-gun fire, airmen were being scalded. Some of them died. The design was negligent.

'You don't see the English making basic engineering errors like that.'

Reinhold arched his eyebrows and spread both hands incredulously, 'Are you serious? They have trouble building machines that look like they can even fly. Haven't you ever seen their absurd FE and DH designs? They look like a cross between bath-tubs and toppled windmills!'

Beerenbrock had recovered from the earlier embarrassment inflicted by Lehmann. Now he had an opinion to offer, 'They would probably say the same sort of things about us. The fuselage of the Albatros DIII looks like a packing crate.'

'It's designed to absorb external impact.'

Lehmann agreed, 'Maybe it's just incidental, but either way it's hardly a flawed concept.'

Beerenbrock knew as much about it as anyone, 'I know what it's designed for, and it is based on the same structural principals as egg shells and crustaceans.'

Lehmann dismissed the argument, 'The construction is stronger than a damned egg. The same can't be said for the lower wing, of course.'

Reinhold tried to bring them into the present, 'The English pusher types were last year's contraptions. The newer Sopwiths and SEs are vast improvements. Unfortunately.'

Beerenbrock scowled, 'I wasn't complaining about the FE2s. I prefer those boxes to the latest Englishmen - it was a damned Pup that ruined my jacket.' The Sopwith Pup was one of Britain's newer creations, although it was already past its peak effectiveness after less than a year at the front. In the context of the war, that was a success story: sometimes a design was obsolescent within a few short months. In the most extreme cases, some were ineffective before they even entered operational service.

Von Bülow had started the thread and was not about to relinquish control so easily, 'The English and French have missed a significant point. I would go so far as to say an obvious point.'

There was the mandatory polite expression of curiosity. He expanded, 'I would refer to the respective traditions of the various military branches.'

There was a confused look on the faces of the other men. Flying machines were a recent innovation. They had no history, or traditions. Von Bülow accurately interpreted the bafflement, 'The French are too flamboyant and the English are too conservative – they have good bloodlines, but have learned to hide behind their moat and now rely on the Royal Navy too much. Last year our High Seas Fleet gave them a bloody nose at Jutland and they won't risk a repeat performance.'

Lehmann had recently scored his second combat victory. Despite this minor accomplishment, he wasn't actually in a position to ask questions as an equal. It didn't deter him. He had a firm belief in himself and his abilities, 'The French are butterflies, the English are moths. You are implying that Germany has the ideal balance.'

Von Bülow was pleased that his latest asset – for that was how he viewed Lehmann - had grasped the concept so quickly. It re-affirmed the truth as he saw it, 'Look at how they paint their aircraft. The English cowardly try to conceal themselves in every drab shade of olive or brown. While the French are not quite so pessimistic, they decorate their machines with such mundane motifs as tame farm animals. I have personally seen ducks, chickens and storks.' No-one felt the need to draw undue notice to themselves by pointing out that storks were not found on farms other than by a chance visit by the wild birds.

Reinhold doubted the validity of von Bülow's assertion, 'That hardly makes a difference, I would say. Identification for individuals can't be discerned over any great distance.'

With the bit between his teeth, von Bülow had some momentum, 'It plays on their minds! These are not bold symbols. The French are defeated before they even see us in the air.'

Beerenbrock made a wry observation, 'I'm sure that part of the reason for their fear is because our own machines have two guns while theirs have just the one. To say nothing of the superior altitude advantage we enjoy.'

'You are underestimating the importance of morale, Beerenbrock.'

'No, I am attributing it to other factors. Tangible ones.'

Von Bülow sensed dissent in Beerenbrock's comments. He sought to convince the other, 'The Germanic people have always had strong martial traditions, right back to Hermann when he smashed the Roman legions at Teutoberger Wald.' Reinhold instinctively sought out Becker to share a moment. Then he realised that Becker was dead, having never learned the true identity of Hermann. It saddened the veteran to have sold the poor fellow short. Von Bülow was unstoppable, 'We are proud of our history. You can see it in every aspect of life: in our bearing, our music, our artwork. Instead of seeking inspiration from domestic animals, we adorn ourselves with heraldic beasts and wild creatures, and runic symbols of blood... and death!'

The brief speech may have seemed a little too fanatical, but it rang true. Reinhold's Albatros was decorated with a sword thrust through a heart; Beerenbrock had a black axe crossed with a spear; Lehmann's personal emblem was a shield quartered in blue and white. Other planes in the *Jasta* were painted in bold colours depicting dragons and boars, or macabre images associated with the dead. And it was not only von Bülow's *Jasta:* most aircraft in the entire *Luftstreitkräfte* were adorned with flamboyant designs that proclaimed the fearless identities of the men who flew them, even though many of those in question had not yet done anything to deserve such a fearsome reputation.

Reinhold's attention had deviated from the discussion at hand, 'What happened to Becker's dog? The large one? I haven't seen it around.'

Beerenbrock had been new to the *Jasta* when Becker was killed and didn't remember him, 'Who?'

Lehmann knew the answer, if not the relevance of the question, 'Typhus. I think the mechanics fed it for a week after Becker died, then it ran off.'

Beerenbrock ignored the distraction. His view of the world was a pragmatic one, where individualism was little more than an expression of the ego, 'Maybe the French are the braver men? We shoot at farm animals; they hunt dangerous beasts. And they do it all with inferior weapons. Which is more worthy?'

Von Bülow was insulted at the suggestion, 'You talk as though we are cowards!'

'I just don't agree with the picture you are painting. We use camouflage on our aircraft as well. What else do you think the various lozenge patterned fabrics and mauve schemes are intended for?'

Von Bülow had no ready answer to that. He felt that this turn in the conversation was allowing facts to get in the way of a good theory, 'It doesn't invalidate the points that I have made.'

Beerenbrock inclined his head in a show of deference that was nothing of the sort, 'However you wish.'

Von Bülow gave him a glare and stalked out. The others stood in uneasy silence, unsure of what they had just witnessed but knowing it would not go unanswered. Reinhold recovered before Lehmann, 'What are you doing, Beerenbrock? Now you've upset him.'

'He's just likes to hear his own voice. We don't have to go along with it.'

'You'll make an enemy of him.'

'Using his logic, does the skull painted on his machine indicate that he accepts that he is a dead man?' No-one had anything to offer. 'He only cares about one thing, and that's his Tusk. He has three victories more than me. That's nothing.'

Lehmann scoffed, 'Nothing? It's double!'

Beerenbrock nodded at the fact, 'And he had more than a year's head start. I'm winding him in. If I catch up to the bastard I'll let him know about it.' He nodded again for emphasis. Though the details that he had presented were true, it was completely ignoring the fact that most of the perceived lead time had been prior to the advent of the *Jastas*. At that time nobody had done much by way of shooting down enemy aircraft unless they were allowed to fly one of the scarce *Eindecker* machines, and those were allocated to only a privileged few. Von Bülow had not been one of them.

Reinhold felt the need to offer a warning, 'Keep your head down, Beerenbrock. There's only one big dog on this hunt and it's not you.'

'Someone should muzzle him.'

Chapter 13

July 1917: The Hand that Feeds

'I was thinking…'

'How novel.'

Yvonne's insults were without surcease. Von Bülow retaliated, 'I was wondering, could it be that I am the one who killed your husband?'

Where does the need to wound another human being come from? Von Bülow seemed to have direct access to the source. Nor was Yvonne averse to twisting the knife, 'No, I heard he died with honour.'

He narrowed his eyes at the insinuation, 'You have spirit, but that is no more an act than your pretence of virtue at our first encounter.'

'What if I had told you that I was a whore? What would you have done?'

He caressed her cheek then, even as she turned away from his touch, 'My dear Yvonne, I think I would have tried to rescue you.' He sounded sincere, but she couldn't tell.

She was mortified at the very idea, and continued her campaign of rebuffing him, 'You rent my time. You don't own my feelings.'

'Keep your blubbery feelings.'

'You are so cruel. Are you really representative of the rest of your countrymen? Heaven help us! No wonder the civilised world wants you all dead in unmarked graves.' Her aggressiveness was an attempt to mask the agony inside. *What have I done to deserve a bastard like this?* The answer was there for all of France to see: deserve has got nothing to do with it.

Yvonne threw caution to the wind in her need to lash out at von Bülow, 'What I wouldn't give to see your expression when you find that I have taken my life.'

It was a bridge too far. He struck her in sudden fury, rocking her head back.

Yvonne's cascading tears mingled with snot as she cowered from the expectation of another blow. Von Bülow remained as still as a statue, as hard, as cold. He stared down upon her without pity, 'You will never suggest such a thing ever again, or you will regret it.' He leaned down and twisted her face until she was looking into his eyes, 'Do you understand me?' It came out as a hiss.

There was unmistakable fear in her eyes, and she was too frightened to speak. 'Answer me!'

Her response was barely a squeak. Though it was impossible that von Bülow understood the language of rats and mice, he appeared satisfied with the attempt.

Why does this pig think I don't already have a mountain of regret in my life?

*   *   *

Max Beerenbrock's stocks were rising. Since April he had claimed more kills than any of the other pilots in his unit, and was now second in the *Jasta's* rankings. Only von Bülow remained ahead of him. Otherwise, it was business as usual.

Tension remained in the air as a result of the latest combat. Rossler had shot down two Spads and this time there were plenty of witnesses. He was still willing to eyeball von Bülow from across the room, having never forgiven the commander's refusal to confirm his second kill. That Beerenbrock had gained from the episode and had since added considerably to his total was not lost on the others. Some of the non-commissioned pilots made a few mental adjustments whenever this was mentioned: Beerenbrock minus one, Rossler plus one.

Von Bülow was caught up in the rivalry and he didn't like it. He felt that decisions had been made and everyone else needed to accept the fact and move on. In any event, it was too late to have second thoughts. Beerenbrock was strutting around like a rooster and it wouldn't hurt the man to lose a claim to another pilot now and then, but his reputation was much enhanced and there had been no further instances where his victories had been disputed.

'I am happy for him. He keeps me on my toes. A bit of healthy rivalry never hurt anybody.'

Mellerhorst was not fooled. Von Bülow didn't like anybody challenging him for primacy within the *Jasta*. There were many pilots with a higher profile under the imperial flag. Tellingly, the haughty aristocrat never sought any of them out on those rare occasions when the cream of Germany's flying men were brought together.

He looked at the latest set of orders to have arrived. Von Bülow's presence had been requested to test-fly the latest crop of prototypes. After that assignment was completed he was scheduled for two weeks leave. Maybe the break would help his mood.

Or maybe he would fret that the more time he spent away from the *Jasta,* the more impetus would be provided to Beerenbrock's scoring spree. That was more likely.

But orders were orders and Mellerhorst was not reluctant to point it out, 'You can't just refuse.'

Von Bülow knew it, but he didn't have to like it, 'Things are too chaotic here.'

'It's a war, Sebastian, things are supposed to be chaotic.'

'It isn't a complaint or a refusal, merely an observation.'

'Well, the whole world is an imperfect place, so you should fit right in.'

Von Bülow grumbled, 'You sound like my mother.'

'Forget it, Sebastian, I'm not packing your bag for you.'

'By the time I get back something else will have gone wrong in my absence.'

If you count Beerenbrock overhauling your total, then yes, it will have gone wrong. Max will do his utmost to upset that little applecart.

Mellerhorst went for a stroll outside. He overheard two armourers discussing the latest development, 'Rossler got another two. Spads. There are witnesses.'

'The Old Man isn't going to like that.'

'He'd rather a finger in the eye.' It stood out like a sore thumb.

*   *   *

'Is it normal to have no power?' Perhaps it was not the most diplomatic way to open a conversation, but von Bülow felt that the most important attribute of a test pilot was honesty. It rated above flying ability simply because prototypes were inherently dangerous and were expected to kill people. If a test pilot did not cut immediately to the chase, lives were put at risk. There was no place for ambiguous statements.

If it was not the endorsement that he had been asked to give, von Bülow didn't care. Had the High Command wanted a rubber stamp they should have visited the local post office instead of summoning a seasoned veteran and asking for an expert appraisal.

In his opinion, the Pfalz DIII should not be put into production. He couldn't see how it was in any way superior to the equipment that they had already been issued with. If anything, it was worse. Disrupting the main industrial effort on the factory floor and replacing it with processes that would doubtless contain as yet unresolved problems was a recipe for disaster. The Germans were already outnumbered in the air. Why add to their woes with more logistical problems?

'Thank you, Sebastian. That will be all for now.'

Knowing he had caused offence, von Bülow tried to minimise the damage to his career, 'I am not in a position to know everything there is to know about the development of new procurements. I'm just a man who flies at the front. If you are intending to evaluate the Pfalz further -' The glare he received confirmed the intention, '...then I am quite happy to recommend one of my own men to assist in the matter. He has a good record and I don't really want to lose him, but for the good of the Fatherland we must all make some sacrifices. I'm sure he would be very eager for the opportunity. He has an excellent feel for mechanical issues. Very likely he would accept a posting to any unit being equipped with the new type to aid in further field testing.'

'What is the fellow's name?'

'Max Beerenbrock.'

Chapter 14

August 1917: Regrouping

Charlotte Gerard had a problem, and that problem's name was Yvonne Coiffard. The dear girl had the face of an angel and the body of a goddess, but her temper came from the Devil himself and would get them all into trouble sooner rather than later. An old rumour was still circulating about a public incident involving a beautiful girl and a German officer and, if the girl in question happened to have been Yvonne, then everything that had transpired since made perfectly good sense.

Life was hard. There was no denying the fact that France would be a better place with the Germans gone, but only the war would decide how soon, if at all, such a thing would happen. However, the sad fact was that the immediate present needed to be negotiated before any daydreaming could be indulged in.

Charlotte decided to act. She put the kettle on to boil...

'Hello, Yvonne, how are you this morning?' The discolouration on the young woman's face had not entirely faded.

'Charlotte?'

'Come and sit with me.'

Yvonne did as she was bidden. One didn't refuse an employer without good cause, especially when the only job available provided you with free lodging. What harm could come from sitting across a table? 'Do you wish to speak with me?'

'Yes; the German who has taken an interest in you.'

'In me? That's true.' There were ladies, and then there were whores. Each female sub-set had their own brand of humour. One could argue that the comment would have been offensive in more polite company.

It startled a laugh out of Charlotte, 'My! I had not expected a sharp wit first thing in the morning.'

Yvonne was not at her best, but there was rarely a time when she was. As a young wife, she had despised prostitutes. As a young widow she still despised them, only now her opinion had a very unhealthy dollop of self-loathing piled on top of it. 'What about him?'

'What are we going to do about him?'

Yvonne sagged in the chair, 'There is nothing to do, other than his bidding. You know the threats that he has made.'

Charlotte steepled her hands as she rested elbows on the table. It was not a mannerism that would have been taught to her by her mother. She was careful with her next suggestion, and also apprehensive, 'Have you thought to bind him to you?'

Yvonne looked confused, 'How so? And to what end, so that he can lead me around like a prize heifer?'

'He is a bad man, Yvonne. You know this as well as I do. Make him fall in love with you, and perhaps he will not be as terrible. I think that he wants to. He is halfway there already, to my mind.'

As expected, the suggestion angered Yvonne, 'Hatred is all that I have left in this world, Charlotte. I had thought you knew it. How could you want to hurt me like this?' There were tears gleaming in her eyes. To say no would be resigning herself to abandonment.

Charlotte owed Yvonne nothing, and could easily find a replacement much more pliable.

But the look offered to her by the older woman was calm and apologetic, 'Yvonne, I would never ask you to deny your heart. All I am suggesting is that you win his – the better to tear it out.'

'I don't understand.'

'He harms you more when he is angry, and nothing angers him more than your scorn for him.'

'If nothing can hurt him more, why act any differently?'

Charlotte was rueful, 'I feel as you do towards him, but you are the one who suffers for it.'

'What would you have me do?'

'Be gentler to his feelings.'

'You mean pretend.'

'Look at us. In this line of work we all pretend.'

Yvonne sighed. It was her most common response in these times, and a natural reaction for someone whose soul had been punctured.

'Dear child, you have seen the very worst of men but some of them were born with good hearts.'

'That isn't all they were born with.' Yvonne bowed her head and lamented, 'The good ones are dead.'

'Not all of them.' Charlotte traced the outline of the yellowed bruise, 'You have the face of an angel.'

Yvonne's smile was lopsided, 'Must I now fight you off as well from trying to pull off my drawers?'

Where has the innocence gone?

'You must insist that he no longer pays for your time.'

'He is not stupid, Charlotte. If you really want him to fall in love, let him think that I want his child.'

Charlotte frowned, 'Why would he believe that more than the other?'

There was a burning intensity now evident in Yvonne, 'When he puts one in my belly?'

'No! I cannot see a happy ending if you allowed such a thing to happen.'

Yvonne was harsh in her assessment, 'Happy endings are for children at bedtime.'

'What will you do if you have a Boche baby? I know that our government has approved infanticide in such circumstances, but I do not think that you would be able to live with yourself – if in fact he doesn't kill you himself.'

Yvonne was frightening in her absence of emotion, 'If I find I am with child, I believe the filthy pig would be most affected if I drowned myself. I shall do it for France. There is nothing left for me in this life. If the death of a whore can discomfit a German, maybe it will be enough to tilt the scales of justice as I stand before The Lord.'

The other woman enfolded her in an embrace, 'Do not consider such a thing. We all learn to adjust to the pain.'

Yvonne understood pain better than most, 'What would you have me do, once he loves me?'

*　　*　　*

Captain Lewis-Hamilton and Ross Burke had enjoyed separate leaves in England, but again found themselves closeted together. They had been co-opted into teaching the latest batch of recruits the various skills that would be needed by men bound for squadron service.

'Can I trouble you for a light, skipper?'

'All you ever do is trouble me in some shape or form.' Lewis-Hamilton handed over the requested article.

Burke cupped his hand as he struck a match, shielding the flare from the slight breeze. He puffed on the cigarette, 'They want us to teach these blighters, but haven't told us how.'

'It's my second stint instructing. It was the same the last time.'

'Well let's have at them.'

There seemed to be a never-ending supply of new recruits. Generally speaking, they mostly came from similar backgrounds: many were straight out of school, and those that were a little older usually had interrupted a university education or else had walked out of their clerical occupations. Manual labour and most trades did not feature on the resumes of these aspiring candidates, although there were exceptions, as there are for everything.

They were invariably young – the older breed had already been processed by the military system – mostly unmarried and keen to sample every aspect of the world that their limited life experiences had so far denied them. Danger, excitement, alcohol: the list of possibilities was restricted only by individual inhibitions, and men who wanted to fly in the first place had few enough of any such qualities. For most of them, they had signed up for the ultimate experience of Boys With Toys.

Again, there were exceptions. Some had made respectable starts to their lives, and others had transferred to the RFC in order to get away from the squalor of the trenches. But they were a minority. The bulk of the men who formed the core of the squadrons had signed on for an occupation that would have no relevance to the skills that would be required for gainful employment once the fighting ceased. That simple fact would only matter to the ones who made it home. It was a problem for another day, a far-off day.

Lewis-Hamilton stood at the front of the classroom. He had not spoken to a group in this type of setting in a very long time and surreptitiously wiped sweaty palms on his trousers. For some reason, speaking to strangers was a lot harder than if they had been men with whom he was familiar. He was unpleasantly reminded of being forced to do public speaking in front of his classmates at school. It wasn't so long ago, and he felt the familiar worm of doubt.

Across the room, one of the other instructors was looking out of the window. He was clearly bored but if he had the least idea that Lewis-Hamilton was uncomfortable, he gave no outward sign. *Where to begin? A joke?* That's often how the C.O. began proceedings, but nothing came to mind. *I know what I'm doing, just say something. Anything.* The silence stretched. The uninterested instructor shifted his focus from whatever had been outside the window and gave his full attention to the front of the room. A faint smile twitched across his face, but it was fleeting. *If this was a physical drill I'd just make them do another set of press-ups while I gathered my thoughts.* But it wasn't a drill.

He cleared his throat, 'Look for the Hun in the sun.' *Oh, God, did I just say that?* Aside from the throng of recruits, there were other veterans present for this introductory class, enough to make Lewis-Hamilton appear like a politician on a soapbox. Burke was beaming from ear to ear, enough in tune with the discomfited pilot that he was relishing the moment. *Damn the man!* 'You've no doubt heard the saying?'

Heads nodded. They reminded the instructor of baby birds in a nest vying for a worm.

All of a sudden, the unwelcome bout of nerves dissipated. Lewis-Hamilton decided to start afresh, 'It's good advice, but it's not everything.

'In the coming weeks we are going to cram you full of information that you need to know if you're going to be of any use in action: flying, gunnery, navigation, photography. Attention to detail. There's a lot of theory, but seeing as how most of you are just out of school, you'll be used to the format. What you can expect to struggle with are the rudiments of practical aeronautics. Before you get the chance to fly solo, you'll first need to satisfy your flight instructor when you are in the air on dual flying. Half of you won't graduate, and some of you may even be killed, though that's less the case now than it was a year ago.

'You may think that you are here because the RFC is expanding, and it is, but understand that fighting the Hun is a deadly business and losses are inevitable. When all is said and done, when you are to be assigned to a squadron it will be because they have lost someone – you are replacements. We'll train you as much as we can, get you acquainted with the necessary routines, and familiarise you with the local area. I know it's obvious when plainly spoken, but getting your bearings from the air is crucial. It's a lot different to when you are on the ground. The scale is different, and you won't fully appreciate that fact until you have been up for the first time.'

Heads nodded again.

'One thing that you won't be doing here is meeting the Hun. In France, he isn't so considerate when it comes to allowing you to do your assigned task. When he has put the wind up you – and be assured, he will - it's easy to lose your bearings. We've lost men in combat who flew in the wrong direction once they became disorientated. Not too many chaps find their way home if they venture too far towards Sauerkrautland - not our chaps, I mean. The Huns don't have that problem at all. That's where they live.' There was polite laughter.

Lewis-Hamilton was warming to his task, 'As a rule, the chaps in my squadron, and by extension I would assume in every squadron in the RFC, are of good family, and are well educated, physical specimens. I would therefore infer that the rule of thumb would dictate that they are more intelligent than the average infantryman. Further, your typical Hun airman conforms to this template as well.

'Here is the crux of the matter, though: men of similar backgrounds and interests could reasonably be expected to get along if placed alongside one another. However, problems arise when there is just one thing that becomes totally unforgivable.

'I myself have suffered the unpleasant experience of keeping company with Australians, and though it may be true that they enjoy their cricket, it is also true that the very fact of their convict ancestral roots makes any contact with them quite excruciating. For reasons that I have not been able to fathom, they take a perverse pride in their barbarity and wear it like a regimental citation.'

Burke sat there with arms crossed, more annoyed that Lewis-Hamilton had lost his stage-fright than at the barbs being flung his way.

Basking in the attention, Lewis-Hamilton continued, 'We probably have more in common with the fliers of Hunland. But, as in the case of the crude southern folk who reluctantly bend their knee to the crown, there is a bit of a problem with Germans. Essentially, they started a war with King George, and every time since then, whenever I meet Fritz, he has tried to kill me rather than clasp hands together in friendship. Of course, I am obliged to reciprocate, and am pleased to announce that I have had some small measure of success in the matter. I am by no means suggesting that when this beastly war is over I shall not shake my enemy's hand, but merely that until victory is ours I shall be doing my best to minimise the number of possible future amicable encounters by dispatching forthwith our jolly acquaintances with good old three-oh-three calibre whenever I happen upon the chance to do so.'

'Hear, hear!' The encouragement seemed genuine. Burke was unimpressed with the men who had said it. Raw cadets were just babes in the woods.

The senior instructor continued with his monologue...

The replacements were conferring, and had taken some time to absorb much of that which had been offered by way of advice, 'Small measure of success? How many victories does he have? I heard it is only two.'

'That's what I heard as well.'

They noticed that one of the old hands had taken an interest in them. His accent was broad, coarse and uncultured to the ears of these young men. He confirmed their query, 'Two. How many do you want him to have?'

'Err, no offense intended, sir. He just made it sound like he was understating himself with false modesty.'

Burke summed them up with a shrewd look, 'Well, you've got Milord pegged, alright.'

The new boys almost writhed with pleasure at the approval shown by the grizzled veteran. He pricked their bubble, 'Would you call two victories a grand score?'

There was a hesitation and the men exchanged a shifty look, 'W-well, not grand, *per se*.'

'So then, maybe it is a small measure?'

'I suppose so.' The answer was delivered in a small voice, though it was evident that getting grilled by a colonial was far from palatable. He was no spring chicken, either, and clearly knew his way around.

'You young fellows no doubt come from a good school. You are bright, ambitious and full of yourselves. None of that matters here. You're more likely to get invited to dinner than I am, but I can only recommend that you forget about eating with the correct cutlery, shut your mouth, open your ears, and learn from your betters. Either that, or become the reason that more replacements are sent through with every lot of rations.'

Ross Burke ambled off, satisfied that he had cowed the callow youths. Though he had a lot of criticism for Lewis-Hamilton, these pups hadn't earned the right to an opinion of their own.

The rebuked cadet delivered a parting shot that was designed to save face, though not in a voice loud enough to be heard over any distance. Schoolboys the world over had perfected the technique, 'So who does he think he is, the vulgar man?'

'An Australian, I should think.'

'A geriatric one, at that. How old do you think he is?'

'At least forty, by the look of him.'

*　　*　　*

'What is in this tin?'

Von Bülow was lying back with one hand folded behind his head as he stared at the ceiling of his room through a haze of cigarette smoke. He didn't even look around. There was only one tin. He answered idly, 'Buttons.' He scratched his armpit.

Yvonne rattled the small container. The clatter within was consistent with the claim. 'Do you need more?'

'Yes, that is the idea.'

'What do you mean?'

He leaned across and traced the curve of her bare hip, 'Open it.'

Yvonne prised off the lid and fingered the contents, then tipped them onto the rumpled bed sheet. Each button had a tag tied to it, 'I don't understand. They are different, and don't match the buttons on your uniform.'

'They are souvenirs.'

Yvonne was confused, so he elaborated, 'Some pilots collect pieces from the machines that they destroy: serial numbers and other mementoes. I decided that it would be much more practical to collect the buttons from the men who flew in them.'

She picked up a button at random and scrutinised it. It had what appeared to be crusty flakes of dried blood embedded into it. She examined another. This time there was evidence of charring, 'These men are all dead?'

'No. Some lived.'

'And you cut these from their bodies?'

'That's the general idea.'

'Why are there cardboard tags threaded to them?'

'Those are labels, numbered in the order that I collected them.'

Yvonne scrutinised them, 'Where are numbers three and four?'

'There aren't any. It isn't always possible to visit a crash site.'

Yvonne went back to her sorting, eventually finding what she was looking for, 'This one? This was the first?'

He gave it a cursory glance, nodding. 'I gave him two hundred rounds and he came down alive. I shook his hand. It was a proud moment.'

'Why was he proud?'

Von Bülow smiled benignly, 'I wasn't talking about him.'

There was an edge in her voice, 'Was he an Englishman?'

He smiled at her poor attempt at guile, but if she truly wanted to know then he felt compelled to burst her bubble, 'No. The first eight were all Frenchmen. But the rest are English.'

Yvonne swallowed her revulsion. He watched the interplay of conflicting emotions with mild amusement. She announced boldly, 'I am not sure if this is grand enough. Your friends – don't they have better relics than buttons to one day show to their children and grandchildren?'

'My grandchildren will respect me for my deeds, not my trinkets.'

Her eyes twinkled at the notion, 'Are German children really so different to the French?'

He looked confused, 'What do you mean?'

'Children love their grandparents for many reasons, but none of those reasons are founded in respect. Not to begin with, not until they are grown.'

Von Bülow was unimpressed by the triviality of her reasoning, 'Well, I am not fighting the Kaiser's war for the sake of my grandchildren's opinions towards me. It's hard to think so far ahead when right now lives are measured in weeks and months.'

Yvonne held the button in her palm, 'How many buttons do you intend to collect?'

He lay back again, apparently once more interested at something on the ceiling, 'As many as I can get. I would like to wear the Order for Merit, and I am not alone in the aspiration.'

Yvonne propped up onto an elbow. Von Bülow watched the effect that this had on her upper anatomy. She feigned not to notice, 'How is that said in German?'

He was nonplussed, 'We don't use German. The Order is only known by its French title, but airmen call it the Blue Max.'

Yvonne knitted her eyebrows together, 'Germany has stolen a French medal to use? Why do you want a French medal?'

'It isn't a medal.' Her lack of comprehension in the finer points of the matter was flawed in so many ways that he didn't know where to begin. To explain the difference between an order and a medal, or the role of the French court in German politics – to von Bülow it was all too tedious. On the other hand, Yvonne's seriousness and her look of concentration were very appealing.

He altered course in the same way that men are wont to do, and with the same motive in mind, 'Have you noticed that we no longer argue all of the time?'

Yvonne stretched out, catlike, and lay facing him, her every action deliberate, 'What is the point? Life is short, and we should make the most of the situation.'

He smiled in fondness, 'I know exactly what it is that we should be doing the most of.'

Of course you do. Yvonne resigned herself to another round of sweaty rutting, and made a mental note to argue with him more often for appearance's sake. She purred in his ear, 'A good man will always win hearts.'

Chapter 15

September 1917: Expansion

'Mellerhorst!'

The adjutant's head peered into von Bülow's office, 'Yes?'

'Come inside and close the door.'

Mellerhorst did as he was bid, then awaited further instruction. Von Bülow waved at him impatiently, 'Come in, I don't bite.'

'Is everything all right?'

'Reinhold or Lehmann, what do you think?'

'Ernst has the better record, and seniority.'

'That isn't what I asked. What you say is a fact – I am after an opinion.'

Mellerhorst smiled crookedly, 'An opinion? Well, then, my opinion is that Reinhold should be passed over.'

Von Bülow growled, 'That isn't how it should be construed.'

'Call it whatever you want, Sebastian. He should stay. Lehmann and Rossler need to provide the leadership for the new *Jasta*.'

'I never said anything about Rossler.'

'You asked for my opinion.'

'On Reinhold and Lehmann.'

'It seems that you have made up your mind on the matter. Is there anything else?'

Von Bülow was not about to let him off so easily, 'What do you have against Reinhold?'

'Nothing. The four best pilots in the *Jasta* are the three of you plus Rossler. In fairness, two need to stay. Reinhold is a calming influence on the new men, and Lehmann is friends with Rossler.'

'I'm not letting Rossler go. He's too valuable.'

'Is this the same Rossler whom you dislike because he isn't an officer; the same man who you have denied confirmation of victories?'

'It is my way to get the best from him. You can't say it hasn't worked.'

'You don't like him!'

'What has that to do with anything? Running a *Jasta* has nothing to do with popularity and friendship.'

You got rid of Beerenbrock. But saying it aloud would be like kicking a hornet's nest. 'Lehmann might have something to say about it.'

'Let him bleat.'

'You are seriously suggesting that none of the best men are to be transferred?'

'Not Reinhold or Rossler. Lehmann can have any other four men of his choice.' He reached for his coat, 'I am going out. I will return later this evening.'

Von Bülow was in a surly mood as a result of this latest turn of events. Yvonne savoured the moment, knowing that he would not be so pushy towards her.

'I have been instructed to supply a cadre of pilots to form a new *Jasta.*'

Yvonne wasn't sure what that meant, or why he even bothered her with things of no importance. Uninterested, she didn't ask for clarification. As ever, he interpreted the silence as a courteous invitation to say his piece, 'Unless I hear otherwise, it means that I'll lose either Reinhold or Lehmann for certain. Both of them are due for a command and they have the requisite experience.'

She wasn't even listening to his boring drone. Then, in the background, the tail end of a phrase entered her consciousness, '…will weaken my unit.' Yvonne's ears pricked up as he continued, 'I'll probably get replacements without any ability whatsoever. I hadn't considered the impact that this would have on the existing formations when they are asked to do this sort of thing. It stands to reason, though - the best units are comprised of men destined to be promoted to other commands.'

Yvonne was unsure how much of the one-sided conversation she had missed, so she hazarded a guess, 'Have some of your fliers been killed?'

Von Bülow was irritated by the question, 'Have you been listening to anything I have said at all?'

'I'm sorry, I find it all so confusing. You said that you didn't like a person called Lehmann. I think that's what you said.'

He waved his hand in the air, 'I didn't say anything of the sort!'

'But didn't you say you wanted him to fly with another squadron?'

'No.'

'Then I don't know why you are telling me these things.' For good measure she put on her huffy face.

'I said I had to decide between Reinhold and Lehmann to recommend for promotion to a command position.'

'Because they are better fliers than you?' It came out so innocently.

He spluttered, 'Better? How does that thought enter into your head?'

'I just thought that it would be easier to lead a squadron if there was one pilot who outshone all of the others. Didn't you tell me that once?'

Von Bülow was now feeling peculiarly defensive, 'It helps…'

Yvonne nodded at the point she had made, but von Bülow was not about to leave it there, 'I am the most accomplished flier in my *Jasta*. No-one questions it.'

'Because you have killed more Frenchmen?' There was more accusation than question in the statement.

'No, because I have more victories. It is not quite the same as you are implying.' He took a perverse pleasure in adding, 'Although it is indeed true that I have killed more Frenchmen.'

Rather than becoming incensed, Yvonne turned mischievous, 'How many buttons do these others have?'

'I have told you once before, every man has a different custom. They don't collect buttons.'

'But if they did?'

'Four each.'

'So few?' She simpered, 'No wonder they don't collect buttons – they wouldn't have enough to secure their flies.'

Von Bülow found such talk from a woman deplorable, even if she was only French and a whore. He pretended not to hear the vulgarity.

Yvonne grilled him some more, 'Who is the other pilot who you need to get rid of?'

'It's not about getting rid of them! Especially not Reinhold; he has been a loyal friend since I have known him.'

More worms of doubt were fed into von Bülow's mind, 'You should keep the loyal ones. The others, do they ever save your life?'

Von Bülow rolled his eyes. *It is the Inquisition all over again*, 'That applies to all soldiers.'

'Do they ever remind you of it?'

'You will never understand, Yvonne. It is men's business. Do not let it trouble you any further.'

But she was not done. The bit was between her teeth, 'Four doesn't seem to be very many buttons. Is it that your men are no good?'

'Who said they were no good? I never said anything of the kind.'

'But you said they only had four buttons. You have a lot more than they do!'

'If you must know, one of the others has five. Rossler.' He didn't bother correcting her persistent use of 'buttons'.

'Then why are you not thinking of making him a leader?'

It was sometimes a burden to explain such things, but her chatter just wouldn't stop, 'He is not an officer.'

'Why not?'

God above! A child doesn't have as many questions.

She had one more thread to pick at, 'Will you give Lehmann some good fliers to accompany him, or is it better to keep them for yourself to help you to stay alive?' It was certainly a clumsy attempt, but Yvonne doubted that von Bülow gave her any credit for creativity at all. To him, she had one purpose only, and it didn't involve the use of her brain.

'Everyone protects their comrades. No man has eyes in the back of his head.'

'Guynemer flies alone, no?' Yvonne was risking more than a reprimand with the question. There was a complete blackout on all externally sourced information in the occupied territories, and everything else was heavily censored. No articles written about France's premier fighter pilot could be found on this side of the front line, but his reputation had filtered across into the public domain even so. Yvonne could not reasonably be expected not to align herself with a national hero, but it certainly underlined how fluid allegiances could be for those who were sleeping with the enemy.

Von Bülow was unhappy with the obvious admiration that had been directed towards an enemy combatant. Yvonne gave him a lopsided smile, 'It is so complex, no?' She laid a warm hand upon his forearm, 'Why should you help Lehmann? He is no friend of yours. Keep the best fliers for yourself. Then they can save you if you need them to. Who cares if they are catching up to your silly button collection? If some of them have more, at least you will have men to be proud of. If Lehmann is as good as you say he is then he should be able to fight without any help from his friends. You have said many times that character is more important than all the rest. Let him prove himself, and you can try to stay ahead of the one called Rossler.'

'You do not grasp the situation. I should have kept quiet on the matter.'

'I am sorry if it seems like I am questioning your bravery. You know more about flying than I do. I am not really part of the war. Rather, just a small person caught up in it all.'

'Do not concern yourself with that aspect. I will look after you.'

'What if you are killed? You have said it can happen.' She looked vacantly into the distance, 'Not that I didn't know it already.'

Von Bülow had no answer to that one.

Yvonne gathered herself for the last word, which was a thing that all women have practised since antiquity, 'Will I ever meet any of the men who have helped you? Or have I done so already but just didn't realise it at the time?' Coming from a prostitute, the comment had only one meaning no matter how innocuous it sounded. The tip of her tongue poked enticingly through those lips, just in case von

142

Bülow needed to be convinced of the inference. He looked into her eyes again, and as usual they were bleak and predatory.

Von Bülow summoned his adjutant, 'I have changed my mind. Here is the new list.'

Mellerhorst read the names, 'Are you sure?'

'What don't you like about it? There is Lehmann and Rossler, just as you advised.'

'Sebastian, you have denuded the *Jasta!*'

'You exaggerate.' He pointed a stubby finger at another list, 'Reinhold, Hartmann, Wintger, Bahlmann, Kruchelsdorf: all are capable veterans.'

'Hartmann has just one victory, and Bahlman has been shot down twice this month. He is burnt out.'

'Do you have anything against the others?'

'Wintger hasn't claimed anything since his ring finger was shot off three months ago.'

'Find Reinhold and send him to me.'

'I am to get this approved?'

'Give it to Lehmann and see if he wants any amendments made to it.'

'Oh, I'm quite sure he'll find it very satisfactory, Sebastian.' Mellerhorst went in search of Reinhold. He found him with an armourer. They were checking every round in some ammunition belts that had not yet been loaded into his Albatros.

'Ernst, von Bülow wants to see you.'

'Now?' There was a look of annoyance on Reinhold's face. 'It's not like I'm wasting my time here. Any irregularities in these links will be liable to cause a jam - a hazardous outcome, as you know.'

'It isn't your job to do the armourer's work.'

'I've got a personal stake in the task.'

'Well, you might re-evaluate your priorities after you have seen the commander.'

Reinhold turned to his companion, 'You will have to finish this on your own, Hans. Try not to miss any.'

The non-com grinned at him, 'Don't worry about a thing, *Herr Leutnant*. I like the look of your face. These will all find a new home in a Sopwith or Spad.'

Reinhold punched him lightly, 'Or between an Englishman's ears, hey?' He turned to Mellerhorst, 'What does he want?'

The adjutant looked meaningfully at the armourer and said nothing. Reinhold sighed and made a beeline for von Bülow's office.

He knocked on the door.

'Enter.'

'Franz said you wanted to see me, Seb?'

Von Bülow passed over the list that had Reinhold's name at the top, 'Which of these men are a hindrance in combat - relative to the others, I mean?'

Reinhold read the sheet and smiled at von Bülow, 'Is this a trick question? I see my name here.'

Von Bülow waved him away, 'No. I mean the others.'

'Is there a mission being planned?'

'Which ones?'

'Bahlmann is the worst of them. He's finished mentally – you should ground him. Wintger is alright as a wingman, as long as he doesn't have to do too much.' Reinhold looked almost apologetic, as if his opinion was a betrayal, 'Nothing against him personally, but we've seen it happen before: a man is wounded and then sometimes finds it difficult to regain his touch.' He hesitated, 'Kruchelsdorf drinks too much, though I'll admit it doesn't seem to hinder him.'

Von Bülow was lost in thought, so Reinhold had to ask instead of waiting for an explanation, 'What is this list?'

'You have been passed over for promotion. Lehmann has been preferred and he asked to take Rossler and some of the other old hands with him to provide the core for a new chaser unit.'

'And these are the ones that are staying on?'

Von Bülow nodded.

'Did he consult you at all, or is he friends with the Chief-of-Staff?'

'Why would he know Thomsen?'

'Well what, then? This is very confusing.'

Von Bülow leaned forward, 'It was my decision, Ernst.'

'May I ask how you decided the issue?'

'I had thought to give Lehmann a helping hand. We can start anew here. You and I can do this, Ernst. It is why I kept you on instead of putting your name forward for the position. I apologise for that. I know that you were more deserving, but I need you with me. Mellerhorst agrees that you are the best man for breaking in replacements.'

'Can we at least keep Rottenberger?'

'It's not all doom and gloom. They have bumped me up to *Oberleutnant*.'

Reinhold felt the devil's bony index finger stirring within his brainpan, 'Congratulations.'

145

Chapter 16

October 1917: Replacements

One of the new men was unaware that von Bülow did not wish to be disturbed when eating. Ever. It was a minor detail - an irrelevant snippet of information, but before the fellow could be clued in it was too late. He now found himself standing at attention before the commander's table, a victim of circumstance, 'I believe in acting fairly towards all of my men, but you must learn that you may never interrupt me at mealtime.' Von Bülow reconsidered his advice, 'In fact, to avoid confusion, never interrupt me at all. Simplifying the options may be easier for you to understand. *Dummkopf.*'

The poor man was left standing at red-faced attention in front of a dozen witnesses. Uncertain and humiliated, he didn't realise that he had the silent sympathy of every man present.

'Reinhold!'

Resignedly, Reinhold presented himself before his commanding officer, 'Normally you head off these fools before they become a nuisance. What sort of wingman are you?'

'Sorry, Seb.' The dining room was hardly the most likely place to be enforcing military protocols. Using a casual form of address was the most that Reinhold was prepared to do to remind the other man of their history together.

'These idiots need to learn some respect and it may as well start with discipline. Every time we go up they scatter across the sky at the first sign of trouble. I've seen chickens panic less when there is a fox afoot.'

'I'll tell the men not to disturb your meals.'

Von Bülow continued as though he hadn't heard, 'Instead of protecting the leader, it has become every man for himself. The experienced pilots have closed up shop and are looking after their own skins rather than trying to shoot Englishmen, and the new pilots are useless. Those that survive are sometimes doing so by the slimmest margins. The ground crews spend more time on repairs than general maintenance.'

'We have lost our most experienced men. What did you expect? It will take time to get things back to normal.'

The commander was still peevish, 'Mellerhorst recommended you as the best man to break in new arrivals. Get on it.'

Von Bülow marched past the assembled aircraft as mechanics and armourers swarmed all over them. Mellerhorst had fallen behind, and was left to catch up as best he could. He was given the opportunity to do so when the commander noticed that one of the Albatros DVs was undergoing alterations to its livery. A black and yellow heraldic eagle was being obliterated from the side of the wooden fuselage.

'Whose is this?'

Mellerhorst was expected to know the answer to any question concerning every detail in the *Jasta,* no matter how trivial. This time, if that had been the only information at his disposal, he'd have had no idea. He knew the previous owner of the machine, and he recognised the men undertaking the work, but lately there were too many replacement pilots to know who had been assigned to which aircraft. He made an educated guess, 'Weber.'

Von Bülow button-holed the painter, 'Where is Weber?'

The man pointed, 'Over there, *Herr Oberleutnant*.'

Von Bülow went marching in the direction indicated. Mellerhorst trailed behind, refraining from pointing out that there was no regulation regarding personal markings. It did not take them long to locate the man, 'Weber!'

The replacement pilot saluted, '*Herr Oberleutnant!*' Very few soldiers were ever reprimanded for observing enthusiastic discipline. Weber may have been new to chasers, but as a soldier he was no novice. And there had already been stories circulating about this particular commander; von Bülow was a known martinet. If there was ever a time to relax, that time was in the future.

'You are changing the personal marking on your machine?'

'It's not my design. It belonged to one of the fellows who were posted out.'

Von Bülow knew full well who the emblem belonged to; they had flown together for long enough. 'Rossler.'

It was just a name to Weber, 'If you say so. I never met him.'

'I read in your files that you were promoted from the ranks?'

'That's correct.'

Von Bülow nodded at this and abruptly departed with Mellerhorst in his wake. Weber was left with the impression that he had done something inappropriate.

The crew chief came and stood in front of him, 'You want the entire Orion constellation? That's a lot of stars.'

Weber collected himself, 'No, just enough to make it recognisable.'

'May I ask why?'

Weber smiled, 'Being new to the *Jasta*, I can hardly yet claim to be a hunter, now can I?'

'There's no rule that prevents you from dreaming.'

The pilot shrugged, 'I took a hit a few months ago. Anti-aircraft. The damage left some sizable chunks missing – the resulting pattern had a remarkable resemblance to Orion, but instead of stars it was written in holes.'

'Isn't that courting fate?'

Von Bülow was still to be seen disappearing into the distance. Weber pointed him out, 'I met a fellow who knows that one. He said that Richthofen once invited him to join JG I, but von Bülow declined the offer.'

The chief scratched his head, 'Never heard that one. Did he say why?'

'Apparently the offer didn't extend to the command of one of Richthofen's *Jastas*.'

A curt nod, 'Well, if the story isn't true it should be.'

'You don't like him, then?'

'It's not the first word that springs to mind. Hard – that's the first word... Might I ask who told you the story?'

Weber was reluctant, but not rude enough to refuse outright, 'His name was Max. Let's keep his last name anonymous in case the story is just a malicious lie.'

'I only know of three Maxs. It can't have been Immelmann, because he was killed before Richthofen made a name for himself. That leaves Müller and Beerenbrock as the likeliest offenders.' Weber tried to look nonchalant, but he failed. The older man cackled, 'You can play cards with me any time, *Herr Leutnant*. Of those two, I'd put my money on Beerenbrock, though only because I know him personally. It could just as easily have been the other fellow, by his reputation.'

Weber admitted defeat, 'You'd win the wager.'

'Ask Richthofen if it's true.'

'One does not simply walk up to royalty and ask for an autograph, much less the scurrilous details of an ill-founded rumour.'

'He isn't royalty though, is he?'

'What world do you live in?'

*　　*　　*

The adjutant looked at Burke and he was not amused, 'Your papers aren't in order, Ross.'

'Bloody hell, Dave, don't give me grief over it. Clearly there's been an error on the part of the Brass Hats. Another one.'

'I don't see it, myself. You haven't been posted back here. You'll have to go on over to the station, hop on a train and report to your new squadron.'

'Don't bullshit me. This is my unit. Ask the others what they reckon. Ask the C.O.'

'No need. It's in print right here before my eyes, on your orders.'

Burke folded his arms, 'A typo.'

'There's no mistake, you stubborn bastard.'

'See here, if you won't fix it, I'll be having a bit to say to whichever newspaperman I can lay my hands on. I'll be damned if I'm going to fly with another mob. I'd rather transfer out of the RFC, and if you don't arrange for me to get posted back here – and I mean today – then there'll be all sorts of noises being made right up to the fucking front door of the War Office.'

'You realise that right now you're AWOL?'

Burke's face was stony, daring the staff officer to put him on report.

Harding had no wish to draw the unwanted attention of Whitehall. Things were far better when business proceeded without the interference of the upper echelon, 'You bloody colonials - always getting above your station. Wait here, I'll talk to the Old Man.'

Burke nodded again, 'Why I even needed to ask is something I'll never fathom.'

The adjutant looked daggers at him and stalked away. *It's bad enough fighting the damned Germans. Why do we have to put up with all of this nonsense from people who are supposed to be our allies?*

*   *   *

Slugger Sloane sat on the wheel of the partially disassembled Bristol, leaning back with ankles crossed. His friends sat in various postures of relaxation around him. They were taking a break from working on the machine and idly watched as the officers played another interminable game of cricket. A human being would not be human if he could not find something to gripe about, 'Do they ever do anything else?'

'Do we?'

Only one man could get away with questioning Sloane, but he was harmless enough and didn't have an enemy in the world - except the German army of course, to say nothing of the Austro-Hungarians or the Turks. But in the civilised world, no.

Sloane pushed him, 'You'll do, Limerick. Give us the one about the Hun.'

The skinny lad was only too happy to oblige his friend:

'All hail the Bloody Red Baron,
Whose name we suspect may be Karen,
Because no man would fly,
Gaudy planes in the sky,
No way is the Baron a Darren.'

Sloane laughed like a loon. 'That's why we keep him around! Young Limerick has a true gift.'

No-one was likely to argue with Sloane. His nickname was well earned. A former amateur boxer with a quick temper, he was renowned for his appetite for hard liquor. He usually had a hip flask ready at hand, and wasn't averse to acquainting himself with its contents. Despite his aggressive nature, he was popular in the squadron because he also happened to be good at winning bizarre wagers.

Feared for his fists, and respected for his ability to hold his booze, Sloane's true calling lay in predicting the winners in races contested by the squadron's inveterate gamblers. The animals being fielded were not horses or dogs, but a motley collection of snails and slugs favoured by the men who collected them wherever they could be found. Garden plants and upturned bins were continually picked over by men starved of normal forms of recreation.

'There are over two hundred men in the squadron: mechanics, armourers, riggers, fitters, clerks, cooks, batmen, transport drivers. Only about fifty of them fly – the rest of us keep the show running. We are the ones who do all of the work, and they get the glory.'

'It's called getting killed.'

'I'm just saying that there is some credit due to us.'

'That's called pay.'

'Sounds like you want a union in the army. What a lark.' Sloane tilted his flask and gulped a slug of the fiery liquid. He scratched a cauliflower ear, 'We should have a team in the cricket. We can be the home team. The fliers can be the visitors – it's not like too many of them spend a lot of time here before they get the chop.'

'I agree. The teams should be reorganised: officers against enlisted.'

'That's how it's always been, anyway - us and them; it's just more of the same.'

'That would give us some variety at least.'

'What do you mean?'

'The officers keep getting themselves killed. They're always blooding someone new. Can they bat? Can they bowl? How soon before they retire hurt?'

The mood turned grim and reflective, 'Let them have it while they're still drawing breath.' They started to mooch off back to work, but paused when they heard the approach of a vehicle. The truck was open in the back, and the men who were seated there dismounted from the tailgate when the truck groaned to a halt.

Sloane grunted in recognition, 'Here are the latest new chums.'

The cricket game ended with the arrival of the truck. On board were men who had recently been posted from England to St Omer, where they had awaited assignment to a squadron for days or even weeks, depending upon the intensity of the fighting.

Rarely did an innings run its full course. Interruptions were the rule rather than the exception. The truck pulled to a standstill and then the oddest thing happened, 'Backa?'

Ross Burke faltered in mid-stride, which was answer enough for the newcomer, 'I'll be blowed. Backa Burke!'

Burke turned on his heel to confirm with his eyes that the voice belonged to a voice from his past, 'Bugger me. It's No-one.'

There were uncomprehending looks among the small gathering at the incomprehensible dialogue between the thickly accented Australians. 'Why aren't you in the AFC?'

'Why aren't you?'

'Even they have their standards, sport. But I thought for sure that they'd have let you in. A fellow Aussie with a mug as ugly as that – it'd boost the morale of every other sod who chanced to look into a mirror - you know; not as bad by comparison.'

Lewis-Hamilton broke up the reunion, 'Burke, George V has rules pertaining to the correct use of his language. He doesn't approve of laxity in its usage, nor do I see why I need to tolerate it or suffer for your lack of education. Everything works perfectly well as it was designed.'

Burke's respect for protocol was as great as his respect for authority, 'Forsooth, gentle thy tongue, Milord. To mine ears cometh the interminable utterance of more of Ye Olde Nonsense. Nary a day passes wherein thou fail to spout such wanton foolishness. Indeed, it be timely that you were informed that grammar was taught unto myself through the erstwhile study of such worthy tomes as written by none other than the good William of Shakespeare, whose manner of prose predates that of your noble King by some considerable hundreds of years. Fie! Should I scorn the traditions of centuries past for no other reason than that his ancestors and their peers have become fickle men of High Snobbery?'

'Excuse me?' The question was equal parts indignation and a request for clarity.

'What I mean is that since you Poms don't talk like Old Willy anymore, how is your grammar better than mine, given that he was there first?'

Did Burke have no sense of decorum? It seemed that he did not. If the exchange left an inconsistent impression upon the new arrivals, that was too bad. They could pass judgement if they were still alive in a month's time. The flight leader gave curt instructions to them, 'Close your mouths. Grab your kit. Your quarters will be shown to you directly.'

The man identified as No-one spoke again, 'So what advice do you have to offer, Backa?'

'It seems that it may be too late to give it to you.'

'Oh?'

'Don't enlist.'

'Is it all as bad as that?'

Burke made an expansive gesture that incorporated the entire airfield upon which their unattended aircraft were assembled, 'Listen, mate, we get new crew in here every other week. Have a look around. Do you see a queue waiting for their turn to fly?'

The new Australian frowned at the inference, 'They say that the most important attribute that binds crews together is strong character.'

'Do They?'

'I take it that you don't agree.'

'I'm just curious to see how these chaps of superior character spot one another, and why the weak characters meekly accept their lot.'

'Well, by definition...'

Burke interrupted, 'Here, Bert. I'll give you a head start on the others. New crews are generally assigned to fly together, unless there are gaps in existing pairings of pilots and observers.' He gave a penetrating stare, 'As is the case if one is killed, for instance.'

'And that is likely?'

'Just don't volunteer to fly with Burrows. He's short odds at the moment, and that *is* because of his character, for want of a better word.' There was a pause, 'Of course, if none of the others want to fly with him, someone will have to be assigned to him. Try not to let that be you.'

'How do I avoid it?'

'Tell one of the other new fellows that he's a veteran. If that doesn't convince them, you're fucked. As an Aussie, you'll get the shitty end of the stick every time.'

'Is it as bad as that?'

'You stupid drongo. You should have joined the AFC. Why do you think we formed our own Flying Corps in the first place?'

*　　*　　*

Mellerhorst had wearied of von Bülow's constant griping, but there was nothing he could do but listen to the endless litany of Weber's alleged faults, 'Just another upstart former NCO. With every battlefield commission that is handed out the purity of the officer corps is diluted even further. When the last peasant is elevated, who will we have left to command?'

The adjutant idly rubbed the scar where his body had been pierced, wondering if the depths of von Bülow's snobbishness had ever been plumbed, 'There are many airmen and soldiers who have been commissioned on merit. Erwin Bohme, for example.' He realised too late that he shouldn't have brought up the name.

'Supposedly Boelcke's best friend. In his eternal gratitude the bastard sent a great man to his death. I'd rather not have friends like that.' Von Bülow's animosity overlooked the fact that he had himself been saved from destruction on a number of occasions by his enlisted pilots. Unable to view the lower classes with anything other than suspicion, he was left with no recourse other than bluster. To hold his tongue in the absence of evidence had never been his way.

'You know that Weber and Bonninghauser flew together as a crew before they arrived here? Mostly reconnaissance, as I understand it.'

Von Bülow had not known. 'How long?'

'Quite a while. I don't know exactly, but it was near enough to a year. You can check their files.'

Von Bülow wondered how things would have worked out had Hockheimer survived. Of course there was no way to know, but it would be an interesting exercise to watch how things transpired for the newcomers as they flew in separate aircraft for the first time.

*   *   *

Bloody April seemed a long time ago, but just six months had passed and few had forgotten why it had been given the epithet. That terrible month had been a particularly harsh experience for the airmen of Britain and France, and the Albatros DIII was the main reason for that fact. But April was gone now, and though the Albatros was every bit as good as it had been at that earlier time, the Allies had narrowed the gap. They now had better equipment of their own, and perhaps more importantly, in quantity. They were at last able to fight fire with fire. As a rule, the English and French aircraft still carried half of the firepower of the German designs, but they had a numerical advantage. In any given combat, they were still able to put a comparable number of machine-guns into action. Man for man, the Germans gave each airman superior equipment to that of his foe, but more eggs were in fewer baskets.

Perhaps more significantly, machines such as the SE5 and F.2B had much better performance qualities than that which had gone before, whilst the newer Sopwith Camel matched the German designs in firepower. Keeping pace with their partners, the French had overhauled the Spad to such an extent that the latest mark was an improvement over its earlier rendition in almost every department. The Albatros was still good, but it had lost its decisive edge.

Everything boiled down to life expectancy. In April, on average, an English aviator could expect to last just two weeks before he fell in battle. However, this decimation was the lowest point during the RFC's brief history to date, and was not fully representative of the normal course of business. During quieter periods in that same year, three to four months was the more normal rate of attrition.

The ebb and flow was unpredictable, and heavily influenced by who had how much of what. England had taken their turn at receiving a beating early in nineteen-seventeen and Germany's airmen would have the same thing in store once the balance of air power reached a tipping point. But that was in the future. Right now things were in the balance.

At this time, one of the shortcomings of Allied aircraft development was that most of their machines were only equipped with a single machine gun firing forward. Others - and the Brisfit was one of them - also sported another gun for rear defence, though this was of more limited use in an offensive capacity. When it came to placing shots into a target, the Germans had a decided advantage. Instead of being forced to bang away one shot at a time like a woodpecker - tap-tap-tap – a top shelf *oberkanone* of the *Luftstreitkräfte* would spew forth a much higher volume of fire, which would unceremoniously chew up their unfortunate prey, who was then spat out so as not to satiate too quickly the hunger of the rampant pilot.

For some, and in truth in these days it was more than some, there has been a day in a life that has redefined an individual for the worse. There is no going back, no doing things differently. Knowledge gained came in the form of regret and self-remonstration, and a resentful recognition that lives had been irreversibly changed. Further, recognition of this metamorphosis did not sneak up unawares - it was immediate, as was the understanding that the new reality had taken a permanent form.

Burrows was wracked with the pain of loss and guilt. *If I had applied more rudder... if I had applied less... if I had closed the throttle... if my first shots had hit...if I had been born under the sign of Aquarius... if... if... if. If.* The litany never ended.

Other men seemed to take the loss of their fellows more or less in their stride, though Burrows had never found comfort in the fact. Despite not being naturally inclined to minimise the suffering of others, his burden had only been increased by the nature of his personal circumstances. As a rule, the loss of one crewman generally resulted in the loss of both: far more two-seaters were shot down with no survivors than ever returned home with casualties aboard. So far as he knew, Burrows was the only man on the squadron who had ever lost an observer in combat. If there were others, he had not been apprised of the fact.

Though his machine had been repaired, the various strategically placed patches told a story of their own. And now he had a new man sitting in that same seat, living and breathing just a few feet away from the pilot's cockpit; a new man whose life Burrows was responsible for, and to whom he could make no guarantees.

Second lieutenant Adam Burrows was not coping well.

Throughout the course of history, tragedy has struck in many forms. Some were caused by natural events that could not be easily influenced by an individual: flood, fire, disease, famine. Others were brought into being through artificial means, and war as an extension of politics was one of those.

For an entire generation, the resetting of personalities was often caused by direct exposure to the violent nature of warfare. Different people were affected in different ways and to varying degrees. The brain is a complex organ. Consequently, the same triggers could have unpredictable impacts on each individual, and much of this reflected their exposure and attitudes to the events that had been part of their formative years. Some men had few illusions about what to expect from combat and were thus able to reconcile the facts. Others found themselves unable to accept their situation, or to adjust to it.

Burrows had once felt that he was destined to be central to the inner workings of the universe. He had believed he had possessed the potential to be The One. This narcissistic view was typical of many people his age. It fostered a sense of entitlement based on opportunities not yet seized and on having noble blood flowing in their veins - though without the need of petty patents to prove the claim.

Now that Burrows had the reality of the Western Front shoved fully into his face, his perspective had altered. It was a sobering experience. Finally he understood that wishes were not horses. Moreover, he was appalled to discover that those of his pals from school who lacked his latest insight probably took the evidence of his downfall as confirmation of their own exulted state of being in the future of the world.

The face in the looking glass was not one that he respected anymore. His eyes now had a cast to them that spoke of a diminished character - one which had been unable to stand up when it counted.

As Burrows stood deep in contemplation by the side of a barn that had recently been converted into a workshop, not far away a small group of men had taken a break from their duties, each sprawled beneath the wing of one of the Bristols. An impromptu recitation started up. The format was nothing new:

> There once was a Digger named Dave,
> Who dug a Turkish hag out of a grave.
> She was mouldy as shit,
> And was missing a tit,
> But was not an unwilling sex slave.

> Alas, Digger Dave's corpse was stolen,
> In a state betwixt rancid and swollen.
> She'd turned sort of green,
> And smelt quite obscene,
> Plus when fucked hard, her head went a-rollin'.

> Poor Dave at last tracked down the thief,
> He needed some oral relief,
> Or perhaps doggy style,
> Oh, how he missed her dead smile!
> But the bastard had sold her as beef.

As the bawdy verse wound down, Limerick received hearty claps on his back. Instead of taking all of the credit, he offered an explanation, 'I heard it from a chap in the Lancashire Fusiliers who had fought the Ottoman's back in fifteen when they were over there doing Churchill's work.'

A wry observation was made, 'Not as wholesome as *Long Way to Tipperary.*'

Another chimed in, 'Not as festive, either.'

'Or boring.'

The enlisted men sitting with Limerick noticed that Burrows was not far away, 'Look at him, lurking in the shadows as though he's invisible.'

'Not to the Huns, he isn't. Stitched him up neat as you please, as I heard it.'

'That was his observer.'

'Same thing. Poor bastard.'

'Burrows?'

'Either one. Take your pick.'

Limerick wasn't fond of officers, but nor did he hate them. They were just different, and to be avoided on account of it. But he had noticed that the enlisted men weren't the only personnel who hadn't warmed to Burrows. He carefully looked around, then gave the slightest nod towards the flier. He didn't want to draw attention to himself by conspicuously marking the pariah, 'He's afflicted, that one. You sometimes see it in livestock; they walk away from the sick ones. Got to feel sorry for the fellow who spots for him: the Aussie.' Limerick felt as though he had put a hex on the man. He cast his eyes down.

Sloane rubbished the lad, 'When have you ever seen livestock? You live in the city.'

Limerick eyed the bruiser, 'I've been around.'

'Sure you have.'

'Ask the others if you don't believe me.'

'Hey, Tyson, has Limerick been around?'

Limerick blustered, 'I mean about the livestock!'

Tyson had been asked a question, but didn't answer it directly, 'Leave Mister Burrows alone. It's macabre enough without making light.'

Though he was too far away to have heard any of the conversation, for his part Burrows hated the crudity of that sorry excuse for a poem. He had heard more than his share of the other trash of the same ilk being recited by the peasantry that made up the ground crews. It made him sick to the stomach. *If that sort of humour is representative of the typical soldier fleshing out the armies of the British Empire, maybe the war isn't such a bad thing after all, given that this is the same class from which the infantry are drawn. The boors deserve to have a good blood-letting.*

Once upon a time, Burrows had resented that such infantile minds had the same rights under the law as he was entitled to. Those cretins were wasting oxygen that a decent man could have made better use of, should he be offered the gift of immortality in exchange for their mediocre lives. Burrows completely understood the concept of vampirism, and the benefits that it could have bestowed upon humanity.

These days, it was all irrelevant. *Give the ignorant an equal share of the Earth's bounty, and let the Devil have his way with justice.*

He stored the thought, with every intention of incorporating it into his next letter home to Maud. He had once gotten sterling advice from a professor: *If you have a thought, write it down before it is lost to the world forever. It may be a gem, it may be fool's gold, but if there are none to judge its value then it is worthless.* These days Burrows was less concerned about his legacy to future generations, but it was the last of his old habits worth hanging onto. What Maud must make of it all was a mystery. He was a different man to that which she had known, but her correspondence to him gave no sign of recognising his downward transformation.

Most nights his sleep was fitful at best, and each day he awoke to the same reality that he had tried to evade. In between, he wrote letters to Maud, now less out of love and more as a way to occupy his time. When his hands were busy, his mind had something to distract it, at least a little. Some letters he was unable to bring himself to post, out of concern for her worried reaction to them. It was all a waste of time, but his whole life was a mockery now.

Every night, he snuffed the lamp and lay down to sleep, but the pattern never changed. He didn't expect it to.

*   *   *

'They keep falling, the good ones. Last month it was Wolff and Voss. It's almost as though the Blue Max has a curse upon it.'

'And from what I've heard, Richthofen hasn't been the same since he was shot in the head.' It was next to impossible to keep Germany's trump card out of any conversation concerning the best battle fliers. These men were amongst the most prolific scorers in the *Luftstreitkräfte*, and were hugely respected by their peers.

The men had just been talking idly among themselves about matters relating to their own circumstances. The conversation was tangential to the thoughts of von Bülow, but he felt no reluctance in hijacking it to illustrate his own perspective, 'Unfortunately, the good pilots are generally destined to assume their own commands elsewhere. The successful *Jastas* are stripped of their experience, and then have to rebuild. What I wouldn't give to have the likes of Beerenbrock and Rossler back again. Rottenberger also.'

It was an admission few of them had anticipated. Von Bülow had a degree of notoriety when it came to drumming good pilots out of his unit.

'What about Lehmann?'

'There's no need to be selfish about it. You can't keep all of the good ones.'

Reinhold kept his opinion to himself. Weber didn't, 'I didn't think you liked Rossler?'

Von Bülow had no knowledge of how the man had known about his relationship with the troublesome NCO. Though it was a fact that Rossler had clashed with the commander on occasion, it had been before Weber's arrival. Von Bülow wondered who the gossip could be. He surveyed the room and decided that of those present only Reinhold was trustworthy. Knowing he would be butting his head against a wall if he embarked upon this particular line of inquiry, he took a different tack, 'He had merit. He was an example to many.'

Kruchelsdorf was slouched in a chair in his rumpled clothes. He peered at them all through bloodshot eyes, 'All men are equal when the lead is flying. Equally brave... or dead.' He subsided.

Von Bülow was not ready to extend credit to any man who didn't wear an Iron Cross, and even then he was grudging if they did not also hold a commission, 'I disagree. Wolff was brave. Voss was brave.' He made an all-encompassing gesture of the new men in the unit, 'Don't compare this lot to them.'

Kruchelsdorf was in a partially impaired state, otherwise he would not have contradicted his commander, 'If you ask me, bravery is shown when a man of lesser ability flies to meet the man who he knows will probably kill him.'

'I didn't ask you. If you want to find bravery, you don't need to look any further than the man's name. If it contains 'von,' then you have found your answer: Schleich, Tutschek, the Richthofen brothers.' Though he didn't specifically mention the fact, it was patently clear to everyone present that the commander was referring to himself as well. His sneer was enough to confirm the idea to any of those who lacked the requisite wit to make the connection.

Kruchelsdorf could not help but respond to the jibe, 'What about Max Müller? Don't forget him – he's no knight.' Von Bülow looked like he had bitten into a lemon. Müller was a former non-com, widely known to dislike the officer class though he was now himself commissioned. A Bavarian by birth, not even Prussian, he was one of Germany's most successful living chasers. Only Richthofen and Gontermann were currently ranked higher.

Von Bülow refused to give satisfaction to the wisecracking pilot, 'And he never will be, the peasant!' It was barely adequate as a riposte, though his expression told of a different interpretation: eloquence was unnecessary. After all, he had not risen to a position of authority through the employment of flowery words.

The smugness was wiped off his face in an instant when Weber suggested in a tone of complete innocence, 'Yvonne, another von to heap praise upon.'

There were several species of silence that met the remark. Most of the men present were uncomprehending of the reference. Bonninghauser and Reinhold looked momentarily awkward. Von Bülow was deathly.

An orderly chose that moment to look into the room, '*Leutnant* Mellerhorst? Telephone call.' The adjutant excused himself from their company. He was happy to get away from the viper's nest.

Von Bülow turned his back on Weber and crossed the room. He drew a line through the roster and pencilled in new names, 'Tomorrow Weber and Bonnighauser can fly the first mission. Your leave is cancelled.'

Weber was furious, 'That isn't fair!'

He received an inscrutable look from the commander, 'Tough luck.'

Mellerhorst re-joined them. He addressed the men present, 'I've just had word. Heinrich Gontermann is dead.'

Kruchelsdorf muttered from the back of the room, 'Gontermann was brave.' Given that he was drunk, his impersonation of von Bülow was credible.

Chapter 17

November 1917: Striking the Mark

Von Bülow had unsurprisingly fallen asleep, and was now snoring. Yvonne lay awake staring at the wall. In the moonlight she saw the tin full of buttons resting in its usual place on the bedside table. She sat up and pulled on a nightgown, then lit the kerosene lamp.

The tin did not move. How could it? It was not alive. If anything, it represented death in blood, fear and fire.

She was captivated by its significance.

After swinging her legs off the bed she leaned towards the table, then picked the tin up and held it before her eyes. *Such a plain, everyday item.*

Having lit a lamp, she opened the tin and looked within at the jumble of labelled buttons. She picked one up and held it to the flickering light. Number eight. *The first eight are all Frenchmen. But the rest are English.* How many did 'the rest' signify? Two at least. Yvonne wondered how many more victories von Bülow had added since he had made the comment, and if they were still all Englishmen. She could count how many buttons were in the tin now, but she didn't know how many there had been even a few weeks ago. There was no answer to be had.

Her attention went back to looking through the contents of the tin until she found number nine. She untied the string, then did the same for number eight. The labels were attached to new buttons. Yvonne derived an unusual satisfaction from her petty act. Quashing her mounting unease, she set nimble fingers to the task of mix and match.

She was not even a minute into her sabotage when a finger traced a line down her spine, 'Are you enjoying yourself, Night Witch?' At some point von Bülow had stopped snoring and Yvonne had not noticed.

She trembled beneath his touch, and this time it was not in revulsion. There was a quaver in her voice, 'What are you going to do to me?'

He chuckled, 'Do? Why do I have to do anything?'

'You aren't angry?'

'Why would I be angry?' There was no obvious inflection in his voice to provide any hint to his true state of mind. Yvonne took it as a bad sign.

To admit out loud that she had meddled with his trophies in order to make him appear foolish would have been a mistake, though neither was under any illusions as to her intent. 'I'm sorry.'

'Can you put them back into the correct order?'

Yvonne's reply was hollow and small, 'No.'

'Then I fail to see how being sorry is any sort of remedy.'

'I'm sorry.' Reiterating remorse at being caught in the act has never been taken seriously by an injured party, but even so, the strategy of offering repentance has never been abandoned by offenders. Even in religion it is a cornerstone.

'Perhaps instead of feeling sorry, in future you could consider exercising prudence.'

Yvonne was crying now, not knowing how much damage she had caused, or how much would be taken out of her hide. Von Bülow had seen her tears before, many times, and was inured to their intended effect, 'The buttons are only tokens. If you think I have superstitions about them then you are insane. You could piss on them and no-one will know they are less than I claim them to represent.'

She refused to believe that he was without any sentiment in the matter despite every other aspect of her interactions with the man. Not knowing of any response that would not trigger von Bülow's ire, she wrapped herself in silence and hoped to view the morrow through un-blackened eyes.

He clasped her shoulder and she flinched. Though his touch was gentle, he was a master of misdirection. This time, though, his voice was only curious. Tone was generally not something he had ever been able to properly disguise and a she felt a degree of relief, 'Why?'

Yvonne turned to face him, and her face was streaked with tears. He brushed them away with a thumb, 'Is this an attempt to look ugly? Here, you've missed a bit...'

She sobbed at his humour and at her own pathetic state, 'I'm sorry.'

'Three times? Is this a curse you are putting on me?'

Yvonne was living on raw nerves, 'The only good thing to come of his death is that he loved me to the end. He never had time to tire of me, or to wish for another. You'll never understand what it means.'

Von Bülow may have been brutal, but he was not stupid. He had the sense to see that she was referring to her husband, although he lacked the tact to sympathise, 'He left you. What else is death, but abandonment?'

'You don't understand.'

'What is it you want of me?'

She shouted at him then, 'I'm not talking about you!'

'Then you're right, I don't understand.'

'Leave me be. Just go away and never come back.'

Von Bülow had lost interest in the topic, 'Maybe I'll write a letter to the High Command and tell them that it is no longer convenient for me to be stationed here, and please can they transfer me to another sector?'

Grief was no impediment to the detection of sarcasm, nor to meting it out, 'If you go, maybe then I'll miss you.'

What is this shit? Women and their lack of reason! Despite the thought, von Bülow knew that he had been bewitched. It was evident in the small things that he noticed about her: the tilt of the head unique to this being; that confident walk when she was unconsciously in a different space; the slender hands, elegant but made bolder through professional usage.

Yvonne was beautiful, and he knew it as a fact. Here she was, crying whilst dressed in an old gown, and it wouldn't have lessened her to wear a potato sack. The scene was one of familiarity, and von Bülow briefly glimpsed how a marriage might be something that brought a feeling of belonging even on a bad day.

In this moment the effect of her physical form was muted by her mood.

It is the eyes… always it comes back to the eyes. They were hard to like because they were almost always flinty and uncaring, and yet sometimes they had a vulnerable luminosity, though it was only a whore's trick. At other times those same eyes provided a gateway to the soul, where fear and suffering resided. It was precisely to witness some of Yvonne's complex human side that motivated von Bülow to deliberately provoke her. At least, that was what he told himself on the rare occasions when he thought about it.

Right now he didn't desire to witness a manifestation of fear, now that other parts of Yvonne's mind had surfaced. So he simply sat there as she cried. He had no support to offer, because that required knowledge of a specific problem, and there was none that he could discern. Sometimes the only thing to do was to wait for the storm to blow itself out.

He sat beside her until she eventually cried herself to sleep.

Yvonne was puffy the next morning, and her hair was in disarray.

'You look like you could do with some beauty sleep.'

He received a poisonous look, 'I think you meant to say 'some more beauty sleep'.'

Von Bülow smiled, 'No.'

It was time to put the smug bastard into his place, 'You have never told me that you love me.'

Even though the ambush had been sprung without prior warning, it failed to take him unawares, 'I don't.'

'You act as though you do.'

'You and I, are we so different? You act as well.'

'Do you sing my praises to anyone who will listen?'

'No. It should be enough that I say them to you.'

'Then you don't love me.'

'If you want me to say it three times I will. That's the magic number with you, no?'

Yvonne gave him a searching look. She took her time about it, 'Maybe one day you'll understand.'

'Maybe one day I'll be dead.'

Please let it be soon. But she said instead, 'Well, there is a war on, as you know firsthand.'

'Have I done something wrong again?'

Again? When did you take a break? 'I believe that every person is unique and I am not an exception'

'Excuse my French, but is that not a contradiction?'

'Do you love anything?'

'Steak. Rare, garnished with spring onions.'

The flippancy of his answer had a kernel of truth that infuriated her. She pressed him further, 'And what of your men? Do they love you even though you do not love them?'

'It would be a reasonable assumption, though respect is their likelier sentiment.'

Yvonne was brusque, 'I have to go to work.' It was a cruel reminder that he didn't have sole rights to her body.

Von Bülow shrugged as if he didn't care, 'So do I. I have some more buttons to collect.' And that was his way of letting her know she didn't have a monopoly on reminders.

*   *   *

Despite the fact that they flew in the same aircraft, Ross Burke was something of an enigma to Captain Lewis-Hamilton. The young flight commander could never shake the feeling that his observer held the rest of the squadron in low esteem. It seemed that simply because he was on the other side of Hill Thirty, Burke had a right to claim superior knowledge to those of lesser years. He would never answer a question seriously, and though this was irritating to the Englishman, he nevertheless persisted, 'Smoke?'

Burke took the offering, 'Ta.' He lit it and inhaled, then blew out a perfect ring before it dissipated before their eyes.

'I have a question.'

Burke sighed, 'Here it comes…'

Lewis-Hamilton gave a slight frown of annoyance. He didn't notice that the frown registered on Burke, or that it caused an imperceptible crinkle of amusement in the corner of the older man's eyes, 'Why didn't you transfer to the Australian Flying Corps when it was formed? I know that they were asking for applications from within the RFC.'

'Mate, I know your opinion of Australians, but even they have their standards. Besides, I know that you will one day appreciate the experience of exposure to the wider world even if currently you have your nose halfway between your arse and a tea party.'

The pilot was not new to insults; they came out almost every time the dumb Aussie opened his mouth. He simply could not fathom the reason for it. Stymied once more, he gave the game up and went looking elsewhere for a friendly conversation.

Bert Noone had overheard the exchange, 'I heard what you said, and the question still stands.'

'Did you used to peek at your sister in the bathtub as well?'

'What sort of question is that, Backa? I was in it with her!'

'You would be.'

'I grew up in a drought and we bathed together. Two in the tub raises the water level as you well know.'

'Fucking Archimedes has a lot to answer for.'

'So why didn't you join the AFC? I've asked you once before.'

'Once? That'd be the day.' The real reason was quite simple, 'The skipper might have too much attachment to his school tie, but one thing that he can do is something that matters very much to me; he knows how to get home every day. If I transferred to an Aussie squadron I'd just be assigned to someone who is unproven, and my dear old mum would finally see my name in the paper.' The reference to the published casualty lists was inherently understood.

'We could apply for a transfer together.'

'I once saw men jump from a burning RE8 because they didn't want to sizzle. It makes you wonder.'

'Isn't that a mortal sin, deliberately taking your own life?'

'For Catholics, maybe. But I'm not sure it counts even then, given that they were dead men either way.'

'It was still a deliberate act.'

'Sometimes there are no easy options.'

Burke didn't know what else to say to his old friend. Pointing out that Noone was not exactly a seasoned campaigner seemed crass beyond belief, but the fact that the man didn't even realise the implication was more proof than Burke needed. He wondered how to let the man down gently, 'Remember when we went grape picking in the Hunter Valley? The first day we were paired with experienced pickers and made bugger all money out of the job.' Noone shrugged, not sure of the relevance. Burke nodded, 'I was on my side of the vine, and the other bloke was on his side. I couldn't see how he was filling his bucket so fast when mine took forever. The whole crop had to be stripped, but I didn't see that the bastard was taking advantage by grabbing the bigger bunches on both sides for himself, and leaving the scraps for me. Then he'd move to the next plant and do it all over again before I could catch up.'

'Yeah, I remember. The same happened to me. You wanted to punch him in the head.'

'I would have, too. In the end, the simpler solution was to figure out the game and prey on the ones who came along later. They either work it out or call it quits.'

'We did all right after the first few days, as I recall.'

'Yeah, but how many didn't figure out the trick? Pack your bags and go home.' *Was the reference too obscure?* Burke had no way of knowing, and certainly no way of asking.

Noone pointed his chin at the distant form of Lewis-Hamilton, 'You don't like him much, do you?'

'The toffee-nosed bastard deliberately bowled me off a no-ball once.'

'Why didn't you block it out?'

Burke scowled.

*   *   *

Boom. The gunshot echoed across the field. Von Bülow was practising with his carbine again.

The new men in the *Jasta* had finally found their feet - those that had survived - and now they were beginning to register their first claims. The commander was reminded of the first time he had been asked to assemble a group of strangers into a cohesive fighting unit. That had been just over a year ago. It seemed much longer.

Boom. Bonninghauser was watching from a distance with Reinhold, 'What has he loaded it with?'

'Extra powder.'

'Isn't he afraid that it will blow his hand off?'

'Are you afraid of being killed when you face the English?'

'It's an unnecessary risk, if you ask me.'

Though von Bülow probably would have said that no-one had asked, Reinhold was built differently, 'I think he is practising for when he goes to Africa. He wants a small bore, but never said anything about the number of grains per cartridge.'

'He needs to get through the war first.'

'He believes he will.'

Boom. Bonninghauser was not all idle questions, 'It seems that he is spending more time on the range with every passing week.'

Reinhold had noticed the same thing, 'He is going through a dry spell. If you can't put shots into the enemy, practice is the next best thing.'

'He hasn't got any since I've been here.'

Reinhold hadn't known it was so long. The new pilots must have been thinking that von Bülow had lost his touch if they were celebrating victories and the commander wasn't. Potentially, it could undermine his credibility. 'How long have you been here?'

'Nearly two months.' *Boom. Boom.* 'How good is he?'

'If you want to shoot for money he'll empty your pockets soon enough.'

Von Bülow looked like he had finished for the day. He had tucked the weapon beneath his arm and was trudging back towards the onlookers. He rebuked them without venom, 'You'll never get any better by watching others.'

Though von Bülow hadn't yet shown his dogfighting prowess to the newer men, he was not without presence. Bonninghauser didn't mind mining the man's brain, 'What is your preferred method?'

Ordinarily the commander didn't mind blowing his trumpet, but he still felt that if people didn't listen to him every time he spoke he was hardly obligated to give an encore. Having been asked a direct question, he gave a minimalist response, 'Sun at your back; shoot from close range.'

It was standard fare. Everyone used that method and Bonninghauser found nothing new in it to harvest. There were two ways to draw von Bülow into a conversation. The first was to ask him how good he was; the second was to ask someone else about their own abilities. If one didn't work the other was guaranteed to. 'What about you, Ernst? Which of your kills went exactly as you had planned?'

Reinhold was immediately reminded of a Nieuport which had erupted in a fireball. It was a thought he preferred to leave alone. He greatly preferred to see his adversaries survive, though it was widely accepted that firing a machine gun at a man could be to his detriment.

Von Bülow had no such qualms, 'Holding your fire until the last minute gives you an excellent opportunity to plaster your quarry, and I'll admit that it is crudely visceral. However, there is no greater satisfaction than clinically walking your bullets into the cockpit and placing a single bullet into a man's skull. Of course, the Maxim's rate of fire complicates matters – as a rule half of the poor fellow's head is taken off. But the process is one to strive for if you aspire to achieve perfection.'

'You have done this?'

'Just once: that day I was in a different place. Time actually seemed to slow and I was able to make exactly the shot that I wished for. I imagined the target's next move, and anticipated my own reaction. From there it all unfolded as I had foreseen. Everything deliberate. Mechanical. Exact. Once you have had such an experience, you want to do it again. It completes you. You understand God. To relive that day is what spurs me on; to find the perfect combination that connects you to the soul of the man you snuff out. But to get to that place where time stands still, you must first stand upon the precipice and look down. When you have been to that place, religion makes perfect sense.'

It sounded bizarre. Bonninghauser had never considered such a feeling. But seeing the animation in von Bülow made him wonder if it was at all possible to achieve. He looked at Reinhold, who had a bleaker outlook, 'For the rest of us, there is usually just the shambles of flames and mangled bodies.'

Von Bülow had more to impart, 'The simple truth is that a man can do everything right every time he flies. Then one lapse and he is dead. This is especially so if the error occurs when the enemy has seen you, or sometimes just if your number is up. Like it was for Boelcke. A man like him is not killed by mortals.'

Reinhold agreed, 'The successful hunter has superior awareness and he makes the right choice without hesitation.'

Von Bülow nodded, 'And luck. One cannot overstate luck. It is as important as character. Maybe more so.' Von Bülow was the best marksman in the *Jasta*, though he was not always aware of everything else around him when there were upwards of a score of aircraft swirling about, with most of them after his blood. He had been riddled with gunfire enough times that he had acquired a healthy dose of respect for the French and the English, 'Even the best pilots fall, and for me this is proof of luck – both good and ill.'

Bonninghauser made light if it, 'Perhaps it would then be better to practise with dice rather than firearms?'

Von Bülow ignored him. Reinhold was also dismissive, 'If target practice and dice games won wars, the Kaiser wouldn't require us to risk our necks for him. He'd hand out bravery awards for shooting clay pigeons.'

'Don't waste your luck on dice, Bonninghauser. Save it for when you are flying and maybe you will live a little longer.'

Chapter 18

December 1917: Winter Sports

The officer's mess was a low-key environment where the pilots and observers spent much of their down time. Lewis-Hamilton was propped on a bar stool as he was pontificating on Burke's propensity to tell tall tales. Percy Wiggan was his reluctant audience of one, 'The story about the ear is untrue. He confided to me that actually it was bitten off when he was attacked in his sleep by an echidna.' The assertion was met with a mildly drunk but sceptical look. It was not lost on the patrol leader, 'You know - a spiny ant-eater. I doubted it myself when he told me. I have seen a picture of one of those animals, and they don't seem very fierce at all except for the spines. But Burke has informed me that there are all manner of strange creatures where he comes from: spiders and snakes and yowies and such. Echidnas need to defend themselves against many things. It seems plausible, and why should the man seek to deceive me?'

Wiggan's philosophy had always been that the simplest answer was probably the most likely, 'Australians are generally uneducated, and my experience of them these last few months has led me to conclude that they are compulsive liars to boot.' With an emphatic raising of his drinking elbow, he emptied his glass in one last gulp. To punctuate his announcement, he added a beery belch.

'Surely it can't be the case in every instance.'

'Believe what you will; you're the one who has to fly with him. For mine, give me a man of good schooling every day of the week, and a church service on Sundays.' He punctuated the pious statement with another burp.

Wiggan pointed at the orderly behind the bar, indicating his empty glass. Another was brought forth, 'Look at them, colonial riff-raff.' He pointed dismissively at the two Australians as they kept each other company in a quiet corner of the room.

Burke and Bert Noone were hunkered down together, deep in discussion about the rugby league competition back at home. There were huge gaps in their knowledge on the current state of the game, which they had not attended live since the nineteen-fourteen season. Consequently, they were more focused on the events that they remembered from the years prior to their war service. Their lack of connection with the present status of the renegade competition underlined how far out of kilter the war had knocked things.

'Billy Cann – he was the best in the business. Never had a bad season, and tough as nails.'

'Yeah, he could tackle all right, but the best? No. Put your money on Messenger.'

'Wrong team. Show some bloody allegiance.'

'Fair call: Cann, then. But his name suggests he keeps close company with swagmen. Get it? Billy can?'

'Very original.'

'No wonder South Sydney were so dominant in those first few years. Throw in McCabe and the Butler brothers and you've got the basis for a good team.'

'I met Harry Butler once.'

'I was with you.'

'Oh. Yeah, you were.'

'I preferred when they played Hallett in the centres. They should never have switched him to fullback.'

'Who, then?'

'Jim Davis.'

'No, he was better in the forward pack.'

'Maybe, but there were enough forwards to go around that it hardly mattered.'

'Word is that young Horder is coming along quite well.'

'Well enough to not volunteer to join us over here where the crowds don't cheer you on without an accompaniment of automatic weapons.' And that observation killed their enthusiasm for reminiscing about their favourite club team.

The conversation had turned sour, but stayed on topic. Burke noted, 'Interesting that Balmain is winning the competition every year now that the war is on.'

'Are they the only team whose players aren't signing up for the AIF?'

'What other reason can it be? Before I got on the boat they were just a mid-ranked bunch, no better or worse than the Dirty Reds.'

'Now there's an unflattering name, but no worse than Newtown's. Who calls themselves the Bluebags? It sounds like they enjoy being kicked in the balls!'

'They're a shit team, too.'

'They ought to change their nickname to something better. Modernise. How about the Biplanes?'

'Jesus, I can tell you're not a Newtown supporter with a stupid suggestion like that.'

'Or a Balmain supporter, either.'

'Balmain. Maybe their players are the only ones with brains in their heads, staying at home where it's the fans that scream, not the participants.'

'Brains? Footballers?' They laughed at the stereotype.

Noone leaned backwards, tilting his chair far enough that he risked injury to his spine in the event that he should overbalance, 'I wonder if the ladies still swoon over them, or are they now handing out white feathers at the ticket gate to blokes refusing to enlist?'

'How hypocritical people can be, judging those who refuse to fight, while they happily sit at home themselves.'

Burke and Noone peered morosely into their beer, each pondering the world in a brief silence. Noone resumed where they had left off, though neither had noticed the pause in the conversation, 'They're fickle bitches, all right. But what do you want them to do, Backa? Join the infantry?' *Women in the army? The very idea was ludicrous.* Neither of them would ever have any notion that the Russians had already raised all-female battalions, but their collective ignorance of events so far a-field was hardly unique amongst the armies that fought on the Western Front.

'I need another beer. Where's Drummond?'

'He won't be anywhere to be seen if it's his turn to buy.'

'The miserable sod.'

'I'll go and find some of the new boys, then. They may as well be useful for something.' For some reason, Noone didn't consider himself to be a new boy anymore - not since the latest intake had arrived. Burke considered the elevation to be premature.

Combat veterans had their fair share of stories to impart, and if they chose to tell them they invariably had a willing audience. For Ross Burke to open up, first he needed to be plied with alcohol. It made him unusually eloquent at times, 'The first time I flew over the lines I ran into the enemy. How about that? No time to familiarise myself with life at the front - just straight in at the deep end. We were at seven thousand feet and there were Albatroses all over us...'

One of the listeners felt the need to interrupt, 'You mean Albatri.'

Drunken eyes swivelled unsteadily, 'Huh?'

'The plural for Albatros is Albatri.'

Burke was dismissive of the new kid's opinion, 'Bullshit.'

Another fellow added his tuppence's worth, 'Actually, it's Albatros. The same as applies to fish or deer.'

The Australian didn't care, 'Or blithering idiot. You're barely old enough to wipe your arse, boy. Keep your school book wisdom for Mummy. Do you want the story or not?'

'Sorry, Ross.' Ordinarily, Burke would have shut up shop and told them to leave him alone – either that, or punch someone in the face - but he was luring these foolish rabbits into his snare and was prepared to put up with their ignorant attention to useless trivia.

'So there we were at six thousand...'

'You said seven.'

'And I also said to shut your mouth, but you didn't seem to hear that part.' He glared at the others and almost called it quits. They correctly read his intention and became instantly submissive. *Stupid Poms.*

'The Hun bastards were shooting the blazes out of us and we lost a thousand feet while some hoity-toity Pommy kids graced the world with everything they know about grammar and diction...' Burke looked meaningfully at them, but they wouldn't meet his eye. All except Noone, who winked. 'The most dangerous place to be when you are flying is not at high altitude, but just above the ground. When you hit the ground you are dead, so being actually on the ground isn't the most dangerous place. The last place that most airmen fly before they are killed is just above the ground. Think about that.'

He nodded at them again, 'So being at five thousand...', Here Burke paused for another interjection but none was forthcoming, '...wasn't too alarming except for the bastard Huns and their Spandaus.' He sagely pointed at one of the boys who had dared to interrupt him. Burke was at this stage very drunk, 'That's a machine gun, in case you didn't know.' It was an attempt to provoke more theoretical knowledge from the upstarts, but they were wary of him now.

'Of course, the other thing to worry about being at four thousand feet is how far it is to the ground.' His speech was ponderous, and especially difficult to decipher for those of the Englishmen unused to the thick accent, 'That's the worst part. There's nothing scary about being just above the ground. Lots of people fall off ladders and out of trees and live to tell about it. But not from three thousand feet.'

Burke could see that they were starting to smell a rat. The constant loss of altitude was about as subtle as a brick through a window. He grinned at the prospect of what lay ahead. Whether they read his look correctly or not was immaterial. If they thought he was just a slobbering drunk, so much the better. He forged ahead, struggling for continuity in his inebriated state, 'From seven thousand feet to two thousand, chased the whole time by Albatroses. And you know the worst part?' He leaned forward conspiratorially, and they leaned in imperceptibly in response to his cue, 'We were on fire.'

The claim prompted some justified scepticism, 'I beg your pardon? How did you get down safely from so far up? You haven't a mark upon you!'

'Are you calling me a liar, fella-me-lad?'

The look on Burke's face forbade any notion of doubt. He cowed his audience with his intensity, 'If I said we burned the whole way down, that's what happened. His Lordship landed us in No-man's-land and we ran nude back to our lines, our very clothes having been incinerated while we wore them. The infantry said that they'd never seen the like: me with my cock wrapped around my waist to keep it from tripping me over, and His Lordship modestly covering his spare pinkie with a scrap of string.'

'But it can't be done. Despite the physical impossibility of surviving after falling in flames for seven thousand feet, you are hale and hearty! Not a mark upon your body.' Mentioning Burke's mutilated ear seemed meaningless in the context.

'I said it was my first mission, no?'

'I don't understand.'

'Brand new. Green. Too green to burn.'

There was a pause of several heartbeats as the implications were sorted by the various men. They let out groans as they realised that they had been duped.

Burke took one last shot, 'Did you know that the word 'gullible' has been omitted from the latest edition of the Dictionary?'

'Really? Why?'

There's always one.

*   *   *

Black branches speared into the lowering sky like the antlers of a deranged stag. There was dampness in the air, and snow-melt had trickled down the coat collar of the young man as he foraged in the forest. He padded softly over the partially buried trail, game-bag slung across his shoulder as he kept a sharp eye out for anything interested in his furtive doings.

He trekked homewards, hunched against the cold, mittened hands fending off the supple branches and twigs that seemed bent on flicking his eyes out. One of them had raised a welt on his cheek. He rubbed it with painfully tingling fingers, but the only sensation was the rubbery numbness of chilled skin.

In the distance, he spied the familiar form of the house he had grown up in. He imagined that it would have looked different only in detail even if it had been constructed of gingerbread. *If Mother hears she has been compared to a witch, well, the look on her face would be worth skipping a meal to see.* He revised his thought. *No, the meal comes first.*

When he finally arrived home, he scraped his boots clean on the bottom step, and then released the latch, letting himself inside as quickly as he could to prevent the warmth within escaping.

'Volker, is that you?'

'Yes, Father. I'm back.'

'Come in from the cold.'

Volker Bartels removed his boots and brought them inside, placing them close enough to the fireplace to allow them to dry, but not so close that they would be ruined, 'Just one hare. The other snares were empty.'

'If the game-warden catches you you'll be sorry.'

'If we don't eat we'll all be sorry.'

'Yes, yes, I wasn't chastising you.'

The younger man removed their next meal from the jute sack in which it had been carried home, 'Shall I skin it?'

'No need, your mother has idle hands, it will give her something to do.'

There was a female snort at the comment, 'Idle hands? Something to do?'

Harald Bartels had a twinkle in his eye, 'Besides chatter.'

Volker smiled at the by-play. His family would have been very happy if it wasn't for the shortages. 'I saw sign of deer in the snow. I can go out again before the tracks are covered if you wish it.'

'No, no, the hare will do. Otherwise your mother will start complaining that she's too fat.'

'Start complaining?'

Another twinkle, 'Well, if not her, then me.'

'And when do you ever complain about being too fat, Harald?'

The twinkle was now accompanied by a mischievous grin, 'I'm never too fat, dearest.'

The comment was duly processed, then answered with a squawk of indignation.

Harald chuckled, 'There, that's what I wanted: the squawk.'

'I don't squawk!'

'Call it what you will, but the hare won't skin itself.'

The domestic routines took over, and harmony was duly restored to the small household. Volker's mother had vanished to the kitchen to prepare their evening meal.

'Father?'

'Yes, Volker?'

'I'm seventeen years old.'

Pale blue eyes peered over the rim of the spectacles that perched atop Harald Volker's nose, 'How fortunate that you learned your numbers at school.' The tone was mild, but both of them knew where the conversation was headed.

'I will be called up soon. If I leave it any longer to volunteer I won't have the option to choose service in your old regiment.'

The elder decided to take the lead, 'There is such a thing as service to the state.'

'I have been brought up to believe so.'

Harald nodded, 'Unfortunately, affairs of state are not always pure. Never. I mean, never pure.'

Volker knew that his father would keep him out of the war for as long as possible, even if it meant hiding him in the cellar, 'Often there is no choice.'

'There are ways to tell whether the politicians are making the correct choices.' He paused, 'My mistake. What I meant to say was that there are ways to tell that they have made incorrect choices.'

'How?'

'The obvious one is when they put a rifle in your hands.'

'Can you please be serious?'

'I am very serious about this, Volker.'

'There must be more to it than that. War is the result of failed political strategy.'

'Yes, it is. But it is very difficult to govern when there are lies and compromises every way a man turns.'

'And now you'll tell me that you can tell their lies, because their lips move.' Volker was just pre-empting his father's pet turn of phrase.

'You are an astute boy. I am very proud of you.' Now Harald's face did turn serious, 'You'll either volunteer or be drafted.'

'I know.'

'You want this?'

'Do I have a choice?'

'Life is full of choices, Volker.'

'I thought that you would forbid me from fighting until I had no other option.'

'I? Forbid? No, no, you will make your own decision in this matter, and not blame me if it all turns to shit.'

Volker looked aghast. He had never heard his father use the word. That one utterance, more than anything else, told the young man how far opposed the older man was to the idea of enlisting in the Kaiser's army.

Harald had used the word for effect, and he saw that the strategy had worked for now. But life had to go on, 'In the meantime, you can go back outside and bring in some more wood for the fireplace.'

'Yes, Father.'

Volker made his escape, relieved to be away from the awkward situation, even if the price to pay was a renewed exposure to the elements. He pulled on his wet boots and went back outside. As he closed the latch, he heard an unfamiliar drone in the distance.

Though Volker Bartels had never seen an aeroplane, nor a zeppelin, he had heard tales of them and knew the sound for what it was. He crossed the yard to see if he could get a view unobstructed by trees, but it was not to be.

The sound gradually decreased in volume, then before it petered out, ended with a distant explosion. Firewood forgotten, Volker ran back into the house.

'Father, I think a flying machine has crashed nearby!'

'Did you close the door behind you in your hurry to tell me of it?'

He had not. The lapse was attended to, then the conversation was picked up again, 'What would it be doing this far away from the fighting?'

Harald Bartels was a firm believer in keeping things simple, 'Possibly it has lost its way and run out of fuel.'

'Can I go and see it?'

'Maybe we'll go out tomorrow.'

Volker knew better than to press the issue. To ask twice was folly.

'Where is the firewood that I sent you to fetch?'

The young man performed the task, but each trip outside caused him to look into the distance at unexpected possibilities.

*   *   *

'A man walks into a bar. The barman says, 'Watch where you're going!''

The pub was packed with servicemen, and that usually meant that there would be a fight at some stage. Inter-service rivalry was inevitable, and most encounters resulted in a considerable amount of damage and no few cracked heads.

'Hey, what do you call a dog that doesn't heel?'

'Gangrene!'

'Syphilis!'

'C'mon, that one's not even new.'

'Remember the time we borrowed linen from the hotel clothes line?'

The story in question was not very old at all, and was recalled amongst hoots of laughter, 'The old bastard came out and accused us of thieving...'

'...Drummond told him to shut his trap if he knew what was good for him - it was three against one...'

'The cranky bastard went back inside and came back with this bloody great mongrel and said 'Now it's three against two!''

'And Hump, he says, 'We should have brought Barry, that'd even things up nicely.''

'Fucking Barry!' The image of the docile nanny filled them with mirth.

191

Ross Burke was deep in his cups, and it was not the first time. His eyes were as red as an outback sunset and as unforgiving on an Englishman. They were the ones who had involved Australia in the bloody war, and the adventurous aspect had ended just as soon as the shooting started. To have joined up expecting anything different was inexplicable to a man who had grown up with firearms. He was no different to a rabbit for the cooking pot, and was a fool not to have realised it immediately. The recruiters had done a good job; that much was certain. Men who were otherwise sensible had flocked to do their bidding.

All that was left to him was to take it out on those around him. He had no hesitation in that respect. As usual, his heavy Australian accent was a draw card and he had another captive audience hanging off his every word. The topic today was his mangled ear, and only Bert Noone knew the game he was playing, 'It was my sweetheart who did it. The local black fellas have a custom not unlike blood brothers – you know, where you cut yourself and press the wound to mingle with your mate - only you get your sweetheart to bite your ear off instead. It's a sign of your love.'

The best audience was an unsuspecting one. The nature of the fighting seemed to offer up a never-ending supply of new victims, 'My God! Do you have to bite her ear as well?'

Burke laughed loudly, 'Don't be a drongo - that'd make her ugly. You Pommy bastards ask the stupidest questions.'

'But it makes you ugly as well!'

'Jesus Christ, she doesn't want me for my ear!'

Humphrey Drummond was famous for two things: his deep pockets and his odd habit of drinking beer in a way that was just plain wrong. His friends leaped enthusiastically upon every excuse to rag him for either one.

'Here you go, Hump. Have a beer, my treat.'

Drummond gratefully accepted the proffered pint and lifted it to his lips, noisily slurping the foamy head whilst leaving the amber liquid to be consumed at leisure, 'Ah, froth!'

The act drew the usual round of mock horror, 'Jesus, where did you grow up?'

Smacking his lips, Drummond beamed back at them, 'Have you tried it?'

'I haven't stuck my finger in my bum either, but I know not to.'

The atmosphere was bubbly, and the men continued making as much noise as possible while ignoring the rumble of the artillery in the distance. Before long, glasses had again been emptied, 'Whose shout is it?'

Drummond's response was entirely predictable, 'Not mine – I'm out.'

'Piss off! It's your turn, don't be cheap.'

The miserly observer resisted, as he always did, 'You mean frugal.'

'Same old story. Why do we even drink with you?'

'To see Humpty drink his fucking froth: no other reason!'

'Remember that time we ran afoul of those French infantry?'

'In the pub? Yeah, that went south pretty quickly.'

'Drummond wrapped a bottle over the back of their sergeant's head as I recall.'

'Now that was a cheap shot.'

'Hump would call it frugal!'

Burke was immersed in the sound of the place, but he also had a sixth sense. He located the source of his unease - a couple of sappers were surveying him from across the room, 'What are those bastards looking at us for?'

'Probably they can't believe that I'd be talking to a sheila as ugly as you are.'

One of the men who had been eyeballing them got up and wove an unsteady path to their table, 'You're the one called Burke, aren't you?' His foot may have been wearing a wobbly boot, but his diction was far more precise.

'You needed to go to a posh school to work that out?'

The enquirer bristled, 'What do you have against an education?'

'Only that it gives your lot a sense that the rest of us are too stupid to count past ten unless we remove our shoes.'

Wiggan heard a fragment of the exchange as he shoved through the throng on his way to the bar. He saw no reason not to add his two bits, 'Do Australians wear shoes?' The comment fell on deaf ears. *Pearls cast before swine.* Wiggan doubted that he'd bother making the effort again.

The chap who had identified Burke had taken a sudden dislike to the rude Australian, 'Can you count past twenty without taking your trousers off?' The change that had come over him was nothing out of the ordinary in the long and proud history of excessive alcohol intake, 'I was conscripted, but I hear that you volunteered. Remind me again who the stupid one is?'

The comment was fired off with one aim in mind, and it worked. Burke threw a punch. The room erupted into instant chaos as fists and missiles flew with gay abandon. Someone threw a glass that struck Drummond squarely on the forehead, which sat him on his rump looking as dazed as a cow attempting algebra. Shouting, swearing and the crash of furniture and fittings drowned out the outraged protests of the publican. Broken chairs and smashed glass littered the establishment within minutes. Later generations may have been tempted to describe it as a war zone, but these brawlers were under no such illusions - they had seen the real thing, and the experience bore little valid comparison to their act of wanton vandalism.

It didn't take long for the sound of shrill whistles to announce the arrival of more serious trouble. The alarm went up, 'MPs!'

Burke grinned like a maniac at his friend, 'Better get the hell out of here, No-one!' They ran for the exit, and they were not the only ones. The doorway had very quickly become a bottleneck, so they baled out of a window instead, laughing excitedly as they ran down cobbled streets. Looking back, they saw that the military policemen were lustily swinging away with their truncheons.

The two friends stopped to catch their breath, 'You stupid bastard, Backa, that idiot was itching for a fight.'

'Well he got one, didn't he? Right in the mouth too, so who's the stupid one now?' Burke inspected his hand and blood ran freely from knuckles that had been cut by English teeth, 'Fucking hell, the Huns have been shooting at me forever and not a scratch, but as soon as I try to have a quiet one at the local some kid from the church choir busts my hand.'

Bert Noone laughed it off, 'I'm pretty sure it wasn't quite what he had in mind.'

Chapter 19

January 1918: Home to Roost

A squadron was a tightly knit community in which everyone knew everyone else. As in other closed societal groupings, not everyone got along amicably. Even so, it was normal practice to all pull together. The very nature of active warfare meant that there were steady losses, but not all of these affected everyone in the same way. Many of the casualties had not yet had time to cement firm friendships and their disappearances often passed with little more than polite regret.

Others had had time to bed down, and when they were lost the pain was acute. The period of acceptance varied, but if a man could survive the first three months, his chances increased dramatically. Even so, it was no guarantee of survival. Many servicemen became fatalistic, but to deny friendship with everyone was impractical. Instead, they watched and waited and based their decisions on that which they witnessed over time.

Adam Burrows was not someone who had won the hearts of the men around him, but he had outlived many of his peers. He had not sought affection, nor received it. The men of 'B' Flight flew with him because it was their job to do so, and they protected him as far as they were able. He was not the newest man in their formation, but they had no faith in his ability.

Wiggan surreptitiously eyed Burrows across the room. *The man has had enough time to learn the trade, yet still he rides his luck. And luck will only go so far.* The veteran signalled to the barman for another drink.

*   *   *

There were no longer any snails to be found, so Sloane and his cronies settled down to a game of cards. There were the usual grumbles, 'Nice, the dog-eared corner you're trying to hide is the queen of spades.'

'No matter, the ace is missing from the pack.'

'And the six of hearts.'

'Stop looking at the cards so closely. Try to pretend that it's a full deck and none of them have tell-tale marks.'

'Pretend? If I'm going to pretend, why not invite myself to fucking Buckingham Palace?'

'To what end?'

'Just because.'

'I wonder if there are snails in the palace garden?'

'Why wouldn't there be snails?'

'Because there's better entertainment to be had there than racing the stupid things, that's why.'

Limerick was trying to figure out how to escape from the game. He was useless at gambling, and if it wasn't for Sloane the others would have robbed him blind. In the distance, he made out the form of Burrows. Corporal Tyson saw the direction of his gaze, 'What do you make of him?'

Hardly needing an excuse to abandon the faulty deck of cards, the others switched their attention to the officer. Sloane gave him the once over, 'He doesn't say much, does he?'

Limerick rephrased it differently, 'If a mime is in a burning aeroplane and he screams all the way down, does anybody hear him over the noise of the engine?'

Tyson was not amused by the callous remark. He was at his core a decent human being who didn't relish the trauma that was evident in others. 'Hold your tongue if you've nothing decent to say.' The group watched to see if Sloane would react to the NCO for the reprimand, but the burly brawler let it pass through to the keeper. That in itself was telling evidence that Limerick had gone beyond acceptable limits. Each flier had a difficult enough job to do as it was. The least they could expect was the full support of the various ground crews.

Tyson had other fish to fry, 'Break's over. Back to it.'

There was no griping about their job. The task was boring but necessary. Cold fingers sorted through boxes of ammunition, each round checked before being painstakingly inserted into empty belts or drums. It made far better sense to find imperfections in live ordinance now, rather than to hear that a gun had sustained a blockage when things got nasty in the air. There were ways for aircrew to clear their weapons when aloft, but in the event that they needed to do so, they generally had other things occupying their minds.

'This is a lot simpler than what the riggers have to put up with.'

'Aye.'

In many ways, loading ammunition was as simple as shelling peas. But checking every wire on an airframe for the correct tension prior to every flight just to keep everything in the correct alignment? That was a different prospect entirely.

*   *   *

They had just landed and the Bristol was partially shredded, 'I thought you knew how to shoot?'

Burke was in no mood to argue the point. He was just happy to be alive.

Lewis-Hamilton saw Wiggan walking over to him. Having rebuked his observer, he now offered thanks to his saviour, 'I was in a spot of bother there, old boy - right up until you came and put the wind up the blighter.'

'I saw he had you cold. What happened?'

'That Australian is so ugly, normally the mere sight of his face is enough to scare off any Hun who latches onto me. Not this time, though.'

Burke was laconic, 'Gun jammed.'

Wiggan nodded sagely, 'You should look after it better. Might not be so lucky next time. The last thing you want to be is a Flamingo.' He pronounced it Flame-Ingo, with the accent on the first syllable. It was Wiggan's way of describing a burning bird.

The flight commander was grateful for Wiggan's timely intervention, but sometimes his foot got in the way of his words, 'Lucky you were on the spot, Percy.'

Wiggan smiled, 'You keep on believing that.' He sauntered off.

Lewis-Hamilton rubbed his jaw, 'What does that mean?'

Burke believed in enlightenment, 'Wiggan knows you think his continued success is based largely on luck, and he doesn't much care that you have only got two.'

'For Heaven's sake, how on Earth did he hear that in what I said?'

'It's the King's English, Milord. Lends itself to all kinds of misinterpretation.'

'Not the way you use it.'

'My point exactly. Would you like some lessons from an uncouth Aussie?'

'I've had rather too many of those as it is, I'm afraid. Thanks all the same.'

*   *   *

Corporal Tyson came to stand before the armourers and he didn't appear too comfortable about it. The threat of Sloane was always present, and that one didn't care who felt his fists so long as it couldn't be proven. If Tyson was nervous, it was because he thought that there was a beating in it for himself somewhere in the near future, even if bashing an NCO would have the boxer put on a charge.

As reluctant as he was, Tyson was just the messenger. He hoped that Sloane understood as much, though he doubted that it would matter much to the thug, 'Limerick, you have to report to Captain Harding's office. He's asked to see you. I think the C.O. is there, too.'

Limerick glanced nervously at Sloane, 'Do you think they know, Slugger?'

Sloane shrugged without concern, 'Only one way to find out, lad.' He shooed the boy away with his fingertips.

Tyson made to go with him, but he was stopped in his tracks by Sloane, 'If this is what I think it is, I'll be wanting some names. The ones who ratted him out.'

Tyson didn't know how to respond, except that trying to hide behind his rank was entirely the wrong option. Sloane had said his piece, being a man of few words, 'Go on, then.' Tyson made his escape, pretending to everyone, including himself, that he was on official business and not fearing for his skin.

The further he left Sloane behind, the safer Tyson felt. The same circumstance had the opposite effect on Limerick. He was full of trepidation, and it made the corporal curious, 'What's this all about, then?'

It was no time to make a confession, 'Sorry, Corporal, I really couldn't say.'

If Tyson was up for a beating, he at least wanted to know why, 'You are damned lucky that Sloane looks out for you, that's all I can say. You'd better hope that the Major knows it, too.'

From then on, no further words were exchanged. Tyson escorted the boy to the adjutant's office and knocked on the door.

'Enter.'

'Hello, sir. Here's Lyme, as requested.'

'Ah, yes. Thank you, Corporal, you may go.'

Tyson abandoned Limerick to his fate and found somewhere else to be. Somewhere away from Sloane's usual haunts.

Captain Harding beckoned to Limerick, 'Hello, Lyme, do come in.'

Limerick saw that the squadron commander was not present and he took it as a good sign. The adjutant wasted no time in bursting his bubble, 'If you are wondering where the C.O. is, I'm afraid that he has had to make an emergency visit to the latrine. He'll be back presently, I'm sure.'

Limerick was feeling very flighty. Harding helped him out, 'Feel free to stand to attention when I speak to you.'

Limerick straightened but had nothing to say. Harding helped him out some more, 'I'm sure you are curious as to why you have been summoned.' He came to stand before the younger man. Like everyone else, he towered over him, 'Lyme, Richard. That is the name on your file, is it not?'

A dumb nod.

'I didn't catch that?'

'Yes, sir.'

'We've all heard your funny little ditties, and they are good for a laugh. Very clever.'

'Thank you, sir.'

'Oh, you won't be thanking me, I can guarantee you that.' Harding peered down at the smaller man without meaning to be too threatening. He failed. 'I can't say that I'm happy that you have thought it amusing to laugh at the rest of us behind our backs.'

Limerick was genuinely confused, 'I'm sorry? What?'

'It's clever, in a way. Punning, I mean. A boy who composes limericks, then enters the army under an assumed name because he is underage. Richard Lyme. Lime, Rick. Even more amusing when your real name is connected into it all.'

Limerick was unravelling. He had no idea what was going to happen to him. A court martial? What then? Surely there would be time served in a military prison? Maybe they wouldn't let him out until he was eighteen and then send him straight to the trenches? He started to get light-headed.

Harding was watching his turmoil, 'How old are you, Richard Green?'

'Seventeen and four months, sir.'

Harding walked over to his desk and checked on some notes, 'And you volunteered for the army fourteen months ago?'

'Yes, sir.'

'Well, you wouldn't be the first.'

'No, sir.'

'But to invent a fictitious name so transparent that it drew the notice of every man and his dog – that's insulting. Do you really think that your betters are as stupid as all that?'

That's what this is about? 'Sorry, sir, that wasn't my intention.'

'Oh, you'll be getting intention. Take that one to the bank.'

Footsteps approached. They belonged to the C.O., who glanced quizzically at Harding, 'Well?'

'This is Richard Green, seventeen years.'

The C.O. sized him up, 'You should still be in school.'

There was no right answer and Limerick knew it.

'Drop your pants, Green.' Limerick saw Harding's reaction and knew that this had not been discussed between the two officers. He fumbled with buttons and fastenings, then stood in his underwear with his trousers around his knees. He was too frightened to question the order, let alone refuse it.

'Small clothes as well.' More fumbling resulted in exposed whiteness that had never seen sunlight.

There was silence within the room for fully thirty seconds.

The C.O. owned the script, 'You are a schoolboy, Green.' He circled Limerick to stand behind him, making a pretence of inspecting those soft cheeks, 'Have you ever been birched? I can't see any scars.'

'Yes, sir.'

'I'm required to hand you over to the authorities. Do you think it fair to first get six strokes across your buttocks for putting me in this situation?'

Harding looked like he was about to say something but a stern look stopped him.

'Yes, sir.'

'Boy, I will swing my arm harder than any of your house masters, I swear it.'

'Yes, sir.'

Time dragged. No word was spoken, no action taken.

Eventually, 'Pull your pants back up, Green.' There was nothing more beautiful about the army than blind obedience, 'If we were in an infantry unit I'd be a lot less impressed. The truth of the matter is that although I lose men almost every week, you fellows in the ground crews have it about as safe as a man can get in this army. For argument's sake, let's say you were kicked out and then re-enlisted when you came of age, then went out and got yourself killed. Do you think your parents would thank me for it?'

'No, sir.'

'How do you know Sloane?'

The question seemed unrelated to that which had gone before, but Limerick knew the connection and answered promptly, 'We attended the same school.'

'He's seven years older than you. It doesn't count.'

'We live three doors apart on the same street.'

'You joined up together and he looks after you. A fair assessment?'

'Yes, sir.'

'What's in it for him?'

'He likes my sister, sir.'

'That's not going to go too well for him if you get killed, is it?'

'No, sir.'

'Just out of curiosity, does your sister like him?'

Limerick looked confused all over again, 'Er, I don't rightly know. Sir.'

The C.O. laughed in genuine amusement, 'Good Lord! You young ones certainly weave tangled webs.' And that came out of the mouth of someone who had only recently turned twenty-six, though in nineteen-seventeen in France, everything was relative.

'You are an armourer, I understand.'

'Yes, sir.'

'Are you a good one?'

'Yes, sir.'

The major nodded at this, 'Then more fool me if I get rid of you.'

Limerick didn't think it would be wise to agree that the C.O. was a fool no matter who asked the question. He said nothing.

'Out.'

The boy made to leave, but was stopped short with a gesture, 'One last thing. If I hear you have made up some snide little verse to commemorate this day, I'll take it out of your hide. Are we clear on that?'

'Yes, sir. Thank you, sir.' Limerick escaped before anyone could change their minds.

The adjutant observed, 'Buttocks.'

'Eh?'

'I've never heard you use the word. It's always been 'arse."

'I doubt that any of his masters at school would have used the lay term. Thought it would have a better effect if I made him feel like a boy. Which he is.'

Harding asked what was still on his mind, 'Do you want me to have him arrested?'

'Forget it, David. The whole thing will cause us too many problems.'

'So, do nothing?'

'That's the general idea, yes.'

'You could end up in hot water over this if anyone finds out about it.'

'They pinned a DSO on me. That was for a lot worse than hot water.'

Harding nodded his acceptance of the decision.

The C.O. had one last line of questioning, 'Which flight is he assigned to?'

'"B" Flight.'

'Lewis-Hamilton's?'

'That's correct.'

'Didn't he have a weapon malfunction on his last stunt?'

'Yes. Or rather, his observer did.'

'Did you hear Green say he was a good armourer?'

'Yes.'

There was short pause, 'Well, it happens.'

Chapter 20

February 1918: Casualties

Once inside away from the cold, Weber removed his flying helmet and ran a hand through his sweaty hair, 'Phew.'

Reinhold pulled up a chair, 'That's a lot of adrenaline for no result.' He tried to rub some feeling into his face.

'I thought I had the bastard.' They had just returned from what had promised to be an uneventful patrol in the frigid conditions. Unfortunately, someone on the British side had conceived the same idea, no doubt reasoning that the Germans would be unlikely to go up in poor weather. If the decision had been left up to Reinhold, that would indeed have been the case. Instead, the small formation had encountered a reconnaissance patrol flying at three thousand metres in the vicinity of Polygon Wood. The gunners in the Bristol two-seaters had put up a stout defence, then their pilots had pointed the noses of the machines to the west and dived for the safety of their lines.

The combat had been frustrating for the German airmen. That the F.2s were fast enough to outrun the Albatros formation was bad enough; that the Englishmen should exercise the right to do so simply rubbed salt into the wound.

'If we'd seen them sooner we may have been able to cut off their line of retreat.'

'Never mind, Weber, some days go in your favour, others do not. At least we got in a few shots before they sorted themselves out.'

'I think I hit one.'

Reinhold was dubious, but didn't want to appear too unsympathetic, 'You've already got an Iron Cross – you should know by now you have to do more than say you hit them.'

Weber grinned, 'If I'd burned him they'd have been warmer than I was. It hardly seemed fair.'

To top it all off, one of their aircraft had landed heavily when they had returned home. Kruchelsdorf had misjudged his airspeed and had not been able to correct the error in time. He had nosed over onto the frozen ground. The shattered propeller was at that moment being replaced by a cursing ground crew.

Because one of his machines had been damaged, von Bülow was looking for someone to crucify.

$*$ $*$ $*$

From his window, the C.O. had seen the ambulance rush to intercept the returned patrol. The vehicle had since departed, and the squadron adjutant had arrived with the latest news. The senior man spoke first, 'Who got it this time?'

Harding took off his hat as he made himself comfortable, 'No-one.'

'Well, that's all right, then. Get these planes repaired.'

'Bert Noone.'

'What of him?'

'No-one.'

'Yes, I know who you mean. What about him?'

'He's dead.'

'You just said… Oh.'

'Sorry, sir. Should have been more clear.'

'Noone. He was an observer, if I'm not mistaken?'

'Yes.'

'Who did he fly with?'

'Burrows.'

'Burrows. Isn't he the one who…?'

'None other.'

'And Burrows' first observer? What was his name? I don't recall.'

'Smith.'

'Smith. Yes. No wonder I didn't remember him. How's Burrows doing?'

'What you'd expect, I'm afraid. Though he's been on the edge for a while now and nothing has come of it.'

'If you count No-one as nothing.'

'Quite.'

'It wasn't a joke, Harding.'

'No, sir, of course not.' Harding decided to cover his indiscretion by raising another matter, 'I heard Bowe is running a book on him; Burrows, that is. He's the favourite to get the chop next.'

'William Bowe?'

'The very same.'

'What in the name of the Lord has the clown got himself into this time? Betting on which of these fellows is the next to be killed – for pity's sake! Who else knows about it?'

'Most of the fellows are putting money on themselves to make it. A handful have even gone the other way – a benefit of sorts - to help their families if the worst happens.'

'Jesus.'

'Some of them are doing all right out of it as a result.'

The C.O. didn't ask which ones, 'What about Burrows?'

'Frankly, I doubt that he cares too much one way or the other.'

'I'll ground the poor boy.' Burrows had to be one of the loneliest people on the Western Front right now, and that was saying something.

The adjutant had a suggestion, but was at a loss as to how best to proceed, 'I don't mean to sound callous...'

'I'll put up five quid to say you'll fail.'

Harding pretended that he didn't hear, 'Sending Burrows on leave just because of some personal difficulties seems premature. Two dead observers is a pittance compared to what the rest of the army is suffering; at least in the context of what the infantry endure every day.'

'You see? I'd have lightened your purse if you had accepted the wager.'

'Or...you could put Bowe in with him instead of the next luckless replacement.'

The C.O. chuckled evilly, 'That would certainly simplify things, David.'

'Except he isn't qualified for the job - Bowe, that is.'

The major twirled his moustache, 'No, that's true; although sometimes people are given jobs that they aren't qualified for and nobody knows any different.'

'You're not seriously considering it?'

'I'll have a think about it while you go and find the slimy bastard.'

Harding departed.

Harding returned, this time with Bowe in tow. The C.O. was straight to the point, 'Bowe, if you persist with taking bets on my men, then by thunder you'll be facing a firing squad.'

The entrepreneurial soldier knew that he was flogging a dead horse, but made the only argument that he felt had any sort of chance, 'I understand your reluctance, Major, but the men have invested rather heavily in the pool.'

'It wasn't a discussion.'

'I can't pay them back!'

'You should have thought of that beforehand.'

Bowe looked set to continue the argument.

The C.O. glared at him, 'I am not remotely interested in your occupation before you put on a uniform. This ends now. I'm not even going to try appealing to your sense of decency because it stands out like dogs' balls that such a thing is no more than idle fancy. And don't try to implicate anyone else if you come back here beaten black and blue. By the Christ, if I see or hear so much as a false rumour about you again, I'll shoot you myself.' He leaned forward, 'See here. You're a smart man, Bill, you know I have the authority to do it.' He leaned forward further, 'And even if I didn't, there's precious little you could do about it after the fact. Consequences be damned, but I'd make you a wager at any odds you please that a squadron commander during time of war is believed over an immoral raconteur such as yourself any day of the week.'

Bowe was mild with his response, 'I'd agree with you, though I take umbrage at your accusation of low morality.'

'Don't test me any further. You'll find that military law is not as elastic as its civilian counterpart.' That a senior ranking officer had to have such a conversation with an enlisted man may have given lie to the claim, but both of them knew it was a fact.

The amateur bookie made his escape, trying to figure how he was going to fix the mess that had been dumped on his lap.

Harding was thinking along similar lines, 'He's more trouble than he's worth, that one. He can scrounge practically any item that a man can afford to pay for, but at the end of the day he's only in it for himself.'

'Draw up his transfer papers and get him out of my squadron. Let him become someone else's problem.'

'That's hardly a solution, sir.'

The C.O. growled, 'I never said it was a solution. I said it could be someone else's problem.'

'What about Burrows?'

'Put him on a train to Paris.'

*   *   *

Lewis-Hamilton knew that Burke was struggling with the loss of his friend, and he was ill-equipped to deal with the problem. The last few days had been hard on the Australian, and it was just as well that they had been kept grounded because of poor weather conditions.

Wiggan noticed the patrol leader's quandary and wondered how much would filter across to their next mission together. Feeling a twinge of apprehension for his own uncertain future, he decided to say something, for to do less was putting too much faith in divine intervention. If he gained nothing else from this war, Wiggan had learned that it was more prudent to take every reasonable precaution, and then trust in God.

'Hello, Wiggan.' Lewis-Hamilton gave a minimal nod in the general direction of Burke, not wanting to be too obvious about it, 'A bad business.'

If it was pity he sought, he had spoken to the wrong man. Wiggan had no sympathy for anyone: not Burke; not Noone; not Burrows;

not Lewis-Hamilton, 'He should have kept his distance. The new ones hardly ever last.'

'He wasn't exactly new'

'You know what I mean, but it's impolite to disparage a man.'

'Remember Dunhill?'

Wiggan hadn't thought of the man for a while, 'What of him?'

'I haven't thought of him for a while, that's all.'

They both paused for reflection, and Lewis-Hamilton's mind went back to the previous year, 'Remember when he nearly hit the bloody goat that day our game got strafed?'

Wiggan's brow crinkled, 'Vaguely. I thought that was Ryker?'

And from the depths of a misremembered past, their thoughts returned to the present. Lewis-Hamilton was unable to shake his unease regarding Burke, 'It must be hard, though, given that they knew one another before the war.'

'It'll be a sight harder on you, skipper. The dumb Aussie will be thinking of other things for a while – not ideal when he's supposed to be your other set of eyes.'

Lewis-Hamilton drew a bead on Wiggan, 'I appreciate your concern.'

'You should. If Burke isn't keeping his eyes peeled and you get yourself killed, it will stack the odds more heavily against those of us who are flying alongside you.'

'When the war is over, you should become a mercenary. You seem to have an instinct for it.'

Wiggan shrugged. He knew that he had discomfited the patrol leader, but the man should have known better than to allow his own observer to become too friendly with a replacement. *Circumstances be blowed. Friends are for before and after the war. Right now they're nothing but a liability*. Wiggan had enough awareness to keep the opinion to himself, knowing that his view was in the minority.

Certainly it was unfair that Burrows was shunned, but most people believed in luck, and Burrows was unlucky, plain and simple. Fair or not, it was prudent to keep one's distance. Wiggan mused that it was probably the primary reason that prey animals had fewer friends than predators.

*　　*　　*

Reinhold accompanied Weber and Bonninghauser on their trip into town. The car pulled over next to the curb. Weber announced, 'This is the place you are looking for.'

Reinhold climbed out, 'Wait here.'

Bonninghauser's tone was mild, but there was an impish gleam in his eye, 'Take your time.'

'Very funny.' Reinhold strode purposely to the front door and knocked.

Charlotte Gerard answered the door, 'Hello?' She looked less than impressed to see an unknown German on her doorstep, though she would have been even more put out had a particular known German presented himself.

'May I come in?' She stepped to one side. As he brushed past her Reinhold tried not to show disapproval at her cloying scent.

'How may I help you, sir?'

'Excuse me, madam. My name is Ernst Reinhold. I wish to speak with one of your girls.'

Charlotte was cautious, 'Is there something wrong?'

'I am here with news of *Oberleutnant* von Bülow. Please fetch the lady in question. I believe her name to be Yvonne.' The madam realised that there was no point trying to pretend that no-one by that name worked there.

'Is he dead?' She was careful not to put any inflection into the query. Reinhold's face may as well have been carved from stone. 'I will find her at once, *Leutnant* Reinhold.'

As he waited he took in the surroundings. Everything was neat and functional, without being extravagant. Anything of value had long since been sold to buy essentials. The curtains were drawn. The sofa was unappealing. There was no artificial lighting.

Shortly the older woman returned with Yvonne. *So this is Sebastian's tawdry whore.* He felt her professional eye upon his person and it discomfited him. *A woman's appraisal shouldn't be so frank.* 'You are Yvonne?'

'Perhaps you remember me better as Simonne?'

Reinhold was unperturbed by the jibe, and answered as if he was unaware of it, 'I have never set foot inside this house, nor any other like it. Please excuse my ignorance in the matter of aliases and alibis.'

'You wish to speak to me, sir?'

'Sebastian is in hospital. He has been wounded in action.'

Yvonne paled. 'Oh.' It was not the gut reaction she had been anticipating in the event of such news. 'Is it bad?' She tried to deceive herself that the question was simply one of good manners.

'Bad enough, but he'll live.'

Her equilibrium made an adjustment, 'His cock can't have been shot off, then.'

Reinhold was taken aback by the comment. He admonished her for it, 'I would have thought you to be less callous, in the circumstances.'

Yvonne's eyes narrowed as she jutted her chin out, 'What circumstances would those be?'

Reinhold was now on uncertain ground, 'I was given to believe you were fond of one another.'

'No.' Had the word been made of inflatable rubber, a dozen knives couldn't have made her tone any flatter.

Reinhold mulled over the turn of events. Yvonne interrupted his thoughts, 'Are you married, *Leutnant?*'

Though he had come to discuss the affairs of others, his own personal life was off limits - especially to a common prostitute, 'That is none of your business.'

'It is just that you are not wearing a ring, as your friend does not.'

Reinhold stood a little straighter, 'That should tell its own story.'

'I believe he takes it off because his wife is elsewhere.'

Brows furrowed, 'Sebastian isn't married.'

'Fiancé, sweetheart: it doesn't make any difference. He certainly has another girl tucked away.'

'No, miss. There isn't anyone else. Only you.'

Yvonne digested the information, 'Well, we live and learn.'

Reinhold touched the brim of his cap, 'I have come here on a misguided impulse, I see.'

Charlotte smiled at him, her humour not unkindly, 'You have not been the first to do so, nor, I expect, the last.'

There was the smallest twinkle in his eye at her byplay, 'Good day, ladies.'

He walked back outside, and saw Weber throw his hands in the air in a parody of disgust. 'Why the pantomime?'

Weber appeared surly, 'You have just lost me a bet. You weren't inside long enough to engage in any horizontal dogfighting.'

'More fool you, in that case. I told you I wasn't here for that.'

'And I told you that von Bülow's misfortune wasn't relevant to the slut.'

216

'How do you know if it was or wasn't?'

'It's written all over your face.'

Reinhold nodded. He probably did look foolish in the eyes of the world, and chanced a glance up at the curtained window to see if anyone was mocking him from within the shadows. He was unsure whether he detected a subtle movement or not.

Bonninghauser had the triumphant look of victory about him, 'Ten marks, Konrad – pay up. I told you that Ernst had still not learned that it can be used for purposes other than pissing.'

Reinhold was not to be diverted by the banter, 'Which of you two was it that discovered this whore was with von Bülow?'

Bonninghauser chuckled, 'Only by accident, Ernst. I saw them linking arms an hour after I boned her. It didn't take a lot to discover her real name wasn't Simonne.'

Reinhold sighed inwardly at the crass expression. His attention turned to Weber, 'What's your story? You can spare me the details.'

Weber shrugged, 'I just paid him back in kind after I found out. How many times has he swung his dick in our faces?'

'None.'

'You know what I mean.'

'Has it ever occurred to either of you that it's better to just stay out of his way?'

Weber was un-amused, 'You were there when he was shot down, Ernst. Did you see anyone else trying to head off the bastard that was after him, or did you want me to stay out of the way then as well?'

'That's your job, Weber. Don't pretend that you were doing him a favour.'

Weber didn't have a response to the obvious statement of fact. Bonninghauser was not so slow off the mark, 'It was just self-interest on Konrad's part. He wanted to kill the fellow that clobbered von

Bülow. It would have allowed him to claim to be the better man. As it happens, he was too slow and the Englishman got away. Now we'll never know.'

'Stop talking shit.'

Bonninghauser gave Reinhold a friendly slap on the back and draped an arm over his shoulder, 'There's no need to be so serious all of the time, Ernst. Of course, you can still go back inside if you are feeling frustrated with the world.'

Reinhold was thoughtful, 'It is a strange thing. She claims there was nothing between them, but as I turned to leave there were tears in her eyes.'

'Ach, you should know that women like to put on a show, even if they don't mean it. For mine, I'm happy enough just to grab a handful of that wonderful arse.'

I am glad that Frieda is cut from a different cloth – now that is one woman worth going home to. It is the thought that he will one day be with her again from which Reinhold drew his strength. Day after day he put his life on the line, steadfastly flying his frail machine through a storm of gunfire. Oddly, it was less frightening to him because he had a perfect world to go back to when it was finally over. It all seemed so counter-intuitive, because there was more for him to lose personally if everything turned sour, yet each time those flimsy wheels touched the ground after a patrol, Reinhold felt closer to God and one step closer to home.

'Where to next?'

'I think we had best get back to the war.'

Yvonne was sitting on the sofa with her face buried in her hands and the flow of tears would not stop. The dread had ebbed away, but she still felt like she was standing on shifting sands, 'What is the matter with me, Charlotte? This is what I have been praying to hear for more than a year.'

Charlotte sat beside her, comforting with an enfolding embrace. There were no words right now, because von Bülow was not dead. He may yet come back with a vengeance. Anything said out of place could draw any reaction from the poor girl; hence hugging, but no talking.

Please don't turn on me for encouraging you to destroy him.

Lucie emerged from the kitchen with a hot cup of coffee for her distraught friend. The beverage was a limited resource, so only the one cup had been prepared; there was not enough for them all. Yvonne gratefully accepted the brew, but started sobbing again when she realised that it must be from the ration supplied by von Bülow. Charlotte and Lucie had no idea what had caused this new outburst, and they were not inclined to ask.

'I should be rejoicing at this release from his filthy touch.'

Don't be too premature with that particular celebration, child.

Yvonne continued to cry, and eventually her sobs turned to sniffles. She sat quietly. In a small voice she finally professed, 'I don't know what to do.'

'Life is complicated, Yvonne.'

Chapter 21

March 1918: Time Out

Burrows took a room in the Hotel Elysée Palace. There were other military personnel staying there as well; it seemed that they were the main clientele these days. Most of the guests wore the faded pale blue uniform that identified them as Frenchmen. *Horizon blue, they call it. Such a pretty name, and so much more evocative than plain old khaki, but no better protection for all that.*

Sitting alone at breakfast, it was not long before he attracted the attention of a small group of British officers eating together at a nearby table. Seeing that he was on his own, they invited him to join them. Burrows passively accepted the offer.

'Des Maxwell.' Amid finger pointing and nodding of heads, further introductions were made, 'This is Davison. Gordon. Barnett.'

'I'm sorry? Gordon Bennett?'

'Barnett. I'm Gordon. He's Barnett.'

'Adam Burrows.' There followed handshakes all around. By the time the brief formality was over, Burrows couldn't remember any of their names.

'The concierge says that this is the place where they arrested Mata Hari a few months back.'

Burrows' look was blank.

'You know, the dancer? They shot her.'

'For spying, not dancing.'

'And a trollop to boot.'

'Which was irrelevant to her shooting.'

'I don't think a courtesan is the same as a trollop.'

Burrows sat in silence, knowing he had made another mistake. He had nothing to contribute to the conversation, 'Excuse me.' Leaving his food untouched, he rose abruptly and left the table, not bothering with sliding his chair back in. Adjusting his service cap, he walked out of the building.

'Poor chap, I've seen that look before.'

'Probably why he's on leave.'

'Should we go after him?'

'Best not. If he wanted the company, he'd have kept his arse parked.'

There were sights to see in the French capital. Maud had always wanted to come here. She had been fascinated by the Eiffel Tower, the theatres and cafes, the exotic names of the streets, and had always felt the allure of cultured destinations. Burrows had privately thought it had been a pipe dream. Commoners didn't travel the world.

But here he was doing just that - travelling the world. It meant absolutely nothing to him.

He wandered aimlessly, and the only reason he didn't go back to the hotel was that he didn't want to run into the men he had rudely walked out on. Eventually, even that was insufficient, and he shambled back the way he had come.

The sun had risen less than three hours ago and already his day was done - a complete waste of time. It summed up his life. Time yawned before him, and he had no way to fill the void. To be killed in action was not something that bothered him anymore, because the alternative would mean lingering in this No-man's-land of the mind for far too long.

Burrows took a bottle to his room for company. He sat looking out of the window for the rest of the day, but if asked what he had seen through the pane he would have drawn a blank. He didn't go down for a meal in the evening. Instead, he lay awake into the night, waiting for the dawn.

Eventually he slept. Though he craved blackness, he dreamed once again of death and suffering. This time he fancied that his skull had been bashed open, the fragments needing to be put back together. Even though Burrows slept, he somehow identified that he was in that state. Without waking, he wondered at the peculiarity of the fact. Usually such cognition would have woken him, but he stayed immersed in the artificial moment.

Come morning, the first image in Burrows' head was of broken bodies and blood. Smith and Noone had morphed into a single entity which he was unable to separate. The way that they had died reminded him of his dream. The metaphor for his sanity was easy to identify.

Every day the pattern was the same. The first images to appear in his thoughts were the faces of the fallen. They stood behind him and breathed directly into his ear and down his neck, refusing to blame him for what had happened. Invariably this was accompanied by an intense yearning to overthrow reality and to achieve an alternative outcome. If only the chance could somehow be seized upon to do just one thing differently on those terrible days - days that were relived in a perpetual loop within Burrows' brain. *Or maybe just the first of those two days? Surely its prevention would have voided the possibility of the second?*

By the time he had taken stock and noticed that he was alive, the fact had become irrelevant. Where once his life was a constant cause for celebration, continued existence had now become no more than a distorted curiosity.

Since Smith had died, Burrows lived in torment. He had yet to waken with a smile on his face, whereas once upon a time happiness had been his default setting. He didn't bother wondering at the change, accepting that even if he ever forgave himself – and that would be a long time coming, if ever – force of habit would have destroyed everything his face would remember by way of assembling a joyful expression.

When he washed his face in the bathroom basin, the habit of inspecting himself in the mirror remained, though he tried not to make eye contact with his reflection. Those eyes - how they stared back at him! Burrows thought that they looked different to the way that they had used to. Now they were knowing, haunted and lacking sparkle. He attributed this change to his belief that he was now a murderer and a coward. *I have failed as a human being in ways that are unfathomable to a cow or a pig.*

Burrows newfound perspective was that humanity was flawed. The proof of it was in the way that children looked at men in uniform with a kind of quasi-religious awe, and were inspired to want to be like them. It seemed to be wired into the younger generation that warriors were a superior caste, and the viewpoint was possibly consistent throughout the millennia, regardless of culture or creed. This preoccupation with martial deeds would almost certainly hinder their personal development to the point that they would never fully grasp the truly meaningful values in life until it was too late. Again, the conclusion was based on firsthand experience.

The inevitability of the process drove Burrows to the point of despair. It was no new feeling. By now he was used to living with demons. Though it would never be comfortable, he drew upon the familiarity of his oppressive burden to see each day through to another empty conclusion.

Some days Burrows became bogged down and wallowed in the mire of his mind until long after the sun had set. Other times he was not as debilitated, though he constantly mourned the men he had killed, and felt guilty if he caught himself feeling sorry for his own situation. It would have been wrong to say that he accepted his lot, because acceptance is a poor choice of word and did not adequately describe the lengths that he would have gone to in order to have the chance to have done things differently. Saving Noone would not have been enough, because by the time Burrows had met the Australian he had already proven himself to be a useless failure. What he really wanted was for Smith to have lived.

When friends die, the routines that are associated with them are destroyed. Old routines are inevitably replaced with new routines. Every morning, once he had mercilessly thrashed himself all over again, and torn off any scabs that threatened to heal his mind, Burrows' first order of business was to assemble the tatters of his soul. This enabled him to present the world with a face that showed the façade of a functioning human being. The act didn't fool everyone - not by a long chalk. Others who had been where he was — they knew, and no words needed to be spoken.

Those who had not been to the same place tried to understand, but it was the understanding that a virgin has pertaining to the act of sex. The only way to know for certain is to experience the reality. Nothing else will suffice, but once you have taken the step there is no going back.

Burrows knew that there was a brotherhood of souls who shared the same bonds with him. But brotherhoods were over-rated, being mostly consisted of men with too little in common other than foul deeds and physical proximity. In hindsight, he would have willingly traded the experience for his old self. Eligibility into this particular peer group wasn't worth the acquired knowledge. At some point, the government would commission the design of a commemorative ribbon to distinguish Burrows and his uniformed fellows from the run of the mill. *What is a coloured ribbon worth? Maud could have obtained one from the local haberdashery for tuppence.*

Each new day the same thoughts took their turn tumbling around in his mind. The only difference was the order in which they appeared.

How long until this wretched holiday is over? Not long enough. Too long.

*   *   *

Reinhold had become the *de facto* leader of the unit, at least until they learned more about the wounds suffered by von Bülow. There were those who hoped that the commander's injuries would keep him away for long enough that a permanent replacement could be named. It was unspoken, but Reinhold was the one most favoured for the position, though nothing was certain. In these situations it was an accepted practice to bring in an outsider. That way there was less likelihood of familiarity undermining the new man's authority.

'I'm going to the hospital. Does anyone want to come with me?'

Weber volunteered. Reinhold was surprised that there were any takers at all. They commandeered the staff car and drove away.

Kruchelsdorf was unable to comprehend it, 'Weber is going to see von Bülow? Am I missing something?'

Bonnighauser had a few insights into his best friend's motives, 'Probably he wants to finish him off. Either that or he just wants to see the bastard suffer.'

'For mine, it's enough to know that he is. Suffering, I mean. Breathing the same air is too high a price, if you ask me.'

'I've never understood why Reinhold stands by him?'

'My guess is that he understands that war is hell – he's just doing his bit to appreciate the fact a bit more by standing closer to the stench.'

The rot of gangrene and the overpowering smell of antiseptic assaulted their senses. Though the atmosphere lacked the chaotic urgency of an aid station, the hospital environment was oppressive in its own way. It was an odd sensation to experience, because it was a lot better place to be than over the Western Front, unless you happened to be one of the many men who would never recover from their wounds. Loss of sight, limb or sanity: few men would prefer those fates to facing death in battle, even if it meant a fiery death.

They made enquiries and were directed to the relevant wing. The area was massive, and beds were crammed into it with no space to spare, each one occupied by a picture of misery. The visiting duo located von Bülow, who was propped up and swathed in bandages. His arm was splinted but he smiled as he recognised them, 'There are men worse off than I am in here. Did you smell the burns ward on the way in?'

Weber nodded, 'We smelt it.'

'Sometimes it wafts across to us. Maybe the doctors do it deliberately to keep us from complaining too much.'

Weber didn't voice his opinion that it would take more than an occasional bad odour to suppress von Bülow's natural urges.

But the commander did look the worse for wear. Reinhold enquired, 'How do you feel?'

The injured man's eyes seemed out of focus, 'My head feels wrong. Every other part of my body hurts, but my head doesn't feel right.'

'You've got a concussion.'

'I've had that before. But this is worse. The whole front of my face feels like it is in the wrong place. Behind my face, the front plate of my skull, I mean...' He trailed away, not making sense even to himself. Disorientation, headache, inability to concentrate without head pain - these were the things that he knew to expect. His eyes felt as though he had been looking directly into the sun for too long. It was an activity that airmen were all familiar with, the better to spot a stooping hunter, 'It's too bright.' But the oddness of the sensation in his face was more disturbing to him than the rest of it. He wondered if he would be permanently impaired, but left the thought unsaid. What would happen, would happen. It could not be undone. He reasoned that if he was cognizant of the possibility of brain damage, he probably didn't have any.

Reinhold tried to divert attention to other things, 'I have some good news for you. Your kill was witnessed.'

Von Bülow tried to track the path of the conversation. Eventually he blinked, 'My twelfth. How did the rest of you manage?' Sometimes the best way to cope was to get straight to business.

Reinhold shrugged, 'Wintger was killed. Only myself and Koenig got out in one piece. Everyone else was shot to bits.' It wasn't entirely true, but it was a salve to the wounded man's battered self-image. There was nothing that they could offer to ease his battered body, though.

'Not a lot that you can do when you lose oil pressure. Just ride the beast until it throws you.' And it had thrown him. Von Bülow's safety harness had been neatly snipped by a bullet. Half of him had been safely strapped in and the other half had been thrown violently clear of the wreckage - at least, that was what it had felt like. His body seemed like one giant bruise, except for his arm, which he wished felt like a bruise. It had been shattered. And of course, there was his head, 'There's not much time for fear, but you have plenty of time to wonder how bad it will be.'

Weber smiled with the unique brand of mirth reserved for unfortunate situations, 'I heard it was bad enough for you to shit in your pants.'

Von Bülow laughed weakly, 'Not for the first time, either. What about you?'

Weber could have told his own stories about fouled underwear, or he could have told of the Camel pilot he had killed. He did neither, 'I tried to get the SE5 that shot you down, but he pulled away. Too quick.'

'What SE5? I had a Bristol on my tail.' The two types were distinctly different in appearance. It would have been hard to mistake them.

Weber didn't know how to give von Bülow enough breathing space, 'I saw it clearly. It was an SE5.'

'Ernst?'

'I never saw any of it. I had so many Camels crawling all over me I thought I was in Mesopotamia.'

'I know one of those square cut bastards when I see one, Weber. It wasn't an SE5.'

Weber said nothing, but it was the way in which he didn't say it that conveyed his opinion that von Bülow was an idiot. Nobody called von Bülow an idiot - either out loud or telepathically – not if they knew what was good for them. Despite being injured and sedated, he still had fight in him, 'Who do you believe in these circumstances: the person directly involved, or the bystander?'

Weber considered himself to be a learned man, and knew he should have been tactful when dealing with an invalid, but he had lost his patience, 'Usually in these situations it is only the bystander who survives; so yes, the bystander is more reliable.' Other than that he was largely immobile, von Bülow may have taken a swing at the other officer.

Deciding that their fallen leader was not actually benefiting from the visit, Reinhold left him a bottle of champagne which he had smuggled into the ward, hiding it under the man's pillow. He doubted that it would avoid detection by the nursing staff for very long, but that was von Bülow's problem. The commander knew it, too, 'I'd better pass it around before it gets confiscated. Some of these fellows have it a lot worse than I do.'

Reinhold looked around. There was a lot of suffering to see in such a small area.

Von Bülow pointed, 'Him over there - ' Reinhold couldn't determine exactly who was indicated, '…last night the poor bastard must have been dreaming about his nurse. He woke us all up in the middle of the night calling for help – thought he was bleeding to death. It turns out all that needed to be cleaned up came out of his cock.'

The visitors laughed at the mortification that it must have caused the soldier, 'Well, better that than to be proved right!'

They stayed a while longer, then bid the injured man good day. The two visitors wove their way out between the rows of beds and exited the cramped room.

They were waylaid by the matron before they made it out of the front door, 'One moment, please, gentlemen.'

Reinhold checked his stride, 'Yes, madam? How may I be of assistance?'

'My staff has reported to me that you have brought contraband into the hospital.'

He creased his eyebrows in what was genuine confusion. By the time he had registered the accusation for what it was, Reinhold's body language had acquitted him in the stern eyes of the senior nurse. She looked at Weber and his manner told a different tale. She reassessed her conclusion, 'What is the name of the patient you came to visit?'

Reinhold answered, 'Josef Hockheimer, 41st Cavalry Brigade.'

The doubt was evident, 'And yet you wear the pilot's badge.'

'The forty-first was my old unit.'

She looked at Weber, 'And you?'

He nodded amicably at the other pilot, 'I'm with him.'

The matron didn't believe a word of it. She nodded to them, 'Well, have a nice day. Stay safe, *Leutnant* Hockheimer.'

'It's Reinhold, madam. Hockheimer is the friend I was visiting.' He hid his amusement at the clumsy attempt to trip him up. They exchanged insincere pleasantries and went their respective ways. Reinhold hoped that von Bülow had already started drinking, because otherwise he'd never get the chance.

'Who's Hockheimer?'

'I knew him once.' The answer was terse and offered no elaboration.

Weber left it alone and reflected on his argument with von Bülow. Unamused by the confrontational aristocrat, and without giving notice that he was changing the topic, he expressed his dissatisfaction, 'He has a face badly in need of a fist.' The German word for the concept was *Backpfeifengesicht*.

Reinhold was pensive on their return journey, 'How would you have done it differently?'

Weber pretended to consider the question, 'I'd have amputated his legs and sewn his lips together, and accidentally poked him in the eye. Maybe it isn't too late to go back...'

'That was a fight that we should have avoided. Everything was against us. There must have been forty of the bastards.' He was referring to the dogfight that had injured von Bülow and not their visit to the hospital. Sometimes it was hard to tell from the context.

'In fairness, we didn't see the others until after we had gone for the Camels.'

'That's no excuse.'

Weber shrugged, 'Not for the first time. It just went wrong for us. It happens. What do you want - safe passage? You're in the wrong game, my friend.'

'Lehmann used to steer clear if things looked unfavourable. He didn't lose men because of his pride. Von Bülow used to criticise him for it; even called him a coward to his face. I suspect it's one of the reasons that he refused to back out even though it looked bad.'

'That was before my time. Sounds like a sensible man. What happened to him?'

'Lehmann? He has his own unit now.'

'I should transfer. Does he have any vacancies?'

'I heard that he makes the new men fly the Pfalz until they have proven themselves.' It was hardly a unique circumstance. Most *Jastas* that were still partially equipped with the type resorted to the same measures, 'Still interested?'

'Would it make any difference if he knew that I had six Englishmen?' Actually it was four: Weber's first two victims had been French, but he didn't feel compelled to split hairs.

Reinhold smiled at him, 'Don't worry, Konrad. You saw how badly Seb was banged up. You'll be safely dead before you have to listen to him again.'

'If they make you the new commander, you'll need to distance yourself from the others. You'll be perceived differently, and you'll also be treating others differently.'

'Have you been reading books again?' But Reinhold knew it was the truth. Even though it was less obvious in some men than others, the job moulded the leader: possessing executive rank precluded equality. When a man has the power to order another to his death, that fact will always be in everyone else's consciousness.

Mellerhorst was the first to meet them upon their return. 'News just in – we have a new commanding officer. Congratulations, Ernst. It's overdue.'

Weber offered his commiserations, 'You poor bastard.' He gave Reinhold a mock salute, then shook his hand and wandered away to find Bonnighauser.

Mellerhorst had some advice, 'You can't be one of the boys anymore.'

Reinhold wondered if the adjutant had earlier shared his thoughts with Weber. 'I've always been a little apart from this lot as it is. Too many of them are new, and Kruchelsdorf is just a piss-pot.'

'Do you want him out?'

'My God! Will you give me a chance to absorb the news?'

'You must have at least considered the prospect before now? You've had a few days.'

'If the English can't kill him, why should I want to get rid of him?'

Though Reinhold was referring to Kruchelsdorf, Mellerhorst was moving on already, 'In a way you're lucky that you are succeeding von Bülow. The others may not have liked him, but it could work in your favour. You'll need to impose yourself eventually. In the meantime the habit of discipline will hold, plus they'll appreciate you more, simply because you are not him. They'll follow you willingly enough. Relax, Ernst.'

'Poor Seb. You could see the strain was wearing him down. He wanted that last kill too much, and overcommitted. He was always driven to prove himself.'

'He told me that he was experiencing odd sensations. A greying of the mind was how he described it.'

Reinhold was surprised, 'He admitted to a weakness? I don't believe it.'

'Can you have known him so poorly? To him it was another thing to keep smashing into until it disappeared. Weakness? No. An obstacle.'

'Yes, that fits better.'

'He had a few other ideas that nobody knew about. An interesting man if you file off some of the edges.'

Reinhold was becoming intrigued despite himself. He had known that Mellerhorst worked at von Bülow's bidding, but some things were just clutter when the reality was mortal combat. 'Anything I need to know?'

'Need? No.' Mellerhorst considered a few possibilities, 'He had me look at some of the armourers reports and log books - that sort of thing. He wanted me to see who was performing by analysing actual returns. Rounds of ammunition per claim for selected pilots etcetera. He wanted to introduce a roster based on what people were actually doing rather than what everyone thought was the case.'

'That doesn't sound like Seb at all. By his own admission he wasn't academically inclined.'

Mellerhorst waved it away, 'He was happy enough to delegate the task. It's not as if he was ever going to do it himself.'

'Did you do it?'

'I did. Not in any great detail, but I used some of the reports that had been filed. I even had Rossler's details, though he's not here anymore.'

'What did you find?'

'His motive. That became clear even before I showed him my work. One of the things he wanted to prove was that the enlisted men were underperforming.'

Reinhold appreciated the dedication to a cause, if not the cause itself, 'You fiddled the figures, didn't you?'

'I have a war to run, not this stuff. It took half a day as it was.'

'It's nice to know that my adjutant can't be trusted to do his homework.'

'Oh, I did it, Ernst. It's just that I saw which way it was headed so I gave it short shrift. According to my findings, von Bülow had a higher rating than Weber and Bonninghauser, but you beat him and so did Rossler and Koenig.'

'Koenig?'

Mellerhorst noted Reinhold's expression, 'Yes, that's about what Sebastian looked like as well when I told him. It turns out that Koenig very rarely comes home with significant damage to his Albatros. Did you know that? I didn't. I had to assess the extent of the damage by factoring in the cost of parts and the time taken to make repairs. It isn't thorough, and the ground crews beg and borrow from everywhere they can, so a lot of what I concluded may not be very accurate.'

'What about Kruchelsdorf? You haven't mentioned him.'

'Sorry, he sometimes fails to fill out his log book after a mission. Insufficient information. On reflection, Sebastian didn't even ask about Kruchelsdorf when I mentioned Koenig.'

'Seb has more victories than anyone else in the *Jasta*. You could have worked it differently.'

'You two are so alike in some ways. That's what he said as well. I told him I'd incorporated Richthofen's reports to prove its validity. He had a bit of a pout and let it go.'

'Where did you get hold of Richthofen's log?'

'I didn't. It got von Bülow off my back.'

'No wonder we never heard about it.'

'It's not a terrible idea, though, Ernst. It could be done. Boelcke had his own set of rules to follow – everyone knows his principles. Maybe we can add to the depth of knowledge.'

'I thought you had a war to run?'

'Fokker would probably be interested in the idea. He's very astute when it comes to piecing together the work of others.'

'Yes, that seems to sum him up. Look, kick it upstairs if you want to, but leave it to the professors and engineers to pursue if it's worth doing. It's more their field anyway. You've got more than enough work to do here.'

Chapter 22

April 1918: Fallen Eagles

The rattling rhythm and jolt of the train had lulled Burrows into an approximation of relaxation as it brought more men in uniform to the front. When it finally lurched to a halt, he was heartily sick of the carry-on of the other passengers who had crammed into every spare nook. Disembarking from the crowded carriage, he was almost immediately accosted on the platform by the squadron's duty NCO, who relieved him of his valise, 'Welcome back, sir. Good leave?'

'Ever been to Paris, Corporal?'

'Can't say I have.'

'I shouldn't bother, if I were you.'

'Very good, sir.'

Burrows left it at that, and the driver was not so dense as to fail to detect the officer's lack of enthusiasm. They drove in silence for the rest of the trip.

Harding saw the vehicle arriving and went to meet the returning pilot. He looked Burrows up and down and concluded that the time off had been a wasted effort, 'How was Paris?'

'Quiet.'

The adjutant would have been remiss to have failed to impart the latest offering, 'Don't expect the same here. You're rostered onto tomorrow's dawn patrol.'

Burrows nodded. It was not unexpected, nor undeserved, 'Who's going with me?'

Harding could have misinterpreted the query and trotted out the familiar names of the other crews in 'B' Flight, but that would have been avoiding the issue. Uncomfortable in the presence of Burrows, Harding had the decency to squirm at the starkness of the situation, 'The Canuck.'

'Donovan? Why isn't he flying with Hooper?'

'Hooper has an ear infection. He's in hospital.' It was a common complaint for open-cockpit fliers. When a man wasn't in the line it was usually because he was either incapacitated or occupied with other military assignments, such as training the next lot for the job. There was no getting away from the war for very long.

'Is anyone else dead?'

Harding didn't appreciate the lack of tact, but couldn't bring himself to look Burrows in the eye, 'No.'

'Well, give it time.'

Next, Burrows tracked down Donovan. There was little he could say to him, but avoiding the man would have seemed churlish. 'Hello, Henry.'

If Donovan was unhappy with the arrangement of being paired with Burrows, he gave no sign of it, 'Hello, Adam. Back from Paris, then?'

'Just in time, so I hear.'

Donovan nodded, but he had been one of those who had been avoiding Burrows for the last month or so, and there was no way to properly break the ice. Burrows wasn't about to build a bridge between them either, 'I'm for bed.' It wasn't even dark.

'I'll see you in the morning, then.'

'Good night, Henry.'

Sleep was a thing that Burrows tried to postpone, though, like death, it too was unavoidable. It lured him with its false siren song, where the dead were brought back to life for him, even though as they were individually greeted he knew in his core that it was all untrue. Dead was dead: the Holy Bible was for those who elected to live in denial.

You have killed your friends, but in your dreams they forgive you, and you cannot grasp why this would be. Were positions reversed, and you were dead at their hands, would you have forgiven them? The answer is yes, of course you would have. They were your friends after all, and they lived for you.

But it was not the same. Burrows knew that he would never forgive himself. History is full of stories of those who sacrifice their lives for others and religions are founded on the act. But those who remain; what of them? Are they grateful to be alive but burdened by a debt that cannot be repaid, one which can only be extended to others still living; a curse handed on to those who will never be thankful for receipt of it? Only the guilt can be passed on with surety. The rest is a phantom.

Every night Burrows opened the shutters of his mind and insistent memories that refused to be held at bay seeped back into the forefront of his consciousness, whispering evil secrets and refusing to blow away. Every thought was shrouded in a thick, impenetrable black fog, and when it dissipated, however temporarily, all that remained revealed itself in the form of stark, uncompromising reality.

To face the truth was hard; to deny it an impossibility. Burrows knew that he was forever lost. The person that he had become was not one he had ever suspected he could have been, nor would he have accepted the transformation if he had been given prior warning of the choice. *What a fool I have been! Of course I had been given prior notice. If my eyes had been open, I would have seen what the war would bring to me.*

Burrows' inner turmoil kept bubbling away in his brain in a perpetual process that had come to resemble a grotesque combination of merry-go-round and Ferris wheel, a heinous contraption constructed solely for the purpose of continually stirring the poison in his head.

In the darkness, he whispered what no recruiter ever said aloud, 'The war requires sacrifice, and no man is exempt.'

Burrows was roused from sleep in the darkest hour before dawn. A hand shook him by the shoulder, 'Time to get up.'

Rising so early was no longer a hardship, unlike the first few weeks when his body had rebelled and left him with an urgent desire to know the whereabouts of the nearest latrine. He was instantly awake, and having gone to bed in his clothes he wasted no time in finding his way to the bathroom. Intending only to splash water onto his face, he decided that shaving could wait another day. A trim physical appearance may have counted on parade, but it was completely irrelevant when flying.

Burrows looked once more into the mirror and changed his mind. He found a sliver of soap and took up his razor.

To the casual observer, the wounds of the mind are not as obvious as those that the body can carry: crushed limbs, splintered bone and gouting blood cannot be easily swept aside, nor can the treatment of such injuries be delayed. But the mess within the mind, like any internal damage, is more difficult to diagnose. Though no man or woman could see the trauma, Burrows knew only too well that it was there. *The pressure that builds up behind the eyes – how long will it take to lessen, and will it ever go away?*

Not for the first time, he considered excising the pain with the judicious placement of a bullet to the afflicted area. Should he have acted on the impulse, he knew it would be with a complete absence of fear, either of pain or of eternal damnation for taking his own life. In the end, what stayed his hand was consideration for others. Mopping up the blood of corpses was a grisly business. Furthermore, someone else would have to fly the mission in his stead.

With poorly lathered cheeks, Burrows stropped his jowls, taking care to avoid nicking himself. His control was not all it could have been, and a thin trail of blood soon ran from his upper lip. It stung but he didn't care. *Tempting, to make a deeper incision - not a nice way to go, but there are many ways that are much worse. I know this because I have seen it.*

Burrows fought the urge to open his throat, when just a single slice would have solved everything within minutes. To resist the whim was another small battle, and the more battles of this type that he won, the harder they became to face up to. None of them felt like victory, and one of the motivations that kept him breathing was the knowledge that a continuation of his suffering was a fitting punishment for his sins. *The pain belongs to me, and the cure is my responsibility and mine alone. I do not intend to be a burden to those who knew my better incarnation.*

Again he looked to his reflection as though it was a separate entity. He superimposed faces from his earlier life onto the image: family, friends, fiancé. *If you don't know the details of my guilt, you won't be able to use it against me, either in careless error, or deliberately the next time we argue. My pain is a bad enough wound without the added risk of deliberate misuse, deserved though this may be.* The face in the glass was haggard and gaunt. It had nothing to say to him.

If he had nothing to say to himself, what could he ever say to those who loved him? *'You have known the best of me, but you were not there with me that day, and I in turn shall not discuss any of it with you.'* Nobody deserved to hear those words, for they would not understand such a denial of confidence and the rejection would certainly be hurtful.

Burrows did not desire to inflict those wounds upon anyone, believing that he carried enough to go around. There were no words that an ordinary man could write that would have adequately conveyed their entire meaning. Only a poet could attempt to make an approximation, and a poet was not an ordinary person. That was the true value of poets.

One last inspection of his grim reflection showed that the distinguishing features of his face had changed minimally over the years, yet now they had become infinitely unfamiliar. It was the result of learning one of life's hardest lessons: you cannot save a life by force of will alone. That once innocent face had been carved by the knife of a cruel craftsman. All Burrows saw was a parody of a human being, a wooden golem with a wooden face and a wooden soul. His thoughts were typically mournful; *I used to be a real boy.*

A strong headwind buffeted the bullet-riddled Bristol, causing tension wires to whistle and sing in Burrows' ears. He couldn't hear much of anything, and the remorseless roaring in his mind would have overpowered his senses in any case. Flying over the enemy lines on the way home, he was oblivious to almost everything around him, even the anti-aircraft fire that everyone knew as 'Archie'. The vastness of the sky showed how little he mattered.

He paid no heed to his surroundings. If a German Albatros had swooped upon him, he would not have seen the threat until it was far too late. Unconsciously, he kept formation with the other aircraft on the patrol, but though he shared a physical proximity, he was far away.

There is loneliness, and then there is emptiness. The first state includes a feeling of missing out on what life has to offer, an aspect of unfairness and of opportunities denied. The second state is barren, a void where self-worth is missing and where one's misfortune is a direct product of personal failure.

From the ground, the world was large. The sky on a clear day had an endless aspect to it, and a big man could be made to feel small in the world. From the air, this perspective was radically enhanced. A cathedral that rears above you when you stand before it is but a speck when seen from a bird's viewpoint. It was easier to be lost when flying high above the earthscape - a surreal place where man was never really meant to be.

Seeing the world with an angel's eyes revealed that all life was puny - less than nothing. A man's errors were his own, but the world was indifferent to them in any case. Burrows was meat in a bag of skin and nothing more. He had never been anything, not even in better times when he had daydreamed that he had the power to change his own corner of the world. To have once possessed a sense of belonging was proof of his delusion. Everyone died, and if it happened now – all at once - it would cause less stir than a zephyr in God's universe. If a man could think, it was proof that he was less than nothing. The war made sense, in its own way. It emphatically rammed home to the willing student that all in life had no meaning, that striving for a goal was a pointless endeavour, that even if your contribution made a difference to other people, and even if it was appreciated in a hundred years time, or a thousand, ultimately it was only recognised by ignorant beings who failed to understand their true place in the complex tapestry of eternity.

Flying above the world, all of this made perfectly good sense to Burrows. Anyone who wanted to feel at home on the ground was denying their reality. A pilot could land his aircraft - his mind demanded it, and force of habit and obedience to a lifetime of conforming to rules is a very strong reflex to deny. How much easier would it be to come in too fast, too steep, to plough one last furrow in land that was only recently farmed, but which now had an excess of blood and bone for fertiliser?

The ones who still believed in friendship would have likely attributed his death to an accident, or if not quite an accident, then at least to a mind that had lost its strength of will because it had been subjected to forces and experiences that it was never meant to endure.

And even if they didn't believe it, what matter? There was no meaning in the scriptures. God was an unknowable quantity. Any combination of words formed by groping in the darkness in an effort to try to interpret His will were inadequate and could never be agreed upon by any two otherwise rational minds. It wasn't even a failure in translation from different languages and cultures across two thousand years of fractured history. Rather, the error was due to a sustained refusal to believe that ultimately there was no purpose. The mass-delusion that is humanity had no true concept of what God wanted, if He even existed at all. When all was said and done, He felt the same compassion for those created in His image as He did for the lowliest insect. And like the brain of an insect, the brains of men were unable to encompass their mediocrity. Nothing else could account for the sustained slaughter that consumed thousands of lives every day.

Behind Burrows, the still form of Henry Donovan lay slumped, held in his seat only by a safety harness that still served its purpose, though the need for the restraint had become redundant. Burrows had seen it all before - it didn't take the liberally splashed blood from a leaking body to paint a picture of the poor man's fate. Bert Noone had occupied the position only a few weeks previously, sitting in that same seat, dying in the same way. Before that, Smith had met his maker, the first of three sacrificial offerings presented by Adam Burrows to the gods of war.

There are many ties that bind men to the Earth, and it is the very existence of these ties that assist in defining humanity. Some bonds are real, others symbolic, but all of them have a value to those who possess them, though the actual value may be restricted only to those who know their full meaning.

Some ties come in the form of promises, and if broken they are potentially devastating, though the physical reality may be otherwise unaltered: if you hadn't seen an aging relative for any of the final five years of their life, how can their death at any point during that period matter in real terms?

Other ties are objects, and these tokens are often one's most treasured items, especially when they represent the memory of a loved one who has died, who is absent, or who has promised you their soul. For Adam Burrows, the silk scarf that he wore into battle was his most cherished talisman. It had been given to him by his fiancé on their last morning together and it was the last thing that she had ever touched while they stood close together for that last time, hand in hand. He had never washed the fabric – to have done so would have removed every last trace of her physical presence, and that was something he could not bring himself to do.

When a mind can take no more, when it has been completely consumed with self-loathing, what better way is there to inflict punishment upon oneself than to cast aside everything from which a man once drew strength? Who deserves love; who understands? If others dare to offer their forgiveness, is that not a sure sign that they do not grasp the enormity of the crime?

To be legally permitted to kill other men, to be absolved of blame for the act: these are things that only occur in wartime for the common man – different rules apply to the power brokers, while serial killers dance to their own tune - and though some may take it in their stride, others cannot. To murder a man is a stressful act, regardless of the context or legality of it. Whilst many soldiers are able to accept the harshness of combat as an aberration in behaviour that can be pondered at a later date, Burrows knew that he was not made for this lifestyle.

Unbinding the scarf that Maud Lanning had given him as a constant reminder of her love, he held it aloft in one hand and unhesitatingly opened his fingers. It was instantly snatched away in the gale, lost to him forever. He felt regret at the gesture, but his loss was fitting. Loss was what he deserved.

Burrows' mind wandered, dwelling on details that would forever be branded into his memory. Blood seeped into his vision, and he realised that he must have been hit, though of course not fatally, as had befallen his companion. He wiped a hand across his face and the sticky mess blemished his glove.

Despite his despair and all that he had believed about his will to live, Adam Burrows did not want to die right now. Had he been given a choice – yes or no – he would have elected to go on living. There was no joy in his continued survival, nor hope of redemption, but even so life was what he deserved. To die and have his suffering end; where was the justice in that? To live in perpetual torment was the better fit. The margins either way were small. To be largely ambivalent about his fate was sad in its own way, but the time for actually caring had expired.

Within the deepest well of his consciousness, there always lurked that ghostly fragment of his better self that would not yield. If he could survive this day, he would have an opportunity, however small - one day far in the future - of a life that included belonging and an ounce of happiness. That even the smallest part of him still harboured hope disgusted him for his perceived selfishness. To have stripped everything from his fellows and still expect something for himself was unworthy.

It was true that there had been no intent. It was true that he would undo that which had been done if he was able to change the past. It was true that what had been done could never be undone, and good intentions counted for nothing when the result was suffering. There was a saying: *the end justifies the means.* For Burrows, it was equally true that the result counted more heavily than the best intentions.

On that day, as Burrows flew his battered F.2 over the picturesque landscape of France, he again fought the parasitic demons of his mind. They were like the tide: powerful, tireless, unrelenting. He was just one man, forlorn and beaten, exhausted beyond the physically exerting task of combat flying. He had little resistance to the compulsion to fly his plane into the ground and end his internal conflict. If he won today's battle against self destruction, he would wake to greet another day, and there would be more of the same. The face in the mirror did not relent. Each time he confronted himself in that reflection, he saw what he had been, and what he had become. If he gave himself up to the forces of reason - and more importantly, the forces of gravity – well then, tomorrow would be free of trouble.

The gash to his forehead did not seem to have any relevance and he was steady at the controls. Then, seemingly all of their own volition, his hands sought to sequester his mind with the intention of flying straight into the ground. He had to consciously keep the aircraft level. His body was betraying him, trying to take the easy option by giving up. He felt his mind abandoning him as well. A lifetime of acting in concert made it very difficult to separate the role of mind and body, but Burrows was determined to prevail over his defeatist physical reaction.

Ultimately, his determination overwhelmed his reflex. Relief at securing victory came at the expenditure of an enormous amount of energy. Burrows was wrung out at every level. He was drained beyond belief, and the relief of winning out over an unexpected mutiny by his own body allowed him to let down his guard. Exhausted, he was unable to remain awake.

The Bristol fell out of formation, and by the time Burrows was able to rouse himself, the aircraft was in a terminal spin. Witnesses later said that they saw him appear to lose consciousness as he slumped at the controls, and when the wreckage was inspected, his head wound supported the observation.

*   *   *

The first two years of the war had seen only sporadic incidents of men attempting to kill each other in the air, armed with anything from handguns and steel darts to grappling hooks. Besides a complete lack of knowledge on how to achieve their goal, the number of aircraft available to all of the combatants at that time was negligible compared to later developments. If nineteen-sixteen had been a time for baby steps for the men learning to fight amongst the clouds, then nineteen-seventeen saw their coming of age.

Hardly anyone remembered flying in the halcyon days of nineteen-sixteen. Mostly this was because a year and a half had passed since then and life expectancy in the intervening period had been a lottery.

It was also a question of numbers: only a very few airmen had begun operational activities prior to nineteen-seventeen. As such, ninety-five percent of all aerial combat losses until the end of the war occurred from that point onwards.

Nineteen-eighteen was shaping up to be even worse than seventeen. The huge numbers of experienced airmen on both sides meant that there were horrific losses amongst the new personnel. Nineteen-eighteen was a crucible of fire that exterminated beginners. These novices were analogous to newly-emerged butterflies, picked off the branch by predators before their wings had properly dried. The Allies now had assumed almost total control of the skies. Only when the Germans were able to assemble concentrated formations were they able to wrest back air-superiority, and even then it was temporary and strictly limited to the immediate vicinity that had been given a priority for reinforcement.

German aviators accepted that they would usually be outnumbered in any given situation and learned to fight accordingly. The best pilots were afforded opportunities to add to their totals, and because they usually fought over their own side of the front lines, these were only confirmed if wreckage could be found to substantiate their claims. The men who fought for Britain and France did not have to prove their kills to the same stringent degree, and as such there was far less accuracy in the Allied score-keeping. Historians would argue about this for the next hundred years at least, but their pedantry did not have any bearing on the progress or outcome of the war.

A target rich environment presented its own difficulties. Quite often an Englishman would survive in battle simply because he had friends that were able to help him out. The man who would have claimed him was often denied victory because he was forced to abandon the chase in order to live another day. Other occasions would see a small number of Germans engaged by a larger enemy formation, and thus have little chance of success. It was just such an action that had seen Werner Voss killed late in nineteen-seventeen, despite the fact that he had scored hits on all of his adversaries.

The Pfalz DIII was deficient in almost every facet. It had poor performance compared to the aircraft it went up against. Its rate of climb was abysmal and it was unable to ascend to the same altitude as other aircraft in order to gain a positional advantage from the top perch. Its handling characteristics were sluggish, and to compound the problem further, it was prone to stalling and was difficult to recover if it went into a spin.

The difference between good and great is measured in small increments: inches per foot, seconds per minute. For the three-dimensional nature of air-to-air combat, each split second advantage is massive. A top-notch pilot is not superior to a novice by an order of magnitude. His response times are not twice as quick, he cannot see for hundreds of miles. The margins are much smaller.

For an Olympic sprinter, the gap between triumph and losing is measured in hundredths of seconds. The athlete who wins multiple gold medals is not much quicker than the one who comes dead last every time that they compete in a Final, but the differential is massive when it is results that are rewarded. In a foot race, the reward for success is a trophy, and though enamelled trinkets are also given to successful combat pilots, the real reward is that they live to fight again.

The human eye can detect miniscule differences in all sorts of details. Though not markedly pronounced, smaller units of measurement register in the minds of those who know what they are looking at. It is something that all living things have practised every day of their lives. Complicated motor skills can be performed beneath the cognitive level. To carry a tray of food up a flight of stairs generally requires no more than exercising due care. Solving the technical aspect of the task and deliberately coordinating every movement of the hands and feet is not necessary. Considering the complexity of the function, accidents are rather few.

In contrast to this, a novice pilot is in an alien realm, one where powered flight is a new technology. He cannot know every trick and relevant skill in the book except through repetition. While he is still learning his trade he is at his most vulnerable. Failure to adjust quickly to new circumstances will not be forgiven indefinitely. Sometimes even the first error is fatal.

At the other end of the continuum, a veteran knows the skills he needs, and they are ingrained. He does not need to consciously decide on a reaction, because it has become instinctive. That the Pfalz DIII was inferior to other fighters to the tune of around ten percent in so many aspects of its measurable performance cannot be understated. For every inadequacy, a pilot needed to compensate with extra levels of experience, reflex and luck.

Yet the longer he was able to survive, the more a Pfalz pilot took his life into his own hands. As if poor performance was not enough, the method of manufacture of the airframe was flawed. Over time, the fuselage would warp as its plywood shell seasoned and started to dry. For many pilots this never became an issue – they were usually killed quickly because of one or another of the multitude of shortcomings of the blighted machine – but those who lived longer were better advised to discard an ageing machine for a newer one before it deteriorated.

Max Beerenbrock had risen to command in the usual way: someone higher in the food chain had been killed. By now everyone accepted the reality of the process. Today he was on patrol with just three Pfalz DIIIs clumped with him. The sky was partially covered in layers of broken cloud, leaving plenty of room to hide in three dimensions. Because the very nature of clouds is to continually morph and shift, a strong possibility always existed that the enemy would be encountered by chance. Sometimes reduced visibility was not such a good thing.

The patrol cruised roughly parallel to the meandering route of the front lines, with the intention of trapping any intruders before they returned home. Beerenbrock had a mantra that forbade his men from venturing into enemy airspace. That way if you encountered trouble you were more likely to make it home. It also meant that the trigger-happy infantry didn't get an opportunity to send a few shots in his direction when he crossed over their position. As always, he was adhering to his own directive.

Today the wind was blowing from the east, though a westerly wind was more usual. Though the Pfalz lacked a decent overall performance, the direction of the breeze would assist in any interception closer to the lines. Conversely, it would also hinder any attempt to make a swift getaway. Because Beerenbrock refused to venture over the line that delineated friend from foe, in the event that he should be shot down, at least it would be on the German side of the lines. It wasn't an ideal situation, but it was nevertheless preferable to being made a prisoner, assuming of course that any downed pilots survived their re-acquaintance with *terra firma*.

Far below in the distance, six German aircraft were engaged in operations against the front lines. They were AEGs, armoured aircraft designed to resist small arms fire from above and below. The ground crawlers were under attack by at least twenty Spads. It could have been more; the view was obscured in places by the very same clouds that provided Beerenbrock and his men with their concealment.

By this stage in the war it was expected that most Spads encountered would be the latest model - the Spad XIII. It was a fast machine which was able to leave the Pfalz DIII standing still. Its armament was also an improvement on the earlier French designs, and it could match the best German fighters. Worst of all from Beerenbrock's perspective, the new model was hard to distinguish from the earlier Spad VII from which it had evolved.

The AEGs had had enough and turned to head home. The French fliers had other ideas. Beerenbrock didn't think there was much chance that any of the Germans would be harmed. It was akin to throwing pebbles onto a tin roof, and the sound would be about the same. But to knock enough holes into the metal monstrosities to do significant damage to them would have to entail equal parts luck and determination on the part of the French airmen.

Immediately, one of the German machines was seen to crash. Beerenbrock was forced to revise his thought. The machine may have been largely bullet-proof, with armour plating for the cockpit, but it didn't make the crew immune. They were vulnerable to fire from directly above.

Though it was unlikely that the Spads would be able to do further harm, there was also a code of honour to uphold – you didn't leave your friends at the mercy of the enemy. As unlikely as it was that another AEG would be picked off, their crews would hardly be appreciative if the small Pfalz patrol left them to their fate.

Rather than flying away and saving his skin by ignoring the events unfolding below, Beerenbrock elected to attack despite his hideous disadvantage in numbers – to say nothing of pitting Pfalz DIIIs against Spad XIIIs. He positioned himself up-sun and assessed the situation further. He didn't have too much time to consider his options; the two-seaters looked unable to extricate themselves from their predicament.

At a distance, one of the French squadrons appeared to be at least partially comprised of Spad VIIs. Beerenbrock might have been mistaken in his identification, and if he was it could be a costly error. Not usually one to go glory hunting, he was loath to pass up the opportunity for an easy victory, if indeed that's how a Spad of any variety could ever be described. He opened the throttle and piled in. His men followed in a line astern formation, assisted by a forty kilometre an hour tailwind.

Their surprise was total, but Beerenbrock's men failed to destroy any of the Frenchmen on the first pass. Rather than being stung into action, the Spads were initially thrown into a state of confusion. The Germans capitalised on the opportunity. Schmidt poured fire into one of the enemy machines, but instead of crashing, the French fighter put its nose down and tried to extract itself from the battle. Other Spads shepherded their friend away from danger, daring the frustrated German to interfere further.

Focused as they were on the other Pfalz, the Spads had not counted on the fanatical determination that Beerenbrock possessed that day. Committing to combat against insurmountable odds required something special. Flying directly at the nearest of the protectors, he let fly with a long burst from his twinned Maxims and flayed it like a slave under the lash.

Smoke began to emanate from the motor of the targeted machine. The German veteran noted its identification mark – a red seven - before it sped away in the general direction of Germany. *Maybe the*

253

pilot has lost his bearings, or perhaps he is dying… Beerenbrock couldn't see if the machine had crashed or not, but that was the least of his worries. He and his men were in a dogfight that realistically had only one ending: once the Spads regrouped, they would hose the Pfalz DIIIs full of gunfire and there would be no going home for anyone who had an allegiance to the Kaiser.

There hadn't been much of an alternative. The AEGs had needed assistance and no man of conscience would have left them to their fate. Beerenbrock checked every part of the sky about him as quickly as his head could turn. He needed to know how many Frenchmen were about to fall upon him, in what order, from which direction, and when. His brain processed everything that was fed into it via his hyperactive eyeballs.

And here they came. One of the French fighters fastened onto Beerenbrock and opened fire. The shots flew wide. The Frenchman then miscalculated his airspeed and overshot. The situation was suddenly reversed and Beerenbrock squinted through his gun-sight, in time to recognise the model as a Mark VII. He fired, briefly, just a dozen rounds in all, then quickly looked over his shoulder to see if he had collected more followers. His men were shielding him. That was their job, but it wasn't an easy one. If they failed to hold off even one tyro, Beerenbrock's failure to check his rear would kill him. He returned his attention to his front and fired a longer burst. The Spad went down, descending in gentle loops and curves until it piled up in a heap far below.

Another section of Frenchmen had assembled and came boring in at the men protecting the leader. Their objective was to get amongst Beerenbrock's wingmen and isolate someone, preferably someone who would be easier to kill than their formidable commander. There were certainly enough Spads to force the issue. The Pfalz formation needed to close ranks and stand firm, and provide covering fire for each other if it was at all possible.

The Allied scouts came at the Pfalz DIIIs in droves and clung to them like insects on flypaper, incessantly hammering away with their machine guns. The gunfire wove a latticed pattern on the wider canvas of the sky, connecting the lives of men hell-bent on killing each other. The Spad pilots were determined to eradicate the planes painted with the black crosses, especially now that they had suffered their own losses.

To the east, the AEGs had seized on the moment and were trying to extricate themselves from their predicament. Unable to render assistance to the men who had intervened on their behalf, they took the option to cut and run. Beerenbrock's men were on their own now. They barely had time to consider the ingratitude of it all, even though in reality there was no other option for either party.

The French split their forces. Half tried to prevent the escape of the two-seaters, the others set upon the four Pfalz DIIIs. It looked as though the French had elected to use the increased firepower of the Spad XIIIs against the armoured AEGs, with Spad VIIs assigned the task of harassing the Pfalz pilots.

Beerenbrock may not have had any say in the matter, but it didn't mean that he couldn't experience a sense of relief that the enhanced Spads had decided to look elsewhere. He had done his part. What befell the AEG boys would play out as it would and no blame could ever be attached to him. He also had enough time to appreciate that at a personal level, his odds of surviving the day had radically improved.

Miles away, the Spad that Schmidt had damaged in the initial attack was rapidly becoming a dwindling speck in the distance.

Another scout came at Beerenbrock, but he had plenty of time to turn and meet it. Flying head to head, neither man had time for more than a hurried shot. As both planes hurtled by close to one another, Beerenbrock dived away in a violent turn. It was a manoeuvre that he would have never attempted with an Albatros for fear of tearing off a wing. The Frenchman had started to pull away but he seemed to have lost control of his rudder. If he escaped, landing would be a tricky prospect. Beerenbrock intended to put the issue beyond doubt. He closed to point blank range. The other man looked directly at him, his face a mask of terror.

Beerenbrock raked the enemy plane from nose to tail and shot it out of the sky. A bonfire of burning gasoline plummeted to earth, where it advertised its own funeral pyre with a thick column of dirty smoke.

Abruptly, the sky started to empty as the enemy planes began to disperse. The French had called it quits. They must have been short on fuel; Spads were not in the habit of running from a fight when they had the benefit of overwhelming numbers, not even if one of the German fliers was on the warpath. They had the firepower to even the score, but not an adequate reserve of fuel. Not today.

For his part, Beerenbrock was not done. Far below, he detected a solitary aircraft snaking its way homewards. Unfortunately, the Frenchman was betrayed by his own trail of smoke. The German leader nosed his machine into yet another power dive and made a course to intercept. As he drew nearer, he was able to distinguish a red seven. He had found his man again, the same one that had been singled out at the beginning of the dogfight. Beerenbrock was unwavering in his resolve to administer the *coup de grace*. He flew in close to the Spad and blew it to hell.

With no-one left for them to fight, the small formation of Pfalz DIIIs regrouped and steadily climbed for altitude as they set a course for home. Surprisingly, they had taken only token damage in the free-for-all. Satisfied that they had done enough for one day, they couldn't wait to return home and regale their comrades with the story of their exploits. It would be something that they could dine out on for months.

But the first order of business was to survive, and in order to achieve that aim they must not relax their vigilance. Nobody had warned other enemy units in the area to stay clear of the deadly team. If they were sighted by a prowling Allied patrol, all that would register would be easy pickings, handed to them on a platter courtesy of the considerate Pfalz factory at Speyer.

Schmidt waggled his wings to attract his leader's attention, pointing out a cluster of Spads six hundred metres below them on a westward heading. These were newer models and in a dogfight they were markedly superior in performance to any German machine then in service. At the bottom of the pecking order, the Pfalz was dead meat.

For all of its vices, the Pfalz had one redeeming quality: loiter time. With an endurance of two and a half hours, it could stay airborne when most other types had cut short their patrols and gone home, assuming of course that they had taken off at the same time. In combat, this was only an advantage to a pilot good enough to survive, and the poor overall performance of the type masked its only positive feature.

Max Beerenbrock had been one of the first pilots to fly the Pfalz in combat, and he had enjoyed immediate success. But until today, only one of his victories had been scored after the time he would normally have been forced to turn back for want of fuel had he been in another machine. Today had been different. Had he still been flying the Albatros DV, Beerenbrock would have only had time to bag his first victim before fuel became an issue. Most pilots who flew the maligned design never fully appreciated the extra time they had to play with; certainly the pilots with other equipment did not envy their poor cousins.

Unlike the Albatros, the wings of the Pfalz did not come off when extra G-forces were placed on them. For this reason, Heinrich Gontermann had flown the type whenever he went looking for balloons to burn. He could dive onto the target with a reasonable expectation of success. Balloons had been his specialty.

Beerenbrock was not Gontermann. He had only ever flown one mission against a balloon, and his wingman had been killed that day. Though he hadn't attempted to replicate Gontermann's methods, it didn't mean that he was ignorant of the strengths of the Pfalz DIII. His speed in a dive would be enough to overhaul these Frenchmen, but they would soon be swarming all over him if they decided to come out of their corner swinging.

The Spad XIII pilots were either complacent or tired, or possibly the pale colour scheme of the German fighters rendered them invisible against the backdrop of the clouds. Either way, the French seemed oblivious to the recent action as they mosied across the battle area on what must have been for them an uneventful day. Beerenbrock signalled to his men to hang back, reasoning that a lone hunter may be able to insert himself into their midst through stealth.

The wandering Allied patrol failed to detect the threat as Beerenbrock carefully stalked his prey, edging ever closer with each passing second. Lining up the last man in the formation, he moved to within fifty metres and fired into the belly of the trailing machine. It gradually lost altitude and fell away from the others. The Spads proceeded on their way, unaware of what had befallen their comrade. How they did not hear the shooting could not be explained.

Beerenbrock followed the stricken aircraft on its lonely descent. His men reappeared like wraiths from the cloudbank and fell in behind him. Together they dogged the crippled Spad until it ploughed into a field. Heidberg machine-gunned the pilot as the man climbed out and scrambled for cover.

Beerenbrock looked across for confirmation of the kill, and received the thumbs up from Schmidt. *That's one, at least. How many of the others will be given is anyone's guess. All four? No chance.*

*   *   *

Percy Wiggan was sorting through the small pile of personal effects that had belonged to Adam Burrows. Normally the job fell to a man's closest friend on the squadron, but Burrows had none that fitted the description. Mostly it was letters from home, but there were also the usual tokens such as hair clippings and a ring, presumably from Burrows' fiancé. Burrows had also kept a diary. A photo of a plain looking young woman bookmarked the leather-bound cover. Wiggan assumed that it was the girl Burrows had sworn himself to, else what was the significance? A sealed envelope completed the inventory. It was unmarked, so Wiggan would need to open it to find out whom to send it to.

He opened the diary and started to read.

Unsurprisingly, it contained details of missions flown and Burrows' thoughts regarding them. Clearly he had been unhappy during his time at the front – Wiggan knew he would not have won a prize for guessing as much – and much of this came across in the spidery script. Wiggan skimmed most of it, but there were some entries that echoed his own views. He slowed down to take in more of the detail.

Burrows had never communicated his unhappiness to anyone, so far as Wiggan knew. They had all known he was struggling, but it was the English way to persevere without complaint. *If only more people subscribed to the practice.* Wiggan himself always showed a stiff upper lip, though he knew that on really bad days his chin gave the game away with its inevitable tell-tale tremble.

But to commit thought to paper... Wiggan knew that many people did it, but had never considered that anything other than dates and deeds would ever be mentioned. He had always assumed that a diary was an unofficial log book and nothing more. Upon further reflection, he saw that he had been naïve in his belief. With his curiosity now piqued, he delved deeper into Burrows' notes.

There was the usual fluff pertaining to everything that a schoolboy dreamed, and how this meshed with the reality of flying training and squadron life. The facts were bare, and so far as Wiggan could tell, accurate. What stood out was that Burrows over-thought his situation, and condemned others for showing insufficient regard for the plight of their fellows.

Wiggan disagreed with the dead man's assessment. He felt that Burrows' opinion was not justified and that the words had been written in spite of the man's tenuous grasp on reality. Yes, the facts supported the various condemnations if looked at in a certain way, but conclusions had been drawn based on false assumptions that did not allow for mitigating circumstances. Much of this was due to Burrows' strange innocence, though Wiggan felt that the man's scathing portrayal of his peers had more to do with social awkwardness.

Wiggan wondered if others committed character assassinations in their various journals and diaries. *Surely it only applied to those who had no mettle?* He thumbed through the pages until he came to an entry that clearly showed that Burrows did not merely fail to fit in, but had seen the full face of war:

It grieves me that I have promised Maud an amazing life together, not because it was an impossible ambition, but because it has now become so hard to reconcile with what I have seen we are capable of when propriety is shunted aside to make way for barbarous deeds...

The writing style was simple in its presentation. Clearly Burrows had known his grammar, but when it came to conveying his thoughts he lacked subtlety, though it was precisely this quality that made the script easy for Wiggan to follow. Everything was stark. Indeed, it was a true reflection of all of Burrows' interactions with his fellows. He had always been very easy to understand because there was never anything that he tried to hide. For him, life was simple. Wiggan had always felt that Burrows was too young for his age; for some reason there were always a handful of people who simply didn't know how they were supposed to think or act. Even before his decline had become evident, Burrows had been an outcast.

Wiggan doubted that he would be missed. *The man is a basket case. Was. Damn, reading his thoughts makes him come to life.*

And yet...

Much of what had been written was also true for Wiggan. Often he felt isolated from the world, and he wondered how many others in the squadron were concealing their anxieties behind a mask of normality. To find that he had common ground with Burrows was disquieting. It made him feel weak, because Burrows had been weak.

Done with scanning the diary, Wiggan opened the sealed envelope. He assumed it was one of those that were to be delivered in the event of death. If need be, he could reseal it later.

'Dearest Maud,

Do not mourn me, my dear. The man you loved ceased to exist before I died...'

There really was no need to read any further, but Wiggan kept on in case he had been mistaken in judging the tone of the content. When he was satisfied, he set it aside. There were three pages in all. The last two did not receive so much as a glance.

He then turned to other mail. Burrows had received a lot of correspondence from his girl, and Wiggan opened one to see if there was anything juicy to be had. He was disappointed to discover that everything was very chaste and prim, though the woman was fixated on the multitude of dangers that she fancied were to be found in France: some of them were completely nonsensical. More telling, she professed to studiously poring over the published casualty lists with an obsessive and morbid dread. *Serves her right, tempting fate in such a manner. Well, she won't need to do that anymore.*

Lewis-Hamilton chose that moment to make his entrance, 'Hello, Wiggan, anything interesting?'

'No, only the usual stuff.'

'The mail has just come in.'

Wiggan's enthusiasm grew, 'Anything for me?'

'No.'

The enthusiasm dissipated, 'Why tell me, then?'

'There's a letter for Burrows.'

'But nothing for me? If you needed it, there's the proof that there is no God.'

'You're sorting his belongings. I thought you should have it.'

'Who's it from?'

Lewis-Hamilton read a name from the reverse side of the envelope, 'A fellow called Athol Lanning.'

Wiggan shrugged. The name meant nothing to him.

'What was the name of that girl he kept banging on about?'

'His fiancé. Maud.'

'What was her surname?'

Another shrug. Wiggan reached across to the pile of letters and checked addresses, 'Here it is. Maud Lanning.'

'So, her father, then.'

'Father, brother, uncle...' Wiggan held out his hand and the letter was passed across to him. He opened it and read briefly. His brow furrowed, 'I'll be damned.'

'Yes?'

'It's a good thing that poor old Burrows got the chop – this would have killed him for certain.'

Lewis-Hamilton took an educated guess. 'The wedding's off and she left it to Daddy to break the news? That's a new approach. Wretched girl. Does it give a reason? Not that it's any of our business, I suppose.'

'As a matter of fact, it does. Maud Lanning was killed in a Gotha raid last month. Her father considered it his responsibility to inform Burrows. He calls him Adam, of course. It looks like the old boy was fond of the young fellow.'

'Nice to have the approval of your future in-laws.'

The import of the timing was not lost on either man. Lewis-Hamilton groped for the right phrase to sum it up, 'Ships that pass in the night.'

'The *Titanic*, you mean.' Wiggan paused in reflection, 'You'd say it was the best thing to happen, in the circumstances. Notwithstanding the loss to each family, of course.'

'You could take the letters back and deliver them in person, now that you're heading off to Blighty for a few months.'

Wiggan still had a few days to go before he was tour-expired, and felt uneasy that Lewis-Hamilton had taken his survival for granted. But he said nothing about it, as merely mentioning the fact that he still had flight time ahead of him would needlessly be risking the wrath of fate, 'No thanks. The postal service is paid to deal with awkwardness, not me.'

It was an odd situation. Wiggan saw that the other man was looking at the letters strewn about, 'Most of these need to be sent back home, but the diary is not for a mother to read. It would cause more harm than good. There are other letters that I'd withhold as well. One in particular'

'Too morbid?'

'That'd be it. Things get lost in the post all of the time.'

Lewis-Hamilton nodded his agreement, 'However you wish. It's not as if anyone will thank us for sending it on, or cry foul if we don't.'

A short while later the two men had assembled the small stack of offending material into a neat heap. Without ceremony, a match was set to it. As it burned, Wiggan observed, 'Nobody would ever want to read this sort of thing anyway. It's too depressing. History is about kings and queens and the dates that wars are fought. It's not about trivial rubbish like this.'

'Shakespeare wrote about star-crossed lovers.'

'Like I said: rubbish.' Like Burke, Wiggan held the playwright in low regard, and didn't much care if he had offended his flight commander in saying so. In his opinion the only good thing about Shakespeare was that he was long dead. For his part, Lewis-Hamilton was indeed offended by the comment, but dismissed the thought from his mind. People like Wiggan may not appreciate the civilised world, but that was not the world that any of them were currently residing in. If the ignoramus could shoot straight, Lewis-Hamilton required nothing further from him.

A leaf from one of the burning pages curled and was lifted by the heat of the fire into the still air. It briefly wafted about until it gently drifted onto the ground directly in front of the pair. The paper had blackened, but upon closer inspection Wiggan could still discern some of the detail in the handwriting. He put the toe of his boot onto it and gently applied pressure. The evidence was crushed into a fine grey powder, lost to the world forever.

*　　*　　*

Beerenbrock felt solid earth beneath his feet and he was more grateful for the fact than he could remember. The last Pfalz had barely trundled to a standstill when Schmidt came running over to him, and the man was more excited than a monkey with a snake, 'Max! How did we manage it? We are all back in one piece and I saw four go down!'

'You saw them?'

'Your three and one to Wesser. Mine got away.' He didn't seem to care at all about his own score. Surviving against heavy expectation put the smaller disappointment into perspective.

265

Beerenbrock was not at all surprised that his men had not been able to confirm all of the kills. They'd had more Spads crawling over them than an infantryman had lice. That they'd had any opportunity to witness any activity other than that which was immediately in front of them - and more importantly, behind them – was mute testimony to their considerable experience. No-one knew more about survival than the men who flew the Pfalz for Germany.

'You missed one. My bag is four.'

Schmidt's smile widened even more and he shouted to the sky, 'Ha!' He pumped both of his fists towards the heavens.

The adjutant arrived amidst their impromptu celebration. Other personnel were also gathering around and for some reason they were not greeting the returned fliers with their usual warmth, particularly given the jubilation of the recently returned.

Beerenbrock looked again at the staff officer. Through long association, he could read the man. Something was amiss. As the adrenaline in his system dissipated, he struggled against the mountain of exhaustion that was piling onto him in the wake of his colossal achievement. His foggy brain could not shake the sense of impending doom. *Has another mine been detonated? Is there a breach in the lines again?* 'What is it? What has happened?'

'We have just heard word…' the man faltered, and there were tears in his eyes. Beerenbrock had forgotten his crowning moment, and awaited the next words. Whatever they may be, they must be calamitous, 'Richthofen is dead.'

266

Part II: Fokker Swansong

Chapter 23

April 1918: The Dead Baron

'Richthofen is dead.'

The words caused the blood to drain from Beerenbrock's face. He felt it ebb like the tide and drop into his belly - a nauseating sensation that reminded him of swallowing hot, salty blood. The words were a death knell that erased all of his elation. Beerenbrock knew that the adjutant was not referring to the younger brother. No. There was only one Richthofen – the man had been by far the best of the chasers ever since he had been hand-picked by that other icon, Oswald Boelcke. Boelcke himself had once been larger than life before he had been reduced to the form of an inspiring memory. And now Richthofen.

The loss of their premier pilot had spread like wildfire through Germany, and had rocked the populace. The wake of his death left a void in their collective martial consciousness. In a war where men died in untold thousands, the loss of just one had been met with disbelief. Very few of those who mourned him had so much as seen the man let alone known him, yet the public image of what he had represented led to a sense of bereavement on a massive scale. Those who knew him wondered at this phenomenon knowing that, though his reputation had been hard earned, affection for a complete stranger must be a bizarre notion to anyone wishing to take the time to think rationally about it.

The timing of Beerenbrock's own momentous battle had thrust him directly into the spotlight. He knew that Richthofen's death had left a large black hole that many wanted filled by a replacement hero and like it or not, circumstances dictated that he was a prime candidate. Over the course of the next few days he had received calls from generals and newspaper reporters and had found it to be tedious. Nevertheless, he had spoken to all of them.

The men who had flown with him had also been hounded. The details of the epic fight had become the stuff of legend. Schmidt had himself only damaged one of the enemy machines, but the attention that he had received on account of it left him wondering how much worse it must be for his leader. He caught sight of Wesser and Heidberg sharing a cigarette, 'What do you make of it?'

Wesser didn't need clarification, 'It's created quite a fuss, eh?'

Heidberg agreed, 'I've heard a few say that it couldn't be done. But we were there, and there are bodies to prove it.'

Schmidt was curious, 'Couldn't be done? Did someone call Beerenbrock a liar? Who?'

'He claimed to be a war correspondent, but wouldn't identify himself. I punched him in the face.'

Wesser had been present at that confrontation but didn't remember anything physical. Instead of contradicting Heidberg's version of events, he confirmed it. Though it wasn't true, it should have been, 'He had it coming.'

'Have you heard that they are considering him for the Red Eagle?'

Schmidt had heard no such thing, and wondered who Heidberg's source was. The Order of the Red Eagle was reckoned to be unattainable, a far rarer achievement than the *Pour le Merite*.

270

Richthofen had one of course, but it had taken him seventy kills before it had been bestowed upon him. No other pilot had even been considered for such an exalted honour.

Clearly Wesser had not heard the news either. Thinking out loud, he found an uncanny parallel, 'They'll call it the Red Max if it happens.'

The 'they' that Wesser was referring to were the members of the *Luftstreitkräfte*. When the first airmen picked up the Order for Merit in nineteen-sixteen, it had very quickly been dubbed the 'Blue Max', in honour of Max Immelmann. Though Boelcke had received his own Order on the same day, 'Blue Oz' did not have the same ring to it. The Order for Merit had been around for a century and a half, and it said much that the army did not have its own slang term for it. Pilots were a new breed of warrior, and some of their innovative mindset came across in the way that they looked at tradition. Now it appeared that another prestigious order was up for grabs, and another Max was involved. Furthermore, calling it a Red Max also referenced Richthofen's inclusion very graphically, due to his famous battle colours.

Neither Schmidt nor Heidberg needed to have any of this spelt out for them. They made all of the connections immediately. Heidberg then went one better, 'The Kaiser had better hope that Schleich doesn't draw the same notice.'

Eduard von Schleich was nicknamed the Black Knight due to the paintwork adorning his aircraft, which he had done following the death of a friend. Although he wasn't the only man to choose a black scheme, he was the one to whom the name had stuck. The ultimate state award that a German could attain was the Order of the Black Eagle, though it was restricted to nobility and generals. Certainly Schleich would fall into the former category. *The Black Ed.* Schmidt wondered if Heidberg was making the whole thing up for his own private amusement.

Schmidt considered the rumoured Red Eagle for Beerenbrock. *If such a prestigious award is even being considered, it can only be to assuage the pain of the loss of our greatest flier.* The fall of Richthofen was still resonating with his countrymen, and would for some time. Though the news was shocking, Schmidt expected that ultimately saner heads would prevail. Beerenbrock was certainly a hero and should be honoured in accordance to his deed rather than in response to Germany's anguish.

Schmidt had seen the failings of human beings firsthand. He knew men whose minds were scrambled because of an inability to cope with the violence surrounding them. He also knew that in the long term it would be better that Richthofen had died in battle, though the timing of these things was always a shock and never ideal. But a dead hero would always be remembered as someone whose star had shone brightly - if briefly. Future recollections of him would be reverent and pure, and though being cut down in the prime of life would forever be remembered as a tragic event, in death a man is given no opportunity to sully his reputation with later deeds. Contrary to expectation, most heroes cannot walk tall for their entire lives.

*   *   *

The Royal Air Force was a newly formed entity, having been created from the amalgamation of the RFC and the Royal Naval Air Service, neither of which, on paper at least, were any longer in existence. George Miller was singularly unimpressed with the restructuring. He refused to acknowledge anybody who addressed him as major, and still wore the uniform that the navy had issued him with. The merging of the two services was only a few weeks old, and consequently most of the men under his command had still not traded their accoutrements for the trappings of the RAF. Only personnel who had arrived since the newest branch of the armed forces had been announced sported any of the new kit. The squadron commander expected the stain to spread fairly quickly.

Miller was a navy man and proud of it. He had no intention of hanging up his iconic white cap and replacing it with a grubby imitation. There was a consensus amongst the senior men serving in his squadron that the hard-won identity of the RNAS was being stripped away.

Now he stood by the motor of his recently landed Camel, listening to the various pings, ticks and hisses that it made as it slowly cooled. He tapped his tobacco pipe against the hot engine block. The charred remains of burned residue tumbled out and sprinkled onto the grass. 'Barker, I'm heading off to the crash site in ten minutes. Have a driver ready.'

'I'll see to it.'

'Thank you.'

Miller crooked a finger at his senior man, 'Callaghan, are you coming for a gander?'

It wasn't often that German aircraft were brought down on the British side of the lines, and because the latest action had happened close to their aerodrome, neither man wanted to pass up the opportunity to collect a souvenir or two.

A map was produced and shown to the recently press-ganged driver. Fingers jabbed at map coordinates and a quick course was plotted; they then sat back to enjoy the ride. By the time that the car arrived at the scene of their latest scrap, a section of infantry had been posted to guard against the advances of curious onlookers.

In the last year, German aircrews had never seemed to be able to make up their minds as to whether it was more appropriate to advertise or disguise their existence. Consequently, their machines were decorated on the one hand in camouflaged patterns of mauve, green and brown, and on the other by striking colours meant to be seen from afar. Stark contrasts of light and dark shouted for attention on many aircraft, with stripes, spiralling swirls or checkerboard patterns some of the common themes. Most often encountered were combinations of black and white, though some other colours were almost as popular, most notably red, which together with the black and white of Prussia, inadvertently advertised the flag of Imperial Germany. A few machines also displayed bold statements, with daring slogans written on wings or fuselage in what amounted to three dimensional billboards. What those scrawlings may have meant was lost on Miller. He did not read German.

When the men of the *Luftstreitkräfte* flew in large formations, their sheer variety gave the impression of a random assortment of painted birds all flocking together in a common cause. It was no accident that the English had dubbed them circuses. On the other hand, when a proudly adorned plane went down, its confident sense of menace was put back into perspective. Each German aircraft was a flying machine just like any other – no more, no less - and they were fragile.

The crashed Pfalz that Miller and Callaghan had come to see had left pieces strewn all over creation. Callaghan made an obvious observation, 'He won't have walked away from that prang, I wouldn't think.'

The two officers jumped out of the back seat and went on foot for the last forty yards. The infantrymen met them halfway. Miller picked out the senior man, 'Hello, Sergeant. I've just come over to have a look at my handiwork.'

'I've orders that there's to be no looting.'

'Fair enough, too.' Miller then casually enquired, 'My understanding of the concept is that it pertains to the act of taking items of interest that don't belong to an individual.'

The NCO solemnly inclined his head in agreement.

Miller continued, 'Well, as I've already said, this chap is mine.'

'Sorry, sir, it's the property of His Majesty's government now.'

'My arse.' Without waiting for a response, the indignant airman coolly strolled past the bemused soldier and proceeded on his way to inspect the wreckage. Callaghan kept in step beside him. Both correctly assumed that no-one intended to shoot them for their trespass.

The motionless body of the German pilot dangled upside down in what was left of the smashed cockpit, still suspended in his safety harness. Blood had pooled on the ground directly beneath him, though it was no longer dribbling from his mouth and nose. Miller and Callaghan laboriously unbuckled the corpse and laid it on the grass, then rolled the dead man over onto his back. His pale face was streaked with congealing gore.

Empty eyes stared up at the sky, unseeing. No longer capable of responding to the intensity of the sunlight, the pupils had dilated, which almost obliterated the colour of the iris. There was no blink reflex when a fly walked onto the glazed surface of the eyeball. Miller was unperturbed by the scene, 'This is a first for me.'

'What do you mean?'

'Getting an opportunity to see my handiwork up close; the others have usually gone down on the other side of the lines.'

Miller bent over the German and proceeded to strip off the multiple layers of clothing that had been worn as protection against the cold. He removed the man's gauntlets and saw that there was a wedding band. It wouldn't slide off the stiffening finger at the first attempt so he moved on. Miller unfastened a wristwatch and then patted the man down, searching in each pocket for valuables.

Callaghan witnessed the methodical procedure without batting an eyelid, 'Don't you want to cut off his finger for the ring?'

'No, these infantry chaps can have it if they want it.'

'They're here to guard the body.'

'They haven't done much of a job so far, have they?'

'I suppose not.'

'They'll have it off in no time and blame it on us. Who'll ever know?'

By this time the outer layers had been removed and Miller started searching inside the tunic. Feeling the detail of the torso beneath his probing fingers, he was able to gain further insights into the extent of the fallen man's injuries. The body was sodden where it had been punctured and the chest was misshapen, with the bones of the ribcage now aligned in the wrong places.

'Do you want anything for yourself?'

'Does he carry a pistol?'

'No.'

'Then the watch will be sufficient unless you feel particularly attached to it.'

Miller passed the item over without fuss. Finally he found what he was looking for, 'Here we go.' He extracted a small booklet and read what little German he understood, then slid it into his breast pocket. He nodded amicably at his friend, 'Not a bad haul: one Iron Cross and two medals, plus identity papers and a photo of a widow.'

'How do you know it's a widow?'

'Does he look alive to you?' The metal awards were the usual types: one was the basic pilot's badge, the other was recognition of wounds sustained in action.

Miller motioned to the Tommies that were hovering nearby, 'This chap's name is Siegfried Heidberg. You might want to remember that particular little detail, otherwise the poor beggar's grave will have to be unmarked.' There was every chance that would be the case anyway. Burial with full military honours was a noble concept, but one which was rarely practised.

As an afterthought, Miller bent down and picked up the dead man's gloves which he had earlier discarded, then surveyed the wreckage scattered about, 'One more thing.' He picked his way over towards what was left of the starboard wing and with crude slashes to the fabric covering removed the plain black cross that identified the nationality of the machine. The older style Maltese Cross had recently been superseded, though the reason for doing so was unknown to the Englishmen. *Maybe they did it in anticipation of celebrating the demise of the RNAS.*

Vandalism having thus been satisfactorily completed, Miller waved a casual cheerio to the sergeant, 'It's over to you now, my good man. Have a nice day.'

The two officers briskly walked back to their vehicle and climbed aboard. They were promptly driven away. Miller tossed the leather gloves onto the front seat, 'Here you go, Harry, have these for your troubles. They might come in handy if we haven't taken victory by Christmas.' It was an old joke, Christmas having been promised far too often as the latest date that the war would end.

The enlisted man beamed with pleasure, 'Thanks awfully, sir.' He was mindful not to address the C.O. by his new rank.

*   *   *

'Smoke?'

Callaghan accepted the offer, 'It can't hurt.' He lit up and blew out a perfect smoke ring.

Miller held out the bottle, 'Drink?'

'Thanks.'

'I'd offer you a guinea but your hands seem to be full.'

Callaghan set his glass on the table and crushed the glowing cigarette into an ashtray.

'Too late.'

Callaghan nodded equably, 'In case you were wondering, that's the reason that some of the boys call you The Guinea Pig. Behind your back, of course.'

They reclined at leisure, listening to the drum of the rain on the roof. In all likelihood it would be too wet to fly on the morrow, so they took the opportunity to get plastered. If circumstances changed, well, they wouldn't be the first men to rue a night of bingeing.

Miller gave himself over to introspection. He sat quietly, and Callaghan flopped onto a nearby lounge and left him alone. Both men were feeling the strain of constantly being in action so they had locked themselves away from their subordinates. Ray Barker acted as a formidable buffer to anyone who attempted to intrude on their privacy.

In the last few weeks, the squadron had sustained a higher loss rate than they had been accustomed to. It was a pattern that Miller had seen before and he had the grace to remind himself that even though he had become somewhat hardened to the experience, it didn't make his ambivalence right. When rational thought couldn't solve a problem, there was no harm in resorting to superstition -

naval tradition had an ample supply of those, 'Any sailor will tell you that killing an albatross is bad luck.'

Callaghan had lit another cigarette, 'A canny move, that, by the Hun - naming his aeronautical inventions with the objective of thwarting the evil intentions of our navy fliers.'

Miller grumbled, 'Not that we are anymore – naval, I mean - at least, not strictly speaking.'

'Perhaps that's the reason that they formed the RAF: to un-jinx us. How many do you have?'

'Albatroses? Just the one: a two-seater, C type.'

Callaghan mused, 'It seems that all of the rotten luck was his, then.'

'No, those fellows put down in a field and are living the high life courtesy of His Majesty's prisons.' There was a pause, 'No, the bad luck was with the LVG that I put away that same morning.'

Callaghan squinted through the blue haze that he had exhaled, 'I recall that one, I think.' He, too, had cause to pause, 'It's odd, but I seem to recollect you clobbering him, when mostly I only remember the ones that directly relate to me. And the really bad ones, of course, like The Collision. The others blur a bit, and I blame that on the French for making their wine so readily available.'

Miller continued, not entirely pleased to have been reminded of The Collision. That day had been a low point, 'To say nothing of the men lost since I first arrived here. Whether it's bad luck to kill an albatross or not, Albatroses have certainly killed enough of us. And then there's Knight, who didn't die but probably wished he had.'

'It was almost good night for him, all right.'

Miller wouldn't have tolerated the pun from anyone else, but the man who now led 'A' Flight had been around and he understood. Moreover, he had been there that day; a blood-stained Callaghan had been one of those who had put the shattered man into the attending ambulance. Knight had never been seen whole again.

The various reminiscences left the pair looking red-rimmed into the middle distance, though the solidity of the wall across from them gave lie to the view.

From the outside looking in, a casual observer would have drawn the conclusion that the veterans didn't look after themselves very sensibly. A lot of their established behaviour patterns were inconsistent with common sense. When they were tired they smoked. When they suffered from headaches brought on due to excessive exposure to the fumes of their engines they smoked some more, then drank to compound their misery. Instead of eating, they often fell asleep at the table.

Most of the senior pilots in the squadron had seen more than their fair share of action. Conversely, the newer men were trying to acclimatise to their new existence. The chronic exhaustion that dogged every one of them during periods of increased military activity caused regular lapses in concentration. Often simple instructions were misunderstood, forgotten completely, or simply resulted in aimless wandering until such time that the offender had been given clearer direction. The inability to properly start or complete a task was more or less taken for granted, as long as the failure did not interfere with operational requirements.

Their collective tiredness was on a scale that none of them had considered possible until they had actually experienced it. Men in dire need of a bath had been known to go to bed fully clothed because it was too much effort to remove their boots. Sometimes those seated at the table were often too hammered to hold a fork properly, or too poorly coordinated to navigate food to their mouths - the previous week one of the fellows had been sent to the infirmary because he had accidentally stabbed himself in the cheek. Only when blurred vision prevented them from functioning at all did they generally acknowledge that it was time to get some shuteye. By then, sleep was either instant or maddeningly impossible.

Reliving key elements of the past in a repetitive loop caused some to experience an emotional void. Others suffered from bouts of irritability, or else manifested symptoms of depression. To face the inevitable sameness of tomorrow was daunting enough for those living a mundane existence; when the daily routine included an expectation that friends could be lost – how much worse was that? That some of those losses were caused by avoidable errors of judgement only compounded the issue. That more men didn't die when so many were similarly debilitated was nothing short of miraculous.

Miller marshalled his thoughts, 'I feel bad for him, you know.'

'Stripping him down like that?'

'Huh?'

'The fellow you killed this morning.'

'No, I don't mean him. Richthofen.'

'What about him? He's been dead for over a week. Or is it two? I don't recall.'

'How knackered do you think he was, doing what we do but also being constantly scrutinised for it? What I mean to say is, if we were so preoccupied with him over here, how much more attention would he have copped from his own side?'

'Well, maybe that contributed to finishing him. Serves them right.'

'Or he just ran out of luck.'

'Why do you feel sorry for him?'

'I'd have enjoyed comparing notes with him after the war. Now he'll never get to meet me.'

'How do you know he'd have wanted to?'

'Why wouldn't he? I've got the soul of a Spartan.'

Callaghan snorted, 'Yeah, the Ah-soul.'

Miller made a face, but did not deviate from his train, 'Was he a jolly fellow, I wonder - a man of principle?'

'A chap can shoot straight and not have principles. Neither is necessarily related to the other. Look at Grace, by way of illustration.'

'Who?'

'William Gilbert.'

'I don't remember him. Was he one of ours?'

'The cricketer.'

'Oh, him. I'd forgotten we used to have pastimes.'

'The man could hit a ball with a stick pretty effectively, but he was still a scoundrel, by all accounts.' Callaghan didn't believe in starting a new paragraph for a new topic. He was thinking again of the dead Pfalz pilot, 'I regret not taking his boots, in hindsight.'

'They were ruined. A bullet took off one of the heels.'

'That would have added value to them, in the circumstances.'

'Too late now, I should say. He'll have been buried in them.'

Chapter 24

May 1918: Hot Air

Lehmann greeted the assembled members of the *staffel* in their lounge, 'Good news, men. We are trading in the winged ammo crates made by Albatros Works for the new Fokker that was tested during the winter trials at Adlershof. Conversion training starts in two days' time. We'll be leaving tomorrow.' He paused, 'Time for one last mission. I need two volunteers for burning a kite balloon at first light.'

The pilots looked askance at one another, avoiding eye contact; everyone except for Rossler, who just stared ahead at nothing. There was a good chance of being killed in an attack on a balloon. They were always heavily defended by artillery and machine guns, with each weapon ranged in to the altitude that the *Jasta* pilots would need to fly in order to make the attack. Due to the transfer order, anyone not on the mission was guaranteed to survive for a few more weeks, barring accidents. No-one wanted to die, but refusing to volunteer was an acknowledgement that you were prepared to sacrifice one of your comrades.

Lehmann immediately realised that he had made an error in revealing the two orders together, but there was no going back. There would be no volunteers for this one. He was sure of it.

Two hands were raised. Both were new pilots without experience. Lehmann waved them away. They were crestfallen, knowing that their first taste of action was now to be delayed until after they learned to fly the new machines. Rossler gave up the pretence of looking into space. A few facial muscles configured differently, and now his face showed disgust, 'I'll do it.'

'No you won't. Your Military Merit Cross has been approved and I'd like to see you wear it at least once.'

The veteran NCO shrugged. He had felt the same way about it. No longer in danger of being slated for the mission, he looked about, curious to see who was going to draw the wrong straw. There were no takers.

Lehmann made up his mind, intent on putting an end to the charade, 'Kluth, you will fly with me tomorrow.' Kluth didn't like it, but there was little he could say when Lehmann had said he would go as well. Lehmann was already regretting his decision. *And this is what it means to lead.*

Rossler had to shove his oar in, 'I thought you said you wanted to see me at the awards presentation, *Herr Oberleutnant?*'

Lehmann gave him a hard look.

He went to bed early that night, but sleep eluded him.

Lehmann and Kluth were dressed for the cold of the pre-dawn air. Their ground crews were the only other men about. Those not on the mission would sleep as long as they were permitted. Lehmann didn't want to be on the flight. He was up to his eyeballs in paperwork. He knew Kluth didn't want to be here either, but other than that he was too fond of his own skin the younger man had no reason to be anywhere else.

'Stay on my wing, do as I do. Maintain speed and separation and don't fire until I do. Try not to get killed.' The words were not required in any case as Kluth was one of the four best pilots in the *Jasta*. They climbed aboard their respective machines.

Lehmann pressed the starter switch and his engine roared to life. *That will wake up the cowardly bastards*. The thought lightened his surliness. He looked towards Kluth who was positioned not far away on his right wing. The other Albatros had also fired up. Lehmann couldn't hear a thing over the bellowing Mercedes, so he waved a hand at the fellow. Higher rank, bravery awards: none of it counted for much when you flew these missions. Mostly a flier knew that on any given patrol he could run across hostiles, but these scripted jaunts were the worst. A man knew in advance precisely what he was in for - other than the end result. The bullet with your name on it: who knew when it was made or where it currently resided? It may have not even left the factory floor yet.

The chocks were pulled away from wheels and the ancient Albatros DVs trundled forwards. An increase in throttle saw the ground speed increase across the grassy airfield, up-scaled bicycle wheels bumping over clumps and tufts of grass as they kept that massive windmilling propeller from smashing itself to bits on the turf. Lehmann left the ground only marginally before his wingman. Once airborne the ride suddenly became a lot smoother.

Lehmann took his bearings and set a course for the waiting balloon. Kluth trailed in his wake.

The sky was decorated in streaks of pink and orange, and layers of mist nestled between the treetops not very far beneath. The plan was for both aircraft to hug the ground for as long as possible. This would mask their approach and hopefully make it more difficult for any French or English fliers out and about to see them in the fog.

They'd be harder to spot at this height as well. When there is only the open sky as a backdrop, aircraft are easier to notice; dots become blobs that then take form at an alarming speed. After that, the shooting begins. Lehmann wanted to avoid that part of the show if it was at all humanly possible. Ground fire on its own was bad enough to endure.

The two men followed the natural contours of the land as far as practicable while trying to balance the need to remain undetected with their desire to get the job done as quickly as possible. Before long, they spied the bulk of the dirigible in the distance. Lehmann narrowed his eyes in grim anticipation. It floated there, plump as a fresh cow pat, inviting someone to put a foot wrong and have their day ruined.

There was no time for subtlety. Sooner or later they had to reveal themselves. Better to get it over and done with and then return home for breakfast. The pair opened their throttles and bored straight in.

The thing was huge. Massive. Ominous. They always were. Lehmann couldn't help but be intimidated by the sight. He always was. He noticed that the ring of guns sited on the ground around the base of the balloon had started shooting. Muzzle flashes were quickly obscured by the smoky haze of burnt cordite. Small-arms ammunition zipped and buzzed past him. He could almost feel their need to bite him, and he clenched his teeth and sphincter in awful anticipation. Anti-aircraft artillery exploded in close proximity, leaving filthy smudges of decaying smoke hanging in the air before it slowly dissipated. Its acrid smell burnt his nostrils. He was drenched in the sweat of terror.

Pull the cocking lever. Sight down the barrel. Press the trigger. Short bursts only. 7.92 mm ammunition flew across the rapidly decreasing distance, piercing and passing through the bloated bag, allowing hydrogen to escape and mix with the oxygen in the outside air. When the mingled gases reached the right proportions, the whole concoction would ignite from the heat of the hot lead being shot into it. And the balloon would be destroyed.

A simple process in theory; in practice it was somewhat trickier. The gasbag was huge – it needed a lot of ventilation before it would burn. That meant a lot of bullets. Short bursts of fire prevented the machine guns from jamming, but it also meant that fewer rounds were being sent down range. Also, it was tempting to close the distance as quickly as possible and then get the hell out of town. The faster the aircraft, the harder it was to hit for those manning the ground defences. A pilot's chances of living to fight another day increased, but his increased closing speed meant that he had less time to shoot holes into the priority target.

If you got it wrong and survived to tell the tale, there was every possibility that the balloon would remain operational: somewhat perforated, but essentially intact. You'd need to run the gauntlet again, or condemn another man to the task. So you did it right the first time.

The gunfire didn't let up. Lehmann's ears were ringing from the proximity of the concussive detonations. He could see the morning sunlight peeping through countless holes in his wings, and he had also heard the distinct sounds of splinters being ripped out of the plywood construction of the fuselage. A tension wire pinged as it was severed. He shut down the stampede that was starting in his mind and concentrated on keeping a steady rhythm of fire aimed at the kite balloon. Short bursts. Short bursts.

The balloon loomed in front of him, growing before his eyes like some primeval swamp monster rousing itself for a meal. A small basket roughly the size of a bath-tub hung tethered beneath it. The two men inside were making final adjustments to their static lines before they leaped into space and prayed for deliverance whilst dangling below their mushrooming parachutes. They had not been prepared for the speed of the attack, and were doing their best to make up for lost time. The first man jumped, hoping to be able to steer his way clear of the burning mass if and when it began to follow him into hell. The second man was not so fast. Lehmann watched as he seemed to stagger, then in slow motion toppled from his perch. Arms and legs pin-wheeled as he dropped like a stone.

Lehmann watched the falling manikin out of the corner of his eye as he ceased shooting. He steered his machine in a graceful arc around the bulk of the blimp and hurtled past. For the first time he looked for Kluth. The second Albatros was glued to his tail, just wide enough to have had its own clear shot at the target. Lehmann looked to his rear. There was no monstrous bonfire glowing in the sky. The dwindling kite balloon was being winched down to safety as the gunners on the ground were no doubt preparing for the German pilots to come around again and press home their attack.

It would have been suicide. Lehmann and Kluth put their machines as close to the ground as they dared and fled for home. Breakfast was not in their thoughts at all.

Lehmann removed his headgear and made his way in silence to the debriefing room. Kluth trudged beside him. There was a cluster of men waiting for them. One of the replacement pilots couldn't contain himself, 'Did you get it, *Herr Oberleutnant?*' The answer was a stony silence. Rossler told him to shut up. Nobody told Rossler he couldn't talk to an officer that way.

Lehmann looked at Kluth and spoke to him for the first time since they had landed, 'Did you see it?'

Kluth roused from his lethargy, 'The observer? He was hit, I think. Quite a sight.' He clammed up again.

Lehmann elaborated, 'We didn't burn the kite, but it was damaged and one of the observers was killed. It was why we didn't finish it off – and it won't be repaired before we head out, so no-one else is going after it again today.'

He directed his next words to the adjutant, 'Falkenhoff, get things finalised in preparation to leave. I'll be in my office.' He stumped away.

Rossler put an arm around Kluth's shoulders, 'Let's get a drink into you, my immortal friend. Then some hot food.' They headed in the direction of the bar.

'They didn't get it, then?' Clearly, the question was aimed by one stupid novice at another.

An hour later Lehmann's grimed and greasy crew chief sought out his boss, 'The damage is mostly superficial but quite extensive. Nothing that can't be fixed, but it will take time. Why even bother when you won't be needing it again?'

'Are you trying to make this someone else's problem, Schilling?'

'No-one in this *staffel*.' He made it sound like a virtue.

Lehmann hardly cared himself, 'If you can't repair it before noon, leave it alone. I'll take someone else's machine and he can drive out with the staff.'

'I'll see what can be done.'

'If the seeing means that I catch you playing *skat* you'll quickly find my boot in your arse.'

'I'll try to be discreet then, *Herr Oberleutnant*.'

'You cheeky bastard.' Lehmann was always hard to read. It was impossible to tell if there was a twinkle in his eye; one's attention was always diverted to the rest of his sour face, and by the time his eyes drew a second glance, they were devoid of any humour.

*   *   *

Fenton had been a book binder in civilian life until someone in the military had the bright idea that such an occupation would translate nicely into learning to become a rigger. The notion had worked. The wee gnome-like man knew what it meant to appreciate methodical processes. What he could not tolerate was shoddy workmanship and short cuts.

Imagine then his dismay at learning that the latest addition to the squadron was a man who epitomised everything that Fenton loathed. Worse yet, the newcomer was popular in ways that a dusty book binder could never be. The new man had somehow insinuated himself into every nefarious activity that could be found. He had already proven himself to be a decent scrounger, and in all probability had other less worthy attributes. The middle-aged rigger had a very good notion of why William Bowe had been moved on from his previous address.

Besides his everyday duties Fenton had modest literary aspirations, although he acknowledged that he lacked the proper intellect required to write a work of any real substance. Yet, as many people have done, he kept a small journal in which he periodically jotted notes to himself. Given that Mister Bowe was here to stay, Fenton resolved that he may as well make the most of a bad situation and decided to compile a detailed study of the man - the better to form the basis for a fictional blackguard. If he ever succeeded in writing a book, it would surely be an easier endeavour if there were copious notes to reference.

Whenever Fenton inked his fountain pen, it was attending to the smaller details that provided him with the most joy. A simple turn of phrase or a judiciously placed adjective were the things that the wordsmith derived the most pride from - details that he knew would in all likelihood be glossed over by the main part of his future readership and appreciated by too few. Yet it was these few that the writer was appealing to, even though he never anticipated actually meeting them, or learning the least thing about them as individuals.

Fenton reflected on the last thought. Every day he witnessed men flying off to do battle. From time to time one or two failed to return. These men also performed to a faceless audience: namely, German fliers. Neither party ever conversed with one another unless the exchange of gunfire could be interpreted as a hostile form of Morse code: dot-dot-dot-dot-dashed-hopes.

As the rigger mused over the anonymous nature of human interaction, the approaching drone of aero engines told that the morning patrol was returning. Shielding his eyes, Fenton counted them in. This time, there were none missing. If Callaghan's flight had nothing to report, so much the better; there would be less work for the ground crews.

With the Camels safely home, the pilots' morning duty was fulfilled so they headed off to occupy themselves with their various habitual restorative therapies. A few hung back to discuss the quirks of their aircraft with the men who mattered. With the flying done for the time being, it had become the turn of the maintenance crews.

Men swarmed over the machines like ants devouring an insect. They were methodical, not stopping until they were satisfied that no problem was left unresolved. The war relied upon their efforts. Lives depended on them, also.

It was an endless procedure. Through sheer volume of repetition, each day's work had become streamlined. Though new problems constantly popped up, the ingenuity shown by the men charged with keeping the show on the road was nothing short of inspirational. Some engines were stripped down and reassembled; others were given only a cursory examination because they had not long ago been given the full treatment. Cables, spars, fuel lines: if it could possibly have been damaged it was inspected. If a part could not be replaced - and this was the rule rather than the exception - it was repaired. It was not unheard of for oil lamps to be burning late into the night.

Fenton had once again become fully immersed in his assigned task. Every wire on the airframe existed for a reason. If any were too tight or too loose, the whole structure would be pulled out of square and the balance of the machine would be affected. Then - funny things could happen. In such a circumstance the pilot in question, if he got back home alive, would be posing some very interesting questions.

Finally satisfied that he had done a thorough job of inspection, Fenton sat on his customary empty oil drum and lit up a cigarette. Out of the corner of his eye, he watched Bowe. The slimy new fellow sidled over towards him and the rigger did his best to hide his annoyance at the intrusion. *Think of it as an opportunity to study the details of his character and mannerisms.* 'Hello, William.'

'Bill to my friends.'

That's what I meant.

'Charlie Turner says you have your letters.' Fenton raised an eyebrow at Turner, who answered with a shrug that may or may not have passed for an apology.

Fenton deliberately twisted the words, 'Yes, the mail came in yesterday.'

Bowe seemed to accept the misunderstanding at face value, 'You write poems and such.'

'The collective interest in my affairs is somewhat surprising, given the general lack of curiosity until now.'

'Maybe we could compare notes?'

'Compare… notes?'

Bowe gave Fenton a friendly pat on the shoulder, 'Perhaps our interests coincide? Have a think about it.' Without further elaboration, he was on his way.

Fenton looked at Turner, 'What was that about?'

'I've heard he's handy at a lot of things. Take your pick.'

'I'm quite sure he'll get along quite nicely without my services.'

'Well, he said to take time to mull it over before you decide anything.'

'There's nothing to discuss. A man should never do a deal with the Devil.'

'I don't understand?'

'It's a contraction of 'not ever'. N'ever. The apostrophe has fallen from common usage.'

Fenton tried to dismiss Bowe from his mind. *The man is a devious worm - and don't forget to write it down.* It was as easy as forgetting maggots in stew. At that point one of the others trotted out a little ditty:

> 'Of all of the Huns that have flown,
> Richthofen's name is the most overblown,
> But the guns of Roy Brown,
> Shot the Red Baron down,
> On his grave scarlet poppies have grown.'

Turner nodded towards where Bowe had last been seen, 'He was singing that little gem on the way back from the latrine this morning. Said he made it up himself.'

'A bare-faced lie, if I am any judge of worth.'

'You either like the poem or you dislike the man?'

'Correct.'

Fenton had listened to the rhyme without enthusiasm. The form appealed only to the basest elements in the social fabric, and for that reason alone he turned up his nose. Certainly some thought had been put into the construction of the verse, as evidenced by the reference to the species of flowers that were the first to pop up in these climes whenever the soil was freshly turned. That these days the earth was dug up more regularly by gunfire than the plough made no difference to the plant. Belatedly, he noticed that the wording would have looked visually appealing if it was in print for, though they had a different accent, the end of each line would have looked similar to every other.

The book-binder-turned-rigger doubted that William Bowe possessed even the miniscule degree of skill needed to construct puerile verse of such crude subtlety. Almost idly, he decided to check with his mess mates to see if anyone had noticed the structure of the composition, 'That particular rhyme appears to have been assembled with more care than the usual run of the mill I've come to expect.'

Turner could hardly believe his own ears, 'You like it? That's a first. You've always said that the art of writing poetry was dead and that no true bard could claim worthiness until his work had first proven itself by enduring for a hundred years.'

'I stand by the statement, though I must profess surprise that you listened.'

'You just said that you liked it.'

'I said it was interesting. It's not the same thing.'

Nobby had a tangential observation, 'The Australians are claiming it was one of their own did it.'

Turner had no idea what the man was talking about, 'Did what?'

'Did for the Baron, is what. Ground fire.'

'No surprise. To listen to them, they're winning the bloody war single-handed.'

'I'll make a wager that the Americans will be worse if they ever decide to pull their finger out and take their place in the line. They've been here long enough now that they'll have already sired brats on the teat.'

'You're probably right. Kaiser Bill will throw in the towel a month after the Yanks fire their first shot, and that will be the reason the war is won - in their minds, anyway.'

Bowe's meagre contribution to the arts had been forgotten. The men went back to their work routines, arguing over other unimportant matters and as usual Fenton was not moved to participate, 'What will they call this war, I wonder, when it is done?'

'The Machine Gun War.'

'I'd go with that.'

'What about The War. That says it all - the scale and finality of it.'

'That's what everyone calls their own war.'

'The Big War.'

'That sounds stupid. It needs to have a grander name.'

'The Biggest War?'

'For Christ's sake, that's more applicable to Custer, if you know your American history.'

'Huh?'

'Little. Big. Horn.'

'Big horn? I don't understand.'

'Why not ask one of them to show you?'

Fenton decided that he had put up with the incessant nattering for long enough, and decided to shut everybody up with a reference beyond their understanding, 'What about The Icarus War?'

Turner frowned, 'Who?'

Nobby blinked, 'What?'

Fenton was hard pressed to keep the condescension from his voice, 'The Greek who invented wings held together with wax and then flew too close to the sun.'

Nobby immediately saw the flaw in the design, 'Well that's pretty stupid. They'd just melt.'

'They did.'

'See?'

Turner spluttered, 'Pfft! Don't listen to him, Nobby. He's just a poet, and that particular breed are no good for much at all. None of his poems even rhyme.'

'He can't be much of a poet if he can't write a rhyme. It's not a poem if it doesn't rhyme.'

Fenton felt as though he could have had a more stimulating conversation with farm animals, 'Not that hoary old chestnut again...'

Nobby lacked the range of vocabulary available to his fellows, 'What do whores have to do with it?'

With Fenton opting out of the discussion, it was left to Turner to carry the flag, 'There are only three ways to make a name for yourself in this war: win a flipping Victoria Cross for killing the blokes on the other side, being a general who gets his own blokes killed, or writing poems about blokes getting killed.'

'Or being a pilot, fighting heroically above the trenches. Like Albert Ball.'

'He got the Victoria Cross.'

'And he got killed.'

'That's how you usually win the VC.'

'There must be a better way to get one.'

'There is - inheritance. His mum gets to keep it on the mantelpiece.'

'I'm not too sure that Missus Ball thinks it's better.'

Fenton reintroduced himself with a final comment, 'I don't think it's called inheritance if possessions are passed to an older generation.'

'What do you call it, then?'

'Unnatural.' And he left it at that.

Turner scowled, 'Ah, they deserve it.'

Nobby was still wondering about Ball's family, 'Who?'

'The old bastards. Who do you think it was that started the war in the first place? Let them lose their sons as a lesson.'

'But I'm one of those sons!'

'Hardly. You don't fly, and you're not in the infantry. Or the navy.'

'Have a heart, I can still get a bomb dropped on me!'

'So can Londoners. It doesn't count.'

*   *   *

Unsurprisingly, Beerenbrock had not received the Red Eagle, nor a Blue Max. Instead, although he had received a lesser decoration, a party was thrown to honour him. It seemed the appropriate thing to do in the circumstances.

Now that the function's official purpose had been fulfilled, the magnificent ballroom setting that had been set aside became central to the gathering of some the most powerful men in Germany. The décor was stunning and so were the women - resplendent or exquisite - depending on personal taste. If there were food shortages in Germany, no one would have known it by the fare that had been presented. With a few exceptions, if a soldier was not highly decorated he wasn't welcome in this august company. Everything spoke of opulence, from the silverware to the fabric of the curtains.

Von Bülow wore his cast as if it was a badge of honour. He nodded politely to his cousin Karl, 'How are things with you?'

'Life goes on, Sebastian.' In truth, they had nothing to say to each other. The fact they had never been friends as children hardly meant that they needed to come to blows at a formal gathering of their peers. They were grown men now, hardened by war and less prone to the trivialities of the world. At least, that was what they would have had others believe. In truth, some of their shared past was far from trivial.

Max Beerenbrock saw the two standing together and made directly for them, 'Hail, Sebastian, well met!'

Von Bülow turned to see who had greeted him in such a familiarly offensive manner. His response was underwhelming, 'Oh. Hello, Beerenbrock. This is my cousin, Karl.'

'We know one another already. Pfalz pilots don't make many friends. Everyone thinks our days are numbered and they avoid us, so we drink together.'

Von Bülow felt cornered. He had never been friends with Beerenbrock. Having him transferred out of the *Jasta* last year was no accident, and he did not regret it. It seemed that the world was conspiring to make this occasion as awkward as possible. He could scarcely have missed the commotion that Beerenbrock had recently caused, though he underplayed his part, 'You have collected the Hohenzollern since we last met. Congratulations.'

Beerenbrock grinned back at him, 'You as well, I see. A happy coincidence. But I didn't see your face at the presentation. Where were you?'

'I was taking a shit.'

Beerenbrock knew that von Bülow would not have been here voluntarily and he intended to make the most of the occasion, 'The funny thing is that I had to shoot down fists full of Spads for mine, but I heard all you needed to do was break your arm.'

Sebastian could see that Karl clearly found the remark amusing, from the supercilious look on his cousin's smug face, but he said nothing. *He was never one to fight his own battles. Some things never change.* The spiteful thought failed to acknowledge that Karl von Bülow was now himself a leader of men.

For his part, Beerenbrock was only getting started, 'Normally a man gets the wound badge when he is injured in combat. I suppose that would mean taking a bullet? A broken arm, though? I don't think that you should be permitted to wear a wound badge if you hurt yourself falling over.'

The Pfalz pilots enjoyed watching the injured man squirm. Too often had they endured his endless noise. He wasn't saying much now. They excluded him from their conversation.

Karl was curious about Beerenbrock's feat, but wasn't going to ask him directly. That would have been tactless, 'How are your boys dealing with their fame?'

Beerenbrock grimaced, 'Their fame?' He paused, 'I know what you mean, though. Two days ago Wesser shot a Frenchman through the head. The plane kept a true course so he left it to fly on until it ran out of fuel. No-one saw what happened to it after that but someone will have seen it crash. Wesser could have had an easy victory but he'd had enough attention recently. He told me that he was satisfied just in knowing what he had done.'

He was about to say more but Sebastian interrupted, unimpressed as usual, 'It's just a story if there are no witnesses and no wreckage. He probably made it up.' If he had meant to irritate Beerenbrock he succeeded.

An older man chose that moment to join their growing group, 'Karl and Sebastian, I see you are getting re-acquainted.'

They responded in unison, 'Hello, Uncle.'

Karl indicated Beerenbrock, 'General von Bülow, this is *Leutnant* Beerenbrock.'

The general extended his hand, 'Yes. Congratulations.'

Beerenbrock accepted the proffered hand. He would have been an idiot not to, 'Thank you, *Herr General.*'

'How is your arm, Sebastian?'

'It is mending, Uncle.'

Beerenbrock decided to make the most of meeting a general, 'A shame about Richthofen. Has his successor been decided upon yet?'

'Willi Reinhardt, I believe. Do any of you know him?'

None of them had heard of the man. Karl offered his opinion, 'It will be hard to replace a pilot of Richthofen's stature. Eighty victories - that's a lot. Voss and Boelcke are the only others to have scored forty, and they're both dead.'

Beerenbrock shrugged, 'An opportunity to step up for someone. Any takers?'

'What about his brother? He's near the top of the list.'

'Lothar's a better option than most of the others. At least the rest of us are used to someone called Richthofen leading the pack.'

The general listened absently to the predictable interplay, until he wondered why his other nephew was quiet, 'What do you think, Sebastian?'

'I think Richthofen is irreplaceable. We haven't had another flier like him. He would have had a hundred before much longer; that's a record that will never be attained now that he is gone. I think there is a bigger problem, though.' Karl groaned inwardly, divining the course of the next few minutes.

But the general said, 'Go on…' and the die was cast.

'Since the introduction of the Fokker Triplane we have steadily lost our best fliers. I fail to understand how men of their calibre would all run out of luck almost as soon as they convert onto the type. Bongartz is another recent casualty.'

Karl disagreed with his cousin, 'Nonsense. Richthofen bagged twenty or so flying the *Dreidecker*, and that's after his head wound slowed him down. I suppose you want to blame that injury on the Albatros?'

'The Albatros is by far our most numerous machine. Of course people are going to be killed or injured flying it.'

'People are going to get killed flying every type that goes into service. Perhaps the problem is that it's too good? Overconfidence has always been a killer.'

'But our best fliers within such a short time frame? No. The thing is a death trap. The process is too predictable: win the Blue Max, get a Triplane, then death.'

Beerenbrock had seen von Bülow's powers of reasoning in action before, but it never ceased to astonish him that the man would speak them out loud.

The general was taken aback, 'Are you suggesting that the Fokker Dr I be withdrawn? There was an inquiry, as you are no doubt aware, and the problems have been rectified. What else is there to do? It's a good machine and in any case the DVII is due to replace it.'

'I'm suggesting that anyone with eyes in their head can see what is before them, and everyone else is clearly supporting Anthony Fokker in his quest to be the primary aircraft manufacturer in Germany for the rest of this year at least. He must be making a fortune too, the greedy Dutch bastard.'

'But everyone who has flown his new designs have praised them. What would you have us do? Ignore the expert recommendations of our test pilots?'

Sebastian cast his mind back to the previous year, 'It wouldn't be the first time.'

'I would remind you that Richthofen himself was one of the main supporters of the DVII project. You haven't even flown it.'

'I don't mind the Albatros. At least it is proven. But if you have to throw it out and strap me into something new, at least make it German. What about the new Siemens-Schuckert?'

'It has reliability issues.'

'That hasn't stopped the Triplane.'

'There are no issues with it!'

'Ask Richthofen how he feels about that.'

'It's common knowledge that he liked it. 'Climbs like a monkey'; those were his exact words!' A vein was beginning to pulse in the general's neck. Karl knew the sign but Sebastian was ignoring it. *As usual.*

'Monkeys are for circuses.' No pun was intended. Only the English called JG I the Flying Circus.

Everyone could see that this was going to become a heated discussion between Sebastian and his uncle. Karl tried to prevent it from becoming ugly, or worse, public. 'Shall I summon a waiter for drinks, anyone?'

Sebastian waved him away, disgusted by the oily intention, 'I'll get them.'

The general turned to Karl and Beerenbrock, 'Excuse me also, gentlemen.' He headed in the direction of a group of older officers. He walked erect, back ramrod straight with dignity and authority, and no small degree of indignation.

Beerenbrock watched the younger von Bülow's retreating back and turned to Karl, 'Is it always this lively when the von Bülow family gets together?'

'Only if Sebastian is on the guest list. The rest of us are fairly dull.'

'He makes some interesting connections. I've seen it before.'

'My dear Beerenbrock, we've all seen it before. The only connection he never makes is between his brain and his tongue.'

'Fancy pillorying Anthony Fokker like that? If he hates the Triplane so much, what chance do you or I have of convincing him of the merits of the Pfalz?'

'To what end? Even if we won him over, we'd only be rewarded by having him sent to our unit. Who'd willingly choose to fly with him? Getting assigned is bad enough.'

'What are you talking about? You've never had to fly with him. I have.'

'Then you have a small idea of what it was like to grow up with him - the blown-up goat.'

'He'd prefer being called an elephant, I would think.'

Karl grimaced at the reference, 'Of course he'd be telling that one to anyone who'll listen.'

'Usually he inserts it somewhere into an unrelated conversation. Did you know he has a name for his victory stick? The Tusk.'

'My God! There's no limit, is there?'

'If Hindenberg would surrender it, I'd wager marks to a pfennig that Sebastian would use the Field Marshal's baton.'

'Don't suggest it to him; he'd probably have the nerve to ask the man.'

'Then why not suggest it? What would it be worth to see the look on Hindenberg's face?'

'You would see a respected family humbled, Beerenbrock?'

'I believe the word you are looking for is 'humiliated'.' He raised his glass, *'Prost!'*

*   *   *

The hospital had become a very familiar place over the last few months. Mary did her rounds as hundreds of patients slept through the night. There were others who lay awake and even a few who were neither asleep nor awake but lay inert in an unconscious state. Some of the men would be patched up and sent back to the war; others had been wounded badly enough that they would be medically discharged from the army; a handful would die of their wounds over the next few hours, days, weeks or months.

Mary had never properly conformed to the broader scheme of things before she had become a registered nurse. Most of her interests were deemed unsuitable for a young woman. Men tended to shy away from her because they were uncomfortable with her intelligence. She loved the exploration of truth, and scientific journals were one of her principle reasons for being. It had never helped matters that this was invariably combined with a willingness to express her views to all and sundry.

The war had changed everything. Where once she had not suffered fools, now Mary saw individuals whom she would have once considered fools suffering every day. Her perspective had radically altered, and she no longer considered them fools so much as injured human beings who needed gentle hands to aid in their mending.

One of those to whom she would have once turned her nose up was sleeping through the night, assisted by enough morphine to keep his agony at bay. His name was written on a clipboard at the foot of his bed: Knight, E.P. The E stood for Edward, but his friends all called him Ned. To Mary, Edward sounded nicer.

Many soldiers married the nurses who cared for them, but as a rule Mary had never conformed to unwritten mores. Though she had been a nurse on the day she had wed, her husband had not been one of her former patients. He had been hale, larger than life, unbroken. He had been fun. He had been carefree. He had been whole. All of those things had mattered a great deal to Mary and she had never understood why her friends went gooey over cripples.

Now Mary had a new circle of friends. She had transferred here to be near Edward. His wounds had been extensive. The doctors had said that to move him would probably be the end of him. Mary Knight now understood love for a broken man, but she still failed to understand why some women chose invalids over their able-bodied brethren. Only two reasons made any sense: the first was that the man they loved was not a shadow of whom she had once known; he had not been lessened and no memories were stored away of better times. The second reason was more brutally practical: a soldier discharged from the army wasn't going to break hearts by getting himself killed in action. The wounds he bore were likely to be his last, so the foundations of any new relationship had a greater chance to take root and grow.

The girl who had often professed to be a devotee to scientific study had been drawn to a man whose pilot training defied thousands of years of accepted doctrine. Unfortunately, Isaac Newton had enjoyed the last word. Edward Knight's injuries had been sustained in an horrific crash - the direct result of a heavier-than-air object being punished by the forces of gravity for daring to take wing. For thousands of years, nobody had ever believed that camels would ever fly. In nineteen-seventeen someone had defied the convention, and Knight had paid the price.

Mary had stopped sitting by her husband's side as he slept. She had heard too many things said aloud in his sleep, which he refused to discuss when questioned upon wakening. It wasn't that she felt excluded, or lied to. Rather, it was simply a realisation that there was nothing at all that she could do to help him. If she couldn't know his problems, she wanted to spare herself the details. Maybe it was selfish, or maybe it was just a way to preserve as much of her identity as she could hold onto. She had stopped berating herself for it.

Edward was just one of the patients that the young nurse checked on as she did her rounds. One of the other patients was awake, and as she walked past his bed he called out to her, 'Ma'am?' They all knew that she was married, but the honorific made her feel old.

'Hello, Simon, can't sleep?'

'Can I have another shot?'

'I'm sorry, nothing more until the morning.'

He lay in the darkness looking up at her face, 'Am I dying?' His face didn't seem too concerned about the possibility.

Mary didn't like lying, and in truth the man could yet pull through, 'It's only been a few days. Give yourself a chance.'

'I missed the sign.'

Mary looked at him quizzically, not knowing if he was rambling. He elaborated, 'Looking back, I saw that my friends were about to be killed but I didn't recognise the signs until it was too late.'

She nodded, 'Everybody does that from time to time. Hindsight is the least valuable of all of the senses.'

'I have an aunt who could see the future, but claimed fortune tellers were charlatans.'

The nursing profession had shown Mary too many things that could not be rationalised. Living with the suffering of others on a daily basis gave an entirely different alternative to her earlier theoretical perspectives. It was almost as though her entire youth had been spent trying to become some weird sort of scientific nun. The path she had trodden had lacked substance, and consequently she had never felt at ease. But as she had just told Simon, hindsight was rarely friendly.

Given that only the elderly had the years to acquire enough information to make valid comparisons, Mary was beginning to see people's need for religion and felt that trusting in the scriptures seemed to be the easier approach. *Maybe understanding can only be granted upon meeting Saint Peter.*

On cue, the wounded soldier asked the inevitable, 'Do you believe in God? Is there an afterlife?'

She took his hand in her own. It felt clammy, 'Do you?'

'It hardly matters, does it? If there is, I'll be reunited with the dead soon enough. If there's nothing at all, at least it's not as bad as where we are right now - living in the shadow of death - with the imminent loss of our remaining friends looming large.'

'There are always new friends to be had.' Mary sat with him awhile. Eventually the demolished man drifted off to sleep.

She rose to her feet and ghosted through the ward, seeing that every patient was made as comfortable as she was able until her shift ended.

Chapter 25

June 1918: New Faces

George Miller was a man who was at one with his aircraft. He was not a passenger in an unfamiliar piece of gadgetry, but rather an integral part of it. Without the combination of man and machine, there would have been no such thing as aerial warfare in the twentieth century. Technology was no use without an intimate understanding of the nature of the beast. Miller was unlike most of his peers; he understood the significance of odd vibrations and unusual engine noises without having to pore through manuals, or listen to stories relayed by men who had miraculously survived the foibles and vices of their aircraft. When his machine didn't respond in the way that he knew it should he could swiftly identify most problems. This ability was instinctive to a degree, or at least if not instinctive it was nevertheless a skill that most pilots would never be able to acquire past a certain point.

Throughout the history of mankind, some men have been born with an unusual understanding of foreign concepts, and this particular attribute of Miller's was viewed as unique within the environs of his squadron. In another era, he may well have been burned at the stake for his arcane knowledge, but then the same would have been true of every airman and engineer. For that matter, it could have applied to every man who understood gunpowder weapons. The consciousness of the world was being catapulted into the modern era, and as had happened so many times in the past, it was accelerated through military exigency.

Miller's success was not because he knew guns, but because he knew how to extract the optimal performance from his aircraft. Though it was true that he could shoot straight, it was his intimate knowledge of the Sopwith Camel that gave him extra time to make the correct choices when he went into battle. When much of what he needed to know was relayed to him through sound and sensation, he had much more time to use his eyes for what was happening around him. His mind processed vast amounts of data in split seconds, and his reflexes took care of the rest.

To achieve so easily what others struggle to understand is something that often leads to one's successes being taken for granted. His closest friends saw glimpses of this in Miller's dealings with others, and it was most noticeable when he was introduced to novices. Two new men had been assigned to 'A' Flight after a dogfight had gone wrong over Houthulst Forest. They now stood before their formidable leader.

Miller gave them the once over after they had been introduced to him by the adjutant. They looked excited to be here, but enthusiasm was no substitute for experience. The more he saw of men like these, the more it irritated the human being that lay chained and bound in Miller's mind - locked away until such time as its release was warranted. There was still a shooting war to finalise and parole for his conscience was not being considered. 'How many hours do you have flying solo? Nine? Ten?'

They nodded an affirmative in unison, 'Yes, sir.'

'Camels?'

One of them seemed unsure how to answer, which was marginally better than the awkward silence of the other, 'A couple of afternoons of circuits, plus take-offs and landings.'

The other replacement thought that perhaps it would be prudent to contribute something, 'We got some time in at the depot while we waited for our posting. Some machines were ferried in.'

Miller was unimpressed, 'Were they, now?'

They awaited his verdict.

'You know the Camel has quite a reputation for killing men not used to flying it?'

'Yes, sir.'

'The rotary engine, a blessing and a curse, all rolled into one.' The torque of the spinning motor made the Camel pull very sharply when diving to the right. In combat, this was useful as an evasive manoeuvre except, of course, that the Germans were not fools and were more easily able to stay with their man because they didn't have to anticipate a violent turn the other way. Though it was true that the Camel could also pull a decent left-hand turn when climbing – again, because of the engine torque - diving was the more usual defensive response to an attack. In other forms of flying not related to combat, the violent tendencies of the machine still often caused fatalities. In fact, accidents were as likely to be the cause of death amongst Camel pilots as was enemy action.

Miller wondered if there was any way to make the boys understand, 'Did anyone get killed on your course?'

'No, sir.' It was unusual, and Miller doubted that it properly prepared these young men for the reality.

'It's called a Camel because it bucks you off.'

'I thought that was horses, sir?'

Miller was surprised that the fellow dared to speak so flippantly to a man who, to all intents and purposes, was the ultimate authority in his life for the next six months – if he lasted as long. But all he said in response was, 'Everything bucks you off.'

'Even a whore?'

The comment may have been acceptable from a veteran, but from a beginner? No. 'Your future depends on one thing: you either stick with your leader or you become separated. Captain Callaghan will take you on an orientation flight later today. Do what he says or I'll have you off my squadron. Understand?'

They chorused, 'Yes, sir!'

Miller dismissed them. When they thought they were out of earshot, he heard one say to the other, 'A whore? You're so ugly she wouldn't let you on to begin with.'

'At least I know how to climb on.'

No, they hadn't heard a thing he'd said.

It was only then that he looked at the names on the files he held in his hands, 'You cannot be serious?'

Barker took a moment to realise what Miller was talking about. He made a parody of becoming consoling, 'What would you have me do, go to the nearest parish office and have their names changed?'

'What idiot would have assigned them to the same unit? Did whoever it was think they were having the last laugh?'

The adjutant smiled benignly, 'Maybe his name was Smith-Smythe.'

'And endless source of amusement, that's what you are.'

'Well, maybe one of them will get the chop, and it will be the end of your woes.'

'Callaghan is sure to thank you for wishing that upon him. You would know that the last stunt will have him waking up in a cold sweat, if past performances are any indication.'

'Then I'd suggest you get some perspective, George. It's barely worth a mention.'

'Elphinstone and Ellington: how am I ever supposed to tell them apart? They sound the same and they even look the same. Nor can I say that I think much of their powers of awareness.'

*　　*　　*

Sebastian von Bülow took in his austere surroundings. Everything was plain and functional. There was no extravagance; no class. It was a typical military establishment near the front line, and he didn't like it at all. No-one had asked his opinion.

Following his return from injury, he had been posted to another sector of the front. Everyone was a stranger and he now had to familiarise himself with the geography of the area as seen from the air. No longer accessible to him because of the distance, Yvonne was far from his thoughts.

'I hope everything is to your satisfaction, *Herr Oberleutnant?*'

'Thank you, Falkenhoff. I shall get used to it.'

The two men sized each other up. They would be working closely together for the foreseeable future. If they didn't get along it would be more difficult. Von Bülow didn't care one way or the other. His arm still hurt abominably and as a consequence it wouldn't be easy to resume flying. But again, no-one has asked his opinion.

'When a nation has an abundance of war heroes, the lesser ones don't rate very highly, don't you agree?'

'I'm sure you are correct, *Herr Oberleutnant.*'

'You will see that I usually am.'

'Yes, *Herr Oberleutnant.*'

Von Bülow was becoming irritated by the other man. *If he expects to be on first name terms he can look elsewhere.* The new commanding officer masked his annoyance, 'I wish to review the files on the personnel before I speak with them. It will give me a greater understanding of how much training they need to do before they are ready for action again.'

'The *Jasta* has just lost its two best fliers, *Herr Oberleutnant.* They just need to get their confidence back. After the loss of Richthofen...'

'Rubbish. Richthofen was killed weeks ago, and none of them even knew him.'

'Did you know him?'

'I met him. I didn't know him. Do you see me saying it's all too hard because the best ones keep falling?'

'It's a question of morale.'

'These are supposed to be grown men, Falkenhoff. They can be inspired by heroes all they like, but they shouldn't expect to have their arses wiped for them when it all goes wrong. They have their own hands for that.'

'You knew Oskar, though?'

'Lehmann? Yes, I knew him. I wasn't expecting to take his place. None of us ever really know what is in store for us, eh, Falkenhoff?'

'Death and taxes.'

'I will be busy here for a while. Find the file from Lehmann's last combat. I'll want to talk to the surviving pilot, as well.'

'*Leutnant* Kluth.'

'Not immediately. I'll be busy for a while. Dismissed.' Falkenhoff saluted and left the room. Von Bülow opened the first file that he picked up. Hildebrandt. He started reading. It didn't take as long as he had thought it would. He picked up another, then a third. By the time he had read half of them his visage was resigned.

There was a knock on the door and Falkenhoff returned with the requested combat report. He placed it on von Bülow's desk and made to leave. An imperiously raised finger prevented the adjutant's departure. Von Bülow didn't look up or say anything, he simply kept reading. Falkenhoff waited, the model of polite patience. Finally, von Bülow gave his subordinate some attention, 'I haven't read all of the files yet, Falkenhoff. They seem to be painting a fairly uninspiring picture, however.'

'I'm sorry, *Herr Oberleutnant*. You are not inspired?'

'I am not.'

'I am sure you will cope. If you have any difficulties, don't forget to wash your hands.'

Von Bülow's look communicated his bewilderment, 'Why would I wash my hands?'

'It's customary after one has wiped one's own arse.'

Von Bülow reddened. In his entire life, few people dared to defy him to his face. He didn't know quite what to do about it, 'These men are the discards from other units. Most have limited experience, some are here directly from flight school, and there are a number straight out of hospital. The *Jasta* if full of walking wounded!'

'How is your arm, *Herr Oberleutnant?*'

'You may keep your clever comments to yourself or I'll see you alternating your time between peeling potatoes and doing latrine duty - after I have wiped my arse and smeared it on the door.'

Falkenhoff was remorseless, 'You have been out of the line for a few months. In that time the *Luftstreitkräfte* has been restructured. We have had steady losses and the new men have to come from

315

somewhere. Some of the best men have been pulled from their units to provide a core of experience for the weaker ones. The old units have been hit hard! The result is that all *Jastas* have effectively been weakened. The fact that we have the new Fokker is the only positive to be drawn from the entire mess. Unfortunately, I am of the opinion that it is giving us a false sense of hope. And then when the better pilots are lost, as in the case of Oskar Lehmann and Rossler, it only exacerbates the problem.'

Von Bülow knew there were problems. He just wasn't expecting the reality to be quite as confronting. 'If they are not fit, they are no use.'

'Be thankful we have the latest aircraft. Spare a thought for anyone still flying around in a Pfalz.'

'Isn't the new DXII an improvement on the older model?'

'Is dysentery an improvement on typhus?'

'My cousin flies the Pfalz. He speaks very highly of it.'

'I hope you will beg my pardon, but your cousin may be mentally defective.'

Von Bülow smiled broadly, 'On that, Falkenhoff, we agree completely.' He looked at the pile of forms on his desk and shuffled them briefly until he had found the one he was looking for. He waved it in the air, 'This is Kluth. Bring him to me.'

Falkenhoff did not agree that Kluth was no more than a sheaf of paperwork, but all he said was, 'I will do it at once.'

'That was the general idea.' Falkenhoff stalked out. Von Bülow didn't like him at all, but no-one cared for his thoughts on too many things it seemed. He should have been used to it by now. Nevertheless, it grated. *What is the point of command if you can't command respect? It always needed to be earned all over again whenever you were placed*

316

amongst a new group of individuals. It seemed to him that a man's reputation had to be constantly reinforced to prevent it from jading.

Again, there was a rap on the door. Falkenhoff opened it from the outside and ushered Kluth inside.

'Come in, Kluth.' They exchange salutes.

'Thank you, *Herr Oberleutnant.*'

'I have spoken to *Leutnant* Falkenhoff, and I have read the report concerning the loss of Lehmann and Rossler. A piece of bad luck, as I understand it.'

Kluth waited. Von Bülow continued, 'I'd like to discuss a few things with you. Maybe you could elaborate on some details.'

'The report is thorough, *Herr Oberleutnant.*'

'Of course it is. Would you care for a drink, Kluth?'

'No. Thank you.'

'As you wish.'

'What is it you think I have omitted from the report, *Herr Oberleutnant?*'

Was the veteran digging his heels in? Von Bülow had no way of knowing. Maybe the fellow was just being careful. No harm in that. 'Nothing at all, Kluth. But we always get a better feel of things by talking through them. I have all of the standard information in my head: times, altitude, map references, the numbers of aircraft involved. All very clear. I'd just like to know some of the rest of it, the things that don't get written. You are the senior man in the *Jasta.* You have led patrols. I'd like to know what you think.'

'I flew many patrols with *Oberleutnant* Lehmann. It was unfortunate that he snorted a lungful of residual gas in the shell-hole that he piled into. I hope he recovers soon. From all I've seen, it's an unpleasant experience. *Vizefeldwebel* Rossler was a good friend. His death has been very hard on us.'

317

'That is no less than I'd expect. Men who serve together, even officers and enlisted, are all equal when we fly. Class distinctions are sometimes blurry for us. What fork to eat with? What does it matter?'

'I eat with a mess fork, *Herr Oberleutnant.*'

Von Bülow narrowed his eyes and stopped guessing, 'Then tell me this: what aircraft have you flown in the war so far? Your file obviously doesn't list the specifics. It shows the units that you have served in and that's all. I understand that you were on two-seaters before you joined the *Jastas?*'

'That is correct. A little over a year: artillery spotting and reconnaissance. Mostly the Albatros C series, but also DFWs. When I first came here it was the Albatros DIII and then the DV before we took to Fokkers.'

'And you have...' here von Bülow made a show of squinting as he paused for effect, '...four victories.'

'Four. Yes.'

'Congratulations.'

'Thank you.' Kluth suspected that the commander was slighting him - possibly to highlight his own distinguished record, 'I hope that your arm is not giving you any discomfort, *Herr Oberleutnant.*' There was no inflection in the comment that allowed von Bülow to take umbrage to it. He pretended nothing untoward was meant by the remark.

'Thank you for your concern, *Leutnant* Kluth. Now tell me this: you are an experienced pilot and have survived two years in combat. You have flown a variety of different aircraft. I want to know your opinion on the merits of the Fokker DVII. How good is it, really?'

'It is superior to anything I have flown so far.'

'Have you flown the Spad XIII?'

'No.'

'You have fought against them, though?'

'Yes.'

'Is the Fokker better than the Spad?'

'That is difficult to answer, *Herr Oberleutnant*. So far I've only flown the Fokker against the English. You read the report - it wasn't a successful result.'

'Well, how much better is it than the Albatros?'

'It's better. In my opinion, its superiority lies not so much in its top speed as in its general handling qualities. It is easier to fly. It accelerates well, it turns well, and the wings don't come off like they do on the Albatros. You haven't flown it yet?'

'No. My arm.'

'The variant with the new BMW is supposed to be much better. Do you have friends in high places, *Herr Oberleutnant?*'

'Why do you ask?' *The insolent bastard. He would know about my uncle.*

'The Mercedes engine on these machines is a superior version to that which we are used to having, but I am inclined to believe that the BMW-powered models will only go to selected units. If you aren't well connected, I don't fancy our chances of seeing just how good the Fokker DVII really is. In all honesty, though, I would have preferred that the fuel capacity had been increased.'

'There is a shortage in fuel, so that's not the biggest issue. We need men who can fly and expect to live long enough to become an asset to the *staffel*. How many of them are any good?'

'They are all brave men.'

'What would you say if I were to draw up a roster that puts the worst men under your command, and the best ones in my flight?'

'*Herr Oberleutnant*, if you did that, I would ask why you needed my input on the matter in the first place.'

319

Von Bülow didn't like the tone of the man, 'Thank you, gentlemen, you may leave me be.' As they turned to leave, von Bülow remembered he had one other thing on his mind, 'Falkenhoff…before you go?'

The adjutant turned expectantly as Kluth kept walking, 'Yes?'

'I forgot to ask you. Could you procure me a helmet?'

Falkenhoff frowned, 'Yours is damaged?'

'No, that one is fine. A steel one.'

'Would a Hardshell do?'

'Reinforced leather? Yes. I'm still having a few problems.'

The observation had to be made, 'No amount of protection for your head is going to make a difference if you come in vertical.'

Unsure whether the remark was sarcastic or not, von Bülow merely waved the man away. Falkenhoff left von Bülow's office and found Kluth waiting for him outside. The recently interrogated pilot was straight to the point, 'What do you make of him, Falkenhoff?'

'He has quite a job ahead of him.'

'His job is my life.'

Falkenhoff smiled gently, 'Perhaps you should make that your job, Kluth.'

'He's the one, isn't he? Lehmann's old commander?'

Falkenhoff confirmed it, 'That's him.'

'A true bastard, then.'

Falkenhoff raised an eyebrow, 'What did Oskar tell you? He never spoke a word of it to me.'

'It's not what he said. It's how he always talked around it. The stuffy bastard would never criticise one of his peers. Not openly. But he never pretended to like him, either.'

'Maybe they just didn't get along. It happens. It doesn't make von Bülow a bastard.'

'I see you, Falkenhoff; trying to douse the fire before it flares out of control.'

'You're the second best pilot in the *Jasta* now, after von Bülow. The other pilots will need someone to look up to.'

'How did that happen?'

'You were there; you should know.'

Kluth slumped imperceptibly, 'Rossler was better than anyone else I've flown with. I'm not the one to fill his shoes.'

Falkenhoff was not going to disagree with the man, but at the same time he wasn't going to rub his nose in it, 'You don't have a choice. I don't think the new commander has his head far enough into the problem. Give him some time. He's just back from convalescence.'

'His head might not be far enough into the problem, but that's no reason to have it firmly shoved into his own backside instead.'

'Best not to let the others hear you say that.'

'I'm not entirely stupid, Falkenhoff. And neither are the other fellows. They'll see what he is without any help from me.'

Falkenhoff feared the man was right. It would only take as long as it took for von Bülow to open his mouth. He might be competent; he might be brave. There might even be a functioning brain inside his head. None of it would matter when that monumental ego was let loose. *Would he have been any different if he was low-born?* Falkenhoff doubted it. *What about if he had been born an earthworm?* The adjutant had a small smile on his face as he walked into the officer's mess.

*   *   *

Despite general public perceptions, no army was entirely rigid in every aspect of its day to day activities. Military precision was largely a myth perpetuated by endless drills during training and a stubborn adherence to doctrine at the command level. But the overall professionalism of the regular armies on the continent had become greatly watered down, in part because of the mass mobilisations that had started in nineteen-fourteen. The primary task had become to train men to fight - as many and as quickly as possible; the compromise was that some of the spit and polish suffered for it. Every army had degrees of tolerance to individual habits and behaviour, and masked the fact by labelling it as initiative. Nevertheless, it didn't prevent outspokenness nor, in some cases, refusal to obey orders.

And then there were men like William Bowe - men who operated to an alternative set of standards, and as such were considered a vital cog in a huge machine. Men like him filled in the gaps that the infrastructure was unable to accommodate and sniffed out opportunities that were invisible to those who trod a lighter path. Unfortunately, there were sometimes ramifications.

Right at this instant, in full view of the entire squadron, Bowe was being prodded towards the office of his squadron commander by a very angry civilian. Together, they had travelled some considerable distance on foot, and the shotgun pressed into the small of his back had not wavered once. Bowe himself was bleeding from his leg where his skin had been penetrated by half a dozen pellets. Fortunately for him, the shot had been fired from long range and the wounds were minor.

Minor, but now very public.

There were accusations to be answered, and that hefty responsibility fell right into George Miller's lap. Either that or it would become a police matter, and though such an event was not unheard of, it hardly fostered goodwill between the English and their brothers-in-arms.

Having finally arrived at the office of the man he had sought out, the farmer was ranting unintelligibly. Even so Miller, knowing what he knew of men of Bowe's ilk, drew his own conclusions. To avoid further confusion, he sought the obvious solution, 'Captain Barker?'

The adjutant spoke a bastardised version of the French tongue, and was able to convey the gist of the farmer's grievance, 'He says Bowe here was stealing from his hen-house.'

'First things first: tell this fellow to put his gun away. He's making me nervous. It's bad enough that the Huns carry them around. There's no need for every Tom, Dick and Pierre to follow suit.'

The farmer duly lowered the weapon, and then looked expectantly at Miller, who blandly turned to the thief, 'Well?'

'I was long gone from the coop before he potted me.'

Miller was confused by the immediacy of the apparent confession. Caught red-handed or not, the normal tactic in such situations was to deny everything, 'That's it? You admit it?'

Bowe had made the most of hobbling along for miles on a gimpy leg. He had worked out his defence, 'If I was in his hen house, where are the hens I stole? Ask him. Ask the Frog bastard!'

Miller corrected him, 'Ask the Frog bastard, sir.'

'That's what I meant, sir.'

Barker and the farmer went to and fro again, and Barker reported that all of the hens had been accounted for. None had been taken, but there was another problem, 'It's not the hens. It was their eggs that were stolen.'

Bowe spread his hands in innocence, 'And when he can't prove that I took his precious eggs, then will I be believed?'

Miller gave him a wintry look that said, *Not on your Nelly.* 'Empty your pockets, Bowe.'

The accused man claimed, 'They are.' He complied as commanded. The turned-out pockets were empty and no-one had said anything of a carry sack. The farmer looked on in disbelief, communicating his thoughts on the matter to the adjutant, who translated, 'He says that Bowe must have dumped them on the way here.'

To which the scrounger had an easy answer, 'That being the case, he'll find them on his way home, won't he? And then he'll come back and I'll eat my flaming hat.' There was a defiance to Bowe that almost had Miller convinced he was telling the truth. Almost.

Miller exchanged looks with Barker. The farmer saw the glance and looked daggers at all of them. He pointed an angry finger at the adjutant, 'He says - '

'Don't bother, I get the general idea.'

The farmer stormed away empty-handed.

They watched him until he rounded a corner and disappeared from sight.

Miller pinned Bowe with a glare, 'That had better be the last I ever see of him, or you'll be getting more than buckshot in your arse.'

Bowe decided that it was time to ingratiate himself with his superior officer, 'Here, what's this behind your ear?' He plucked an egg from thin air, 'And I believe there's another in your pocket.'

Miller put a hand into his pocket and the look on his face said enough, 'I don't know how you pulled that deception, you crafty bastard, but I don't want the entire neighbourhood around here ever again. Understand me?'

'Yes, sir. Enjoy your breakfast, sir.'

Miller knew for a fact that William Bowe would likely be having a very similar meal himself. 'Go and get your injuries attended to.'

When they were finally alone, Barker saw the funny side of it, 'You knew he'd be trouble, that one. Nasty habits.'

'Be sure to remind me of it from time to time.'

'Oh, have no fear. I will.'

'I don't doubt it.' Miller put a silver lining on his cloud, 'I'm having poached eggs for breakfast. What are you having?'

'You are a true bastard, sir, and I now know why you took him in when nobody else would have.'

Chapter 26

July 1918: Improper Conduct

The summer rain was coming down in torrents, drumming on the roof and temporarily transforming the aerodrome into a quagmire. All flights had been suspended. The veterans saw it as an excellent opportunity to stay indoors, though they spared a thought for whichever poor sods in the infantry would be standing to in the rain, awaiting an attack that was unlikely to materialise. As for the new pilots, they had no thoughts for anyone other than themselves, and were champing at the bit, annoyed that the weather was forestalling their opportunity to come to grips with the foe.

Lieutenants Elphinstone and Ellington had cornered their flight commander, bemoaning the inclement weather. Callaghan looked outside, relishing the squelch and slop created by the heavy rainfall, 'It keeps the Hun grounded, too, you know.'

Like children, the new men wanted to explore the unknown despite being told by their elders that fire isn't something you volunteer to put your hand into. Elphinstone was having none of it, 'How are we to win the war if we can't get on with it?'

You'll rethink that sentiment soon enough. But Callaghan was a cool customer and was content to leave the roulette wheel alone, 'A life where no-one is trying to kill me. Imagine that?'

Lieutenant Upton, the deputy of 'C' Flight, had been given a pup to look after. He had let it in from the rain and now it was chewing on one of the legs of the mismatching furniture. Those who noticed didn't care, whilst those who'd have cared didn't notice. They left it to its own destructive devices, allowing the playful youngster to have its day.

Someone had a record playing on the gramophone. It sounded tinny, and everyone had heard it too many times before to have feelings of affection towards the music. Though this caused mild levels of aggravation, there wasn't anything new to put on and most of the other albums had minor scratches that ruined whatever small enjoyment they had once bestowed.

Elphinstone complained about the quality of the music. One of the men told him to shut up. Barker brought in a packet of cigars and passed them around. Callaghan was appreciative, 'Where'd you get them?'

'What's your interest?' It was answer enough. William Bowe was making his presence known in all circles.

'If the sneaky blighter can get anything we want, why hasn't anybody bothered with trying to get the latest rumours on Kaiser Bill's new horse?'

In the last few months Germany had updated their combat units again. To have expected them to stagnate on older equipment had about as much probability as the existence of luminous fairies. True to form, their latest acquisition had been encountered with increasing frequency. Rumours had filtered across to every Allied squadron and the speculation was much as expected. Whenever a new design was brought into play it dominated the skies and although there were a few exceptions to the rule, preliminary reports on what the Fokker DVII was capable of left the RAF men apprehensive.

The appearance of the newest scout was typical of the earlier marks from which it had evolved. The triangular tailplane and dinner-plate rudder were straight out of the Fokker design manual and very unlike the classically paddle-shaped lines of the discontinued Albatros D series. It also lacked the overall streamlined elegance of that dwindling breed.

Each frame was sheathed in lozenge camouflaged fabric that looked like the scales of a giant reptile, and the simplified national markings seemed to have been stolen from the Middle Ages — specifically, the crosses crudely applied in charcoal or tar to the doors of Plague Houses. It was an apt comparison and only reinforced the image of Germany's obsession with painting macabre motifs on their machines.

The DVII was mean, ugly and deadly. The Germans had stripped their new design to the bone and crammed a more powerful engine into it. They now had a machine that could run rings around the major Allied types.

Callaghan had discussed this new nemesis with the other senior men. Though all exhibited a professional interest and none were surprised about the latest turn of events, it was nevertheless disconcerting to know that the Camel now had stiffer opposition. Not exactly subscribing to the viewpoint that fighting should be fair, they had greatly preferred to shoot from a position of superiority. That time seemed to have run its course and now the boot was back on the other foot. Though they were interested in seeing how much of what they had heard was true, they were filled with dismay at the likeliest way that such an education would come to pass.

The keen interest in the new Fokker was not limited to the old hands. If anything, the newer pilots had even greater cause for disquiet. Elphinstone and Ellington may not have had more to lose with their own lives on the line the same as everyone else; nevertheless they were more likely to suffer than the others due to the fact that they had less experience to draw upon to ensure their continued existence.

Elphinstone was wondering at the veracity of some of that which was going around the rumour mill, 'It's said it can hang on its propeller. Is such a thing even possible? That's a lot of air needing to be bitten. The blade wouldn't have sufficient ground clearance for take-off, would it?'

Ellington phrased it differently, 'I've heard it stands on its tail.'

Elphinstone had a quizzical expression as he asked, 'What's the difference?'

Someone noticed the pup gnawing a chair leg and threw a boot at it. The small creature piddled itself in fright and scampered for safety, finding temporary refuge behind Ellington's legs. He cruelly trod on its skinny tail. Yowling in pain, it fled the room. 'That's the difference - I didn't hang on its propeller.'

Upton was outraged by Ellington's action and called him out. Ellington just waved a hand dismissively, 'My instructor said to kill something every day to get used to the act. Whether a worm or a bug makes no difference, but it helps in preparing the mind for killing a Hun. By that reasoning, the silly dog got off lightly.'

With nothing left to do but find and comfort the mistreated animal, the aggrieved Upton went in search of his pet.

Callaghan had witnessed the entire incident. He looked at Ellington with different eyes, 'That's a bit harsh, I should say, stamping on the animal. Nothing really prepares you no matter what you've been told.'

Ellington had no regrets, 'It can't hurt, though.'

'Kicking a dog is not the same as pulling a trigger on a man.'

'Given this infernal rain, it'll have to do.' Ellington had a question that was very dear to his heart so he changed the topic, 'Of those you've encountered, which of the Hun aeroplanes are the most dangerous?'

'The ones chasing you.' Though Callaghan had not yet faced off against a DVII, he could still have answered the question in a knowledgeable manner. Yet he was unwilling to impart friendly advice to someone who could casually inflict cruelty upon a dog - especially one so little. Ellington grated upon him and had been treated accordingly.

Ellington was none too pleased with the answer, but had the sense to leave off. Ultimately, all newcomers tried to glean stories and helpful advice from the older hands. It was nothing out of the ordinary, but Callaghan was not in an expansive mood. In his estimation, there were easy answers and there were complicated answers, but no answer mattered if it was not heeded.

In Callaghan's experience, the first missions flown in earnest were the most important. The more often a man came home, the more he learned and the longer he lived. It was a simple philosophy, if a rather obvious one: clearly a pilot lived longer if he didn't get killed. There were only so many ways to say it: learning to spot the enemy when he was still a distant speck gave a man more chance of writing up an increasing number of entries in his log book. The more victories that were entered into the book, the happier with himself he would be.

Callaghan was fed up with the inane chatter, 'Give over, otherwise I'll take you out on a patrol and leave you to find your own way back.' Neither of the new men knew the area well enough to navigate with confidence. With enough Huns around to take an interest in them, their chances would have been slim if they suddenly found themselves alone.

Easily reading the veteran's mood, Barker poured Callaghan a shot of whisky. It was downed in one gulp and left the man's eyes bugging out of his head. When he finished his fit of coughing, he held out his glass again, 'Another.'

Elphinstone had erroneously decided that Callaghan's patience must have been restored by the sudden intake of alcohol, because he had another question, 'Is there more satisfaction in clinically dispatching the other fellow with a few well-placed shots, or is there more enjoyment in hosing him?'

Callaghan ignored the man, but no-one had noticed Miller's entrance, 'A matter of personal taste, I should say. Do you eat with a fork or your fingers? Either way, the food still gets put away. I must say, though, I feel sorry for the poor bugger when he burns. Not enough to hold my fire - let's be clear on that point.'

*   *   *

The Albatros Works were still engaged in the task of aircraft manufacture, but instead of building their own machines, they were now contracted to the construction of the Fokker DVII. Consequently, although the Albatros DV was still in service, it was appearing over the front in ever-dwindling numbers. As more units were taking on increasing numbers of the new Fokker, they were passing the older machines to those units not yet earmarked for greater things.

One unit still using the Albatros was one of the first *Jastas* ever created, now commanded by Ernst Reinhold. Mellerhorst was unimpressed by the deteriorating state of things, 'Most of these machines are the left-overs from other *Jastas,* and have been handed to us in a sorry state of repair. The previous owners clearly didn't care about making work for others.'

It didn't amuse Reinhold, either. 'They'd have had a reason, or not, but either way we'll do the best we can. And be thankful you're only flying a desk – I'm the poor bastard who has to go up in them.'

Mellerhorst clapped Reinhold's back, 'It wasn't a complaint for my benefit, but rather for the ground crews – their efforts cannot be understated.'

Reinhold's silence was a statement in itself. Anyone who didn't know the value of their mechanics and armourers was an idiot, and probably long since dead.

The various personnel were preparing for another mission. The rituals were still the same, but Reinhold had been flying for so long now that he couldn't remember much of anything else. He looked at the other men that were going with him. There were old hands and new. Weber and Bonninghauser weren't fresh faces any more - not even close. Those two had supplanted some of the veterans: Bahlmann was now in a sanatorium and Kruchelsdorf had broken his back, though it hadn't reduced his capacity to drink.

Schenk was a new man who now flew Bahlmann's machine and he had kept the original markings. Consequently, Reinhold occasionally confused him with his predecessor.

As engines were warmed up along the flight line, Mellerhorst sent his friend off with the ritual advice intended to thwart bad omens, 'Break an arm and a leg.'

'One day I will – then you'll owe me a drink.'

Reinhold saw the Bristol Fighters before anyone else as they picked their way cautiously through the clotted cloud cover. He signalled to his men and sent them down to do battle. As each

Albatros selected its target from the English formation, Reinhold opened fire. Unable to discern any effect upon the enemy, he swivelled his head to check for threats.

It was as well that he did do so, for a second machine had closed on him and was almost in a position to fire. Reinhold evaded the attack by climbing in a steep spiral turn. Completing the manoeuvre, he found himself positioned behind the aggressor. Careful not to present himself as a target to the observer's gunfire, he gave immediate pursuit before firing again.

The shots flew wide of the target, a miscalculation in the angle of deflection. He swore at himself – those small errors are sometimes the fatal ones. You need to kill the other man before he has a chance to do it to you. Every lost opportunity is a gain for the enemy.

Once again, the wary German veteran checked for approaching danger. Scores of combats over a two year period had given him an acute perception of his surroundings. Air combat was a high speed affair, and death could come upon a man in the blink of an eye. This time there was no immediate hazard to his health. The nearest machine was Bonninghauser's Albatros, and that worthy was all over his intended prey.

With no Bristols on his own tail, Reinhold immediately pressed home his attack on the machine which had gone after him. His original target had long since slipped out of the arc of his fire and was now engaged elsewhere. Reinhold corrected his aim and saw shots pepper the aircraft in his gun sight.

In slow motion, Reinhold's mind belatedly registered the effect of his attack. He witnessed something that would be with him until the day he died: the pilot's head had turned to a fine mist. The man's flying helmet held the remains together in a soggy mass, but Reinhold was under no doubt about what he had just caused. The plane flew true for a short time before it began to list, then started to curl away.

Reinhold locked his focus on the hapless observer, watching as realisation spread over the man's frantic face as he contemplated his fate – if he stuck with his gun he would not be able to access the flight controls, but if he attempted to take control of the aircraft he would be left defenceless against the killer on his tail. Across a distance of mere metres, Reinhold beheld the disintegration of his helpless enemy. Before the observer had time to make up his mind - and there was precious little of that commodity - the aircraft rolled and plummeted towards the ground so far below.

For the moment Reinhold was transfixed, and though the distraction was temporary, any hesitation could be fatal. *Is it my imagination, or can I taste the English flier's brains in my mouth?* There were flecks of blood on his windshield.

He snapped back to the present where very little time had elapsed at all. There was Bonninghauser, closing in on his man. The Albatros was in the blind spot under the tail of the frantically twisting Englishman, and the observer was unable to bring his Lewis gun to bear. The Bristol suddenly dived violently.

Bonninghauser reacted instinctively, but he had nowhere to go and the two aircraft touched - just the lightest brush; it was barely a caress. Both machines were making over a hundred miles an hour. The brief contact at that speed caused both aircraft to shudder. Collision!

Reinhold watched as the drab two-seater spiralled downward, the pilot fighting to bring it back under control. Somehow the descent was arrested, and the perilous trajectory of the F.2B started to flatten out. It didn't last, however, and the broken bird started its inexorable journey towards the larger misery being fought in the desecrated landscape far below. The rest of the descent was terminal.

Reinhold's captivation with events switched to concern for his own man. Bonninghauser was still airborne, though the Albatros now had a section of fabric flailing around where it had been ripped loose from the frame. Knowing his plight, Bonninghauser turned his nose homeward. Reinhold didn't like the fellow's chances; every Englishman would be seeking vengeance for the loss of their comrade, and Bonninghauser was not only the man most responsible for the act, he was also a lame duck. Anyone with a grain of instinct would be keen to finish the job.

Sure enough, several Bristols began to converge on the damaged German. The other pilots in the *Jasta* came to the aid of their comrade as Bonninghauser was forced to decide whether to go all out for home at the risk of over-stressing his airframe, thereby causing more damage to the integrity of his wing, or nursing his machine within safety limits, only to be overhauled and summarily executed. Reinhold reminded himself that just moments before another human being had been given his own impossible choice, and now no doubt lay dead in the wreckage.

Unable to abandon a friend to his fate, Reinhold turned to lend assistance. Before he could head off the assault on the crippled Albatros, he was sought out by other Bristols. He looked at his fuel gauge, and decided that there was nothing more he could do. It was time to go home. The extended range of the large British fighter was another critical factor that would reduce Bonninghauser's chances should the F.2s decide not to break off the action. And why would they?

No sooner did Reinhold have the thought, than two aircraft fell away in a cloud of putrid smoke and fiery debris. He spied a parachute. *Good news and bad, then.* The bad news was that the aircraft was one of his own. For the first time since men had taken to the skies, German pilots had been issued with parachutes. One direct result of this innovation was that any aircraft that fell from the sky could now have its nationality identified more reliably. At least, for now; in an ever changing environment, any successful strategy was always immediately copied by the other side. Imitation was the greatest compliment that could be bestowed, and that truth has held firm for millennia.

Though the loss of the Albatros was bad news, nevertheless Reinhold now knew that the parachutes were actually functional. Even if it transpired that they were not entirely reliable, they were still better than the obvious alternative. There was no better example of this than the fate which had befallen the F.2 observer.

Taking his eye off the drifting silk canopy, Reinhold saw that Bonninghauser was nowhere within sight. He pursed his lips and set a course for home.

Reinhold approached the airfield and saw that he was one of the last men to return. The other machines were either taxiing to a standstill or were already parked. None of those who had landed had crashed, though there was a cluster of trucks and men gathered around the battered old biplanes. He recognised Bonninghauser's markings, and was astonished that the man had made it back.

It raised another question: If Bonninghauser had made it back, who hadn't?

At last the old Albatros rolled to a standstill, and the young *Jastaführer* killed the engine. He sat in the cockpit and fisted his goggles with oiled gloves, before pulling them up off his face. He spat filth from his mouth onto the floor of the machine, then sagged, still buckled in. He closed his eyes and sucked in the clean air.

'Are you all right, *Herr Leutnant*?' It was the voice of his crew chief.

'Am I the last one?'

'We don't know. Some of the men were shot down. We don't know how many.'

'Yes, I saw perhaps two. But maybe one of them was a Bristol.'

'Weber got one, so he says.'

'Help me down.'

'You aren't hurt?'

'No.'

Reinhold clambered down and made his way towards Bonninghauser's plane, 'How are you, Rudi?'

Rudolf Bonninghauser looked him in the eye. It was a wild look — spooked - which was not at all surprising in the circumstances, 'Did you see?'

'I saw. But I've never talked to a man who's done what you just did, because I've never seen one survive.'

'I think I only made it back by accepting that I was a dead man - any further action that I took could only have positive consequences, or at least no worse than I expected.' The combat had left the man grey in the face and visibly shaken. The way he was looking curiously at Reinhold seemed to imply they were two of a kind, 'That's aged me ten years.'

'Congratulations then, you'll outlive the rest of us. We won't make thirty.' Their laughter had cracks in it. Someone with moral sensibilities may not have found the remark funny, but then black humour was not intended for gentle spirits.

Bonninghauser pointed at his wing, 'Probably won't be repairable, my wagon. The spar is badly cracked.'

'We don't have any new ones.'

'There's Emil's.'

'Why doesn't he want it?'

'He has a bullet in his leg.'

'That will do it.' Reinhold wanted to stop the inane conversation, but his mouth wouldn't listen to his brain, 'I'll witness your kill.'

Bonninghauser stared blankly at him. Reinhold realised that the man hadn't fully come back to earth. There was a part of him still fixed in time, reliving the specifics of the collision. Two of them, at least, were still up there in that visceral battle to the death.

Mellerhorst was looking at the pair as though they were a circus act, 'The Englishman was destroyed, Bonninghauser, that's what everyone is saying. Write him up in your log book. And let me read it when you're done: an original entry, for once. Did you fire your guns before it happened?'

'I...I think so.'

'I'll check with your armourer.'

Mellerhorst made his report, 'Everyone is accounted for, Ernst.'

'How bad is it?'

'Two wounded.'

'I fear that the English have had it worse, then.'

'We are still waiting for confirmation from the army of our claims.'

'I'll tell you something, Franz. Bring your dog here and tell me he can't taste the blood of an Englishman on my clothing. And my face.'

'You should wipe it off.'

'I have, but some stains can never be removed.'

'It's the war. It changes men.'

'And then their sons want to be like them. It can never be explained in words.'

'I don't have a son.'

'I'm a son. That's what I meant.'

Mellerhorst considered the statement. He changed tack, 'Bonninghauser should be grounded for a few days. He needs the rest.'

'No, we're short-handed as it is. We'll fortify him with a party tonight. It can help us celebrate another dawn tomorrow, and our victories today, and the fact that none of us were killed in the process.' Reinhold was looking into the middle distance – what would one day be known as the thousand yard stare – and he confessed, 'I made mistakes today - three of them: lapses in judgement or concentration.'

'You know how it can be, Ernst. Sometimes minor errors are fatal; other times gross errors have no consequences at all. The end result is all that counts. How you get there doesn't matter in the least, except for peace of mind.'

'Yes.' Reinhold didn't sound very sure of himself. Today peace of mind was an alien concept.

'Tomorrow will be better than today.'

'For who? People die every day.'

The phone rang. Mellerhorst answered, identified himself, spoke briefly, hung up. 'Congratulations, Ernst, you officially have nine now.'

'I prefer fighting the French.'

'And drinking their champagne. Let's open the bottle you were saving.'

'It was supposed to be for my tenth.'

339

'Consider; there were two men in the Bristol. Your first eight kills were all single-seaters. By my count, that makes ten.'

Reinhold gently prodded Mellerhorst's wound badge, 'If that's representative of your accountancy skills, I'm surprised you weren't sent home for good after your last injury. An adjutant negligent with his administrative duties? I could have you court-martialled.'

'I'd have to do the paperwork on that one as well. We should talk about it over the bottle.'

*   *   *

Elphinstone and Ellington were in high spirits when they landed, and their jubilation was heard by everyone who had witnessed their antics, 'Oui, oui, oui, all the way home!'

Callaghan's thunderous expression told a different story. He grabbed one man by his jacket front and flung him to the ground, then rounded upon the other and struck him full in the face. He yelled at them, 'C.O.'s office! Now!'

Barker had heard the commotion and met them halfway. Seeing the flight commander's ropeable expression meant trouble for someone, and the dishevelled appearances of Elphinstone and Ellington told who. The why of it? That was the question...

Within twenty yards, the adjutant had been given a candid outline of the events that had occurred as the routine Camel patrol had flown the last few miles home.

The two pilots were confined to quarters from the moment that their transgression had been reported to Miller. Nobody had bothered visiting them.

Callaghan had still not cooled off, but Barker was already thinking ahead, 'What are we going to do about it?'

Miller shrugged, 'Wait and see. Maybe nothing will come of it.'

'I don't think that's likely. By now our squadron will be instantly recognisable to everyone who lives around here. They see us every day.'

The senior man turned to Callaghan, 'What's your take on it?'

'I'm still tempted to go over there right now and shoot them both in the legs.'

'Have a drink, instead.' Miller went to his drawer and searched for his hip flask. He poured them all half a glassful.

Downing his share without ceremony, the adjutant was not to be distracted, 'I'm telling you, it won't have gone unnoticed.'

Miller nodded, 'Well, we'll know soon enough.'

He was right.

Within two hours, there was an angry farmer demanding to see them. When Miller saw who it was his heart sank. It was the same gentleman that had caught Bowe stealing from his hen-house. Given that this wasn't a first offence, and especially because the other occasion had been trivialised, Miller expected a somewhat stiffer fight of it this time around.

If the farmer had been angry on the occasion of his previous visit, it paled in comparison to this one. His face was blotched in apoplexy, and spittle flew across the room as he harangued the men assembled before him. He was a tower of burning rage.

Barker translated enough of which was being shouted at them, but really there was no need. The three officers already knew that aeroplanes from their squadron had strafed the man's livestock for fun. Getting a more passionate version of the bare bones of the story was just a waste of time. The man would vent his anger, and in the end he would go away empty-handed.

Miller knew the Frenchman's outrage was fully justified, yet there was nothing he could do by way of recompense. Given that he still had his fair share of Germans to contend with, it was more expedient to try and shift the blame elsewhere, 'Ray, tell him it wasn't us.'

Barker looked at him in astonishment, 'But it was.'

'Just tell him.'

Once the message was translated, the farmer's look of disbelief matched that of the adjutant. More was said, 'He says you're a liar.'

'I thought that might have been it.' Miller tried to think of something plausible to say, but he had drawn a blank, 'Ask him his name.'

'Gaillard.'

'Gaylord?'

'Close enough.'

'We'll just call him Farmer Frog.'

The farmer was unable to follow their byplay, so he pointed at the Camels lined up in the distance, 'Those markings, and the white on the tail: that is the same marking as the machines that shot my Deidre!'

Barker translated for the benefit of Miller and Callaghan.

Callaghan raised an eyebrow, 'Deidre?'

Miller shrugged, 'Must be the name of his cow.'

'This gets better and better. Who calls a cow Deidre?'

Raymond Barker wasn't bothering with the trivial aspect of the Gaelic-named Gallic bovine, now deceased, 'He's got you cold, George. We're the only ones still getting around with RN livery.'

Miller waved away the protest, 'Nonsense. Tell him that white paint is no longer used to identify Navy property. It's all part of the Air Force now. Nothing means anything anymore.'

'I'm not sure I have the right words for it.'

'All the better. We can blame the misunderstanding on language barriers.'

'His cow is dead. I'm not sure that it's a misunderstanding.'

'Just tell him.'

'You are making this deucedly difficult for me, George.'

If nothing else, Miller had now found a use for the Royal Air Force's existence. He could hide behind its anonymity. The source of the small comfort ignored everything that the Frenchman pointed out. Despite every denial, Miller's retention of his uniform was too big a giveaway. Besides which, the aircraft had been positively identified, and whether the markings were outdated or not was a moot point.

Another exchange of broken French followed. Barker had more bad news, 'He says he cannot understand English, but faces have the same expressions regardless of language barriers. He knows you're lying.'

'He's right of course, but how can he prove it?' Miller waved his hand in the air, then irritably added, 'Don't tell him that.'

Barker's tone also now had an edge to it, 'I'm not the idiot around here! It's the other two that made this mess.'

'Yes, well someone has to clear it up and it's on our heads. You may as well do your bit.'

'I say just hand them over.'

Miller lost patience and glared at the adjutant, 'Tell your friend that if he isn't out of my sight within ten seconds I shall put a bullet in him myself if he loves his damnable cow so much.' While he said this to Barker, he pulled out his sidearm and checked the mechanism, then looked up at the farmer to see if the message was getting across.

The Frenchman's eyes were bulging in rage but he had his back to the wall and knew it. He was none too pleased to be rebuffed so insultingly. For the second time in as many months he left their company amid much fanfare, this time yelling abuse and threats at the top of his lungs.

Miller may have treated the wronged man unfairly, but he was not entirely without sympathy for the fellow. 'You could almost say it was inevitable, letting young men loose on the world without proper supervision. I'm surprised this sort of thing doesn't happen more often.'

Callaghan drew his own conclusions, 'Maybe it does but we just don't hear about it.'

'Regardless, I think it's best that we just keep stalling the Frog until he comes to the realisation that walking ten miles a day for nothing is a fruitless activity.'

Barker felt that the entire fiasco could have been handled with greater sensitivity, 'It hardly seems fair, though, if you want my opinion.'

Miller had taken the easier route and could live with the decision. After all, it was only a cow. Nevertheless, he wondered if he had missed a trick, 'Do you have a better idea?'

'Hand them over to the gendarmes and send in a requisition for two new pilots.'

'It doesn't help the farmer much, though, does it?'

'Do you want to make an enemy of him?'

'What can he do that the Kaiser hasn't already attempted?'

'We'd have probably needed to compensate him somehow. How do you replace livestock when there's not enough to go around as it is?'

'That's my conclusion also. Let's keep the Brass Hats out of it.'

'What if he makes a direct complaint?'

'Then we'll just change our story to accommodate our poor understanding of foreign languages.'

'It's seems rather flimsy.'

'It's a cow, Barker. No-one will care. You'll see.'

'I'd still advise a different course of action - something punitive that *Monsieur* Gaillard would agree to be a fitting punishment. You can't just forget about what the idiots have done. We are responsible for them, after all.'

'Forget? Oh, no, I'm not forgetting any of it. We're flying a lot of support for the army right now, and seeing as how The Two Ellies want to shoot everything that moves, we'll send one or both of them out on every mission. We'll be rid of them sooner that way, and it will give someone more deserving a break.'

'Why not have told the farmer as much?'

'In my experience, once you admit to wrongdoing, the floodgates open and every man and his dog wants to have a piece of you. Let's not forget that those clowns did not act on lawful orders, or that Farmer Frog would hardly care about us splitting hairs if we were to tell him so. To him, we're culpable – it makes no difference at all whether we have his enmity or not. Plus, the French authorities will hardly be able to prove his claim even if they believe it.'

'Why wouldn't they believe it?'

Callaghan interjected, 'We're fighting to save his blasted country. It wouldn't hurt to show a bit of gratitude. Has he shed any blood? I doubt it. Sweat maybe, but not blood. The cow can be his sacrifice.'

Barker looked betrayed by Callaghan's response, 'I thought you wanted to shoot the bastards?'

The leader of 'A' Flight shrugged, 'I can have it both ways if I want to.'

For his part, Miller found it interesting to have so much discretionary power at his disposal. Although he knew that he had gone beyond acceptable limits in dealing with this particular problem, taken as a whole it made running his squadron a lot simpler than it could have been. He doubted that British infantry or artillery commanders had been granted as much leeway to run their units with the same flexibility.

*   *   *

'Look, here comes Jimmy.' The poor lad had become Nobby's favourite hobby. If there was fun to be had, it was generally at Jimmy's expense. One of them derived enormous amusement from their various interactions; the other, not so much.

The latest practical joke had been spectacularly successful. The method of construction of the squadron latrines allowed a man to reach down into the hole of the seat in his own cubicle and laterally access that of his neighbour. Nobby had given Jimmy just enough time to get comfortable before he struck. Scrunching some pages from a broadsheet newspaper, the prankster had lit the bundle and shoved the burning mass into the fetid space, waving it under young Jimmy's backside.

The screams of outrage had every witness doubled over in fits of laughter which only increased when the singed victim tumbled out onto the grass and fell flat on his face, having tripped in the tangle of pants around his ankles.

That had been two days ago, and he had still not lived it down.

'Hey there, Jimmy! Has the hair on your arse grown back yet?'

'Leave him alone! He's too young to have had any to begin with.'

Too weedy to fend for himself, the fitter's apprentice had no option but to endure their wit. To have made a complaint would have drawn little sympathy from the C.O. The man would likely have offered to swap places with him.

Instead, he found refuge within the sanctity of his mind, and the promise of a better life once the war ended and he could return home. His favourite daydream was always centred on the existence of Sarah Perry. He pictured her in Hyde Park wearing her pristine white dress, elegant in sun hat and veil with a parasol completing her attire. He had many words to describe her: sweet, innocent, flawless, angelic. But if he had been compelled to choose a single word to sum up her perfection that word would have been 'love'.

'I've seen that look before.'

'Mooning over what's-her-name again.'

Jimmy endured the taunts because he had no other option, but sometimes the only way to get Nobby and his cronies to leave him alone was by showing that he was one of them. As such, he often found himself forced to participate in their bullying of him, if only to pretend that he was unaffected by their unwanted attention. He did have minimum standards though, and mockery of Sarah was something he would not stand for. James Buckland may not have been a knight of the realm, but it was not for lack of purity.

Turner was genuinely curious, but there was no way of asking a serious question without risking the ridicule of his mates, 'So what's she see in you, then?'

True to form, Nobby resorted to smut, 'Can't be his manhood - it hasn't grown to size yet. Either that, or it was shrivelled in the flames.'

Jimmy could handle a bum-burning, but he was scathing when his girl's morals were questioned. Though he knew it only encouraged the others, he was unable to let the insult pass, 'Disgusting, you are. Sarah and I are waiting until we are wed.'

'Foolish lad. Try before you buy, I always say.'

'It's not like that for us. We are in love.'

'Very nice. And how do you measure the extent of your love with your breeches pulled up? By holding hands and whispering in each other's ears?'

'Yes! And with picnics, family meals and outings.'

'Outings?'

'Playhouses and the opera.'

'Well, she sounds like a real firecracker, lad. I don't think I'll try to steal her from you if it's opera that's your ken.'

'You disgust me with your filth.'

Turner decided that it had come time to simmer things down, the better to extend the entertainment before it all got out of hand and ended in blows, 'Here, steady on, he's only larking with you. A bit of fun.'

'It's not funny when you speak about Sarah like a cheap lady.'

Nobby nodded, 'Aye, lad, it's no good if she's cheap. Free is far better.' Crude laughter accompanied the jibe, and he took enormous relish in winding the boy up like a spinning top.

'The innocence of young love: a haven in a horrid reality. There's no place for it at all.'

'Not when there are whorehouses open for trade.'

Every barb was intended to make Jimmy writhe like a worm on a hook. When he seemed to have calmed sufficiently, Nobby threw more fuel on the fire, 'So are her knickers white, boy?'

For his part, Jimmy was both bemused and offended by the comment, 'What other colour would they be?' He blushed a deep crimson at the mere mention of Sarah's intimate apparel.

'Well, maybe she doesn't wear anything at all under her pretty strumpet's dress.'

The young man was shocked at the suggestion. In a state of confusion at the mere mention of such gross impropriety, he flew into a rage. He leapt upon the offender, but Turner and others restrained him. Jimmy continued struggling in their iron grip, unwilling to yield. For such a slightly built individual, he possessed remarkable strength; not enough to compete with grown men, but still...

'Simmer down, Nobby is from Sheffield. He probably can't afford fancy clothes for his wife.'

Nobby had a grin from ear to ear. He'd never seen Jimmy so lively, 'That's true.'

The young apprentice was beginning to tire, and when he finally had no strength remaining, the restraining hands assisted him back to his feet, 'I can't believe that you would talk about your own wife like that.'

'Well what about you, then? Why did you join up?'

'Excuse me? I don't understand the thrust of your question.'

Nobby spread his hands in a placating gesture, 'Well, I joined the army to get away from the nagging cow.'

Turner interjected, 'I thought that it was a horse that you called a nag?'

'OK, so her face is like a horse. But the rest of her is more like a cow. Mind you, I could have had a real looker if I'd wanted one. I just didn't see the point in trying to hold off the advances of every grand Lord and Dandy. They're more grateful to you for noticing them, the plain ones.'

'Plain? I thought you said she resembled a cow with a horse's head?'

'She does. An ordinary cow, like. Not the pedigreed sort, with papers and new halter and such.'

'Mine, I brought her a broom for a wedding gift. She rides it around all night as fancy pleases her, then by day she cleans the house with it. It's used to whack the sprogs when they don't look lively enough, too. Bargain purchase, that was - real quality straw.'

Jimmy was nonplussed. Here they were, making fun of each other as they had done to him all along. *Maybe it was a rite of passage?* It still didn't make it acceptable, the way that they carried on. They were supposed to be grown men.

'Even the C.O. knows how to do it right. He's got some girl eating from his palm, and she has a ring on her finger.'

Jimmy decided that if he was championing the innocent, then it was a natural extension to stand up for anyone who was being maligned in their own absence, 'She's probably widowed.'

'Have it your way then, Squire James.'

*   *   *

Miller marvelled at the quiet cocoon of silence that surrounded him now that the Le Rhône engine had shut down. After a brief reflection, he laboriously climbed down from the cockpit and began the slow trudge across the grass of the airfield. Finally he was indoors, 'Blimey, it's freezing at five thousand! I think my bollocks have retreated into my stomach, and not through fear of the Bloody Baron.' He looked to an orderly, 'Get me something hot to drink!'

'He's three months dead, sir.'

'I said it wasn't through fear of him, didn't I? You think I'd say that if he was alive?' The man scurried away to attend to Miller's requirement.

Ray Barker had some discrete information to pass along, 'Your lady-friend from the hospital is waiting for you, sir.'

Miller grinned at the adjutant, 'Not before I stand in front of the stove and warm up, old boy; wouldn't want to give her the wrong impression concerning my endowment.' You could take a man out of the navy and tell him that he was now a member of the Royal Air Force, but you'd have difficulty in ever removing his crudity.

'Hello, Mary. How's your husband?'

'One day he'll use it again. Until then, you'll have to do.'

'Your directness is part of your charm.'

'I thought it was my intellect that drew you to me?'

'Call it whatever you want, my dear. Ports do change their names from time to time.'

'It never ceases to amaze me that the last thing to appear in a man is maturity.'

'Don't worry, we derive comfort from the fact as well. What should amaze you is what appears first.'

'No, what's amazing about that aspect is that you don't tire of it. Anything new in your part of the war?'

'Some of my pilots have attracted the wrong sort of attention to themselves; and worse, to me. They went and strafed a nearby farm and now the aggrieved party is after my blood.'

'As I said, maturity is the last thing to develop.'

'Yes, well, it's one thing to fuck a friend's wife. It's quite another to shoot up the entire countryside. It's raised quite a scene.'

351

'We can't have that. Better to limit ourselves to cuckolding, don't you agree?'

'Now see here, what he doesn't know won't get me shot.'

'Don't worry, darling, I shan't tell. It's only temporary, anyway.'

'What about you?'

'Nothing to remark upon, really. Just the usual pain and suffering: carrying away amputated limbs in buckets of blood; emptying the beds of those who died in the night to make way for the latest pathetic casualties; holding the hands of those who'll die the next night. Have you considered stopping what you do to make less work for me?'

Miller could see the obvious distress that the conversation was causing, but he didn't know how to rein it in, 'It's not my doing. My Huns have all gone down on the other side of the lines.' It wasn't entirely true, but the exceptions had not required hospitalisation. As such, Miller didn't feel that his reasoning had been impeded, 'Some poor German lass is mopping up my mess.'

Tears welled in Mary's eyes. Miller hated when she did that, 'Don't worry, I'll send a letter of apology when the war is done.'

'And what if you don't make it?'

He reminded her of their reality, 'You have a husband to go back to. I'll be taking what's in my head to the grave, and the sooner the better.'

'I thought you had the soul of a Spartan? That's what your friends say.'

He grimaced, 'That's not all they say, either.' Miller's eyes followed a fly that circled aimlessly around the room, 'Maybe it's time I stood with the three hundred.'

She pleaded with him, 'Don't talk like that.'

'Then let us talk of the future, one where my best friend is overjoyed to learn that his firstborn bears a striking resemblance to the best man at his wedding. You could ask to call the child George, in honour of the King of England - one of three cousins who gave us this jolly war.'

'That isn't funny. We aren't having a baby. I've taken every precaution.'

He smiled wickedly, 'No you haven't, and I should know because we always end up sweaty afterwards.'

'Not to be pedantic, but the sweatiness is during. Afterwards it's cigarettes and a lovely snooze.'

His face was a picture of innocence, 'Do you go to sleep as well?'

'You know what I mean.'

'It all makes perfect sense now, but when the war is over there is going to be some considerable explaining to do.'

'Nobody will know.'

'I meant to ourselves. Will we ever look back on this and make sense of it all?'

'Hold that thought, sailor.'

'Which one?'

'The one where we are all alive, with the luxury to look back.'

'So serious today.'

'Shall we discuss the great poets, then?'

He laughed, but she meant it. He had no such intention, 'How about casting aside our inhibitions instead?'

'And by inhibitions, you really mean clothes?'

'That's the spirit. It's been too long since I've experienced your... intellect, wasn't that what you called it?'

'Do you know what I like most about you, George?'

'I'm sure you want to tell me.'

'Your ready access to copious quantities of alcohol.'

'Happy to be of service.'

'Likewise.'

There was a brief lull in the conversation as Miller completed an interrupted train of thought, 'Byzantium and Constantinople.'

'Beg pardon?'

'Ports that change names.'

Chapter 27

August 1918: Error of Judgement

Miller dreamed, but his sleeping mind was not doing him any favours. Instead, it digested everything he had learned about risk. He had decided a long time ago that there was no part of the war that appealed to him. Of all of the forms of combat that existed, none were any better than any other.

On the face of it, the Royal Navy had the best lifestyle of the three services. They lived in clean quarters and most of their action was sporadic so few casualties were sustained most of the time. Unfortunately, 'most of the time' did not mean all of the time. When a magazine exploded after taking a direct hit, it was not unusual that a thousand men died together. Tragedy on a warship was invariably catastrophic. Whether it was fire on board a battleship or suffocation on a sunken submarine, losses of the 'all hands' variety were all too common.

The infantry were no better off, and entire battalions were sometimes obliterated within hours or days. Generally speaking, though, losses in the line were in ones and twos as artillery shells kept being lobbed onto their heads. Bullets and disease were no less enviable, but for all of his daily hazards, a Tommy occupied much of his time fending off boredom.

For the fliers in the squadrons, death rarely came in clumps. Losses were more spaced out and came in a steady drip similar to water torture as, one by one, men failed to come home. Where the navy sweated on the appearance of the death card in a tarot deck, the army passed around a hand grenade instead of a hot potato. Unhappy with either of those games, the men of the RAF played Russian roulette with each other.

In the balance, Miller had concluded that the infantry must have had the worst of it, not because of the risks they endured, but because of their living conditions. In good weather, they lived in dirty holes with ramparts partially comprised of the bodies of their enemies. If it rained, all they had was mud.

The faceless thousands peered into his sleeping mind. Eventually, they reached out to pull at him with bold, grasping hands, trying to get him to join their bulging ranks.

But it was only Barker shaking his shoulder, 'There's been another accident.'

Miller roused himself. He was only marginally more pleased to be facing reality, and only then because he reckoned he was being paid for his waking hours, whereas sleep was supposed to be on his own time, 'Who is it this time?'

'One of the riggers has walked into a propeller.'

That got the commander's full attention, 'Hell.' He rubbed grit from his eyes, then asked the question again, 'Who?'

'Fenton.'

'I'm only grasping at straws here, but how bad is it?'

Barker only had bad news, 'About what you'd expect.'

Miller closed his eyes for an instant and turned his face up towards the sun. When he opened them again it seemed as though he had hoped that looking skyward could offer an explanation, 'What happened?'

'One of the pups was getting too excited by the noise. He ran over to stop it getting chopped to bits and lost his footing.'

They pondered the scales that God used to weigh the world. Miller delivered his judgement, 'I liked Fenton. He was solid, didn't make careless errors. If he worked on my machine I never had wires slackening and coming loose. Or breaking, other than by Hunnic intervention. The man was a genius.'

'There'll probably be some damage to the propeller.'

Miller could imagine.

'Solid bit of timber, but you don't cut a man into pieces without needing to check everything for problems. It's too late to pick up an engine vibration a hundred miles from home.'

'Which machine is it?'

'Ellington's.'

'Maybe you shouldn't get it looked at?'

Barker wondered if Miller really meant it. As an afterthought, he added, 'The pup is unharmed, in case you were interested.'

*　　*　　*

Marcel Bonnet celebrated his twenty-first birthday by clambering out from beneath an overturned Spad. He had applied too much brake on landing and the machine had nosed over.

Dumont was grinning from ear to ear, in part because it was always amusing to see people trip up, but also because he had not had long to wait to get his own back. Four days previously he had himself landed heavily and bent an axle. Bonnet had been ribbing him about it ever since.

357

The battered pilot may have been shaken by his mishap, but he kept things in perspective, 'At least I still have my health!'

Many others had been less fortunate. The most recent loss had been unusual in that the dead man had crashed because of a minor injury – he had taken a bullet through the palm of his hand. Unable to hold the control stick properly, the slipperiness of his blood had compounded matters. The end result looked as though the fellow had done his best to dig his own grave with a propeller.

Though there were always new ways to be killed, it didn't necessarily require assistance from the two greatest hazards - those being the Germans and the weather. The upside down Spad before them today was evidence of this and had been caused by nothing other than human error. Bonnet had had too little sleep and too much to drink. Had he possessed those commodities in inverse proportions he would not have now been sporting minor cuts and a black eye.

Bonnet and Dumont watched as the ground crew went to work determining the extent of the damage. Though the aircraft had been upended, often the required repairs were minimal and could be effected reasonably quickly. Dumont made light of the incident, 'If you'd wanted another machine you need only to have asked.'

Bonnet gave an elaborate shrug, 'Maybe the bump will fix the infernal tapping in the cylinder head.'

Dumont ran fingers through his black hair, 'I do not understand how your mechanic cannot find the problem.'

'You see? We are alike in our mystification.'

'Perhaps he is not the best man for the job? Have you thought to perform any of the work yourself?'

Bonnet had a poor view of his own mechanical skills, 'I do my work and Louis does his. We do not presume knowledge of the other's field of expertise.'

Dumont pursed his lips in a moue of concentration that made his moustache move in ways that looked as though a mouse had emerged from a nostril, 'It seems that you are making progress, Marcel. All that remains for you is to not presume expertise in flying.' The backdrop of a Spad with its wheels pointing at the sky added weight to the intended belittlement.

'Why would you say such a thing? That particular flying machine is Louis' cherished pet, and he can give it a nice tummy rub while its legs are in the air. I have done him a favour!'

Dumont's eyes twinkled as he scowled, 'I can only comfort myself that we are not close, you and I, if that is how you treat your friends.'

'Only now you realise this? Have you never wondered at the odd flavour of the cigars that I have freely given you?'

Dumont regarded the other with suspicion, unsure if the man was serious or not and wondering how he may have contaminated the tobacco. Then he laughed. There were much worse things to deal with than a few harmless pranks.

Bonnet lit up, and held out the offering, 'You first?'

Dumont smiled uncertainly, shaking his head as he declined, 'You first.'

'As you wish.' Bonnet took a few puffs before he held it out again, daring his friend to accept the renewed offer, 'Here.'

Dumont still smelt a rat, 'I shall pass.'

Bonnet shrugged, secretly amused at the doubt that he had planted.

They stood there together, one smoking and the other not, watching the enlisted men working to right the aircraft. Neither pilot offered to help.

Bonnet was thinking about the fatal crash from a few days ago, 'Roque was unlucky.'

Dumont had his own take on it, 'He shouldn't even have been up that day, but Jolivet was ill and still hasn't recovered. Now Bouvier is also bedridden.'

'Malingerers.'

'I have a theory.'

'Flu?'

'Not about that; of course they have the flu. Flying.'

'There are a few theories going around. Louis is of the opinion that engines can be made powerful enough to double a machine's altitude.'

Dumont wondered how cold it would be at fifteen thousand metres if such a thing came to pass, but all he said was, 'What would he know about it? He can't even locate a fault in the cylinder. He is an idiot.

'There is such a thing as physics. To get an engine powerful enough to increase the ceiling by such an amount would mean building a bigger unit: not just the engine but also the rest of the aeroplane. You only need to use your eyes to see that the most monstrous examples getting about today struggle to fly at all. Personally, I think that the upper limit has already been reached.'

Bonnet knew that Dumont did not have a degree in either physics or engineering, so could not speak with proper authority on the subject, 'As long as you don't forget to search above your position, I think you may believe whatever you wish.'

'The quest for higher and faster is becoming much more difficult. Give me a machine that can turn.'

'I prefer the Spad.'

Dumont looked pointedly at Bonnet's machine, 'Few would think so from the evidence.'

After nineteen-eighteen, a tendency would emerge to gauge the formidability of aircraft technology by simple values: speed, ceiling, weight, range, wing loading. During the first war when flying machines were used, this was not so apparent and no-one really knew which qualities were more important. The fliers themselves were less interested in breaking down the whole and instead concentrated on the complete package. This practical approach made sense, because no value on its own conclusively dictated the worth of a design.

Despite widespread tinkering with almost every part of an aircraft, discussions amongst the first aviators on topics such as horsepower were very rare. Certainly they were interested in learning about their equipment, but during the pioneering years of powered flight the focus of most of their interest was in simply understanding at an elementary level how engines actually worked. This learning curve was always growing, but it wouldn't be until the next generation that airmen became more technically obsessed prior to climbing into a cockpit for the first time.

Bonnet knew that Dumont had more to say, 'Tell me your theory.'

'Ah, finally you ask something sensible.'

'If that's how you feel, I won't bother any more with offering to share my cigars with you.' Bonnet took one of the items in question and rolled it beneath his nose and breathed deeply, the better to savour it.

All that resulted was a disdainful comment on his poor attempt at facial growth, 'I think you have some mange growing on your lip.'

Bonnet made his own riposte, 'You take your life in your hands by flamboyantly parading your own splendour for all of the world to see. A Boche flier could shoot any one of us on purpose, but you are the only one risking being shot by a poacher.'

Dumont was unimpressed that his friend would try to mock him for moustachioed excellence, especially when an obvious attempt at imitation had failed so miserably. Instead of getting down in the muck with the other fellow, he decided to espouse his view of the world, 'It could be that each soul has a pre-ordained number of heart beats allotted to them by God. A little baby may die because he has been given only ten or a hundred; an old man would have many millions.'

He paused for effect and Bonnet seized upon the moment to do a quick calculation in his head, 'So would a small child.'

Dumont frowned at the interruption but elaborated on his thought, 'A man who lives with great excitement causes his heart to beat more quickly than a lazy man. Consequently, we ourselves are more likely to go to an early grave than die of boredom.'

Bonnet gave the idea minimal consideration because it was utter nonsense and, really, didn't deserve any attention at all. *The man is a lunatic if he expects to be taken seriously.* But all he said was, 'A bullet in the head would nullify either strategy.'

'Well, naturally.'

'I think you should concentrate more upon flying than philosophising.'

'My dear Marcel, it wouldn't hurt if you concentrated more on flying, either.' Dumont pretended that his look towards the abused Spad wasn't loaded with meaning.

* * *

Miller had found enough spare time in his schedule to squeeze in a visit to Mary. As he drove to meet her, a conversation with Callaghan from that morning kept buzzing in his brain. Bowe had admitted to one of the fitters that he was taking bets relating to men in his old squadron returning from patrols. No names had been mentioned about how Bowe was gaining enough information to work out the odds that he was offering, and Miller quite frankly didn't care. If there was any truth in the allegation, the man would answer for it.

Miller decided to get Barker to do some sniffing around and see what could be seen. He was sure that something would turn up. In the meantime, he dwelt upon the latest loss of another of England's best fliers, 'Harry, how are you chaps receiving the news about Mannock?'

'No offence intended, sir, but none of us knew him.'

'I suppose not.'

'Did you?'

'No.'

'There's a poem about him that I heard this morning.'

'Oh?'

Harry seemed reluctant to go on, 'Do you want to hear it?'

Miller didn't care one way or another, 'If you'd like.'

The driver was very self-conscious about performing for an audience of one, especially when the man had rank. But having made the offer, he was forced to make the effort:

'An RFC cove name of Mannock,
Sent all the Huns into a panic.
He flew SE5s,
In twisting spirals and dives,
And he had a half decent mechanic.

'But poor Mick, cause he hated The Hun,
Eventually out of luck run,
In the deadliest of games,
He crashed, burned in flames.
Fate caught up with the top Englishman.'

Miller was unsurprised by the content. It was more of the same fare that he had heard before. Only the details were different, 'Bit depressing.'

'Yes, sir.'

'Sounds to me like one of Bowe's efforts.'

'He says he got it from a friend, but who can say where it came from before that?'

Miller agreed, 'Bad news travels fast, but maybe that particular verse would be better off being forgotten. It's disrespectful.'

Harry became acutely uncomfortable in the presence of his superior's censure, so he drove in silence. Miller had nothing further to add. He had other things on his mind; *Who does Bowe know that is giving him current information relating to his former squadron?*

Luckily, Mary was between shifts so they retreated to her quarters together. She still wore her uniform and the apron was smeared with blood left by what appeared to have been a fist that had grabbed hold of her. Miller thought it best not to ask. Mary had a slight frown,

'There was a colonel at the aid station yesterday trying to locate one of his men.'

Miller was moved to comment, 'Sounds like a funny sort of colonel.'

'He was wearing a couple of medals. One of them was a Victoria Cross.'

'I didn't think you cared about that sort of thing?'

'I don't. The surgeon pointed it out.'

'What was his interest?'

'That's what I'm coming to. The surgeon asked the colonel what he had done to win it. The colonel told him it was none of his concern, but that he preferred his other medal.'

'Other medal?'

'It had a blue and white ribbon.'

Miller knew a dozen men who wore the ribbon of the Military Cross, and none of them would have rated it more highly than England's most prestigious valour award, 'Did he say why?'

'He said it was for saving a man's life.'

Miller mulled over the reason, 'Like I said, a funny sort of colonel.'

'Maybe he was only a captain when he performed his deed?'

He nodded equably, 'That's the most likely explanation.'

Mary looked critically at her reflection in the mirror and removed the apron. She patted at her hair, but was not content with the effect, 'You know, George, I had no idea that men were so foul-mouthed.'

'The colonel or the surgeon?'

'Not them, just men in general.'

'Ah.'

'Really! It's all quite beastly, listening to them when they think I can't hear.'

'It serves you right for eavesdropping.'

'But I wasn't.'

Miller crept up behind her and encircled her waist, breathing a puff of warm air into her ear, 'Then be thankful that they consider the company they're in before they open their mouths.'

'I've half a mind to give them a talking to the next time I hear it.'

He smiled, 'No penny for your thoughts, then? You'd do it for free?'

'Seriously, I'm sure that your father never spoke in such a manner.'

'I'm sure you're right. And yet here we are alone together having virtuous thoughts that could only have met with his approval.'

Mary suspected he was toying with her, 'If only you were all as attentive in the classroom, you'd learn more than what is passed down in the playground.'

'You mean the gutter?'

'Now you're making fun of me.'

'Only now?'

She laughed, 'Stop it. You know what I mean.'

'I'm pretty sure that the Saxon tongue is used whenever Englishmen gather in groups of two or more, else how has the language endured? It can't just skip generations.'

'It only makes you all the more hypocritical. High moral standards aren't valid if they aren't always practised, regardless of the company you keep.'

'You could be right. Maybe my men would be reluctant to go forth every day if the ladies could see firsthand the task that they do.'

Mary frowned, 'I've seen.'

Could gentle and brutal be combined into a single word? 'Secondhand.' He doubted that Mary fully appreciated how different mortal combat was

366

to the hospital ward: the smells, the nerves, the rawness. She only had antiseptic and the screams of the wounded, and screams were something missing in a dogfight, unless you counted your own. The wind carried the rest away.

They said nothing for a while, but it was sometimes their custom. Either their thoughts flowed together, or they drifted apart in ways that were afterwards difficult to reconnect.

The room was sparsely furnished, with just one photograph occupying pride of place upon the only table. Miller's eyes were drawn to the grainy image. A naval officer and his bride self-consciously looked straight into the camera, 'Why did you choose him over me?'

'Is that what you think happened?'

'Wasn't it?'

'George dear, I would have said yes to either of you. Edward just asked me first.'

'That's all it took?'

'The whole world had gone crazy. It didn't seem out of place.'

'Your whole life ahead of you: a hell of a thing to do.'

'I saw it as a chance to grab onto something before it became too late. See? I was right.'

*   *   *

Sebastian von Bülow couldn't understand what was so hard about flying and shooting. True, he was himself diminished in the aftermath of his smashed arm, but it didn't excuse the poor performance of the remainder of his men. Not one of them had scored a single victory since he had assumed command almost six weeks ago. He decided to take a different approach, 'Kluth!'

The senior veteran prepared himself for more intimidation from the disgruntled commander, 'The men just aren't ready. We'll have to break them in one at a time. Smaller patrols.'

Kluth was doubtful, 'Won't that be more dangerous?'

'It's a war. What do you want?' Von Bülow had his hands on his hips.

'What do you have in mind?'

'You and I will go up tomorrow to see what we can see. Neither of us has any worthwhile recent experience, so it will give us a chance to have a crack at something without worrying about the others pissing about and ruining the show.'

Kluth could see merit in the idea, but remembered his previous two outings with smaller than usual formations. Both of those had been in the company of Lehmann and neither had been a hell of a lot of fun, 'So be it.'

'I'm done with hunting for now. It's time to go fishing for a change.'

'I'm sorry? Fishing?'

'There is a new squadron operating Dolphins in our sector, so calling it hunting isn't really accurate; we're going fishing. We'll beat up their airfield to stir things up a bit. The English are having things too easy these days.'

'Dolphins are mammals.'

'What are you trying to tell me, Kluth?'

'They aren't fish.'

'They swim, so they are fish. That is an order.'

Von Bülow fastened the chin strap on his flying helmet. He looked at the other man doing the same in the pre-dawn air and smiled, 'You will have done this before?'

The answer was terse, 'A time or two.'

'Well, at least we aren't going after any kite balloons.'

Kluth was not entirely grateful about having to face a lesser evil.

'Don't get yourself killed, Kluth. I need your experience to get this *Jasta* back into the war. Now let's go and give the bastards something to remember us by.'

They mounted up and prepared to venture into the dragon's lair.

Chapter 28

September 1918: Black September

George Miller had started his day well. A DFW reconnaissance plane had fallen to his guns before breakfast. Now he was in the air for the second time that day but this time with the entire squadron in tow in a tremendous show of strength. It was an impressive sight to behold.

A typical squadron was comprised of men of varying degrees of expertise in the fighting trade, and though measuring their worth by their number of victories was frowned upon, nevertheless it was a valid yardstick. Roughly half of all airmen would never know the satisfaction of bringing an enemy aviator down, and of the rest, few would achieve the feat more than once. Pilots with three or more victories were in evidence everywhere, but that spoke more of the extent of cumulative losses than anything else. The journey to even so modest a score as one or two victories was fraught with peril. Consequently, men who had registered combat claims were like gold. Every trick they had learned had come at a price and the experience of each veteran was invaluable.

Every man was on the lookout, alertly scanning below for signs of easy pickings. They checked above with greater attention, with a zeal perhaps bordering on paranoia, for the first hint of an attack out of the sun. A squadron at full strength had almost fifty eyes, though inevitably some of those eyes were new to flying and hadn't yet learnt to spot trouble before it struck. Other fliers happened to be looking the wrong way at the critical moment, but fifty eyes is still a lot of eyes and it was a reasonable bet that at least one pair would spot a threat in time to take evasive action, an act which in itself would warn the others.

On this occasion it was Callaghan who spotted the indistinct forms rapidly descending upon them. That it was one of the most experienced pilots who saw the danger first was not unusual; it was part of the reason that he was still alive to have earned his seniority. Miller saw the flight commander signalling with his fist, pointing upwards. The commander acknowledged him and pulled his Camel into a turning climb. The rest of the squadron followed suit, scarcely affording themselves time to steel for the impending action.

From their superior altitude, the Fokkers fell upon the Camels, machine guns sparkling wickedly as they plunged through the British formation. Tracer bullets laced the sky and the smell of burnt cordite and castor oil were invasive to nostrils whilst gunfire competed with the roar of red-lining engines for the right to overwhelm a man's senses with their assault upon his ears. Adrenaline and blood pumped through every man irrespective of his sworn allegiance.

The first machine to fall away was a Camel. Miller had a notion that the stricken machine had been marked with an 'X', though he wouldn't have sworn on a stack of bibles to the fact. If his identification had been correct, for some reason he couldn't recall the pilot's name. From a certain point of view that was a good sign; not linking a machine to a specific individual meant that Miller hadn't lost one of his established men. Nevertheless there now another letter home to be written - one which would cause some problems for an anonymous family in England; problems beyond the inconvenience of writing words of condolence. Miller had become intimate with that part of the job by now.

His thought about the downed Camel was completed in the blink of an eye, but it had been a distraction that he chastised himself for. Until there were no more Germans duelling with his men, the only thing he had time for was narrowing his focus on the chaos as it unfolded in familiar but unpredictable patterns. Every man strove to turn with the enemy in an attempt to latch onto the tail of his respective opponent, with the uncharitable intention of shooting the poor soul full of holes.

A second machine fell, this time to the Camels of 'C' Flight, who had been in pursuit of a Fokker which had strayed into their path. Upton had flown in close to score strikes on the cockpit, riddling the pilot with bullets. It was the only discernible damage to impact the German aircraft. The Fokker reared vertically before turning over and spiralling earthwards.

The next machine to fall from the sky took the form of a fireball. As the fuel-soaked frame fell, its burning fabric peeled away and writhed in eddies, flames fanned by the momentum of its fall. It must have been visible for miles - a beacon for anyone nearby looking for trouble. Sure enough, within minutes some friendly SE5s had joined the free for all.

The frequency with which Allied scout pilots scored individual victories over the Western Front in nineteen-eighteen was less to do with their considerable ability and much to do with lottery. The simple fact of the matter was that they significantly outnumbered the Germans. On a *pro rata* basis, that meant less sharing to go around. Whereas the *Jasta's* pilots had a target rich environment, their opposite numbers flying for Britain and France had leaner pickings.

With very few exceptions, the men who fought for Germany did not consider themselves to have the better part of the deal.

With the arrival of the unexpected reinforcements, Miller extricated himself from the thick of the fighting. Mistaken identity aside, entering into a free-wheeling combat with so many individuals on both sides was fraught with risk. It was impossible to keep track of every machine swirling about in the man-made mechanical maelstrom; sooner or later someone would stitch him up. Instead, the squadron commander contented himself with prowling the periphery of the action, patiently hanging back until an opportune moment arrived - at which point he could pounce upon an unwary victim.

It was not long before Miller noticed that one of the Fokkers was trying to play the same game of cat and mouse, though with considerably more difficulty. Being outnumbered, the German couldn't simply sit back unnoticed or un-harried. He was cagey, though, and none of the Camels or SEs could corral him.

Miller convinced himself that he had identified the enemy leader. The man's aircraft bore conspicuous white markings on the tail that the other machines lacked. The Camel pilot considered going after him, but resisted the urge. Where was the benefit to shooting a top-notch veteran, if such he was? Germany had plenty of those to spare. One more or one less was not too important in the wider picture, but to willingly go after a hard-nosed DVII veteran was a different proposition to stalking two-seaters.

Miller was no coward, but he attributed his continued survival on assessing risks and refusing to engage an enemy if he lacked enough of a positional advantage. The Fokker pilot clearly had an awareness of his surroundings. He would not be falling victim to any ruse that the Englishman could spring.

I have one life to give, and I'll be damned if I'll be risking offering it up to this bastard. Miller had already seen more than his fair share of the war, and if he decided to give his life to a family as yet unborn, rather than to a murderous Prussian, then who was in a position to fairly criticise him for it?

The dogfight became a massacre. The Fokkers, already hard-pressed, were shot to bits. In total, eight went down, with two falling to a determined onslaught by Callaghan. Some burned, some crashed and one fell apart in the air. Smoke trails, travelling in the opposite direction to which smoke had usually travelled throughout the millennia, followed each of them into the depths of the abyss.

Miller counted four parachutes.

Suddenly, the Fokker DVIIs were gone, scattered like leaves blown away in an autumn wind as they quit the fight and ran for cover. It was all very well for the Germans to flee in ones and twos - they were over their own territory. But any Allied pilot caught over enemy airspace was taking his life into his hands, and that was something that every man did quite enough of as it was without further tempting the fates. Miller's men regrouped, finding safety in numbers. He reiterated the creed: you pick your fights, bloody the enemy, and quit in time to do it all again tomorrow.

And bloodied they had been! Even as the dogfight swirled about him, Miller considered the reasons for the poor showing of the Germans. After all, they had the advantage of superior altitude, and had initiated the scrap. They could just as readily have ignored the Camel patrol and gone looking for easier prey. Instead, they had pitched in and been hammered flat.

During that entire time, which seemed like hours but in reality was closer to twenty minutes, the moment never arrived where Miller felt obliged to re-enter the fray. He would not lose any sleep over it.

There had been more than enough Camels and SEs to deal a significant blow to the Germans. All in all, he considered that it had been a good day's work.

Though Miller had not fired his guns in anger, he had spent his time analysing the enemy for strengths and weaknesses. The mottled *Jasta* had been massacred, and he had a few theories based upon his observations. There were two possibilities that presented themselves as the most likely reasons: firstly, the Fokker DVII was not all that it had been reported to be; secondly, the day's events had involved a German unit with little real combat experience.

Miller knew where he would have put his money. The lizard-skinned machines could only be as good as the men who flew them, and these fellows had been inept. Miller had already clashed with DVIIs a few times and it had curled his whiskers. Besides which, the new Fokker would never have been preferred over other types already in service if it was an inferior design. Today they had not lived up to their formidable reputation: hanging vertically from their propellers as they peppered accurate bursts of gunfire into everyone they shot at had not been in evidence.

Of course, the German commander had not led his men by example and Miller wondered if the unit's poor showing was connected to this. Though he himself had hung back on this occasion, Miller's squadron was used to his absence on patrols. It was more often the case that the three flight commanders took the men into battle, and they usually did so very effectively. There was simply not much call for Miller's services as a flier any more. His role had become more of an administrative one. That he chose to fly at all was just that – a choice.

The violent action had cut the patrol short far quicker than would have otherwise been the case - a direct result of fuel being chewed through at an alarming rate. There would now be a hole in the aerial blanket that the Allies had thrown over the front, but the Camels had done a job and the next patrol would soon plug the gap.

Holding formation as they battled the prevailing wind on their way home, Miller counted his charges. He picked out Callaghan. One Camel was missing from 'A' Flight. Miller tried to recall the names of the men who comprised Callaghan's unit. Two candidates sprang straight into Miller's mind, and their names were Elphinstone and Ellington. He found it hard to separate them as independent personalities. One of the two had been flying the missing machine that had been marked with an 'X'; Miller was certain of it.

Sebastian von Bülow killed the motor. The engine spluttered and died and the windmilling propeller eventually became stationary. He sat in the cockpit, shattered at the events of the day.

Unbuckling his safety harness, he gripped the leather coaming of the cockpit rim and climbed out of his seat. Jumping gingerly to the ground, he angrily brushed past the men who had run up to attend to him. He saw Falkenhoff and stormed past in silence. The adjutant gazed at his back then fixed his attention on Kluth, 'What happened?'

Kluth was exhausted, 'They just aren't up to the job.'

Falkenhoff had already counted the Fokkers as they came in to land, and he knew that half of the *Jasta* was not missing due to an error in navigation. 'Eight?'

Kluth said nothing more, but followed in the footsteps of von Bülow. Whether the veteran's retreating figure was shaking his head in disbelief or disgust, Falkenhoff had no way to know.

The adjutant had every reason to want to stay clear of von Bülow, but he also had the responsibility to keep the unit functional at an administrative level. He knocked on von Bülow's door, but there was no answer. He tried the doorknob, and it was not locked. The door swung open. Falkenhoff let himself into the office and saw that the commander was well on the way to getting himself drunk.

Von Bülow glared at him, 'Did I ask you to come in?' To have said that von Bülow's tone was sharp would have been misleading. Although 'sharp' construes weapons that slit throats, the commander could have more aptly have been described as abrasive - more skin is lost, and nowhere near as cleanly.

Falkenhoff hadn't expected friendliness, 'Some of the ones who have gone down are reporting in. It mightn't be as bad as we think.'

'How bad do you think it is, Falkenhoff? Half of my planes were shot down, and for what? We got one Englishman. One!'

'We?' Falkenhoff knew that von Bülow had taken no part in the destruction of the Camel, and he had tired of the senior man's surliness a long time ago.

The frustrated *Jastaführer* glowered back at him then put his bottle down and enquired, 'Have you had any word on how many dead?'

'Only Braun so far.'

'Good riddance to him.'

Falkenhoff was appalled, 'You cannot mean it!'

Von Bülow was unrepentant, but instead of shouting, all he did was reach for the bottle. He eyeballed the other officer over the rim. There was a quiet knock on the door. Falkenhoff went to see who it was. He spoke quietly to the messenger, then closed the door again, 'Hildebrandt as well.'

Von Bülow closed his eyes and leaned back in his chair. He sighed, 'It had to happen sooner or later. They just can't compete against a better trained opponent.'

The adjutant tried to find the silver lining on a very ominous cloud, 'Well, at least we now know that the parachutes work. A lot of men would have died today without them.'

'They should have.' Von Bülow leaned in closer, 'This is why I was against their use all along.' Falkenhoff remembered no such thing, and it was not as if von Bülow kept his opinions to himself. There had never been a discussion on parachutes, but the adjutant said nothing. The commander continued, 'It is the enlisted men, I tell you. Two of them died today because they refused to engage.'

Falkenhoff tried to calm him down, 'We aren't the only unit taking such losses. It isn't fair that you are blaming these men. They do their best.'

'Fair? What has it to do with fair? If you want to complain about fair why not mention that usually the English are on our side whenever there is a fight with the rotten French? Then they go and do this. Why not cry at the injustice of the Americans siding against us because we sank a few of their ships when their supposed position of neutrality included running arms to our enemies? Fair? What world do you live in, Falkenhoff?' As the diatribe reached its end von Bülow was almost shouting.

The adjutant let the wave wash over him. He had endured many such scenes, and usually they blew themselves out. Von Bülow even seemed to forget his tirades, and if reminded of them, would generally pass them off as a 'heat of the moment' incident. Falkenhoff wished that the aggressive pilot would just go back to shooting Englishmen and blow off steam that way.

There was another knock on the door, and the commander irritably bade the man to enter.

The orderly was nervous. The walls were hardly sound proof and he had heard a great deal of the heated conversation, though he pretended otherwise, 'Excuse me, but we have just had word from *Leutnant* Ehlers. He has asked if we can pick him up.'

Von Bülow nodded his assent, 'Of course, send the truck.'

Falkenhoff volunteered to go with it. Again, the request was agreed, 'We have to look after them, these young officers. They are the future, if only they can survive long enough. The human mind and body are perishable resources, and should be properly cared for.'

This is the same man who wants to cull ninety percent of the population because of their lowly station.

Perhaps von Bülow had divined Falkenhoff's thoughts, because his next words answered the silent rebuke, 'My job is to kill, and to lead others who kill. In order to do so, I require the best men; men of integrity who have been raised expecting to serve the Kaiser.' He was not done, 'This applies equally to the quality of the equipment at my disposal. I will go so far as to say that in the event that my machine is damaged, I will requisition a new one and you should give the damaged crate to one of the fellows who have not shown an aptitude for fighting - the better that my proven talent remain unimpaired.'

Once more, Falkenhoff was aghast, 'Are you suggesting that I assign a faulty machine to one of the new men? You don't think that equates to murder?'

The response was dismissive, 'Think of it more as a practical allocation of resources, Falkenhoff. I'm sure that's how the war has been run from the beginning.'

Rather stiffly, the adjutant excused himself, 'I will go and fetch Ehlers.'

Von Bülow waved him away without wasting another breath. He tilted the bottle back to his lips.

The Camels landed. Miller found Callaghan. The man had an angry weal on his face which was probably caused by embers from one of the Huns he had shot down. It reminded Miller of the time that a spent cartridge had lodged painfully in his collar, 'Elphinstone?'

Callaghan curiously fingered his newly acquired burn, 'Ellington.'

'That's half of the problem solved.' It sounded heartless, but in an environment where friends died on a regular basis, anyone making your life more difficult than it already was received little sympathy.

Miller could see Elphinstone not far away, acutely aware that he was being spoken about. He managed to look stricken and sullen all at once. The senior men didn't care. Miller found the squadron adjutant, 'Captain Barker, put Ellington on the roster for every patrol for the next week. That way one man per flight can be rested every day.'

'Ellington? You mean the other one. Elphinstone.'

'Elphinstone. He'll get the message.'

'He won't fit into 'B' and 'C'. They don't know him, and they don't trust him either. They know what he did. He's unreliable. I don't think it's a good idea.'

'It looks like the Huns are starting to strap cook's apprentices and scullions into their planes these days, so it's probably less dangerous than usual. If he's still alive in a week he can start with a clean slate. That is, if we haven't heard from Farmer Frog in the meantime.'

'The poor bastard is probably terrified of what we'll do to him if he makes any more trouble for us.'

'He should be. Young men with modern weapons and scarcely a brain between them - he'd be wise to keep a low profile.'

380

'You'll only make an enemy of him.'

'So what will he do about it? Throw eggs at us as we fly overhead? I thought Bowe stole them all?'

Barker didn't think it was politic to point out that eggs were easily replaceable if the chickens were kept safe, 'Not him. Elphinstone.'

'Elphinstone? What of him? Is he related to the Duke of York? Or a personal friend to Lloyd George?'

Barker doubted that the Prime Minister kept such lowly company, 'I wouldn't think so.'

'Then he's an enemy who I think I can cope with.'

'That's a bold thing to say about someone who follows you into Hunland with a loaded machine gun.'

'Ellington and his friend -'

Barker interjected, 'Elphinstone.'

Miller didn't appreciate the interruption, 'I know his friend's name!... shot one cow grazing in a field. Between them. It took two of them to line up a cow and plug it. That's pretty poor preparation if he intends to shoot me in the back. He might be an idiot; it doesn't necessarily make him an imbecile. I'm not saying he isn't one, mind.'

The truck pulled over by the side of the road, and Ehlers emerged from within the post office from where he had called. 'Hello, Falkenhoff, I didn't expect to see you here.'

'He's on the warpath again.'

Ehlers furrowed his brow, 'What happened? I hardly saw a thing: I went this way, the Camel went that way, and then I piled up into the trees.'

'Are you hurt?'

'Some scratches only, from the branches. The bastard things have more than a passing resemblance to the birch rod that my father used to exercise his arm with.'

'We lost eight planes. Two dead.'

'Who?'

'Hildebrandt and Braun.'

Ehlers absorbed the news, 'Hildebrandt. How long was he with us? He was already with the *Jasta* when I joined.'

'Five months or so, I think.'

'Shit. I suppose von Bülow is getting fired up about the NCOs again.'

'I won't bother giving you a cigar for guessing as much.'

'Then what about a drink?' A flask was passed over to the downed airman. He observed, 'I get the sense that there could never be enough high-brows to satisfy von Bülow. If he had his way, and there were no other classes within our social structure, how would he feel superior to others?'

'I'm sure he'd find a way.'

'It wouldn't be hard. He's a decorated war hero.'

'He has a hat-full of medals, but I think that the price of attaining them has been far too high for him. When all is said and done, they are just ornaments made of enamelled metal hung on a ribbon.'

Ehlers was still clearly swayed by their allure, 'Maybe so, but they represent so much more.'

Falkenhoff had a way to bring things into perspective, 'You've already got your pilot's badge. Maybe you can catch up with von Bülow by getting yourself a wound badge next.' He pointed at a small cut on Ehlers' forehead, 'I'm afraid you'll have to do a bit better than that, though.'

The pilot dabbed at the cut, but it had already scabbed over. Reminded of his recent brush with death, he enquired after von Bülow's worst day, 'He harps on about the arm, but how did he really break it?'

'It was a crash. Haven't you been listening to him?' The remark was effectively daring the man to lie.

'I had a notion that he may have fallen over in the shower.'

'How would he have done that?'

'No-one could love him as much as he loves himself. He must practise somewhere. Maybe he slipped on the soap?' Together they chortled at the lewd suggestion.

Falkenhoff felt that he had said too much. He couldn't retract his defamatory comments, but he still cautioned his companion about being too loose-lipped, 'Just keep this discussion between ourselves.'

Ehlers knew that they shouldn't have been rubbishing the man, but he wasn't in as much awe of the commander's reputation as he would have been had he seen von Bülow at his peak, 'What can he do about it? He won't get a Blue Max for shooting someone like me. I haven't contributed anything worthwhile to the war effort so far.'

Most men who were shot down fit exactly that description: their lives were regularly cut short before they had done an adequate apprenticeship in the flying trade. The adjutant said as much, 'Twenty such esteemed fellows isn't even enough anymore, either. It's nearer to thirty these days from what I've heard. But I'm sure he'd derive some satisfaction if he could get just one more despite the revised quota. That man's military ambition will always be unfulfilled.'

Ehlers was mournful, 'The same for me. At least he has a start.'

'He's on the edge, Ehlers. All of our men are badly fatigued, but he has been doing it for a lot longer.'

Though he knew it was true, Falkenhoff had long since ceased believing the excuses that he continually seemed to be making for his commanding officer. At some point a man's actions polluted those who were most often in contact with him. Sebastian von Bülow had led a successful Albatros *Jasta* for an extended period – a year and a half - and whether or not he had been a key contributor to the unit's success, the harsh reality was that times had changed.

The man was simply no longer fit to command. Falkenhoff had heard that von Bülow had been one of those hand-picked by none other than Oswald Boelcke, and it was inconceivable that the great man had made such a recommendation based on false witness. Once a much-touted man seen to have considerable potential, the former prodigy would almost certainly be ending his career - and perhaps even his life - in charge of a sub-par Fokker DVII outfit.

Chapter 29

October 1918: Final Adjustments

Miller could tell by her demeanour that something was wrong, 'What is it?'

'He's dead.' There was no need to ask who.

There were no words. He held her gently for as long as she needed him to. She felt frail and cold, 'What are you going to do?'

'I was thinking that maybe you would marry me?' There - she had said it, and on the same day as the death of her husband, no less. *What an upside down world.*

'When?'

'This morning.'

Miller had thought she would have answered the other question, but Mary had known his train of thought, or perhaps it was simply her own. *Of course Ned had died this morning. If he had died during the night she would have come sooner with the news.*

He answered her proposal, 'All right.'

'You don't need to think about it?'

She had always divined his needs. How much closer could two people be? The timing was horrendous – poor Ned – and poor Mary too, engaged on the very day she was widowed. Every morning Miller accepted that he may not see the sunset. With that weight of expectation, he was already living the rest of his short life in the company of men for whom he didn't share an affinity - with a few exceptions. If one possible alternative was to spend many years with this one woman, could he claim to be sane if he passed up on the opportunity? 'No.'

'How can you be sure?'

'It's hard to explain.'

She looked at him expectantly.

Miller ordered his thoughts as best he was able because she deserved the effort, 'When I see the world, it's as though I am looking out of a cracked window. I can't see outside properly because the view is splintered and out of focus. The angles are wrong. Not just the angles. Everything is wrong, and it will never be put right. The glass can't be fixed. Ever.' He tried to say the most meaningful sentence of his life, 'But here's the thing: even though I can't sort out how to make things better, when I see you through that window looking in at me, at least I know how the world is supposed to be, and that is enough because it is all there can be.'

'I think I know what you mean.'

'I know you do. That's why I said yes.'

They hugged, and the war was a long way away.

Mary laughed while tears streaked her face. The laughter was neither sad nor happy, but a mixture of both, and so were the tears.

He brushed an errant strand of hair, 'Yes?'

'Not the most romantic way to organise the rest of our lives together.'

He laughed softly with her, 'No.'

'And on that note, I'm going to ask for one more thing.'

He asked what it was without saying a word or moving a muscle – heart to heart - and she answered him, 'I should very much like to have a child now. You can call him George if you wish.' She gave him a smile that carried knowledge beyond her years, 'After the King, of course.'

'A most unfortunate name in the event that it is a girl.'

'No, then it would be Maud.'

There was no end to the grief that had been piled onto their lives. No wonder each was a refuge for the other. He stroked her silken hair, 'Of course.'

She looked at him beseechingly, 'Please come back from the war.'

Miller made a decision on the spot, 'I am a squadron commander, Mary. I'm sure there is enough paperwork to keep me grounded. And you've given me a reason to want to be.'

His sudden commitment to her was startling, 'Are you allowed to do that?'

Miller had never told Mary that his responsibilities as a commander no longer required putting himself to the hazard, but that he did so by choice. To avoid ruining their fragile moment, he opted for the safer route. The truth could wait until another day. He smiled, 'We'll see.'

*   *   *

Von Bülow was worn out. The last few months had been hard, particularly the previous one. He had heard no few people referring to it as Black September. Since his return to combat his arm had not responded well to the rigours of violent manoeuvre combat, and his loss of mobility had seeped into every aspect of his life. He had not learned to cope with the restricted use of his injured limb, and no victories had been forthcoming against the air armadas that had been launched by the Royal Air Force on a daily basis. Failure to do what he did best drove him to outbursts of epic proportions. Within the confines of his unit, his authority was absolute, and the best defence against his constant ire was absence.

The men under his command knew of his achievements. How could they not when von Bülow recited them chapter and verse every time he came home with smoking guns and nothing to show for it? He had been reduced to the status of a broken and bitter veteran unable to lead by example. The senior pilots accepted the validity of his war record, but even those men's loyalty had been tarnished by direct exposure to the smouldering personality of their leader.

None of the animosity was lost on him. Von Bülow was injured in body and damaged in his soul, but he was rarely blind to that which was thrust directly into his face. If anything, he understood exactly why he was poorly thought of because he shared the sentiment entirely. A man was measured by what he could do. Though he could be given a head start by coming from a family of means, or by deeds of martial excellence, if he failed on the largest stage and did so publicly, then that failure was unforgivable. Even now, von Bülow saw his primary role as a leader of men - born to inspire by virtue of his pure blood and reinforced by his proven valour, all of it witnessed by the pitiful men in the infantry divisions as they scrabbled for their puny lives in the muck thousands of feet beneath his wings. That he was unable to continue as that same person was a corrosive poison in his veins.

For a man already loathing himself, the censure of his charges was accepted, but otherwise of no account whatsoever. Even if he was now a shadow of his old self, none of his men had even approached what he had done in the war. That wasn't the main source of his scorn; rather, though all of them were physically fit, none were his equal even now after his crash. He despised every one of them for it. Their mutual hatred was worn like a magical cloak, one which generated an eternal heat fuelled by no more than fleeting eye contact.

Who can know the inner workings of the High Command? Had decisions been made to improve morale in the over-stretched *Jastas* by reassigning some unit leaders to roles where they were already proven? Was any of it influenced by pressure being applied from below, or did it come from above? Had complaints filtered upwards, as they invariably did, but had uncharacteristically been heeded? Was the balance of the war so critical that any option was grasped at out of sheer desperation?

There was no way to answer any of these questions, and no-one was asking them in any case. Von Bülow received new orders, and that was the end of it. He had been transferred to a staff position in Berlin. Maybe someone had taken pity on his plight as a washed up commander. Lehmann was returning in his stead.

The morning patrol had still not returned as von Bülow was accompanied to his waiting car by Falkenhoff, who was there to see him off. There was no pretence of handshakes. Rather stiffly, the two men exchanged perfunctory salutes to satisfy the formality of the commander's sudden departure.

The adjutant saw no reason not to extend an olive branch as a gesture of goodwill now that he had seen the last of the prickly man, 'Good hunting when you get to Africa, *Herr Oberleutnant.*'

Von Bülow was not one to let matters drop, 'Berlin is not in Africa, Falkenhoff.'

Maybe the elephant will trample him when he finds it.

Kluth brought his men home without incident. He saw Falkenhoff waiting as the Fokker's motor cut out. He pulled off his leather helmet and raised an eyebrow, 'Gone?'

Falkenhoff nodded. Kluth shrugged, 'Please don't tell me that they've named me as his successor?'

The adjutant barked a laugh and was about to respond with his own comment, but suddenly stopped himself. He pointed and exclaimed, 'Those aren't ours!'

Kluth spun around and his eyes widened as he identified the bulky frontal aspect of the machines just now clearing the far boundary of the airfield, 'Get under cover, you idiots!' He followed his own advice as fast as his sprinting legs could carry him. Pilots and ground crew abandoned their aircraft and fled for safety.

As they cowered behind sand-bagged walls, a flight of Dolphins strafed the assembled Fokkers. Some were holed in the first pass. The English came back for another tilt. This time they were met by sporadic gunfire from the ground defences. The attack faltered and sped away before the Germans could mount a proper barrage.

Eventually, Kluth climbed to his feet, 'Could they have followed us home without anyone noticing?' The question was not particularly relevant. He turned his attention to more important matters, 'Is anyone hurt?'

Schilling was already organising the mopping up of this latest minor-scale action.

An hour later Falkenhoff received a phone call, 'Yes?'

Kluth overheard key words in the mostly one-sided conversation such as 'aid station', 'shot' and 'strafe,' and from which he inferred the general drift of the communication. These were not unfamiliar words for men who served in an army during times of war.

Falkenhoff fell silent, and when he hung up the receiver, it was almost as an afterthought. He had a bemused look on his face, 'Von Bülow's car was machine-gunned from the air.'

Kluth paused as he absorbed the information. He had to work through too many emotions to make any sensible response. For lack of anything suitable to say, he made a small circular gesture with his hand. It summed up everything, but he still didn't have the words.

Schilling chose that moment to poke his head into the room with a damage report. He looked at Kluth, then at Falkenhoff. He forgot why he had entered.

Kluth looked at Schilling, 'We've just received word that von Bülow is dead.'

Schilling frowned. Falkenhoff corrected Kluth, 'Shot. Not dead.'

'When?'

'Just after he left here. Possibly the same fellows who had a go at us.'

'Poor bastard.'

No-one had expected feelings of sympathy in the circumstances, but it is always easier to forgive someone who will never trouble you again. And it is never an accepted practice to rejoice out loud - even if that is one's first desire.

*   *   *

Yvonne looked down upon the sweat-drenched sheets. Whether Lucie would live or die was in the hands of the Lord, but either way there would be no happy ending. Yvonne doubted whether the coughing of her friend could be made more painful were she fed a steady diet of tacks and broken needles – each hacking spasm sounded as though the poor girl's lungs were being ploughed through a field of glass shards.

As if the war hadn't been enough, now the world was in the grip of an epidemic of proportions never previously witnessed in recorded history. It may have only been a strain of the flu, but bodies were piling high in the mortuaries at a rate which grave diggers couldn't keep pace with. The extent to which this was happening was downplayed and no reliable figures were ever presented to the public. Censorship within the warring nations had clamped a firm hand over the problem.

To make matters worse, the medical services were already over-stretched with their commitment to battle casualties and all hospitals were short-staffed. Those who fell ill but remained at home, such as Lucie, were actually limiting the spread of the epidemic, though this was not evident at the time.

The contagious nature of the Spanish flu allowed it to spread faster than it would have done in former eras, when humanity had commuted at a walking-pace. In recent times the world had become industrialised and rapid modes of modern transportation by sea and rail assisted the spread of the sickness to all corners of the globe in very short order. Very few countries employed effective quarantine measures and none were spared the ravages of the lethal virus.

In a world with a population just shy of two billion people, up to a hundred million would perish – one person in twenty - before the sickness finally ran its course. Some areas were hit harder than others. In terms of sheer numbers, the virus would kill more people in less than a year than the Earth's most powerful military forces had done in four years of dedicated production-line warfare.

Ultimately, the flu would become less virulent – due in large part to the lethality of the virus itself. Many hosts felled by the deadliest strain died within hours of showing the first symptoms and therefore succumbed before they could pass it on.

At the heart of the problem was the sheer volume of personnel in the military. Some carried the virus to uninfected locales, while those who were more severely stricken were sent to hospitals for further treatment. But herein lay the problem - the act of moving men from one place to another in crowded conditions exposed more of the population to the virus than had the sick remained in isolation.

To Yvonne and those around her, little of this was known and even if it had been there was nothing that they could have done to alleviate it. Furthermore, the widowed prostitute had a history of being trampled by events and none who knew her would have been surprised if she had walked directly into the path of the next catastrophe. Although it was one thing to shout in protest and offer token resistance to injustice, it was quite another to take pre-emptive action. It was a far simpler prospect to live in dread and accept whichever fate lay in the future.

There were many people in the world like Yvonne. Failure to recognise threats and opportunities until it was all far too late has always been a strangely human quality that asks more questions than it answers – questions like, 'when there are so many individuals who timidly let the world happen to them, how is it that their long-lost ancestors ever worked up the gumption to climb down from trees?' It was a question that Charles Darwin never really addressed in his famous work, *On the Origin of Species*.

Yvonne didn't read books and she didn't trouble her days with trying to solve the world's mysteries. There was always more pressing business to attend to. She tightened her shawl and put a hand on Lucie's forehead. *Where is Max? He said he'd be bringing some bread next time.*

393

Chapter 30

November 1918: Parting Shots

Volker Bartels was finished and he knew it.

The wreckage of his aircraft was proof positive that he did not have what it took to survive in this most brutal of arenas. He had only arrived at the *Jasta* two days previously, and had been immensely excited to have a chance to fly against the enemy. In two short days, his prayers had been scornfully brushed aside.

Simply put, the Allies were in a position to fly anywhere over the front lines as they pleased, and newly trained German pilots never had any opportunity to cut their teeth on easy missions. It seemed that every man who flew against Germany was a hardened veteran. Bartels was no fool. With no end to the war in sight he despaired. There was nothing but regret in his decision to volunteer to fly - at least the infantry could hide in holes when the shooting intensified. In the sky there was nowhere to seek refuge. Even clouds couldn't hide you forever. At some point you had to try and make it home.

As he sat in the ruins of what had not so long ago been a perfectly serviceable flying machine, Bartels wondered how long it would take before he was killed. He unfastened his safety harness and shakily climbed out of the cockpit. It was a long walk home.

'Here he is.' Wesser was the first to notice that Bartels had returned. There was no apparent relief at his arrival, and now the young man knew why. His fellows must have seen a dozen men like him come and go and they just weren't prepared to care about him until he had proven himself. If he was already resigned to his fate, how much more so were they - having seen it all before?

The other pilots gave him a drink, then left him to his own devices. A melancholy Bartels sat in one corner and listened to their quiet conversation. For the first time, he understood their behaviour. Almost all of their discussions were centred on one or other aspect of their trade: either that, or inconsequential matters. Very few of them talked of life after the war, because that was not an eventuality that they could reliably plan for. So instead, they talked of the weather and weapons. And drinking. And gambling. And whoring.

Beerenbrock was nowhere to be seen, but Bartels saw that Schmidt and Wesser were as thick as thieves. They said nothing about their exploits from the previous April. Bartels wondered what had happened to the fourth pilot from that day. *Heidberg: that was his name.* Being new to the unit, Bartels had no way to find out. He anticipated that any enquiry about a dead man would be treated with hostility.

The talk had turned to the merits of the Pfalz DXII. Apparently there were none. Bartels could relate to the sentiment, having just been shot down in one. He wondered how much worse the DIII must have been for it to have been replaced by the later model. With nothing to lose, he asked the question aloud.

He was initially answered with stony silence. To them, he was still a new boy too raw to be included in any discussion. Schmidt relented and invited him to join the conversation, then addressed him directly, 'The reputation of the Pfalz as a death-trap is warranted, and always has been. Some fellows do alright in it – Beerenbrock, Gontermann – but they would have succeeded in just about any machine that they flew in. The Pfalz has a better endurance than other types, but you need to be skilled enough to survive against superior machines before this is any sort of advantage. Most of the men who strap themselves into any plane are of moderate levels of ability, and these are the ones who fail all too often. Experience is critical.' That Bartels was deficient in this aspect was left unsaid. The veteran may have been hardened. It did not make him cruel.

Though someone had taken the time to include him in a discussion, Bartels wondered how many more crashes he would need to survive before he felt like part of this group. He was not sure that the requisite experiences would be worth the reward.

'Bartels, the commander will see you now.'

Beerenbrock had his hands behind his back and was looking out of the window. He didn't turn around when Bartels made his presence known. 'Have you met the new man?'

Bartels wondered precisely what constituted new. Erwin Koenig was a nine-kill veteran. Just because he had never served in this particular *Jasta* didn't make him new. *Did it?* It seemed that every unit was a closed society to outsiders. 'Not formally.'

Beerenbrock barked a laugh, 'Formally?' It seemed that he had never heard anything as ridiculous. He went straight to the reason for the summons, 'He's just back from a stint in hospital. His old unit has run out of machines so he's been sent to us. Even if he hasn't made a full recovery from his wounds, he's more valuable to me than you are. I don't have enough machines to go around, and I can't risk those I do have on men who continually wreck them.'

Other than wondering at Beerenbrock's lack of bedside manner and the suggestion that he had been involved in multiples crashes, as opposed to just the one, Bartels was unperturbed.

'What, no protestations of indignation? I've just grounded you.'

Bartels just nodded.

Beerenbrock looked at him suspiciously. *Maybe this one has a brain in his head.* 'I've just saved your life, Bartels - at least for now. I hope you appreciate the fact.' He could see by the younger man's expression that it was still sinking in, 'No doubt you first heard of me in the papers. People believe what they will, and I have heard it said that I am a good man. But if they had seen my dozen worst deeds they would know me as God knows me, and to him I must ultimately answer. When this war is over, if I am still alive, I shan't bother staying in contact with my comrades. Too many of them were present for some of the things I have done, and it will be best if I maintain a distance from them.'

Bartels didn't know how to respond, but Beerenbrock was not done, 'You at least can be spared from such a circumstance. Whatever befalls you in this life, stay as far away from me as you can.'

The commander's directness emboldened Bartels, 'I have a question.'

Beerenbrock's look was not encouraging, 'I'm only twenty-five, Volker. There isn't much that I have had time to do properly in my life. If you take out my military service, I'm hardly more than a boy. Before this, I worked for two years in a bank as a clerk. I might not even have a job to go back to.' A gesture included their surroundings, 'All of this is temporary.' He looked at Bartels again, expecting the replacement to ask the usual questions about the time he had shot down four Spads, 'What do you want to know?'

'Never mind.'

'Just as well. I don't have the authority to approve a loan for you.'

*   *   *

The war was over. Just like that.

Claude Dumont, dapper as ever, sat in the front seat of the car as his driver negotiated the appalling road leading to the front lines. They hit one particularly bad pot-hole, and the small Frenchman was almost catapulted out of the vehicle. He crushed his service cap back onto his head, hoping it would remain there, but without any real expectation that the hope was justified.

He half turned in his seat to address the car's third occupant who was perched precariously in the back, and proclaimed exultantly, 'My friend, I wouldn't have thought a road would give us more of a buffeting than what we suffered at the hands of the Boche guns a few days ago!'

The other officer spread his hands wide, but not so wide that he couldn't quickly grab hold of something should the immediate need arise, 'What can I say, my Captain? Would you rather that we had stayed at home?'

'No, no, you misunderstand. This is a thing we must do.' The car lurched again, its occupants almost thrown to their doom for the hundredth time in twenty minutes. Dumont laughed out loud, 'Ha! That one has compressed my spine even further. If only we had received this treatment last year, I would have been a much smaller man - a quality that would have made me much harder to hit as I hurtled through the clouds in search of our murderous foes.'

'I thought that you had never been wounded?'

'And what has that to do with anything? It doesn't hurt to seize every advantage.'

Their driver had to swerve to avoid an artillery piece that had been abandoned in front of them. He left the road, where travelling suddenly seemed much more acceptable. Dumont would have none of it, 'What are you doing, you imbecile? Trying to kill me with boredom? Get back on the designated path before I have you arrested.'

'Sorry, sir.'

Dumont slapped the driver jovially, 'No, why should you be sorry? We have beaten the damned Boche pigs! We will all get drunk together and celebrate.'

The pilot in the back seat made his own observation, 'Captain Dumont, I fear that we have already been celebrating like that for two days without pause. I have a hangover that makes this drive seem like punishment for doing something that I may have offended you with. If that is the case, please shoot me now. The road is terrible.'

'Ha! You young ones were all made without any fortitude. I fear your mother must have been a lamb rather than the sow which I had originally presumed to be the case, based upon your unfortunate appearance. Luckily for France there were enough older men such as myself to win this war.'

'You are only two years older than I am, my Captain.'

'And so? It still makes me older. I defy you to prove that it is not so.'

The man in the back seat conceded the point, 'It is so.'

'And again I am proven right! The younger generation also lacks the spirit to fight a battle they cannot win. Why do you not argue with me when you know you are wrong?'

There was no chance of keeping the obtuse man down, or quiet. Dumont was in an ebullient mood all right. It was a direct consequence of learning that the war was over and that he was alive - not just for the next week or month, but for a future that spanned untold years. It was almost too difficult to grasp. And to think, this had been the normal state of being just four years ago. Four long years. Four long years in which men had had the names of places like

Verdun branded into their brains. Four long years in which the flying machine had changed from a rare and exotic thing to a tool used daily - as familiar as a common plough horse, and probably more numerous.

In those same years they had been inspired by men such as the redoubtable Guynemer - now dead this last year and a bit. On the other side of the ledger they had learned to fear individuals who would never have been known had it not been for the invention of the aeroplane: Boelcke and Max Immelmann; or Richthofen, for those unfortunate enough to have been born English. On reflection, those characters were all dead as well. *And good riddance.*

The Frenchmen continued to be bashed by the road in a car that seemed to have been built without suspension. Dumont would not shut up, 'The silence, listen to it.'

All that the others could hear was Dumont's blathering; that and the engine of a tortured car with wheels that must have been built square. Dumont didn't need to hear the comment out load, 'That's what I mean, of course. The guns are quiet.' It was the first sensible observation that he had made all day. The artillery on the Western Front had fallen silent before every man in a hundred kilometres was killed. No-one would have thought it possible.

Dumont's eyes refocused, 'Stop here.' He pointed. The two men looked. In the distance, small from this remove, was a German sausage balloon, partially deflated but still tethered to its cable and dominating the horizon. Or it would have been dominating the horizon had they not been so far from it. Dumont ordered his driver to take them closer. With no choice in the matter, the car was put into gear and the gruelling assault upon their bodies resumed.

Their car was parked as far into the front lines as it would take them - any further and the aviators would be in the complex network of trenches. Infantrymen were everywhere, though mostly they had abandoned the need to carry their weapons. Dumont wondered if they were breaching orders by doing so. The captive balloon caught his eye again. It was hard not to when it was only two kilometres from their present location.

'What a grand sight, no? Lieutenant Bonnet?'

Bonnet looked over at the monstrosity that they had attacked just two days previously. The balloon was partially deflated, a result of seeping gas that had collapsed the fabric. It hadn't been shot through as thoroughly as the Frenchmen would have liked at the time of their attack, and an undamaged section had folded in upon itself, trapping the remaining hydrogen inside and allowing the gasbag to remain aloft. There it hung above the battlefield, limp and lifeless. It was a stark testimony to the effectiveness of the Allied aggression in the air during the final stages of the war.

'Have you nothing to say, Marcel? We did this as our last act of war. I am a proud man.'

Bonnet shielded his eyes, 'It looks like...' He couldn't find the words.

Dumont did not have the same problem, 'A battle ensign at half mast. The symbol of Wilhelm's defeat.'

Bonnet's murmur was melancholy, 'Just him?'

Dumont became exasperated, 'Such a baby you are. Did you want the war to last longer because you are not happy with destroying only two Boche machines to my five?'

Bonnet regained his humour, finding himself back on territory that had been familiar not very long ago, 'Sorry, Captain Dumont, I keep forgetting that you have regrets at leaving the Fokker triplanes for me while you prey on the easy ones.'

Dumont gave him a mock bow, 'Triplanes? You speak as though you have shot down more than just one of them!'

Bonnet returned the bow, 'One was all I needed to have something worth boasting of. As you are quite aware, my second kill was one of those hideous DFWs, which somehow you acquired a taste for. I found it quite bland myself. I was simply curious to find out what it was that you saw in the type to bother expending so much ammunition upon them.'

'Ho! And now you say that I cannot shoot straight. I should challenge you to a duel.'

'But I am all alone, my Captain. I should think that you would not be content to attack me unless I could have an observer to protect me?'

The riposte by Bonnet contained a barbed reference which suggested that Dumont was happy to shoot a man in the back. Were it not the simple truth, the older officer would have taken offence. Instead, he laughed at the joke, 'Such a lion you are, Marcel. What a leader of men you would have made, if only you could have brought yourself to shoot at the clay targets offered up by the Boche generals.'

Nearby, some infantry watched their banter. A small group approached the parked vehicle, curious to talk to the airmen - a breed they rarely saw except overhead, and had never met in the flesh. Dumont saw them coming and was welcoming, 'Here are the real heroes of the war. My proud friends, I am honoured to have worn the same uniform as you have. You have done a magnificent job to see this through to the end. France will never forget your sacrifice.'

The dirty soldiers summed up the two decorated officers and the bored driver, unsure how to respond. They decided to state the obvious, 'You are pilots, and good ones by your appearances.'

Dumont nodded, 'No better than you. The difference between us is that airmen have stories written in the papers, not because we are braver - I doubt that it is the case - but because we die in a more visible manner. It is a small distinction, but one that seems to matter to those who have not fought as you or we.'

He was quite pleased with his little speech, and Bonnet was actually surprised that it seemed sincere. The soldiers pointed at the balloon, 'That there? We saw some of our fliers attacking it a few days ago. I don't know how any of them survived. It made us think that perhaps we were not too badly off, with a hole to hide in.'

Bonnet expected his friend to regale his new audience with details of the deed, but Dumont had fallen silent. It was not like him, and especially not since he had heard that there was an armistice. Silent, he wandered a short distance away. The soldiers looked uneasily at Bonnet. Their spokesman was apologetic, 'I am sorry if I have caused the captain any offense, sir. Sometimes it is hard to know what not to say – we all have things best left buried'

Bonnet didn't know what to make of it, 'I am sure it is not the case. And if we were all too afraid to speak for fear of the effect, who would ever speak again? Only the politicians.'

That drew the expected scowls. Bonnet continued, 'But he is a very good pilot, and now perhaps there is nothing left in his life that he will achieve that will matter as much as his service to France.'

'Lieutenant, if that doesn't apply to every one of us I shall take a shit in my helmet and eat my next meal from it.' There was a moment of awkwardness as the speaker realised that he had said the words out loud in front of an officer he didn't know.

Bonnet didn't miss a beat, 'And will that meal be cold, so that at least you will remember your days in the army?'

The soldier laughed ruefully, 'Maybe not so cold if my turd is fresh! Either way, hot or cold, my days in the army will be in my head forever.'

Bonnet nodded, and watched Dumont carefully picking his way towards whatever it was he was seeking. *Maybe they should become engineers? There was surely plenty of rebuilding to do. They could start with the roads.*

Dumont stopped walking. Talking to the infantrymen had disturbed him. He carefully surveyed the ground around his feet. It was just dirt, but not what you would ever expect to see in a normal world. The earth had been churned up many times by artillery fire and no few shovels. Nothing grew in it. It was just a dead sludge. In lieu of any vegetation, wreckage poked out of the surface in places: a broken picket, some buckled corrugated iron. Twenty feet away a wheel with smashed spokes leaned against a tangle of rusting wire. At his feet were some spent cartridges. It was scenery that had an appearance implying that no-one cared, and it went for as far as he was able to see. As he looked about, two fingers still attached to some rotting flesh drew his notice. It didn't help his mood.

The war was over. *What to do now?* All he could think about was his family. His sister had lost her husband in nineteen-fourteen on the Marne, back when no-one felt that red uniform clothing was unsuitable for modern warfare. In the beginning there was no way to know that things would get really bad. She had been forced to deal with personal loss a lot sooner than had most others.

He hadn't seen her in years - not since before she had been left stranded on the other side of the front lines, cut off after one of the

German gains in territory. Living in occupied France, she probably saw German soldiers in the streets from time to time whenever they were granted leave from the front, in addition to whatever garrison troops may have been permanently stationed locally. Dumont wondered what it did to a person to be isolated and unable to fight back. He had a pang when he considered that she could even be dead. The thought had occurred to him from time to time, if ever he permitted himself to become separate from the war. When he saw her again both of them would be very different people. He wondered what they would be able to talk about. *No matter what the war has done to us both, I will help you, Yvonne.*

*   *   *

Pascal Gaillard had slept in the same haystack every morning for a week. Over a period of days he had furtively excavated a cosy nest in which he could hide. It was supported internally by a simple wooden frame, leaving only just enough space to lie down in. The den was warm and kept off the intermittent drizzle, but he had no intention of occupying the position for a minute longer than he needed to.

Each morning he woke before dawn and peered out from the small hole that gave him a direct view of the group of buildings in the distance. Smoke rose from the chimney of the main house, and the degree to which it deviated in the breeze told him how much wind there was. Every morning faint wisps betrayed the remains of a fire that had been untended overnight. The smoky remnant drifted far enough from the vertical to cause him another day's delay.

For the last few mornings, the strength of the breeze had been determined to be too strong. Unhappy with each opportunity lost, Gaillard had become accustomed to wriggling backwards out of his concealment and leaving the hayfield before it was light enough to be spotted by a casual observer at a distance. Every morning it took him over an hour to get home, by which time the sun was up. He took care not to be seen by any of his neighbours, and used vegetation and natural contours to shield his movements whenever possible. Each evening he did the trip in reverse. He knew the way back and forth like his own backyard, and mused that those who had harmed him probably used exactly the same route.

This morning he peered from his vantage point, and the faint plume of smoke did not waver to left or right. There was no breeze at all. The day was still. It was perfect for Gaillard's purpose.

He had just one aim.

He still remembered the day when his son had come home on leave for a fortnight. Armand had brought one of his comrades for a visit. The poor fellow's home had been demolished by shellfire, and no stone sat upon another. For want of a roof over his head, the young man had sought out the hospitality of the Gaillard family - what was left of it. Marie had wasted away barely a year ago.

It transpired that Armand's friend was a skilled marksman, and was often chosen by his commander to pick off enemy officers, machine gunners, runners and snipers. He and Armand discussed matters that the elder Gaillard considered too macabre for men so young, but he knew there was nothing for it. He had listened to their stories out of polite interest, but his ears pricked up when they discussed the specifics of long distance shooting skills. It all seemed very simple to the untrained civilian.

No longer just listening to keep up appearances, Pascal Gaillard stored away everything that they talked about, and he was fairly sure that the boys had not been aware of his interest. Even if they had known of his veiled fascination, he was sure that they would likely have attributed it to the curiosity that non-combatants have pertaining to the unfamiliar but dangerous activities associated with soldiering.

In a world obsessed with destruction, obtaining a weapon had not been difficult. They almost lay around waiting to be found by any interested party. Gaillard had no idea what type of rifle he had in his keeping, but through trial and error he learned the various mechanisms involved in its usage. He was pleased to discover that it was not too complicated, and even if his maintenance was shoddy he didn't need the weapon long term.

So he lay in the hay, isolated from the rest of the world and invisible to everyone except God. He chambered a round, then peered along the barrel and aligned the iron sights into the middle distance. He knew the range to the main yard based on the appearance of various items that could be seen. The objects themselves were of no particular interest to him - unless they walked on two legs. From what he had heard from his guest's conversations, Gaillard knew that when a group of people could be distinguished as separate individuals - but with otherwise blurry features - the distance was roughly five hundred metres. He had tested the information for himself, and had been forced to make some adjustments. For a man on the wrong side of fifty with no proper training, five hundred metres was a very long distance to shoot at anything. It was for precisely this reason that he wanted absolutely no wind. The least eddy of air could spoil a shot over such a range. He would only have one chance.

Getting himself comfortable, Gaillard didn't keep his cheek pressed to the stock of his weapon, nor did he concentrate too hard because it would have ruined his eyesight. There was plenty of time to aim when the sought-after personage eventually presented himself.

On and off, France had been at war with England for centuries. They were natural enemies that had somehow landed in bed together as a direct consequence of confused politics. The friendship between the two countries was not real. It was a temporary expedient - the exception that proved the rule. Gaillard belonged to an older generation of Frenchmen, and he was unable to fathom how Britain and Germany had gone to war against each other. To his mind, the recent alliance that the English had made with France against Germany did not expunge past deeds, or indeed, misdeeds.

England had always stolen from France, and on those occasions that they had failed it was not for want of trying. Whether it was land, livestock or the hearts of faithless women, every slight was enough reason on its own to want to put a bullet into an Englishman. Gaillard may have hated the Germans, but it was tempered with respect; for although the murdering Boches had been busy killing Frenchmen for the last four years, they had also killed their fair share of Englishmen. Following that line of reasoning he felt that, despicable as they undoubtedly were, France's continental neighbours couldn't be all bad.

Furthermore, though it may have been true that unexploded German bombs would be claiming the lives of French farmers and children for decades to come, the fact remained that some of the ordinance was also of English origin. *Did they give even a second thought to this? No.*

Pascal Gaillard would have professed to be a righteous and God-fearing man, and at times a vengeful one into the bargain. He would have been affronted at being called petty. To him, to seek retribution for the wanton destruction of personal property was anything but petty. The blatant disregard that had been shown towards his livelihood may have been pursued by the French civil authorities had he bothered to report it, but he doubted that his losses would have been properly compensated despite the extreme hardship that the war had caused.

The pursuit of justice is never petty, though it may be illegal if looked at too closely. In the high opinion of Pascal Gaillard, his need for vengeance was entirely vindicated and he had no qualms about taking matters into his own hands.

Twenty minutes passed. In the twenty-first minute the door to the main house opened and a uniformed figure appeared and walked out into the yard.

Under his breath, Gaillard swore. He had not considered that the fellow would be unrecognisable at such a distance. He was bareheaded, and no features could be distinguished over that range. At five hundred metres, the face was just a blur. *What practise have I ever had in looking for things so far away? My eyes are past their best, and the only thing I've needed to look for in recent times have been my chickens.*

Gaillard was fuming to himself again - swearing a blood oath for every hen and egg stolen when he himself had been close to starving. Consumed with rage, he took a moment to register that the man he had been staring at had been joined by another.

A man wearing a white hat.

Yes, at last. Today is the day! Gaillard had never been fooled by the arrogant officer's denials, nor had he appreciated being given short shrift when he had reported those instances of wrongdoing. For the English, the alliance with France was nothing but an excuse to run rampant through the countryside - this time with a license to do just as they pleased. Their propensity for thievery proved it. *You shot my cow because you thought you were not answerable for your actions — but I will have my justice and damn the consequences.*

Though the white cloth of the service cap was a blur it nevertheless provided a good reference point. Gaillard aimed directly at it. He was sure that the bullet's trajectory would fall significantly over the distance, but wasn't confident in assessing how much. He couldn't bring himself to aim above the target in case the shot went high. *Aim at the head – if there is drop it will still strike the chest. Or the gut. Or shoot his balls off.* None of the possibilities were unacceptable to the farmer.

For the average human being, it is no easy thing to shoot a man, even with the greatest justification; even with practise. Gaillard had shot foxes and rabbits, but never a man. He steadied himself, slowing his breathing to calm his nerves. He wasn't trying to win a tournament or a trophy; the shot didn't need to hit the centre of the target. It just needed to be a killing shot. Whether the man died instantly, or over a period of days, was immaterial. But Gaillard knew that he only had one chance. If he fired twice, the men standing down-range would be better able to pinpoint the source. He would be hunted down and lynched.

France has won this war, and now we must prepare to renew our eternal differences with the barbarians across the Sleeve. Gaillard did not know that the English term for the strip of water that separated their countries had a different name, nor would he have cared in the least. A bead of sweat trickled down his forehead, but instead of dripping into the eyes, it was diverted once it encountered the hairs of his bushy eyebrows. Gaillard decided that he had better aim a little bit above the target after all. He squinted, and took the pressure of the trigger with his finger. He breathed gently, then just before he inhaled, he fired.

The sound in the enclosed space was deafening and Gaillard almost passed out from the pain in his ears. The rifle's recoil

410

hammered his shoulder, and he knew he would be tender in the days ahead. Ignoring the various sources of pain, he collected his thoughts and looked downrange.

For a moment nothing seemed to have happened. Gaillard cursed his folly, his age, his eyesight and his luck. He did not dare to curse God. But when he looked again, he saw that the man that he had shot at had crumpled. The white hat had tumbled off onto the ground. The fallen man was not moving. The victim's companion was screaming his head off. To Gaillard, it seemed that this man's manner was less indicative of fear, and more to do with the summoning of aid. *How can I read what his manner means when I have never met him?* But Gaillard had other things to worry about. Analysing human behaviour could wait until another day - if there would ever be another day. A gambling man would have given him short odds.

There was a stampede of confusion as more men rapidly appeared on the scene. Amid much waving of arms, some pointing, and no small amount of shouting, men appeared with rifles of their own. Gaillard braced himself. *A rabbit is sooner seen when it runs.* He was not tempted to get into a shooting war with the English; he had evened the slate, but that was only worth something if he lived to tell the tale.

And then...

And then Gaillard saw something which he could not process. One of the men stooping over the prone body was wearing a white hat of his own. *Merde! How will I ever know if it is him?* Gaillard knew he'd never get a second chance to exact his revenge, but also knew that the uncertainty of this particular outcome would eat at him for the rest of his days.

But remorse? No.

Peering anxiously through the small opening that he had shot from, Gaillard saw that the armed men were heading in his direction.

411

They were spaced out in a way that a seasoned campaigner – and Gaillard was not such a one – would have recognised as lacking in adequate field-craft. The Britons advanced more or less in a bunch, each hoping not to be picked out by the shooter as a possible target. These were not infantrymen, but rather squadron personnel whose secondary function was to act as perimeter guards on an aerodrome. In their view, the war was over, and if they could preserve the current state of their collective skins then that was the preferred option.

Only in the direst of circumstances were they prepared to sacrifice one of their own, if that's what it took, but nevertheless they hoped that one man down was the worst they were looking at. Believing that if they were fired upon they would have time to deliver a fusillade of shots into the shooter before he could fire at them a second time was enough motivation to spur them onward. The reluctant soldiers entered the hayfield and, if they appeared grim, at least there was a genuine reason for it.

Gaillard had anticipated being hunted and he lay quietly, unmoving lest the least rustle give his position away. He lost sight of the oncoming patrol. *Are they on top of me? What sort of fool am I to throw away my life because of a cow and some lost poultry?*

The sound of soft footfalls was the only thing that the farmer could hear. The rest of the world did not exist. He daren't breathe, blink or think.

'It's like looking for a needle in a haystack.'

'Are you trying to be a funny bugger? Shit, the war's supposed to be over and we're out here looking for a crazy shooter.'

'The murderous sod could have hidden behind any of these, or that tree over there, or that one there. Mark me, he's long gone.'

'He'd better be, or it's our hides.'

Gaillard didn't speak English, nor understand more than fragments of the spoken word. Most of the tongue that he was familiar with came in the form of obscenities – the first words that anyone learns in a foreign language, provided that it isn't derived from a school curriculum. Not knowing what had been said was its own form of torture. *Have they found me?*

Yet, he lay still, not even bracing for the volley of shots he felt sure were about to be unleashed upon his person. Though he expected to die, Gaillard held himself immobile on the off-chance that the hunters might somehow pass him by. The slightest movement would have been fatal. *If I am dead, then I am dead. But I won't assist the wolves by crying in the wilderness.*

The footsteps were methodical. They took a long time to vanish from Gaillard's hearing, and echoed in his mind for what seemed an eternity. And once eternity had come and gone twice, only then did he allow himself to breathe normally and work some movement back into his cramping muscles. To remain still for so long when so much is at stake may be taxing, but it is never boring. In those instances, thought is narrowly focused in ways that only those who have been in mortal danger can comprehend. And what is more likely to provoke deadly force than to commit murder in plain sight?

They say it is difficult to find a needle in a haystack, but I've never heard of such a needle pricking someone with as much effect. The sweating farmer grinned savagely at the thought of what he had achieved - one man against a foreign army. His hands started trembling as the effects of the adrenaline that had been pumping through his veins started to dissipate. The reaction was the body's way of letting his brain know that it didn't appreciate his recent escapade. Almost immediately he was overcome with drowsiness. Fighting the need to sleep, he used his fear of discovery to remain alert – no easy task – and sudden thirst drove him to sip water from his flask. There was no going anywhere until the sun had travelled the full span of the sky.

Pascal Gaillard waited until darkness had fallen, then without fuss but with determined thoroughness, pulled his hideaway apart so that it would never be discovered. The last thing he wanted was for the English to realise that their man had been deliberately fired upon from a prepared position. *Better that the pigs believe a renegade Boche soldier has fired the last shot of the war, or they'll be paying me another visit at home, and this time they won't be satisfied with shooting the animals.*

When the demolition was completed, the gnarled farmer disappeared into the inky night.

Chapter 31

December 1918: The Last Directive

Oskar Lehmann had started the war as a non-smoker, but like many of his peers he had come to rely on cigarettes to calm his nerves. Since his last convalescence, he had given them up entirely. It was not so much a case of wishing to break a habit, as an avoidance of aggravating his lungs. The dose of gas that he had inhaled in the spring had never been something that had been given enough time to heal. Though the incident had happened only a few months ago, he doubted that he would ever fully recover. It didn't affect his ability to lead now that the shooting was done.

'You've seen the order, Falkenhoff?'

The adjutant's downcast eyes told their own story. He didn't even answer the question. Lehmann sympathised, but had his own solution to the problem, 'I'm not inclined to follow it to the letter.'

Falkenhoff looked him full in the face, unsure whether he had heard correctly. To disobey a direct order from the High Command was unthinkable. Lehmann confirmed his intent, 'Hand over our machines to the Allies? Is it even a legal order?'

'It's the High Command, Oskar. You don't have a choice.'

'The intent is to deprive us of an effective fighting machine. Burning them will do that just as effectively. There is also the matter of honour – the Armistice was a ceasefire, not our surrender. They jumped on us with a billy club under a flag of truce.'

Falkenhoff wasn't too sure that Lehmann's interpretation was the correct one, 'What are we going to do about it? Everyone has had enough. And I disagree about the intent with regard to the DVII. England and France want them for themselves. Taking them from us is just their way to humiliate us further.'

Lehmann showed his teeth, though friendliness was the last emotion he was conveying, 'All the better reason to have misunderstood the order.'

'They'll court-martial you.'

'And do what? Discharge me from service?' He laughed harshly. The pain within his chest made him regret it instantly, and the laughter ended in a weak bout of coughing.

'They could shoot you.'

Lehmann fought his discomfort, 'I doubt it. The war is over. There isn't any need to hold the army together with those sorts of methods anymore. Truth be told, they probably even want us to do it, but are too cowardly to say so.'

'To my ears you are starting to sound like von Bülow.'

'Sebastian? I know you didn't like him, but it doesn't make him wrong.'

Falkenhoff shrugged, 'We'll do it your way, then.'

'Yes, you will. Until I have heard otherwise, this is my unit to command, even if all of my planes have been surrendered to the dirty bastards, or destroyed.'

'Have you heard what the men have been saying about him?'

'Who?'

'Von Bülow.'

Lehmann didn't care one way or the other, 'No.'

'It hasn't been complimentary.'

'He isn't dead; let them say what they will. What is he going to do about it?'

'Burn them. Burn the bastard things!' Lehmann gave his men the order to destroy the Fokkers. They were unhappy about it, but they also knew that the commander was exceeding his orders, and if nothing else, he had earned more of their respect for his stance, and by extension, their unquestioning obedience. This final act may have been a token gesture of defiance, but it was better than going out with a whimper.

They torched the machines, and for those who had been in battle, it didn't look too different from the scenes that they had witnessed in their surreal realm far above the earth, except that no living beings were roasting, nor cordite burning in their nostrils. Even as the machines were engulfed in flames and billowing smoke, the act was sterile, with no horror attached to it. It didn't stop Lehmann's memory from dredging up things better left buried.

The men watched their aircraft burn. If nothing else, the Allied obsession with the Germans' technological edge was both flattering and frustrating. *If only we had been able to match them in actual numbers.*

Falkenhoff's mood was dire, 'I tell you, Oskar, you've single-handedly just sent more machines up in smoke in twenty minutes than you did over the last two years.'

The young *Jastaführer* hadn't considered it from that perspective. It diminished his sense of worth, but he nevertheless appreciated the observation, 'Then they can give me a DFC for it - and the Legion of Honour for good measure.' He cited the British and French decorations in order to punctuate the adjutant's point. Neither one thought it was particularly funny.

Most of the men standing around the inferno had served under von Bülow, and they had not forgotten him - nor forgiven, 'To think, of everyone who wanted to shoot him, the privilege went to someone who didn't take it personally – other than a general hatred for everyone in field grey, of course.'

'That's the least of the wonder. He was shot in the head but the bullet missed his mouth!'

'The Englishman had no choice but to aim for his head - he'd have had no chance of hitting the bastard's heart.'

'Heart? He has one?'

Someone turned to one of the pilots who had not contributed so far to the conversation, 'What do you think, Kluth?'

'To be truthful, I always thought that putting a bullet in him would have been the only way to get rid of him. He was never going to burn; his skin was too thick.'

Lehmann was disappointed that his men could be so disrespectful of a former commanding officer, but the war was over due to a gross betrayal by their own politicians, and though none regretted that the end of the war had arrived, it was only fair to let them vent their anger at the way it had happened. It wasn't as if von Bülow would ever find out about the things that were being said about him. Besides which, though Kluth's comment may have had little affection in it, the statement was as close to the mark as a man could get without possessing a university education. Nor was it an insult. Lehmann said nothing.

These men – they were just like boys who knew that father was listening, who by refusing to reprimand their commentary was implicitly giving consent to continued poor behaviour. Unsurprisingly, they went too far, even though they were familiar with Lehmann's tolerance levels, 'Spare a thought for the driver. The poor bastard's last moments were spent listening to senseless ranting.'

'The Englishmen put him out of his misery.'

Lehmann was curt with his rebuke, 'Cut out your shit and show a little respect for a war hero.' He had the authority to make it stick, and the offenders were shamefaced in knowing that they had pushed their luck beyond acceptable limits.

Chapter 32

July 1919: Legacy

Volker Bartels had come home, but his brief foray into the military had changed him. He wondered what it must have done to the men who had done years instead of just weeks. He was flattering himself. Strictly speaking, he had seen out the last months of the war, but it was also true that the sum of his experiences amounted to just one disastrous combat. It was difficult to put into words, and even were it not, how did it amount to a memoir?

Naturally, his family was glad that he had returned unharmed, but they had no way to understand that he was no longer the same. From all he could gather from reading between the lines, they did not see how such a brief exposure could be traumatic. After all, were there not thousands – millions – of others who had seen and done more, for longer, and been relatively unaffected?

The short answer was: no. The only consolation that the former Pfalz pilot could draw was that lessons must have been learned by the upper echelons: the generals and politicians. Those who had seen the face of modern warfare would never dare risk starting another. Bartels wasn't even sure that there would be enough men in Europe to field a viable army for the foreseeable future. Surely no sane person would volunteer for a rematch?

His one claim to fame was that he had served under the redoubtable Max Beerenbrock. Think then, of Volker Bartels' dismay when he discovered that the name meant nothing to his parents, 'Are you serious? You don't know his name at all?'

His father's answer was mild, 'Should I?'

'He shot down four Frenchmen the day Richthofen was killed!'

The senior Bartels was thoughtful as he murmured, 'I would think that the man who got Richthofen had the more difficult task that day.'

And that was the end of it. Germany had too many heroes and nobody could name them all. Worse, if these mighty lions could not win the war for you, what good were they? And worse yet, if the war was un-winnable, were those same heroes not in part responsible for assisting in the recruitment of men who had little if any chance of contributing meaningfully at all?

Volker Bartels had been but one such man to be lured by reputations. He had been ecstatic to learn that he would be flying with none other than Max Beerenbrock, but he found his father's conclusions disturbing, and no less a betrayal of core values than those he had learned to be integral to the terms of the Armistice that had ended the war so abruptly.

The world had become a different place. New leaders had arisen, and many of them would never have amounted to anything if the assassination at Sarajevo in nineteen-fourteen had not caused such an unreasonable global response. The Kaiser had abdicated and the Romanovs had been overthrown, but George V was still standing and would never have to answer for a war that his far-flung family had presided over. The world was a different place, but only the future would tell if it was a better place.

The guns had fallen silent eight months ago. Today London had been witness to a victory parade in which fifteen thousand men marched the streets to honour their dead. The Royal Air Force had flown overhead as part of the commemoration. As a spectator, Percy Wiggan had been unimpressed by the antics of some of those pilots, flying beneath electricity wires down the Strand just above the heads of the assembled masses. In his opinion it was the height of extreme folly. Wiggan had not survived more than a hundred combat patrols to have it all end in misery because of some drunken idiots.

That had been this afternoon, and now that the show was over most people had gone their own way. There were still clumps of individuals - both veteran and civilian - some mingled together and others standing apart.

Wiggan met up with men he had flown with before he had been posted to one of the handful of Sopwith Dolphin squadrons. He hadn't seen either man in over a year. The exchange of handshakes was hearty.

Essential information was concisely exchanged, and then they fell into familiarity. Some things would never change. For his part, Lewis-Hamilton knew he was running out of time and expected that Burke would do the decent thing and finally come clean, 'I say, Ross, is the story about the echidna true?'

'I'll tell you what, sport: I have to convince people that I flew with an English Lord with a fancy name; you only have to hide the fact that you knew a bloody Australian. Who has the tougher task?'

'But I'm not a lord.'

'I never could tell by listening to you holding court with the new chums.'

Lewis-Hamilton was actually offended, 'Holding court! By Jove, you are an impertinent man.' He forgot about the echidna. Burke's ploy had succeeded. Though his methods differed with each attempted diversion, the results were alarmingly consistent.

Wiggan was of the opinion that if everyone else could see the baiting for what it was, if Lewis-Hamilton was blind to it then he had everything coming. The whole issue was compounded by the simple little fact that it was always more difficult to detect humour in another if one had not already credited that worthy with a minimum degree of intellect. The ragging by the colonial probably wouldn't end until there was an expanse of ocean separating him from his victim.

At that juncture, Wiggan saw another familiar face. He waved a hand above his head, 'Hie!' The fellow had either ignored him, or just couldn't hear over the general hubbub. The other possibility was that his name wasn't Hie.

As Wiggan walked over to the man he searched his memory for a name. He didn't trouble himself with the fact that the fellow had major's crowns upon his epaulettes and may not have had a desire to converse with one not so exalted in status, 'You're Arthur Reid.'

That got the man's attention, 'Do I know you?'

'You were one of my flying instructors.'

It focused the man enough to ask, 'Name?'

'Percival Wiggan.'

'Wiggan?... No, don't recollect. Sorry. Willard? I remember Willard. Can't be you, of course. Willard had a terrible crash. Killed himself and three others.'

Wiggan was disappointed but tried not to show it, 'You really don't remember?'

'Sorry, old chap.' In their early twenties, neither of them were old except by the standards of combat survivors.

'You said that I was one of the better pupils that you had taught.'

'Well, you're still alive and I see that they've pinned a DFC on you, so it shows that I knew some of what I was talking about.'

It was not the answer that Wiggan had expected and he couldn't disguise the fact. Reid didn't know him and didn't care to, 'Listen Wiggle, I used to tell a lot of the boys the same thing. It keeps up morale and all that rot. The new ones have little enough chance as it is. There's no need to spell it out; they'd refuse to believe it anyway. I take it that you never did instruction between stints at the sharp end?'

'No, I was sent to Canada on a War Bonds drive.'

'Half your luck, then.'

'In any case, I wanted to thank you for teaching me enough to stay alive.'

'Here, old boy, you can't be all that wet behind the ears, surely?'

'Sir?'

'You've got captain's rank, and decorated to boot, so you must have been through the mill the same as the rest of us. It's not only ability; there's a slab of luck that you need as well.'

'Thank God that part's done.'

Reid eyed him, 'Not in my squadron, it's not. The new kids: the ones who were too late to see action? They're the worst offenders. It seems I've lost one a month since the end of the war. The idiots keep on trying to prove they have the right stuff, then they go and prang and leave me with more letters to write home to Mother. And then I need to explain to the War Office why I have lost another SE5 when the war is supposed to be fucking over.'

Wiggan hadn't wanted to talk shop. Reid hadn't asked, 'So many ideas and ideals; a generation snuffed out. Is there a Shakespeare or a da Vinci lying amid the dead, forever unknown?'

'Maybe a Shakespeare, God willing.'

A lady of middle years was purposefully walking towards them. A man who must have been her husband lagged reluctantly two steps behind. She was dressed in mourning, though that was a look not out of place these days. Her words were delivered in a questioning monotone, 'If I'm not mistaken you would be Mister Arthur Reid?'

An amused grin crossed his face, 'What, I must have it written a foot high on my back?'

She slapped his face with some ferocity and spat out, 'My son is dead because of you!' With that, she turned on her heel and primly walked away. As the dejected husband shuffled after his wife he turned and stared at Reid. The look could have been an apology, it could have been shame, or something else entirely. It hardly mattered whichever it was.

Reid had a decent hand print forming on his cheek. Wiggan frowned, 'Who was that old biddy?'

'No idea.'

Wiggan made light of it, 'If that's how they feel about you here, best you don't show yourself in Hunland.'

The incident had left Reid subdued, 'I don't think we call it that anymore.'

Wiggan cast about for his friends, but neither of them was in evidence. Everything in life is a loose end. A man may wish to know more of those around him, but inevitably they fall by the wayside and all that is left is in the imagination.

When Wiggan emerged from his brief reverie, Reid had also vanished into the dispersing throng.

Chapter 33

1920: The Visitor

The war had stopped churning out corpses two years ago, but the pain did not end there.

Karl von Bülow turned the small package over in his hands. It was wrapped in plain brown paper. He carefully opened it, and plucked out an envelope. It had his name printed neatly on the front. A woman's handwriting, if he was any judge. The envelope was not sealed. He lifted the flap. It contained a single page. He unfolded it and read:

> Dear Sir,
>
> You will not have heard of me, but I knew your cousin. I have recently learned of his affliction and felt compelled to send a token of my feelings towards him.
>
> Most sincerely,
>
> C.G.

Karl frowned slightly. Curious, he looked at the postmark. It had been sent from France – no surprises there. He proceeded to un-wrap the small item that had come with the message.

He saw what there was to see, pursed his lips, and threw it into the fireplace. He looked at the grandfather clock. It was almost ten. The expected visitor could not be very far away.

There was a knock on the door, and Karl knew who it would be. He greeted the visitor himself. Suits may have replaced military uniforms, but the wearer could never disguise his history so easily. His carriage and manner stamped him as a former soldier, 'Hello. You would be Ernst Reinhold?'

A nodded acknowledgment, 'Ernst will do.' They shook hands.

'I am Karl, Sebastian's cousin. Please come inside.'

'Thank you.' They entered the darkened parlour.

'Please take a seat.'

'Thank you.'

'Drink?'

'Please.'

'Cognac?'

'Thank you.'

Karl poured two glasses and passed one to his guest, 'A toast?'

'To what?'

Karl shrugged, 'Or not. As you please.'

The silence extended, and may have become awkward if either man had been the type who could not savour quietude. Eventually their glasses were emptied. Karl indicated the decanter, 'Another?' Reinhold leaned across and they performed the deed without either needing to stand. Glasses were raised in salute to each other.

'You will be staying?'

'No.' Reinhold did not wish to impose, 'I have just come to see him on the way to other business. How is he?'

Karl leaned back in his chair, 'Recognisable.' Reinhold nodded. Sebastian had always said he and his cousin were opposites. It stood to reason, then, that Karl would be succinct.

'Of course you may see him – it is the purpose of your visit - but first I would ask you something.'

'Yes?' Polite curiosity.

'Ernst, do you know of anyone whom Sebastian kept company with bearing the initials C.G?'

Reinhold furrowed his brows, 'How do you mean?'

Karl fathomed the other's confusion, expecting that Reinhold may have interpreted the question to include any of the scores of personnel he had served closely with during their time in the military, 'My apologies. I mean a woman. Do you know of such?'

For Reinhold the name of the whore came to his mind. *Yvette. No... Yvonne. That was it.* He recollected the time that Weber had made the E-von reference, 'C.G, you say?'

A brief nod from Karl. Reinhold shook his head, 'No, though who knows what name a whore may assume?'

'No, I mean someone who he knew on a personal basis?'

Reinhold shrugged. Certainly the prostitute had known him personally, but the initials were wrong. 'Why do you ask?'

'I received a communication from a woman in France who knew him during the war. She sent a letter of sorts.'

'One of his nurses, perhaps?'

Karl smiled wryly, 'Would a nurse be the sort of person to mail a former patient dried excrement?'

Reinhold was halfway through a sip of his drink as he heard the words, and nearly choked. With watering eyes, he gasped for air, trying to stifle a laugh, 'Are you sure it was dry when it was mailed?' He summoned his dignity, but was unable to keep the mirth from his voice, 'Please do not take offence, Karl – I understand the plight of your cousin – but does it not strike you that Sebastian may have made enemies amongst his friends, so to speak? He wasn't in hospital for an injury to his cock; by his own account that worked fine. Why wouldn't he make a nuisance of himself towards the female nursing staff?'

'He'd hardly be the only man that ever applied to. How much worse would he need to have been to be singled out in such a manner?'

Reinhold shrugged, 'Well, for starters he didn't have full use of his own hand. Who knows what demands he made?'

Karl seemed to have missed the innuendo. He rubbed his chin with his thumb and forefinger, 'You would know that we never got along? It was hardly a secret. I had always assumed from the way he spoke that the two of you were friends - an impression which was further reinforced by your visit here today.'

'And still you opened the door for me?'

'I was merely curious to see whether your tongue was forked.' Reinhold had not expected glib humour from Karl.

'We shared a respect for one another as officers, and flew together until he was injured in the crash. With that kind of contact you make allowances. Friends, though?' Reinhold pondered the concept, 'I'm not sure he ever had any friends since Hockheimer was killed in nineteen-sixteen. We spent a lot of time together, but our tastes and methods were too disparate for us ever to be thought of as friends - to my mind at least. You would have to ask some of the other fellows.'

'Max Beerenbrock thought you were friends.'

Reinhold was non-committal, 'They despised one another, those two. But they had one thing in common, and that was that they were too focused on fighting the war to properly absorb everything else that was in their lives.' He reflected further, 'All in all, not the worst attitude to have given the magnitude of the assignment.'

Karl was tenaciously trying to solve the C.G. conundrum, 'Why not put a name to the letter? If you're bold enough to put shit in the post surely it would have been more satisfying to sign off on it?'

'Avoid retaliation?'

'From whom? Do you think I could be bothered to take the time to repay a petty vendetta, or are you suggesting that my esteemed correspondent is afraid of being sought out in the event of a future war between France and Germany?' Reinhold shrugged noncommittally. Karl was unimpressed, 'For Heaven's sake! That would be paranoia to an extraordinary degree! The Treaty has castrated us. There's no way to re-arm our military without France and England stamping all over us at the first whiff of industry.'

Reinhold agreed with the sentiment, 'I concur. There won't be a war in Europe for another hundred years at least.' He then amended, 'Notwithstanding the Balkan states, of course. They'll never be happy with each other. And obviously the mess in Russia. But the civilised world? No.'

'So what of this C.G?'

'Seek reparations if it will make you feel better, Karl. It's the latest solution to major grievances, apparently.' He may as well have told the aristocrat to fly to the moon. They looked at one another over the small distance between their chairs. Neither had quite expected the other to be so far removed from Sebastian. It was not unwelcome.

Karl climbed to his feet, 'Please, allow me to escort you to my cousin. He is being attended to by my sister's maid.' Reinhold detected a softening in Karl at the mention of his sister; or perhaps it was the maid? The sentiment was overlaid with sadness. *Someone has had their heart broken. The maid, then.*

They made their way down the hallway, Reinhold trailing slightly behind. He idly absorbed row upon row of hung portraits, 'These paintings are all of your family?'

Karl nodded, 'Yes, going back quite some way.' He quietly mocked the splendour of it all, 'It is very grand having every uncle and aunt to look down upon us in our daily endeavours. No-one else would ever be permitted to supervise us – the von Bülow family is far too eminent to have an outsider pass judgement upon us.' Reinhold wondered if this was a subtle hint at his own visit. *Probably not.*

They proceeded slowly, 'I have not noticed a likeness of you or Sebastian. Perhaps I missed them?'

'Not at all. A von Bülow needs to be dead to be on this wall.' Karl seemed pensive. He indicated two pictures hung next to one another. He pointed, 'My parents. When I left the army I returned home just in time to farewell and bury them.'

'The influenza?'

Karl nodded, 'My wife and son are staying with her family until things are sorted here. Partly it is to do with Sebastian. Clara does not want our son to see him until the boy is older. They have been gone for almost two years. I visit when I am able, but it is difficult. Are you married, Ernst?'

Reinhold solemnly indicated the portraits of Karl's parents, 'My fiancé died in the epidemic. I had not seen her in over a year. Her father wrote to inform me.' Each paused to consider their individual circumstances, 'I had thought that we would have had enough to burden ourselves with – what with rebuilding after the war. Maybe I had gotten out of it too lightly?' He paused, 'Yes, there were bad days, but on the whole it was about what I had expected. I saw the strain in others, but that aspect was missing for me.' *Most of the time.*

'My little boy is a source of great joy to me, and my wife is an enormous comfort.' The sentiment seemed inadequate and perhaps even insulting; a wife would want to be more than simply a comfort. Karl had a confession to make, and some things were easier to say to strangers with similar backgrounds than could be said to a loved one, 'There are mornings when I think it would be an easy thing to put a pistol in my mouth.'

Karl looked at the visitor who had come to his home, but there was no reaction. 'How many bullets were fired at me when I was flying? Only God knows, but if He had wanted me to do it, He'd have let one of them hit me. So I don't.' *Suicide is a rational solution to the problems that never go away. When the road has been too hard, when the pain of existence has no foreseeable end, when the injuries to the body and the soul will never mend – then the easiest way to escape it all is to take final control of your own destiny. There is only one reason to want to go on: one has a responsibility to dependants, and that includes preventing the pain of loss that they would be forced to endure.*

Reinhold heard Karl but he didn't care. The man's family was intact and he was complaining. Grief always intruded, but you found a way to make space for it amongst everything else. Instead of saying anything, Reinhold studied the man's family portraits. His gaze roved, and finally settled on a painting that left his scalp tingling. An accurate portrayal of Yvonne was the last thing he had expected to find. His reaction must have been transparent to Karl, who asked, 'You look like you have seen a ghost?' Instantly he realised what he had said, and it weighed on him.

Reinhold looked more closely, 'I have seen her before.'

'No, you are mistaken.'

Reinhold was connecting the dots, 'This is your sister?'

'Anna.'

A von Bülow needs to be dead to be on this wall.

Karl divined Reinhold's next question, 'Drowned. Nineteen-thirteen.' There was obvious pain in the memory, 'My little sister, she was far too young to end like this. I have seen men die most horribly, but this is one I will never erase.'

Reinhold wasn't sure any of the deaths that he had witnessed would be erased.

'They say it was an accident.'

Reinhold checked himself. *They say? How is a drowning not an accident?* It certainly sounded as though Karl wanted to believe it, and was trying to convince himself. He droned on, unable to arrest himself, 'Anna and Sebastian were very close.' Cogs kept turning in Reinhold's head. Karl's voice held a degree of puzzlement, 'I never understood what she saw in him, myself.'

Everything became clear to Reinhold. *Use your imagination, my friend.* But he suspected that Karl would never be able to face up to the reality.

'I shall see that he is cared for, of course. We had our differences, but we are still family, after all.' Karl stood before the likeness, then tore himself away, 'Please, Sebastian is waiting.'

Erna looked down on the drooling husk that used to be a violent and arrogant man. As ever, her feelings were mixed. They had shared a lengthy personal history, bound together by Anna and some very rash choices.

Anna von Bülow had never liked that her cousin used to bully Karl, even though there was a four year age difference between the boys. Sebastian had always made up for his disadvantage in years and size with sheer doggedness. Anna had always ranted about his dominating nature to her best friend, Erna, who for her part was in full agreement. There was just too much of the wild beast in the smaller boy. He had always wanted to be a horseman, a hunter and a wrestler: a man of action. Smoking guns and wicked blades were his passion. Learning that his better-read cousin liked gardening was like a red flag to a bull.

Poor Karl. The number of times Anna had tended to his lumps had made her weep. Erna had never understood the change of heart. One day the two cousins suddenly had eyes only for each other.

Erna saw which way the wind was blowing and had tried to intervene. Harsh words were spoken. Anna's judgement had become clouded, and she had stooped to calling her lifelong friend a jealous peasant.

The maid had been deeply offended by both halves of the accusation. Only a fool would see virtue in the strutting bantam rooster. She said as much, and from that point on they had stopped speaking to one another.

Anna threw all of her attention onto Sebastian, then. Erna saw no compelling reason to go to any more trouble, and poor Karl walked around as though he had been hurled out of a tornado.

Eventually it all came undone. Anna found herself with child and told Sebastian. He denied everything and Erna had wondered if perhaps he simply didn't know about the birds and the bees. In the end she realised that he was nothing but an inconsiderate and selfish bastard - a view that Anna had also belatedly reached. It should have been no great surprise to anyone, because that had been their starting point and he had never acted in any other way.

Nothing was ever said to Karl, but he was the one who found his little sister face down in a duck pond only three feet deep.

And now it all comes to this.

Sebastian sat in a chair all day long, doing nothing. He stared into oblivion and was either deep in thought, or else lacking the simplest cerebral processes. Given that he had never been one to engage in deep thinking, Erna knew which condition to be the most likely. He didn't seem to register his surroundings at all. His head had been broken open in nineteen-eighteen and the surgeons were unable to extract the bullet from his brain without killing him. They said that he was lucky to be alive at all. Clearly the medical profession had a distorted view of what constituted luck.

Erna stared at him dispassionately. She had had almost two years to consider a variety of options. Her vengeful side still wanted to poke pins under his finger nails and contaminate his food. Though in life he was a despicable man, in his current state he was just a breathing object needing constant maintenance. To wreak havoc upon his person would be pointless. A man needed to be aware of his worthlessness before he could understand humiliation.

In the end, Erna was left feeling deflated. This was her lot; to look after a man who had not only caused so much harm in the world, but who didn't have the turn of fortune to die in agony as he had so richly deserved. She could only hope that there was some small part of him that cried in the darkness, but this was merely grasping at straws and she knew it. His eyes were dark and empty pools.

There was an irony here. A friendship was long dead, and the innocent were left to tend to the wounds of the guilty. There was no way out of the situation that would not harm the feelings of a kind and generous employer - himself an injured party.

Ultimately, for most people, revenge was only ever acted out in the mind. The aggrieved tended to plan their schemes but never execute them. Their fear of failure and of being caught usually outweighed baser desires. Subsequent refusal to act is rationalised in ways that convince a person that they have higher moral values and that revenge is too trivial a reason to actually follow through to its conclusion. But to spend so much time plotting and settle for a sterile return was fruitless – what is the point of it if you stand by and do nothing? Someone who plans the perfect crime and reneges on its fulfilment can be accurately described as a coward. No other word was adequate.

Erna heard approaching footsteps: the distinctly soft tread of Karl, and one other. *It must be Sebastian's friend.* They were speaking quietly as they drew near. The visitor continued to Sebastian's room alone. He knocked once and entered, 'Hello. I hope I am not intruding? My name is Ernst.'

'Hello, sir. I am Erna.'

Reinhold let her know that there was more to it than that, and that explanations were unnecessary, 'Anna's maid.'

Erna parried the observation, 'Not any more. It has been over six years, now.'

'I am sorry.'

She looked at him, searching for a clue to his life, 'I know you have also lost friends – how could you not? – but Anna did not deserve to die as she did.'

Reinhold was offended by the comment. This servant couldn't just spout an opinion that condemned others, no matter what her own pain may have dictated, 'Nor did those of my friends who died. Further, they never contributed to their circumstances, other than that they obeyed legal orders.'

The mark struck true. Tears shone in Erna's eyes, 'I am sorry, sir. I did not mean to speak ill of your comrades.' She made another connection, 'How did you know?'

'More to the point, how does he miss it?'

'It is just that he doesn't see some things that are plain to others.'

'To be clear, we are talking about Karl and not Sebastian?'

Erna was earnest, 'Please, sir, he is a good man.'

Reinhold had no personal ties to Karl, so he felt no compunction to speak with any degree of diplomacy, 'He is a blind man.'

'A man sees what he wants to see and disregards the rest.'

'Someone should write a song about that one day.'

She looked down at the motionless thing that was called Sebastian and accused Reinhold, 'Sometimes people choose unworthy friends.'

He couldn't have been bothered to mount a defence, 'I served with him. You will see that he is cared for?'

Erna's dark eyes glittered, 'Oh, yes. Everything that he deserves.'

Author's note

I am unable to identify the time when I first realised that I wanted to become a writer, though I was certainly young. In the same vein I also knew that for most who shared the storytelling dream the goal would probably remain unfulfilled – to present your ideas to a publisher and expect them to welcome you with open arms is the surest path to set yourself up for a fall. Given that it is such a cut-throat industry I felt that my best bet would be to do something completely different – in effect to reduce the field with whom I would be competing by offering up something that others were not. In hindsight, it is plain that the word 'different' needs to have its spelling revised to four letters, such is its appeal in the public's perception – Elizabeth II needs to get onto her Chief of Grammar and Spelling about that one...

The first book that I wrote was not one you'd expect to find in mainstream bookstores. It was aimed at a very niche market – one that certainly had a larger following before the advent of the internet and the mass availability of digital games. After many years of research and experimentation I managed to develop a scaled reconstruction of WW1 air combat based on a mathematical algorithm that I had devised which measured aircraft effectiveness in terms of the following known values: maximum speed, fuel load, weight, dimensions, ceiling, weapon data, production numbers and period of distribution. The results of trials of *Richthofen's Reign* replicated known outcomes and provided me with insights into aerial warfare that I had not previously considered and which I had not read anywhere else.

Unfortunately, because this was my first book and I was attempting to impart a complex system, it was difficult for a new reader to grasp. One of the problems is that everything about the process needs to be understood before you can make any headway at all. It's not a computer sim but it could be, though what it would cost to have it built is beyond my ability to calculate.

I passed a few copies to various wargaming websites for reviews and one of the editors gave me this feedback; 'A hundred and fifty hours to work through from beginning to end? No-one has that commitment! But there is stuff in here which people would like to know about, so maybe you could write a book that details that sort of thing?' Write another book? I'm not sure he fully appreciated just how drained I was at the end of such an assignment - at least not the one that I had just completed. Rather than jumping at the opportunity, I shelved the idea. That was in 2006.

A lot can happen in nine years but his suggestion never really went away. In the meantime I worked on other ideas and other algorithms because I am a firm believer in trying to make a living out of what you are good at. The publishing industry is a hard nut to crack and I felt – and still feel – that an original concept has less competition than the cut-throat business of creative writing. On the other hand, the problem in selling new ideas lies in marketing them and getting people to accept that what you do is not a load of make-believe bullshit.

Ultimately, though, my ambition was always to write a novel and with the hundredth anniversary of the Great War approaching there was always going to be a lot of tangential publicity in the media for anyone who wrote a novel set during that period. With an almost decade old suggestion to write a book on that theme still gnawing away at me, I decided to do a story based on the outcomes of a game of *Richthofen's Reign*.

To make it a more interesting experience for me, the plot was not planned with a specific end in view. Sebastian von Bülow was only chosen as the main character when it became apparent that he was the most successful pilot during the timeframe that culminated in Bloody April, 1917. At that point I started writing the book, not knowing if he would be killed later in the war, but making contingency plans either way. Some of the ideas that evolved from this were then applied to other personalities as I reached the end of the campaign. Because of this lack of future knowledge at the time of writing, in some ways *Fledglings* is a diary. I wrote of the experiences of key characters while they were still alive, and then I had to deal with events when they were killed or injured. The result is that in some places the plot stumbled - and how like life is that? Some sections of the book then needed to be modified to fit the new reality. In a very few instances I took some poetic license and jiggled the action to fit the plot. My final act was being forced into writing a better ending than that which my spreadsheet had told me to do, though it stuck in the craw to do so. I just had to ask myself, 'Do you want a good ending, or would you prefer it to peter out?'

The combat sequences chosen for inclusion in *Fledglings* were largely a product of results obtained in the detail of the dice-generated action that *Richthofen's Reign* is based upon. Every so often something happened that had simply not been considered, and though these may have been interesting as hypothetical reconstructions, the men who actually witnessed them in real time would have had an entirely different perspective. To illustrate this point, I have had more than a few comments made to me pertaining to the inclusion of the word 'barbequed' in the second chapter – being either too out of era or too insensitive - but I kept it in because once you have seen such a thing no other word fits quite as well.

Statistical trends found in *Richthofen's Reign* during the entire war are representative of the historical data, even so far as identifying different periods of intensity for the various sides: the first half of 1917 was a golden period for the *Jastas*, while the latter half of that year saw the balance swing towards the Allies as they brought newer and more effective aircraft into service. The final year of the war was all about Allied dominance in the air.

The one thing that you will never read about elsewhere concerns the fuel loads of WW1 aircraft, which is unusual if for no other reason than that this particular quality is central to so much of that which is written about the WW2 air campaign just a generation later. Working through the process of *Richthofen's Reign* gives a much better appreciation of the Pfalz DIII, something that you will never find written about it anywhere. Similarly, the various Fokkers had a much smaller tank capacity, though their performance in other areas offset this deficiency.

Though the main characters in the book are fictitious, those who are 'off screen' are real. Readers interested in this subject would be expected to be familiar with at least some of the historical figures and it is left up to them to work this out. There are a few giveaways to prompt this conclusion. For example, Manfred von Richthofen - the Red Baron - is mentioned several times but never makes a personal appearance. Also, many of the theories expressed here and there by individuals have serious flaws which should be apparent to the modern history buff and these are included to give those particular

442

readers a feeling that they are getting more out of the story than the casual observer.

Unlike a module of *Richthofen's Reign*, this novel is not solely to do with flying and shooting. Almost every event which happens in *Fledglings* has been modified either from somewhere in the historical record, or else from my observations of the lives of others. Those activities that have no verifiable source are based on principles of human behaviour that I have noticed in group dynamics and most particularly in small-unit leadership. Instead of asking, 'What would Jesus do?' the question has been slightly modified to read; 'What do people do when no-one is around to stop them?'

Some topics that are popular on social media forums did not have the same grip a hundred years ago as they do today and these are dealt with accordingly. For instance, nowhere in the book is there any mention of 'fighter aces' as this is a concept that was retrospectively applied to successful pilots after the war. Though the best men were celebrated to varying degrees – most notably by the Germans - it was not universal. The more common perception was that singling out individuals was something that only the paparazzi would stoop to. Team work was considered to be much more important.

Post Traumatic Stress Disorder (PTSD) is a newly diagnosed phenomenon (relatively speaking) but its symptoms and effects are encountered throughout the pages of this novel. One of the more telling things that I learned when researching this work was that Erich Maria Remarque, author of *All Quiet on the Western Front* – one of the most important books to come out of the Great War - served for less than two months in the line during nineteen-seventeen until he was wounded in action and permanently repatriated to Germany. No-one who has experienced trauma would be surprised at this – it can be devastating in very short order – but that such a seemingly brief exposure had so profound an effect upon him speaks volumes about what everyone else with more extensive combat experience must have endured during the time of their own service.

Norm Mjadwesch
February 2015

For more information about *Fledglings* and a range of other projects, please feel free to visit my website at
<u>toothandclawproductions.com</u>

Richthofen's Reign – a scaled reconstruction of the air campaign of WW1 loosely based on wargaming principles.

Globall – recreating the history of World Cup soccer using individual player statistics.

Formula Won – the history of F1 motor racing in the form of a simple board game.

Broken Castle – recreating the history of international cricket using individual player statistics.